SOUTHERN CHARMER

A Charleston Heat Novel

JESSICA PETERSON

ALSO BY JESSICA PETERSON

THE SEX & BONDS SERIES

An outrageously sexy series of romcoms set in the high stakes world of Wall Street.

The Dealmaker (Sex & Bonds #1)

The Troublemaker (Sex & Bonds #2)

THE NORTH CAROLINA HIGHLANDS SERIES

Beards. Bonfires. Boning.

Southern Seducer (NC Highlands #1)

Southern Hotshot (NC Highlands #2)

Southern Sinner (NC Highlands #3)

Southern Playboy (NC Highlands #4)

Southern Bombshell (NC Highlands #5)

THE CHARLESTON HEAT SERIES

The Weather's Not the Only Thing Steamy Down South.

Southern Charmer (Charleston Heat #1)

Southern Player (Charleston Heat #2)

Southern Gentleman (Charleston Heat #3)

Southern Heartbreaker (Charleston Heat #4)

THE THORNE MONARCHS SERIES

Royal. Ridiculously Hot. Totally Off Limits...

Royal Ruin (Thorne Monarchs #1)

Royal Rebel (Thorne Monarchs #2)

Royal Rogue (Thorne Monarchs #3)

THE STUDY ABROAD SERIES

Studying Abroad Just Got a Whole Lot Sexier.

A Series of Sexy Interconnected Standalone Romances

Lessons in Love (Study Abroad #1)

Lessons in Gravity (Study Abroad #2)

Lessons in Letting Go (Study Abroad #3)

Lessons in Losing It (Study Abroad #4)

FOLLOW ME, Y'ALL!

- Join my Facebook reader group, The City Girls, for exclusive excerpts of upcoming books plus giveaways galore!
- Follow my not-so-glamorous life as a romance author on Instagram @JessicaPAuthor
- Follow me on Goodreads
- Follow me on Bookbub
- Like my Facebook Author Page

Published by Peterson Paperbacks, LLC
Copyright 2018 by Peterson Paperbacks, LLC
Cover by Najla Qamber of Najla Qamber Designs

This book is licensed for your personal enjoyment only. This book may not be re-sold or given away to other people. If you would like to share this book with another person, please purchase an additional copy for each person. If you're reading this book and did not purchase it, or it was not purchased for your use only, then please return it and purchase your own copy. Thank you for respecting the hard work of this author. To obtain permission to excerpt portions of the text, please contact the author at jessicapauthor@jessicapeterson.com.

All characters in this book are fiction and figments of the author's imagination.

www.jessicapeterson.com

❋ Created with Vellum

*Dedicated to every woman who's ever wanted more.
I hope you go after it with everything you've got.*

"I feel that having what you want is more important than having it all."
—Judy Gagliardi Wagner

Chapter One
OLIVIA

Taking the exit ramp off I-26, I roll down my windows. Turn up the country song on the radio. A guy with a sultry southern accent is singing about making out in the back of his pickup truck.

Feels appropriate for my arrival in Charleston, South Carolina. The city I'll be calling home for the next month.

While I wait at the light at the end of the ramp, I glance at the duffel bag in my passenger seat. The edges of the jewelry box I've stuffed into the front pocket strain against the crisp black nylon.

My chest tightens. It's already sore from one thousand, one hundred and thirty eight miles of tears.

And probably for the one thousand, one hundred and thirty eighth time, I see the image of Teddy in my head. Excitement in his blue eyes dimming when, after an excruciating pause, I replied to his four word question.

I'm sorry, but I need time to think about it.

In that moment, I could just imagine my family—my friends—*everyone* putting their hands on their heads in disbelief and asking *what the fuck is wrong with you?*

What *is* wrong with me, *needing time to think* about marrying the perfect man who wants to give me the perfect life?

"But you could have it all!" my mother said, clearly bewildered. "Everyone loves Ted. You don't run from a man like that."

But here I am, running.

Like a coward.

Like an idiot.

It's the only thing that felt right after the proposal blew up in my face the other night. I wanted to say yes to Teddy. But as he kneeled there, offering me the most gorgeous diamond ring on Earth, I got this awful gut feeling that the whole thing was wrong.

Which is laughable, considering how picture perfect Ted's proposal was. He pulled out all the stops: flowers, dinner at a Michelin starred restaurant, flawless four carat diamond. It was so *him*.

But was it at all *me*?

Lately, I've fought this feeling of being suffocated. I don't understand it. I was raised under the banner of "having it all", and I've worked my butt off to do exactly that: have the dream job, the dream house, the dream guy. It's all finally within reach. I just had to say yes to Teddy. But I couldn't. All I could think about as I stared down at the ring was a conversation he and I had had recently. We were talking about my love of romance novels.

"As a professor of feminism in nineteenth century masterpieces, aren't you supposed to, like, be opposed to everything those books represent?" he asked, shaking his head.

Romance is *feminist*. The reply was on the tip of my tongue. Romance is one of the few genres that explicitly puts a woman's dreams and desires, sexual and otherwise, front and center. It's one of the many reasons I love reading it.

But I didn't say that. Ted is not at all supportive of my romance habit—I read at least one a week. When I drunkenly confessed my secret desire to write a full-length romance of my own a couple months back, he laughed and said I had better things to do.

I mean, I get it. Ted has a very specific vision for our future together. As one half of the power couple he sees us becoming—he's a corporate lawyer, I'm a professor at an Ivy League University—I have to stick to the straight and narrow. Ted's always polished and put together, and he encourages me to be the same. He likes when I wear expensive clothes—"Dress for the job you want, not the job you have," he says—and insists we socialize with other well-dressed, like-minded couples that live in the neighborhood we recently moved into just outside Ithaca.

Being with Ted has transformed me into the successful woman I always thought I'd be. So why does *being* that woman make me feel so smothered sometimes?

It's a very privileged problem to have. I recognize that. But I can't seem to kick this feeling. Overcome it.

I start at the sound of a honk behind me. The light is green. I follow the nice GPS lady's instructions and hang a right onto Meeting Street.

I've never been to South Carolina before. The first thing I notice is how damn *hot* it is. The air blowing through the windows is thick with humidity and the salty smell of the ocean. So different from the crisp feel of late September in upstate New York.

My long-ish hair whips in my face, already frizzy. Usually that bothers me. No one appreciates a great blowout more than I do. But right now, hair seems like a silly thing to worry about. So I just tuck my sunglasses onto my head to keep it out of my eyes.

The second thing I notice is that the whole city seems to

be under construction. There are cranes and the skeletons of half-finished buildings everywhere.

Fashionably dressed hipsters mingle with tourists in white sneakers and sun hats on the sidewalks. My car trundles over the uneven pavement that shimmers in the heat of a five o'clock sun. I turn left on Calhoun Street, and then right on East Bay, and all that new construction gives way to the historic charm you see in pictures.

My head is on a swivel as I head south. There's the famous Charleston City Market on my right. On my left, there's a hulking cruise ship in the harbor. Farther down on my right, I get a tantalizing glimpse of a narrow cobblestone alley. It's lined with a series of enormous gas lamps, the live flames like licks of fire. A sign, small and simple, hangs below one of the lamps.

The Pearl.

A restaurant?

I catch a whiff of something delicious. Smoked meat.

Smoked *something*.

My stomach grumbles. It hits me that I'm suddenly hungry—ravenous—for the first time in days. Luckily, I'm in a foodie town. I read a lot about the incredible bar and restaurant scene during a teary Google search last night at The Holiday Inn Express in Harrisonburg. Seeing pictures of shrimp and grits, biscuits and craft cocktails, and fried chicken sandwiches made me feel the tiniest bit better.

The tourists—and the traffic—disappear when, according to my GPS, I enter the South of Broad neighborhood. It's leafy and beautiful, and it's unlike any other place I've been. Antebellum mansions line either side of the street. Shutters and porches and enormous window boxes galore. Gardens teem with flowers and mossy fountains behind wrought iron gates.

Somewhere in the distance, I hear the clomp of horse hooves.

I'm more than a thousand miles from my life in small town New York. And while the distance is real, I feel like I'm even farther away than that. Like I'm on a different planet.

It's terrifying.

If I'm being honest, it's also a relief. I feel like I can breathe again down here.

Longitude Lane is up on the right. My final destination.

After my freakout during the proposal, I decided I needed to hit the pause button on my relationship with Ted. Take some time to myself after the whirlwind of the past three years. In that span, I'd met and moved in with Ted, published my dissertation, and gotten tenure in the English Department at the university where I teach. I haven't had time to step back and process it all.

I also haven't had time to play around with that novel I've wanted to write. No matter how hard I try to quash it, the itch to write this damn thing won't go away.

So I'm taking that time now. I'm going to write, if only to prove to myself that the grass isn't greener and that my life with Ted really is the right life. Then I'll be ready to walk down the aisle. I'm probably just suffering from a classic case of burnout anyway. Some time away is just the ticket.

Surprisingly, Ted was on board with the idea. We agreed to take a real break, which means we're allowing each other to be with other people if that's what we need.

Part of me thinks it's strange that the two of us agreed to such an arrangement. Especially considering the fact that Ted just tried to put a ring on my finger. But he's clearly eager to give me as much space as possible. I want to give him space, too, after the way I reacted to his proposal.

Besides. I want to spend my time in Charleston writing. Not hanging out with other men.

"Go. Sow your wild oats," Ted told me. "When you're ready, come back to me wearing the ring."

His confidence soothed me a bit. At the end of the month, I *will* be ready. I *will* be wearing his ring.

I will have it all.

In the meantime, I'm going to enjoy my freedom. The day after the proposal, I called Julia Lassiter, one of my friends from graduate school. She's a beautiful southern belle who comes from big Charleston money and has a raging crush on early twentieth century female British writers. In true Virginia Woolf fashion, she recently accepted an offer of a room of her own in Barcelona in exchange for teaching at a university there for the year. Ever since, she's been bugging me to use her vacant carriage house in Charleston.

"Get away from all those uptight Ivy Leaguers and come hang down south. Charleston's kind of a wackadoo place. And I mean that as a compliment. It could be just the change of scenery you need to start that novel you know you need to write."

Julia was thrilled I finally took her up on the offer.

Then I called my boss, the English Department Head. She was *not* happy with my emergency request for a sabbatical. But I was firm in my need for a break. There's no way I could do my students justice right now. She finally relented when I convinced her my top notch TA, Christine, could handle my class load; Christine had agreed to take over until she has her baby at the end of October.

So I've got almost four weeks to reset, recharge, and dabble in my book.

I make the turn onto Longitude Lane.

Right away, I slam on my brakes.

"What the f—"

A handful of humungous birds loiter in the middle of the

alley like bored teenagers. They look like turkeys. Or maybe they're geese? They peck at each other. Peck at the ground.

One of them has the balls to look me in the eye for a full beat. Like *I'm* the one holding up traffic.

I wait for them to move, but they don't. I start to sweat. I mean, what the hell are you supposed to do when you encounter birds the size of beach balls in the middle of a city street?

I consider honking my horn. But this little alley is *nice*. I half expect Scarlett O'Hara to come charging out of the house to my left, bottle of bourbon in one hand and a shotgun in the other, telling me she doesn't *give* a damn if I'm tired and hot and cranky, *people down here don't honk*.

On to plan B. Maybe if I get out of the car—

But then a man appears, saving me from what I'm sure would have devolved into a scene from *The Birds*.

Not just any man.

A shirtless one.

A sexy, shirtless, tatted up man.

I watch, my mouth going dry, as he strides out into the street, his broad back to me. He shoos away the birds with one arm, urging them to the other side of the alley.

He is barefoot.

The sting of cigar smoke fills my nostrils.

"Don't be a dick, Dolores," he says, pointing to the only white bird in the group. "I know you understand what I'm sayin'. Get! I told you to stay out of the street. You wanna end up roadkill? Huh?"

He's got a southern accent. More velvety than the guy's on the radio. I feel that velvet on the underside of my sternum. My heart brushes up against it, purring at the sudden softness.

The birds finally meander to the sidewalk. Then the man turns to look at me. Our eyes lock.

I swear to God my normal bodily functions skid to a dead stop. Even my eyes stop blinking.

He is gorgeous. In a scruffy way. He rocks a full beard. Dark, graphic tattoos. His dark hair is wet, like he just got out of the shower, and long enough to be held back by one of those elastic headband things I've only ever seen hot European soccer players wear.

The stub of a cigar is clamped between his teeth. He squints his eyes—they're hazel, more green than brown—against the smoke.

He clearly works out. Thick torso and shoulders, shapely waist. Forearms so sinewy and perfect they make me want to die a little.

The definition of a BILF. Beard I'd like to fuck.

They do not make men like this in small town New York.

He holds a mug of what I assume is coffee in one hand, even though it's almost dinnertime. I get the feeling he's just starting his day. *What does he do?*

He holds up the other hand to me.

"I'm sorry, ma'am," he says around the cigar. Shit, now I'm looking at his lips. His full, expressive lips. "Damn fowl are always causin' trouble."

Ah. So they are *fowl*, not geese.

(Like I'd know the difference. But still.)

Leaning out the window a little, I say, "No problem. About the, uh, fowls. *Fowl*. Heh." I resist the urge to grimace. When was the last time I got flustered around a guy? I'm thirty-two years old, damn it. "Thank you."

"Anytime."

I watch him make his way to the house on my right. All the while blinking back a strong sense of *where the fuck am I?* A half-naked guy with a hot accent just saved me from some *fowl* in the *street*. He seemed unmiffed about it. Like this kind of thing happens all the time on Longitude Lane.

Maybe it does. Maybe wild birds and wilder men are common in Charleston.

If so, this is going to be an interesting four weeks.

Chapter Two
OLIVIA

BILF climbs the steps to his house. It's small and old but, from what I can see of it, spectacular. Glossy black doors. Gas lamps. Ivy climbing up one wall.

Before he opens the door, he glances in my direction again. His gaze—it's got this *intensity*. This unabashed pointedness he's totally aware of.

Makes me feel like I've committed a crime.

My stomach dips.

I look away and hit the gas.

Longitude Lane is less a lane and more like a long alley that's barely wide enough to fit a car. My tires trundle over uneven brick pavers.

My GPS tell me I've reached my destination after I've sailed past the house next to BILF's.

Julia did not mention she had a super-hot neighbor.

Throwing the car in reverse, I check the number on the stuccoed pillar beside a small gated drive.

Yup, this is 7 ½ Longitude Lane.

I type the code Julia sent me. The gate opens and I drive inside, parking my car on the brick driveway.

I look up at the narrow building in front of me. It's small, two stories, with garage doors on the bottom floor and windows on the second. A curving wrought iron staircase leads to the front door on the second level.

The house is painted white with bright blue shutters. The window boxes on the second floor burst with greenery and white and purple flowers.

It just might be the cutest damn thing I have ever seen.

The inside is even cuter. In true Julia style, it's decorated to the nines. Lots of expensive antiques mixed with more modern furniture. The gleaming kitchen is small but exquisite, complete with a French range and marble countertops. There's a bedroom, a huge walk in closet, a tiny bathroom, and a screened in porch off the back.

The heaviness in my chest lifts.

But then it returns with a vengeance when, while I'm unpacking in the bedroom, the ring box falls out of my bag. I sit down on the bed and open it.

The enormous diamond winks at me from its classic platinum setting. My heart palpitates. It's so beautiful. And so *big*. Exactly the kind of diamond Ted would pick. Nothing but the best for him.

"Nothing but the best for *us*," he likes to say.

I close the box with a sharp *clack*. I go over to the tall boy dresser and open the top drawer. I set the ring inside. The sight of the box makes my stomach hurt. So I cover it with a handful of my underwear and shut the drawer.

I'll feel better about everything at the end of the month.

Until then, I'm going to try to forget about the ring. Focus on myself and my writing instead. The more time I spend doing that, the more refreshed I'll be for my return to New York.

I wake up the next morning and forget where I am.

Instinctively I turn my head to look for Teddy on the other side of the bed. But it's empty.

Since we've been together, I can count on one hand the number of times I've woken up alone. I'm not quite sure what to do with myself.

So I head to the kitchen to make some coffee. Always a solid first step.

The Nespresso machine I found in a cabinet whirrs to a stop. I lift my mug of foamy coffee from the maker and set it on the counter, adding a splash of the almond milk I picked up last night at the convenience store a few blocks away.

My head throbs. I spent most of the night staring at the ceiling, thoughts racing. I finally fell asleep around three or four. Even though I stayed in bed until nine—late for me—I feel groggy. Beat up.

Taking a sip of coffee, I grimace. It tastes as bitter as it smells.

I'm overwhelmed by a sudden wave of homesickness. Teddy makes us coffee every morning. A special Columbian blend that he discovered in law school.

In that moment, I miss him. So damn much.

Resisting the urge to pick up my phone and call Ted—we agreed not to contact each other so I could have as much space as possible—I add more almond milk to my coffee and grab a protein bar. I usually stick to light breakfasts. I've got a closet full of beautiful clothes back home that I won't be able to fit in otherwise.

My laptop leers at me from its perch on the counter. Probably should check my email. Make sure Christine is handling my class load okay.

I want to miss work. And I do, but not as much as I feel like I should. I grew up loving Jane Austen, which eventually led to my interest in nineteenth century British literature. I still love Jane. I *really* love my students. They're top notch, smart, and ambitious. Being in a classroom with them is a real pleasure.

But as much as I love teaching, the politics of our department have been difficult to deal with. It's definitely a cutthroat culture, egged on by a "publish or perish" mentality. A lot of the time, it feels like having a gun to my head—especially considering how hard I've pushed myself to climb the ranks within the department.

Even so, it's not like I'll ever leave. Shrinking budgets means it's ridiculously difficult to get tenure at universities these days. Tenure—which I got last year—is every academic's dream. It comes with prestige and security. Benefits. Basically, it opens the door to a very bright future in academia. I'd be out of my mind to give that up.

Doesn't hurt that Ted's so proud of all that I've accomplished. So are my parents. My friends.

Besides. What else would I do? Write steamy books all day?

Even that can't be as glamorous or fulfilling as it sounds.

I'm about to find out.

I tuck the computer underneath my arm and head out to the screened in porch off the bedroom. Julia calls it a "sleeping porch". One of those fancy bed swings, complete with stylish rope supports and a small mountain of Indian block print pillows, hangs on one side of the porch. The other side is occupied by an antique settee and side table.

I notice the bead board ceiling is painted pale blue. The same shade as the sky outside.

The morning is already warm and muggy. I set down my laptop and coffee on the table and reach inside the door for the light switch. Takes me a couple tries, but eventually I find the switch for the ceiling fan. The fan spins to silent life, making the air *just* bearable. Another degree or two and I'll be melting.

I sit down and open the laptop. Password, Wi-Fi, close out the approximately two hundred documents I have open. I'm usually pretty organized. But thanks to the packed teaching schedule I've had over the past few semesters, I'm still playing catch up.

I check in with Christine via email. Sounds like she's got everything handled. I tell her to contact me for anything she needs, and then I log out of my email and open the Word document I've been working on in secret for a couple months. The first line makes me smile.

(Probably Stupid) Idea for Regency Romance that is a cross between Romeo and Juliet and Game of Thrones. Same amount of hot blondes and boobs, more commentary on family roles and of course more penis.

I scoff, curling my legs underneath me. I wrote this one night a few weeks ago, late, when I was avoiding a departmental email thread about publishing schedules.

When I decided to write my dissertation on Jane Austen, I reread all her books. Then I started reading the mountain of literature inspired by her signature blend of wit, social commentary, and romance. Georgette Heyer led me to Elizabeth Hoyt. Elizabeth Hoyt led me to Sherry Thomas, and Sherry Thomas led me to Tessa Dare. Jo Beverly. Joanna Bourne. Julia Ann Long...

I could go on for days.

Clearly I fell head over heels in love with historical romance. To this day, I love nothing more than curling up on a couch, or by a pool, or on a plane with the latest juicy release from one of my favorite authors.

A release I always buy on my Kindle so no one can see what I'm reading. Romance novels are totally my guilty pleasure. Sometimes I'll feel guilty for...well, feeling guilty. But it's an obsession I can't really share with many people. Least of all my colleagues at the university. I distinctly remember one of my thesis advisors calling romance novels "trashy bodice-rippers that are bad for your head."

He didn't need to say they'd be bad for my career. That was just understood. A fact.

I take a sip of coffee. The caffeine is starting to hit me. My heart beats thickly in my chest. I read my outline again. It's actually kind of good. I'd want to read this book.

I think about the hero.

He comes to me, suddenly, fully formed and glorious. He's shirtless. Corded forearms, wild hair, piercing hazel eyes that are more green than brown. He's got a dark past and a soft spot for babies.

My fingers begin to move over the keyboard. They shake a little with excitement.

Fuck it.

I came here to write this thing, and I'm going to do it if it kills me. How hard could writing a romance novel be anyway? I wrote a three-hundred-page academic treatise on Jane Austen, for God's sake. Writing a love story will be a cake walk after that.

An hour later, I highlight the entirety of what I've managed to write—323 meager words—and pound on the delete key, erasing it all.

It sucks.

I suck.

I was right. The grass *totally* isn't greener.

I can't nail my hero's voice. He's coming off as too douchey. I want him to be confident. Commanding. He is heir to a Dukedom, after all. But how do I do that without making him a total prick?

I'm so frustrated that my throat has started to close in. It's also getting really hot out here. I'm sweating.

I look up at the sound of an approaching car, grateful for the distraction. Glancing over my shoulder, I see a black Jeep Wrangler pull up to Mr. BILF's house below. A tall, gorgeous dark skinned woman gets out, dressed casually in slouchy jeans and a t-shirt.

She doesn't even knock on his door. She just climbs the steps, opens the door and moves inside.

"It's me," she calls, closing the door behind her.

BILF's girlfriend?

I don't know why I feel a stab of disappointment. I came to Charleston to get a break from men. Not to find one.

Besides. Even if I was in a finding mood, I doubt I'd have a chance in hell with that guy. I bet he dates models. Artists. Models who *are* artists. I've always attracted more straight-laced, corporate types anyway.

But my heart still skips a beat when a pair of french doors on the first floor of BILF's house open. I'm hit by the smell of bacon.

My stomach rumbles. I glance at my half-eaten protein bar.

A beat later, I overhear a string of expletives that almost make me jump.

"You can tell those dickheads to go fuck themselves." I recognize the rumble of BILF's voice. His words are angry, but his tone is not. He speaks slowly, evenly, just like he did yesterday in the street. "Who cares about critics anyway? I'm proud of the food we make over there. So it's simple. That's the fuckin' point. I make food the way my mama did, and her mama before her. I am who I am, Naomi, and I'm not gonna change for anyone. Least of all a goddamned stranger."

Naomi. Of course she'd have a gorgeous name like that.

I hear the murmur of her voice. I can't tell what she's saying.

Another smell. Something frying *in* that bacon fat.

Maybe it's the budding novelist in me. But I can't help but feel something juicy is going down at my hot neighbor's house.

Juicy and delicious. I'm starving. My usual protein bar isn't cutting it today. Maybe BILF has some bacon to spare?

It's the potential for writerly inspiration—and breakfast meat—that makes me close my laptop and stand up.

At least that's what I tell myself as I head next door.

Chapter Three
ELI

I give the onions in my ancient cast iron pan one last flip. They sizzle and pop over the high heat, browned with bits of the bacon I'd fried up earlier.

Gracious, that smells good.

I was raised in the temple of simple southern cooking. My faith in a nutshell: all good things start with bacon fat, butter, or bourbon. Bonus points for all three. Means I have to spend extra time at the yoga studio. Also means I get slaughtered by critics on occasion.

Both worth it. Although I've never had critics actually bring a restaurant to the brink of bankruptcy before.

I shove the thought from my head. Too depressing.

I dump sweet corn, fresh from the cob and gorgeously juicy, into the pan, along with a handful of lima beans from my garden out back. Wiping my hands on a kitchen towel, I toss it over my shoulder.

"Expecting company?" Naomi asks from her usual perch on a stool at the island. "You're making enough succotash to feed a small army."

I nudge the pan forward, then quickly dip it back. The

onions and corn and beans rise together in a tidy wave, then fall back into the cast iron with a satisfying sizzle. I add a generous pinch of Kosher salt. Give it another flip.

I don't usually cook like this for myself. But I've had a lot on my mind, and cooking helps to clear out all the bullshit. Helps clear out the heavy sense of anxiety that's weighed me down lately.

"Nah," I reply. "Just you."

"As tempting as that *lovely* invitation is," she says sarcastically "Sergio and I have a date. We're grabbing lunch over on Shem Creek."

It's Monday. My restaurants are closed. Means my staff members, like Naomi and Sergio, get the day off.

"But I thought we were in crisis mode," I say, not looking up from the pan. "You know, critics-eating-up-my-new-restaurant-we're-all-doomed-save-our-souls shit. Do y'all really have time for a date when the world is fuckin' ending?"

Naomi calmly plucks an ice cube from her tea—toothache sweet, just how we both like it—and hurls it at me. I hold up my arm a second too late. The cube hits me square in the temple.

I wince. Naomi, being Naomi, cackles. She's worked in my kitchen at The Pearl for close to five years now, pretty much since I opened the place. We cooked side by side until I promoted her to head chef of my new restaurant, The Jam, which I opened earlier this year. Even though she runs her own kitchen now, we still squabble like kids.

"Girl's gotta get laid, even if the world is ending."

"I already told you," I say, gently kicking the ice cube across the floor to Billy, my ten-year-old lab-and-God-knows-what-mix. Billy sniffs at it, not impressed. He sighs. *I feel you, buddy*. "Ignore what the critics are saying, and just keep doin' what you're doin'. There's a reason I made you head chef. You know what's important, and you stick to it. As long as we're making food *we* love, and as long as customers love that food and leave happy—hell, Naomi, you know those are the only things that matter."

I glance at the glossy cover of the food magazine resting beside Naomi's elbow. They printed yet another scathing review of The Jam. One line was particularly brutal: "Perhaps Elijah Jackson is only capable of making one restaurant work. Adding a second to the roster is not always a smart gamble for a chef like him."

Chef like him. Meaning running two restaurants is clearly too ambitious for a simple country boy with unpretentious tastes like me.

Seriously, fuck that reviewer for life.

I've never compromised the faith I have in my cooking. Not once. Awful reviews notwithstanding, I don't plan on starting now.

Then again, I've never planned on closing a restaurant, either. Especially not after the phenomenal success of The Pearl. Something about The Jam just hasn't clicked with people. I don't get it. Yes, today's market is much different from when I opened The Pearl. But people have always loved my food. It's honest. It's made with heart.

I feel anxiety, tinged with panic, edging closer again. I don't want to let it get too close. I'm worried it'll swallow me whole if it does. And then what? The Jam isn't bankrupt yet. We still have a chance to bring it back from the brink. Which means I can't afford a breakdown right now. I need to set an example. Stay positive and upbeat so my cooks and my dishwashers and my wait staff do, too. The idea that all those people are at risk of losing their jobs because of me—

Don't go there.

I quickly turn back to the stove. Grits are bubbling in a pot beside the succotash. Grabbing the towel off my shoulder, I lift the lid with it and stir in a little more half and half and a lot more butter to get the grits nice and creamy. Just how Mama makes them.

The heavy thoughts retreat.

"I know." Naomi puts her hands around her sweating glass. "But I want to make sure we're on the same page here, E. People aren't coming to The Jam anymore. Maybe our food is *too* simple. Especially when you consider all the really cool, different things chefs are doing down here."

Naomi makes a good point. I admire Charleston's chefs for their creativity. There's John Melrose, whose hipster-y restaurant serves Asian comfort food classics with a south-by-central-America twist. Abigail Edmonds is serving up a fresh, New England spin on southern seafood at her place. And at his restaurant, Hank Havens is digging up recipes from a hundred years ago and adapting them for a modern, elegant menu.

"They're definitely pushing the envelope," I say. "But so are we in keeping things simple. That in and of itself is radical."

Naomi nods. "I believe that. Honestly. I don't have to answer to the money, though. That's your job."

One of my least favorite parts about being executive chef. It's also a painful reminder of the nice chunk of change I personally invested in The Jam. If it goes under, I'll never see a penny of that money returned. Earlier this morning I was looking at my account balances, trying not to freak out over the idea that they wouldn't be replenished like I planned they would. They're *much* lower than they were this time last year.

"They won't be thrilled about the review," I reply, referring to the hospitality investment group that I've partnered with. "But I'll just point them in the direction of The Pearl, and they'll go back to being happy."

By some miracle, the bad press The Jam has received hasn't damaged the brisk business we do over at The Pearl.

As proud as I am that we're booked up months in advance, it means most people don't get to eat there. Part of the reason I opened up The Jam (I know, I know, it's way too fucking cute, but I love Eddie Vedder and make no apologies for it) is so more people can experience my food.

"Now you're just bragging," Naomi says with a smile.

I shrug, lighting another burner. Time to poach the eggs. "Damn fuckin' right I am."

The tags on Billy's collar jingle as he lifts his head. He looks towards the open doors. Then he gets up.

Billy doesn't get up for *anyone*.

I turn my head to see a woman standing in the doorway. She's in a flowy silk dress that's way too dressed up for Charleston any day of the week. Least of all a Monday morning. Shiny sandals. Jewelry. Enormous, fancy black shades—designer if I had to guess—that cover half her pretty face.

The only part of her that's *not* impeccably put together is her hair. It's a dark, wild, tangled mess.

It's just fucked hair.

I like it.

I recognize her as the girl who almost ran over our neighborhood's infamous Guinea Fowl last night. If her New York license plate didn't give her away as an out-of-towner, her half-horrified, half-flummoxed expression would have. You'd think I was a yeti from the way she looked at me.

"Hi," she says, putting her hand hesitantly on the doorjamb. "I'm—um—staying next door. I heard some shouting, and I wanted to make sure everything was okay."

Her New York accent dips on *door*. Comes out sounding like *dawr*.

It's cute.

Naomi's eyes dart to meet mine.

"Eli doesn't shout," Naomi says. "But he certainly has a way with profanity, doesn't he?"

I look to see the woman letting out a breath. What did she expect to find? Me threatening Naomi or something?

My stomach dips.

"Shit, I'm so—*shit*, I can't even apologize properly, can I?" I say, fisting my hair in my hand. "I'm sorry if I scared you. The cussing—it's a bad habit."

"One you're awfully proud of," Naomi says.

"Well, yeah," I say. "I mean, I haven't had my coffee yet. I can't be held accountable for the stuff that comes out of my mouth."

The woman's shapely lips curl into a small smile. Just big enough for me to catch a flash of white, even teeth.

"So you're saying you always call people dickheads and make bacon before coffee," she replies.

I let out a bark of laughter.

"Only on Mondays." I walk across the kitchen, Billy at my heels, and hold out my hand. "I'm Eli. I saw you last night in the street, right?"

The woman takes my hand and gives it a firm shake. I catch a whiff of her perfume. Smells sexy. Expensive.

Too expensive for you to afford.

I blink. That's a nasty little thought. This whole business with The Jam has really got me feeling all out of sorts.

I ignore it. It isn't like me to worry about shit like that. I don't need to impress women with money to feel good about myself. Never have, never will.

"Nice to meet you, Eli. I'm Olivia. And right—that was me last night. Thanks for the rescue from the fowl. I was worried I'd gotten lost. Charleston is definitely...interesting."

When I drop her hand, she pushes her sunglasses onto her head. Her eyes catch on my bare chest. They're pale blue and wide. Intelligent.

There are purple thumbprints underneath them.

I notice she's kinda pale. On the thin side.

My kitchens are full of lost souls and misfits and tortured characters. I know a runaway when I see one.

And this pretty girl in her fancy get up is definitely a runaway.

Blame it on the overly friendly southern boy my mama raised me to be. But I want to know what her story is. What she's running from.

And yeah, that just fucked hair doesn't hurt, either. Neither does the idea of having some company for breakfast. I don't want to be alone right now. It's hard to keep anxiety at bay when I'm alone.

"You still look lost," I say.

She clears her throat, blinking, and meets my gaze.

"And you're still not wearing a shirt."

It's Naomi's turn to laugh. "Amen. I've been after Eli for years to dress like a gentleman. Or dress at all. Still a work in progress—the man never wears a shirt at home."

Olivia looks a little alarmed—and a little amused—at the notion.

"Really?"

"Really." I nod, crossing my arms. "I'm always coverin' up when I'm at work. If a man can't be free in his own goddamned home...well, that's a sorry state of affairs right there."

She's grinning now. "The fowl certainly didn't seem to mind. Do you have names for all of them? Or just Dolores?"

"Just Dolores," I reply, grinning back. "She's my favorite."

Olivia's stomach rumbles. Audibly. She quickly puts her hand on her belly, like she wants to muffle the sound.

"Smells so good in here," she says a little sheepishly. "This whole *town* smells good."

Naomi looks at me. I look at Naomi. She knows how much I like to feed people.

She also knows how much I like brunettes.

I'm not a pussy hound. Never have been. But after ending a long term relationship last year, I'm down to have a good time. I pretty much chucked normalcy out the window when I decided to become a chef. Maintaining a normal relationship with the hours I keep and the environment I work in is almost impossible.

Almost. I still believe it can work if I find the right person. A woman who's as passionate about what she does as I am. Figure that's the only way someone will understand why I work and cook the way I do.

Billy is looking up at Olivia now, wagging his tail. She reaches down to give his ear a gentle tug.

"Why don't you stay for breakfast, Olivia? I'm used to cooking for a crowd, and I made way too fuckin' much, as usual," I say, gesturing to the handful of pots and pans on the stove.

Olivia's eyes stray to the succotash. Then they move to Naomi.

"I don't want to interrupt—"

"Sweetie, you're not interrupting a damn thing." Naomi slides off the stool. "As delicious as Eli thinks he looks without a shirt on—"

"Hey," I tease, holding out my arms. "I *do* look delicious. Don't I, Olivia?"

Olivia laughs, even as a blush spreads across her cheeks when her eyes sweep over my torso. She looks back down at Billy and rubs his neck.

"—I'm taken. Even if I wasn't, I'd never, *ever* date this guy. Meaning no offense."

Ducking my lips, I nod. "None taken."

"I'll let y'all get to it." Naomi slides her phone into her back pocket. She looks at me. "See you tomorrow, chef. Olivia, it was nice meeting you."

"You too," Olivia calls after Naomi as she heads out the door.

Then it's just me and Olivia in the kitchen. She straightens, smoothing her dress over her thighs. She looks anywhere but at my chest.

I bite back a smile.

"Take a seat. Breakfast is almost ready." I wink at her when she finally meets my eyes. "Girl, I'm gonna blow your mind."

Chapter Four
ELI

Olivia scoffs as she settles onto Naomi's stool. Billy follows her. Lays down with a *thump* at her feet.

Apparently I'm not the only guy in the room who noticed how good Olivia smells.

How pretty she is.

"Are all southern guys so cocky?" she asks.

"Some of us, yeah." I face the stove and stir a splash of vinegar into a pot of simmering water. Then I turn down the burner. "But I'm one of the few who can back it up. Ever had grits?"

"Nope."

"Aw yeah. You're really in for it then."

Olivia laughs. A small, contained sound. "I take it you don't get many Yankee grits virgins in your kitchen."

"You'd be surprised." I toss her a grin over my shoulder. "So you *are* a Yankee."

"What? Did my accent give me away?"

Now Olivia is grinning, too. She blinks. Like the expression is unfamiliar.

"Among other things." I grab two bowls from the counter

and start to plate breakfast. Big ole scoop of creamy grits goes in first. I top that with the succotash, then crumble some bacon over it. The smell—smoky bacon, buttery beans and corn, starchy grits—is divine. I set the bowls back on the counter. Turning to the stove, I carefully crack an egg into the simmering water. "Where you from?"

"New York."

"Where in New York?"

A pause. Just long enough to let me know she's thinking about her answer.

"Upstate," she says at last.

I watch the white of the egg form a neat little ball. A couple more heartbeats and it'll be ready. I've poached a million eggs in my lifetime. Not afraid to say I know how to make 'em just right.

"Are all Yankee girls so coy?"

"Some of us, yeah."

I smile at that.

Egg is ready. I scoop it out of the pot with a slotted spoon and settle it right in the middle of the first bowl. Now my stomach is grumbling. I'm excited to share a home cooked meal with someone. Been too damn long.

Grabbing a fork, a knife, and a napkin, I reach across the island and set it all, along with the bowl, in front of Olivia. Those big baby blues of hers get even bigger when they fall on the food.

"Wow," she says. "Eli, this looks incredible. Even though I have no idea what any of it is."

My chest swells a little at the compliment. I live for this shit.

Feeding people good food.

Blowing pretty girls' minds by filling their bellies.

The Jam, bankruptcy, bad reviews—they feel about a million miles away right now.

"It's a breakfast grits bowl. You cut open the egg," I say, gesturing to her bowl with one hand while I wipe the other on the towel at my shoulder. "Let the yolk run all over everything. Brings it all together—Mama's grits and the succotash and the bacon."

Olivia's eyes flick to meet mine. They're blazing with...

Hunger?

My heart skips a beat.

Damn if I don't want to know more about the strange mix of vibes she's giving off. Her handshake was confident. Her laugh contained.

But then there's this wild, uncertain longing in her eyes.

On the outside, she's calm and confident and beautifully put together. Minus the just fucked hair, of course.

On the inside, though, I get the feeling she's burning.

"Wow," she says again, her gaze flicking over my chest before returning to the food. "Thank you. So much. Usually I just have coffee and, like, half a protein bar for breakfast. This is a treat."

I cross my arms. "Sitting down to breakfast is one of life's best little pleasures. Eat."

Olivia does as I tell her. She carefully slices the egg open. Smiles when she gathers a little of everything on her fork—yolk and bacon and butter beans and grits—and puts it in her mouth.

A mouth I suddenly can't stop looking at.

Blinking, I watch her eyes roll to the back of her head before she closes them. She lets out a little moan of appreciation as she chews.

"So?" I say, clearing my throat.

Olivia opens her eyes and meets mine. "So I don't think there are words to accurately describe just how incredibly, insanely delicious this is."

She's got this interesting way of speaking. It's somehow smart as hell, refined almost, without being stuck up.

I grin. "Told you I'd blow your mind."

"What are grits, anyway?" she asks, digging out a big scoop with her fork. "And how do you make them so damn good?"

I watch her take one last bite before I turn back to the stove. If I keep watching her—

Well. It'd make me a goddamn creeper, for one thing. And for another, I want Olivia to be able to enjoy my food in relative peace. To take in the flavors, remember them. This is her first time in the temple.

I hope she'll be back. Her enthusiasm—those little sounds she makes—it's a nice reminder of why I started cooking in the first place.

I crack another egg into the saucepan of water. "For simplicity's sake, think of grits as ground up dried corn. They've been a staple down south for centuries. There are a million ways to make 'em, but I like to keep it simple. Add lots of butter, half and half. Sometimes cheese if I'm hungover."

"They're, like, savory oatmeal almost." Olivia's words are muffled around a mouthful of food. "But way better. Do you make them every morning? If you do, I might have to stop by more often."

She's kidding. I can tell by the teasing tone of her voice. But I still give her an earnest look when I turn around with my prepared bowl a minute later. I *like* having her in my kitchen. Anxiety and panic don't threaten anymore. It's just us. Good food. Good conversation.

"I'll make them for you as often as you'd like, Yankee girl."

Olivia's eyes dance. "Don't get ahead of yourself, southern…charmer."

"Fuckin' hell, that *show*," I say, referring to a popular

reality TV show about a rich, ridiculous group of Charleston residents behaving badly.

"It's so awful," she says. "I love it."

"Me too," I say, laughing.

I walk around the island and settle onto the stool beside hers. Her gaze flicks over me. Her nostrils flare, once.

She looks away.

At my feet, Billy perks up. He knows there are scraps coming his way.

"So you're a chef," she says.

I nod, taking a wolfish bite of bacon, egg, and succotash. Damn, that *is* good.

"Yep. Been workin' in kitchens since I was fifteen years old. Mama is an incredible cook, and she passed on her love of food to me. Was a no brainer to come to Charleston for culinary school—I grew up in Aiken, which is about three hours from here. I opened my first restaurant five years ago."

Olivia nodded. "And the rest is history."

I laugh, shaking my head. "Not quite. Few months back, I opened my second restaurant. I wanted to do something simpler. More casual. Critics have *not* been impressed."

"Why not?" she says, shoveling another spoonful of grits into her mouth. I bite back a grin. Girl can't get enough, can she?

"Bastards are tearin' me a new one." I shrug. For some reason, talking to Olivia about this stuff hurts a lot less than it usually does. Although I'd still prefer to talk about something else. "One of the guys called my menu 'basic bitch southern food.'"

Olivia blinks. "That seems unnecessarily harsh."

"Welcome to the restaurant world," I say.

"No wonder you were cursing."

"Yep. That had me going. And the coffee—shit, I forgot the coffee. Want a cup?"

She grins. "Yes please."

I shovel in a few more bites myself before standing. When I have the time, I like to make coffee the Italian way—using freshly ground beans my sister Gracie, a coffee connoisseur, drops off from her coffee shop, and a moka pot on the stove.

I make quick work of it. Grind the beans, fill the moka pot. Set it over a low flame on the stove. It's immediately fragrant.

Before the whole fiasco with The Jam happened, I used to love mornings at home. It's been a while since I felt content like I do now. All thanks to the hungry girl who showed up in my kitchen.

I turn back to Olivia.

"Well." She pushes her empty bowl forward. "Clearly you know how to cook. I don't think you'll have any problem changing up your menu to impress those critics."

I settle my palms on the edge of the island and lean into them. Look at Olivia. "I'm not changing my menu."

She blinks again, her brow scrunching up. "Really? I don't know much about running a restaurant, but I can't imagine bad reviews are all that great for your bottom line."

"They're not." Another shrug. "Worst case scenario, we'll have to close the restaurant. But I'm hopin' it won't come to that."

Now she's looking at me sideways. "You don't sound all that concerned about losing a restaurant. Losing the opportunity to open *more* restaurants. Don't you—I don't know, want to make money? Be a celebrity chef and all that?"

"Of course I want to make money," I say, searching her eyes. "But not at the expense of my happiness. I'm not gonna change my menu. I genuinely love the food we make. I'm proud of it. Cooking that way makes me happy. But changing who I am and what I cook to please some idiot behind a computer? That sounds like my own personal hell. Why on God's green earth would I do something that makes me unhappy?"

Olivia blinks. Her gaze has turned thoughtful.

"But the money," she presses. "The press. Being famous. The security that would buy you—the reputation you'd have—"

"Isn't worth it if I'm not happy," I repeat. "I'm not sayin' money isn't important. Man needs something to live on. But I've got all I need." I gesture to the room around us. "Could I afford a bigger place if I changed up my menu? Got better reviews? Opened more restaurants? Probably. But I love my little slice of Charleston. I love what I do. And that's something I'm not willin' to compromise on."

It seems self-explanatory to me. But Olivia is staring at me like I'm some kind of exotic species she's never seen before.

Like she's never even *considered* putting her happiness first.

Which begs the question: what does she put first? Why isn't it happiness? Yeah, I may not be the happiest guy on the planet right now with everything going on. But that doesn't mean I don't try to prioritize it as much as I can.

The coffee starts to steam behind me. I turn to the stove. Turn the burner off. I grab two mugs and a carton of half and half from the fridge.

Facing her, I hold the carton over her cup. "Half and half okay?"

Olivia hesitates. Then: "Sure. Why not. I'm…"

I wait for her to finish. *I'm on vacation. I'm wanted by the authorities and this could very well be my last meal as a free woman. I'm in agreement that full fat dairy makes life worth living.*

"I'm okay with that," she says at last.

Oh, this girl is running from something all right.

Hiding something, too.

But it's not my place to push her. If she wants to tell me, she will. When she's ready.

I'll feed her in the meantime.

She's careful not to let our fingers brush as she takes the mug.

"Jesus," she says after taking a sip, her voice an octave lower with pleasure. "Do you make the best *everything*? This coffee tastes like liquid velvet."

I grin at her over the rim of my mug. What started out as another shitty morning in a string of shitty mornings is actually turning out to be pretty damn great.

"It's literally my job to make the best food on the planet, so...yeah. Glad you're enjoying it."

Olivia looks down at Billy. "It's not even noon, and already this might be the best Monday I've ever had. All thanks to food."

"Not me?" I say, arching a brow.

She laughs, her blue eyes dancing again. "Maybe if you put a shirt on."

"Never."

"You don't compromise on anything, do you?"

I lick my lips. "Not on things that matter."

Olivia swallows. "I admire that, Eli."

Insert Robert Plant howl here. I *like* it when she says my name. Maybe it's her accent. The sultry voice she's still using as she finishes her coffee.

"And I admire your appetite, Olivia."

Her gaze skips over my stomach. "Unlike me, you clearly keep yours under control."

"Not really." When she spears me with a look of pointed skepticism, I grin. "I eat a lot. But I also bike all over town, and I'm rollin' out my yoga mat whenever I can."

"You practice yoga?" she says, brightening. "Me too. Although I'm terrible at it."

"We should take a class together sometime."

I look at her. It's not an invitation to a date. But it's pretty damn close. Hey, I like hanging out with her. Like how she keeps me out of my head.

I wait for her to turn me down. Tell me she has a boyfriend, a husband. A husband *and* kids.

But I'm not seeing a ring on any of her fingers.

Olivia runs her tongue along her bottom lip. "It'd be great if you could point me in the direction of a studio close by."

"Consider it done. We've got plenty of great studios in town. My favorite is probably Yoga First on Spring Street—hot yoga at its best. Take Peter's class if you can."

Her eyes latch onto mine. A beat of unmistakable heat passes between us. How long has she been here? Half an hour? Half a day?

I want her to stay. It's only gotta be an hour or two until lunch. I've got some basil and fresh peaches—maybe have one of my prep guys bring some of that burrata we made yesterday at The Pearl—I've just got this feeling Yankee girl here would love my southern riff on a Caprese salad. We could eat it on the couch while catching up on that terrible reality TV show we both like.

Going a whole day without thinking about The Jam sounds like heaven right now.

"Got any plans for the rest of the day?" I ask, sipping my coffee.

Chapter Five
OLIVIA

My ridiculously full stomach twists at the honey brown kindness in Eli's eyes.

He's scary handsome. And one hell of a cook. And full of conviction. Which only adds to his distinct, down to earth charm.

He practices *yoga*.

And he's looking at me like I haven't been looked at in a long time. With warm, naked interest.

The air between us crackles with attraction. Energy. He's so easy to talk to. To look at.

Probably easy to fall in bed with, too.

My arousal lights into confusion. I may be on a break from Ted. But that doesn't mean I'm ready to jump into bed with someone else. I still feel so mixed up inside. So raw and tender to the touch. A hook up is not a good idea right now.

What if it's terrible?

What if it's not?

I am going back to New York at the end of October. I have a really great life waiting for me there—the job I've worked a decade to get, the house I've saved for, the relationship I've always wanted. No guy, no matter how delicious he may be, is worth sacrificing all that.

And I have to remember why I came to Charleston in the first place. To work on my book. Which I should be doing right now, instead of ogling this sexy, shirtless chef.

I stand up, my stool grunting against the roughed up wooden floorboards, and look away. Look around the house. It's small. But it's exquisitely renovated in what I can only describe as historic-Charleston-meets-southern-California style. Downstairs is all one big room, done in masculine shades of black and army green, punctuated by pale, antique-looking oak floors and these gorgeous ceiling beams that look like they were salvaged from a very chic barn.

There's a gigantic bookshelf that lines the length of an entire wall. The shelves practically groan beneath the weight of a zillion books stuffed haphazardly here and there. There are also a few bright yellow boxes, marked *Cohiba, Habana, Cuba,* scattered amongst the books. His cigars.

My heart literally skips a beat.

Of course Eli reads. Because the food and the yoga and the tattoos weren't sexy enough.

I catch a few names on well-worn spines. Hemingway. McCarthy. Nikki Sixx's *Heroin Diaries*.

I'm impressed. Although there's a conspicuous lack of female authors and subjects on these shelves. Something I'd be all too happy to remedy.

I push the thought aside. Probably best if I kept my distance from this house. This man. Too much opportunity for distraction.

Still, I can't help looking around a little more. A massive, commercial-style range occupies the opposite wall. An enormous antique table serves as an island and, I imagine, a gathering spot in the middle of the room. Across the space, I glance longingly at the leather sectional sofa in front of the TV. It looks cozy.

And the smell in here—it smells like bacon and delicious man. Eli's cologne, maybe. Something spicy and dark and woodsy. What I imagine Tom Ford would wear if *he* were a sexy southern chef. It's mouthwatering.

Oh, I *want* to stay. Pick his brain some more about happiness and compromise and the supreme trust he seems to have in himself.

But I shouldn't.

I really, really shouldn't.

"I should actually get going," I say. I realize I'm still holding my empty coffee mug. I set it carefully on the island, grateful for the excuse not to look at Eli. "I've already overstayed my welcome. Thanks again for the grits and the coffee—it was seriously the most delicious breakfast I've ever had."

I turn to see Eli studying me. He's skeptical. Knows something is going on, but is too polite to ask me outright what it is.

I'm glad he doesn't. I've felt so...*free* while I've been here. Like I can let my guard down and just relax. Be myself. I can't remember the last time I felt this way sharing a meal with Teddy. I guess I always feel the need to be "on" when we're together. Like I need to fit a certain mold by saying the right things and wearing the right clothes and hanging out with the right people.

But Eli? Eli clearly doesn't give a rat's ass about any of that stuff. Which makes me not want to talk about it. He makes me want to talk about big picture stuff instead. Stuff I haven't talked to really anyone about, except maybe Julia.

Talking to Eli like that would be dangerous. So I won't.

I can't.

"You sure?" he asks instead. "As long as you love to eat,

you'll never overstay your welcome. Stop by anytime, Olivia. You're welcome here, always."

His ridiculously hot southern accent makes the O in my name disappear. *Livia*.

A warm, happy shiver darts up my spine.

I have to get out of here.

Now.

"Thanks," I say. We look at each other for a beat. How do we end this? I can't hug him. He's half-naked, for Christ's sake. So I awkwardly extend my hand like the confused, sleep-deprived idiot that I am. "Sorry I'm running out on you like this, but I...have a lot to do today. It was nice meeting you, Eli."

His lips twitch into an amused grin. I don't think this guy —this big, tatted up, self-assured guy—could be awkward if he tried.

He takes my hand in the enormous mitt of his. His palm is dry and calloused. I feel the press of a strange ridge along my thumb—some sort of scar on his palm. I resist the urge to ask about it.

"Nice meetin' you too." He gives my hand a squeeze that's *just* firm enough. A current of electricity snaps up my arm, making my skin break out in goose bumps. "Hope to see you around."

I give Billy's velvety ear one last tug. Then I turn and dart out of Eli's house like it's on fire.

I'm on fire.

I close the door behind me. Let out a breath now that I'm in the safety of the carriage house. My face feels hot.

The whole world feels hot.

I am completely, uncomfortably, deliciously full.

At the same time, the caffeine from Eli's fancy coffee is hitting me. I'm sleepy and jittery, all at once.

Okay okay okay.

What should I do next?

Write. Yes. That's what I'll do.

I grab my computer and set it on the counter. But instead of opening Word, I open my internet browser and Google "Eli hot chef Charleston".

I get about fourteen thousand hits. Which means this guy is a big deal down here. Not that you'd know it from the way he dressed. Or the way he talked. The way he *was*.

At the top are articles from national newspapers and magazines.

How Elijah Jackson's Simple Southern Fare Changed The Foodie Scene Forever

Star Chef Eli Jackson's New Restaurant a Disappointment With Critics

A Table at Eli Jackson's The Pearl Still Hottest Reservation in Town Despite Struggles at New Joint

Elijah Jackson. Is there a more perfect name for a sexy-sweet southern chef?

I think not.

So he owns that pretty restaurant I saw on the drive in. I'll have to check it out.

I read the scathing reviews of his new restaurant, The Jam. They feel personal, somehow. Maybe because I just ate the food that these critics are lambasting. Food that was incredibly delicious. So good I'd almost call it a religious experience. I'll never look at breakfast—at Monday mornings—the same way again.

Makes me realize just how much I hate my usual Monday morning routine. Recently I've been getting the Sunday scaries bad, which always keep me up half the night. I wake up Monday morning to my alarm blaring with a knot in my stomach and single thought in my head: *how am I going to get through this day?*

I know I can't have hot guys cook me a hot breakfast every Monday morning.

That's not real life.

That's not how the adult world works.

Mondays suck for everyone. Except, apparently, Elijah Jackson.

Which makes me wonder if what I've been putting myself through every Monday morning—every *weekday* morning—is just a shitty fact of life, or a conscious choice. A *wrong* choice. Are all the expensive clothes and makeup and cars indicators of me living my best life? Or are they a kind of golden cage I've put myself in?

Why on God's green earth would I do something that makes me unhappy?

Eli shrugged when he said those words. Like everyone followed their happiness. Their hearts. Not prestige or perfection or expectation.

But Eli is insanely talented. He has the luxury of living this wild, weird life. That isn't the case for normal people like me.

I have to be practical.

How much can I realistically ask of the universe anyway? I have a supportive family. A great job. A man who loves me.

I'm incredibly lucky. People would kill to have what I do. It'd be greedy to want more. Not more stuff necessarily. But more fulfillment. More freedom to be myself, the way I was just now with Eli. It just seems silly to want *fulfillment* with all the very real pain and suffering going on in the world.

I have my happily ever after. And if I occasionally feel smothered by it, well...that comes with the territory. Having it all requires work. Constant, exhausting work. But it's worth it.

Right?

"Hell*looooo!*"

I start at the sound of a familiar voice. Julia is standing in the door, wearing what is doubtlessly a couture floral dress and a smile. I don't think I've ever seen her *not* look like a million bucks.

Leaping from my stool, I dash across the kitchen to wrap her in a hug. Seeing a familiar face after feeling all those unfamiliar...well, *feelings* at Eli's earlier makes my heart feel like it's going to burst with gratitude.

"Oh my goodness!" I say. "Aren't you supposed to be in Spain drinking too much sangria and dancing at the discotecas or something?"

Julia pulls back. Her smile dims a little.

"Yeah, about that..."

I slide my hands down her arms and give them a squeeze.

"Everything okay?"

She licks her lips. "Kind of. I had to cut my semester in Spain short, unfortunately. My dad isn't doing so well."

My heart skips a beat.

"I'm so sorry," I say. "I know how close you two are. What can I do?"

Julia shakes her head. "Nothing we can do at this point. He's pretty uncomfortable, but he seems to feel better when I'm around. So I'm going to stay with him for a while. Do what I can to keep him happy."

I pull her into another hug.

"I'm here if you need anything, okay? Selfishly, though, I'm glad you'll be in town. You sure you don't want to stay here? I'm sure I could find someplace else—"

"Don't even think about it. I want you to stay right here and finish that fucking *book* you told me about. How's it going, by the way?"

Julia is one of the few people in whom I confided about

my secret steamy writing tendencies. For so long I regretted it, because she always brought it up when we visited each other. But now I'm kind of glad I told her. Maybe I need a little push. A little moral support.

I nod at my laptop. "I just got here yesterday. I wrote one and a half pages, which I deleted because they were garbage. So far, writing romance is not as magical as I thought it would be."

"Bless your dirty book loving heart. Of *course* it's not magical. Eighty percent of the time, writing is the fucking pits, whether you're writing a dissertation on the birth of aspirational middle class values in Jane Austen's work, or steamy, graphic, delicious sex in a romance novel," Julia says. "Speaking of graphic sex—I cannot wait to read yours. I'll actually be back at the College of Charleston this semester doing some admin stuff in the English department if you want to swing by. We've got some great fiction writers on staff. Can't hurt to pick their brains."

I grin. "I'd love to. Thank you. So you won't be teaching?"

"Not until next semester," Julia replies, shaking her head again. "Then I'll have my usual course load."

Julia's been teaching undergraduate English down here for years now. Unlike me, she loves it. Then again, that could have something to do with the fact that she's got a trust fund, which allows her to split her time between teaching and indulging in her true passion—antiquing across Europe.

"I haven't seen you in a while. Why don't you stay for a bit?" I nod my head toward the fridge. "I picked up a bottle of Chardonnay I'd love to open. I *am* a writer now. Probably means I should have a glass of wine in the middle of the day. You know, for my muse," I say, using air quotes.

Julia grins. "I am so here for this."

"By the way," I call over my shoulder as I grab the wine

and a corkscrew. "I wish you would've told me you had a cute neighbor who walks around half-naked all the time."

She leans into her forearms on the counter and wags her eyebrows. "C'mon, Olivia, we both know Eli's not cute. He's smoking hot. You think you two might...you know?"

"Absolutely not," I reply. "What about you? Have you ever..."

"Nope." Julia takes the glass of Chardonnay I hand her. "Not my type."

"He's not my type either," I say, sipping my wine. "Totally not my type."

Julia eyes me. "You never know until you try it."

"Absolutely not," I repeat.

"The lady doth protest too much," Julia says, still grinning.

I look away. All the while thinking about how stupid I was to go over to Eli's this morning.

Because now I can't stop thinking about him. I want to get back to writing my book if only so I can hang out with my hazel-eyed, broad-shouldered hero.

The one who looks and sounds an awful lot like my hot new neighbor.

Chapter Six
OLIVIA

I make Julia promise to call me tomorrow before I let her leave. Then I grab my laptop and try to write for the rest of the afternoon.

I wake up early and write the next morning, too.

By ten A.M., I'm ready to tear my hair out. My shoulders and neck ache from being hunched over my computer.

I wonder if that yoga studio Eli mentioned has morning classes.

I wonder if Eli takes them.

Ignoring the jolt that idea gives me, I Google the studio and see that they have an eleven o'clock class.

Perfect. I'll even have enough time to bike there. Eli said that's how he likes to get around town. Figure I'll give it a try.

And honestly, what are the chances that Eli will take the same class? At *eleven* on a *Tuesday*? He has a restaurant empire to run. I imagine that leaves very little opportunity to squeeze in some midday exercise.

The studio is on Spring Street, a little over a mile from the carriage house. So I grab Julia's bike—with a fancy wicker basket, Carolina blue paint, and buttery leather handles, it looks like a Gwyneth Paltrow-approved version of a bicycle living its best life—and head up the peninsula. I saw lots of people biking on my way in, so I figure I'll join in on the fun.

The late morning sun is just getting hot. I stick to the shady side of the street when I can. My legs yawn awake as I pedal, my calf muscles stretching pleasantly with each lazy rotation.

I've decided that while I'm here, I'm not going to rush. For one thing, no one else in this town seems to be in a hurry. Fowl included.

For another, I've always got my foot on the gas back home. If I'm not running to work, then I'm running to a meeting. If not to a meeting, then to the gym, or to the grocery store.

And damn it, I'm tired of running. Maybe it's time I start thinking about why I do all that running in the first place. Because everyone else does it?

I blame my sudden change of pace on Eli's slow, intentional way of moving around his kitchen yesterday morning. The way he made me sit and eat a real breakfast with him, like we were Europeans and the idea of *not* sitting down to a meal was sacrilege.

How he took his time making the perfect cup of coffee.

That *coffee*. If I had to think of a word to describe it, orgasmic comes to mind. So different from Ted's. So *delicious*. I've never had anything like it.

I could've used some of it earlier today. My writing mojo is nonexistent. I just can't seem to get to the actual *story*. I have too much going on peripherally, trying to capture on the page how the characters look and smell and behave in my head. What they want. Their histories. Their weaknesses and favorite sexual positions and clothing.

Then there's the themes I want to get at. The feminism. Matching up the character arcs so the hero and heroine touch on the other's sore spots, which then forces them to confront their demons. And then of course there have to be great secondary characters who drop nuggets of wisdom just when the hero and heroine need them...

Whew. Anyone who says writing a romance is easy has *clearly* never attempted the feat themselves.

Although I have to admit I enjoyed mentally dressing Eli in a riding jacket—no shirt underneath, naturally—and breeches as a stand-in for my hero.

I enjoyed mentally *un*dressing him even more. Even though I knew I shouldn't. Even though thinking about anyone other than Ted was weird. Weird and exciting, if I'm being honest.

I try not to think about what that means.

I pedal up Meeting Street, enjoying the breeze being on the move creates. I can't remember the last time I rode a bike. In New York, I'm always inside or in a car.

It's nice. Especially when my route takes me through the College of Charleston's bustling campus. I'm suddenly curious; I don't know much about it, other than the fact that Julia teaches there.

I ride past as slowly as I can without running any students over. It's very pretty. Very southern, lots of big oak trees draped in Spanish moss and pastel buildings held up by towering pillars.

Out of the blue, I wonder if they have a creative writing program. Julia did say they have fiction writers on staff. On bad days back at my university, I fantasize about ditching my classes on twentieth-century literature and teaching classes on writing instead. On fiction. Romance.

Not that it matters. Teddy would shit a brick if I did something so impractical and...well, kind of strange. I can just imagine him saying something along the lines of, "You're capable of more than that". Or even, "What will people say when they find out you went from teaching premier classes on the greatest writers in the English language to teaching courses on how to write trashy books? Come on, Olivia".

Come on, Olivia. Ted says that a lot. But he's right. I have to keep my head screwed on straight.

It's a quick ride up to Spring Street. The city is much newer and younger up here. I nearly swoon with delight when I see Yoga First is housed an adorable pink cottage beside an even more adorable inn. I lock up my Gwyneth Paltrow bike on the rack beside the door and head inside.

I don't roll out my mat as often as I'd like. Teddy prefers golf—he belongs to a local club near our house—and even though I suck at it, I try to play with him as much as I can. Once I get good at it, I'll start to like it. That's what he tells me, anyway.

I'm immediately hit by the smell of incense. I smile. The funkier the yoga studio, the better, in my opinion. I fill out some paperwork and rent a mat. In the meantime, several people have checked in. Class is going to be crowded.

The friendly woman behind the counter escorts me to Studio A at the front of the building. Opening the door, she peeks inside, then looks at me and grins.

"One spot left. Lucky you."

I thank her and step into the studio.

Yep, it's definitely crowded. Which always makes me the tiniest bit nervous. I'm not exactly a graceful yogi. I wish I could say I've never fallen onto my neighbor while attempting crow pose, but that would be a lie.

It takes me a second to find my spot. Ah, there it is. Up front. Beside a man.

A huge, shirtless, tattooed man.

My stomach clenches.

He's laying face up on his mat, knees bent. I recognize the

swirling script tattooed on his upper ribs, just beneath his left pec.

Eli.

Despite the studio's blaring heat, my blood turns to ice. I don't know whether to laugh or cry.

The teacher, a smiling, ripped twenty-something man with dreadlocks hanging down to his butt, looks at me and points at the empty spot. "You're right there."

"Thanks," I say, blinking.

"You can take your spot now," he gently prods. "Class is about to begin."

I blink again. "Yup. Got it."

I feel like I'm wading into the deep end of a pool as I head for my assigned spot. Eli is facing away from me, so he has to look up toward his eyebrows to meet my gaze.

When he does, he smiles. A wickedly handsome, utterly masculine half-smile that lights up his face and turns my knees to jelly.

"Olivia!" He sits up. "I'm glad you came! You're in for a treat."

The excitement in his voice is obvious.

He can't be this happy to see me.

Can't be.

Can he?

"Why am I in for a treat?" I ask, looking away as I roll out my mat. "Because I get to practice next to you?"

He laughs, the sound a deep rumble in his chest, and reaches out to help flatten the rolled-up edge of my mat. From the corner of my eye, I notice the woman beside him checking him out.

I don't blame her. The guy is gorgeous. And mostly naked.

"That," he says, "and the fact that Peter is teaching. His classes are hard, but you feel so fuckin' good afterward. Like your body and your mind are wrung out, you know?"

I sit down on my mat, careful not to let my knee touch Eli's.

"Exactly why I'm here," I say, turning my head to look at him.

Eli's got one arm draped over his bent knee, making his already bulging bicep bulge even more. To an almost pornographic degree.

Can biceps even *be* pornographic?

I start to sweat. Hope—pray—that I don't make a fool of myself practicing next to him.

"What'd you have for breakfast?" he asks.

I stick my tongue into my cheek, fighting a smile. "Protein bar. Coffee from the Nespresso machine."

"Now that's just plain sad." He shakes his head, clicking his tongue. "Shoulda come to my place. Whipped up a mean fried green tomato eggs benedict. I made enough for two, but since you didn't show, I had to give your plate to Billy."

I give up the fight against my smile. "Lucky Billy."

"Coulda been you, Yankee girl."

Peter calls the class to attention. Eli gives me one last half smile—one last flash of hazel eyes—and then he's getting on his knees and settling into child's pose. My heart skips a beat at the way the muscles in his back ripple beneath his skin.

I begin to wonder if I'm going to make it out of this class alive.

The flow is familiar, thank God. We start with a series of sun salutations. I've always struggled not to rush through my poses. I hold all my tension in my shoulders and neck, and it's easy for my arms to get fatigued from so many chaturangas in a row.

I can't help but notice how beautifully—patiently—Eli moves on his mat. From the corner of my eye I see him flow from one pose to the next as easily as water coursing through a stream. He's taking deep, even warrior breaths in and out of his nose.

My eyes catch on the muscles in his arm. They bunch and ripple against tattooed skin that glistens with a fine sheen of sweat.

If my shoulders are burning like they usually do, I don't feel it.

Peter has us meet in downward facing dog. Underneath the pyramid formed by Eli's gorgeous body, I meet eyes with the woman on the other side of him.

Wow, she mouths, gaze flicking to Eli.

I suppress a grin.

I know, I mouth back.

"Just a reminder to keep your eyes on your own mat," Peter says as he walks behind me. "Find your *drishti*—your point of focus."

Right. I'm here to clear my mind. Not check out hot shirtless southerners.

I do my best to keep my *drishti* on my mat. Even so, I'm aware of Eli moving beside me. His practice really is beautiful. Patient.

I find myself moving patiently too, breathing through the tight pull in my hamstrings and the fire in my quads as Peter leads us through an interminably long series of chair poses. I'm not graceful. But moving more slowly allows me to arrive in every pose and stay there for as long as Peter cues us to.

Once, during a chair twist, I twist the wrong way, and Eli and I end up facing each other. His eyes are kind when they meet mine. My eyebrows go up when I realize my mistake. He grins.

I find myself grinning back, despite the way my legs have started to shake.

His hotness is becoming less intimidating. Probably has

something to do with this generous, down-to-earth charm of his.

By the grace of God I make it through class without embarrassing myself. I even attempt side crow pose—something I've never done before—and manage to fly for approximately half a second. Of course Eli held the pose for what had to be ten minutes. Sitting in my sumo squat, I watched the thick veins and sinews pop against the backs of his hands as he balanced his legs on his triceps.

I imagine what those hands would feel like on me.

Stop. I need to stop thinking about him like this. This fantasy goes nowhere.

Eli and I walk out of the studio together when class is over.

"How good did that feel?" he says, opening the front door for me.

I step out into the sunshine. This *heat* is unreal.

"Pretty damn good. I needed to work off those grits from yesterday," I reply. I nod at the bike rack, where Julia's tricked out bike awaits. "That's me."

"You biked here? Good for you. I didn't have the time this morning. Gotta be at the restaurant in half an hour."

"Oh?" I slide my sunglasses onto my face. "What's on the menu tonight?"

He tucks his mat underneath his arm and looks at me, one eye screwed up against the sun. "Why don't you come find out?"

I flush with pleasure at the invitation. "I did some reading up on you yesterday."

"Uh oh."

"Only the good articles," I tease. "But everyone says The Pearl is the hardest reservation to get in town—that you have to book it months in advance. It's gotta be too late to get one for tonight."

Eli just grins, shaking his head. "Olivia, you just gotta say the word and I'll get you in anytime, at any hour."

I tell myself he's just being neighborly. It's too exciting—too bewildering—to think there's something more behind his kindness.

I cannot think there is something *more* between us.

"Okay," I say. "I'd like that. I'm—I'm pretty much free all night, so...whenever you can fit me in is great."

"How about seven?" he says. "That's the seating for the chef's tasting."

"Chef's tasting?"

"The Pearl seats eighty. But every night, we select ten guests at random to do the chef's tasting. You sit at a big communal table right next to the kitchen, and we feed you five courses of whatever the hell we feel like cooking that day. It's an experience you don't wanna miss."

My stomach dips. In a good way.

"Sounds fancy," I say.

"It's not," he replies. "But the food is fuckin' ridiculous. My best work."

"Better than the grits bowl?"

Eli laughs at that. "If I blew your mind then...well, I just might push you over the edge tonight."

We're standing close.

Were we always standing this close? I can smell the sweat on his skin. Salt. That woodsy, smoky cologne.

I swallow. Manage a smile. "Seven it is. Thank you very much for the invite—I've never done a chef's tasting before."

The sunlight catches on his eyes, turning them into translucent pools of green.

"I don't wanna make a joke about popping your cherry, because we just met and all, but..."

It's my turn to laugh. It brings a lightness to my chest I haven't felt in a long time.

"It's been a while since I had a cherry popped," I say. "I could use a little excitement."

"Happy to do the job."

He's smiling, and I'm smiling, and we look at each other for a beat too long.

Shit.

"So," I say at last, blinking. "Tonight at seven."

"Yeah." He runs a hand up the back of his head. "Seven o'clock. You like wine?"

I roll my eyes teasingly. "Do I like wine."

"Then I'll put you down for the wine pairing, too. My sommelier is a crack shot. She always knows how to make the meal come together."

Jesus Christ, he is relentless. In the best way.

"Sounds great," I say. "See you tonight."

"See you tonight, Olivia." His gaze is steady as it holds mine. "I'm lookin' forward to it."

Then he heads for the parking lot behind the studio.

My hands shake a little when I unlock my bicycle. Yoga always leaves me a little shaky. But I think I'm shaky with excitement, too. A little disbelief.

I don't know what good deed I did to deserve a (temporary) neighbor like Eli. If anything, I feel like the villain of my own story right now. Like I'm tipping the karmic scales against myself for escaping a perfectly nice life. A life *I chose*.

I don't understand any of it. Not Eli's reasons. Not my own.

But my gut is telling me the key to untangling my feelings isn't holing up and licking my wounds in private.

It's telling me to *get out*. Something I don't do often enough, especially by myself, in small town New York.

So tonight, I'm going out.

Chapter Seven
ELI

I'm still sweating from class when I pull up to The Pearl. The ninety degree temperature isn't helping. We're at the end of September, but the heat has yet to abate. When it's this hot outside, it's a fucking inferno inside the kitchen.

Greeting my prep guys who are busy making stock, chopping veggies, and butchering meat, I duck my head into the walk-in refrigerator to make sure we have a supply of clean, wet towels cooling on their usual shelf. The cooks and I will wrap 'em around our heads and necks tonight in an attempt not to die during service. Then I head for the kitchen.

My happy place.

I still get butterflies every time I walk in, even though it's been years since I opened the place. I've known from the time I could walk that I wanted to be a chef. My earliest memories are all about food: sitting on Grandaddy's lap, shoveling my mother's famous potato salad into my mouth with both fists. Watching my uncle smoke an entire pig in a pit in our backyard, then helping him butcher it on a picnic table. Keeping quiet while Mama made mayo from scratch because "noise ruined it".

I love food and I love family. In my kitchen, I get to have both on a daily basis, as the staff at The Pearl has gelled into our own not-so-little family over the years. We have very, very little turnover. People—whether they be line cooks, servers, sous chefs, bartenders, or busboys—like working here. I'd like to think it's because they feel connected to a higher purpose. We're not just filling people's bellies. We're filling their eyes, their heads, their souls, too. There's an exquisite kind of beauty in sitting down to eat good food with good friends. Connecting over cocktails, forgetting worries while savoring a cup of perfect peach ice cream (hand churned, of course).

I try not to think about the family at The Jam. The one that I'm probably going to have to break up soon. Just this morning, I poured more of my own money into The Jam's coffers—an emergency cash infusion to keep the doors open. Things are not looking good over there. So in addition to the money, I'm pulling long shifts in the kitchen there alongside Naomi whenever I can. We're scrambling to adjust the menu while sticking to my "simple is better" philosophy. But no matter how many menu items we tweak, or how many hours I spend pouring over the books or working my ass off in the kitchen, nothing seems to help.

I feel a familiar heaviness settling on my chest. Blinking, I get to work.

Work always helps chase the anxiety away.

So does yoga, and hanging out with Olivia. I was more excited than I should've been to run into her in class this morning.

Just like I'm more excited than I should be to cook for her again.

Pulling a clipboard and pen from a nearby drawer, I start to jot down ideas for tonight's specials and tasting menu. I reserve a spot or two for dishes my line cooks pitch. As hard as they work, it's important to allow them to flex their creative muscles.

I always feed my staff before service, so I make some notes about what to cook for them, too.

I take my time with all my menus. But today, I'm especially thorough. Which may or may not have to do with the fact that I want to feed Yankee girl the best damn meal of her life. Despite the pretty smile Olivia flashed me during class this morning, there was still pain in her eyes. Sadness.

Sadness that disappeared, for a minute or two, while she ate the grits bowl I made her yesterday. A full belly has a way of making things feel a little less heavy.

A way of making you feel a little less lost.

Yoga works up an appetite anyhow. Case in point—I'm ravenous. More so than usual.

I blame it on practicing extra hard because I was next to a gorgeous woman with a hot, strong body. Girl didn't miss a pose. And the way the muscles in her calves flexed during locust pose—

"You sweatin' already?" A guy in a baseball hat and dirty shirt appears at my elbow, dropping a crate overflowing with produce on the counter. "It's not even two! Dang, chef, if I didn't know any better, I'd say you were nervous."

Smiling, I drop my pen. "Nervous? Me? Naw. Just startin' to stress about my veggies being a no-show." I hold out a hand and he takes it, pulling me into a hug.

"How you been, brother?" he asks.

Luke is one of my oldest friends. He and I were dishwashers together at a local fish camp when I first came to Charleston seventeen years ago. I stayed in the restaurant business, but Luke went on to play major league baseball. After an injury sidelined him a few seasons back, he returned to town to play for our minor league team, the Charleston Pirates.

Now Luke splits his time between playing first base and tending to the enormous organic garden in his backyard on Sullivan's Island. Man's got one of the greenest thumbs I've yet to encounter. His produce, all local varieties that have been grown in the area for centuries, is second to none. I buy whatever he's willing to sell me.

Today, that looks like some beautiful collard greens, enormous heads of purple garlic, garnet sweet potatoes, and a whole bunch of leeks. I inhale the rich, sweet smell of sun and dirt that rises out of the crate.

"Better, now that I'm seeing this," I say, nodding at the potatoes. "What do you think? Sweet potato fries? Gnocchi? Maybe a simple syrup for cocktails?"

Luke grins proudly. "The gnocchi, definitely. Maybe throw some of those leeks into a sauce—they're lookin' mighty fine, if I don't say so myself."

"This all looks amazing. No surprise there."

"And The Jam?" he asks. "Any news?"

My mood dims. "We're hangin' in there. How're things with you?"

He shrugs, digging his hands into the pockets of his well-worn jeans. "Garden's good, baseball...not so much. We're 27-81 for the season."

"Ouch," I say with a grin.

"Starting to think my playing days might be numbered." He picks up a sweet potato, turning it over in his hand.

"And why is that?"

He shrugs again. "I don't know. You know that girl I been seein'?"

I scoff. "Luke, you been seein' half this city."

"True," he says, grinning. A grin that quickly fades. "Anyway. This girl told me I was washed up."

"*What?*" I pull back in disbelief. "I hope you told her to fuck off."

He's still looking at the sweet potato. "Definitely got the hell out of there as quick as I could. Whatever. I know I should take it with a grain of salt. And part of me does. But another part...I don't know." Luke shakes his head, finally looking up. "What about you? Heard you had a cute stranger over for breakfast yesterday."

I roll my eyes. "Word travels fast in this city."

"Says the guy who not only loves Andy Cohen, but loves to gossip like him, too."

Laughing, I watch Luke toss the potato back into the crate.

"That's fair. You know how I like to feed strangers. And Olivia was hungry, so..."

"Olivia." Luke pokes his tongue into his bottom lip, grinning. "Haven't heard you actually mention a girl's name in a while, E. Anything you wanna tell me?"

He's right. I haven't mentioned a girl's name in this kitchen since I broke up with my girlfriend last year. I'm not the type to kiss and tell.

But Olivia and I haven't kissed.

Yet.

"She's a Yankee," I say, turning back to my clipboard. "Don't know what her story is beyond that."

"But you're gonna find out, aren't you, you smug bastard?"

My turn to grin. "Hope to."

"Good luck." Luke claps me on the shoulder. "I gotta get goin'—we have a game tonight that we're probably gonna lose. I'll be back on Thursday with another delivery. Got some heirloom acorn squash coming up that are lookin' mighty tasty."

"I'll take 'em. Be good, you hear?" I call after him as he heads out of the kitchen.

Luke flicks me the bird over his shoulder. "Couldn't be good if I tried."

Wasn't that the truth. Man has a little black book as thick as all the Harry Potter novels combined.

Shaking my head, I pick up my pen. Glance at the potatoes in the crate.

Time to rice these beauties and get a start on the gnocchi.

I hope Yankee girl likes pasta.

"Ho-ly *shit*, chef. That's out of this world."

My head chef Maria's eyes nearly roll to the back of her head as she chews.

I smile, turning to run a damp prep towel around the rim of the shallow pasta bowl. In it, the bright orange sweet potato gnocchi—tiny pillows of pasta goodness—glisten in the light gorgonzola sauce I've whipped together. I added a handful of spicy arugula, and another handful of earthy, slightly sweet hazelnuts, finely chopped.

Simple. Savory. Satisfying.

Exactly what I was going for.

"Good, right?" I say.

"Good? Chef, I just creamed my pants. Luckily I keep an extra pair in my locker."

I smile harder. Maria may be only one of two women in my kitchen here at The Pearl, but she's got the dirtiest mouth by far.

Wiping my hands, I cross my arms. "My work here is done."

"Chef." I look up at the sound of my manager Kip's voice. "Our guests for the seven o'clock tasting are all here."

"All of them?"

Kip's lips twitch. "Yes. Including your *personal* guest Olivia."

"Personal guest?" Maria cocks a brow. "You fucking this girl, chef?"

"If he isn't, then he definitely wants to," Kip adds, a mischievous gleam in his eye. "We haven't had a personal guest of Eli's visit us in a while."

"*That's* why you put oysters on the menu," Maria says, nodding. "You want to get her in the mood, don't you?"

I run a hand through my hair. "Keep it down, would you? And my personal life is none of y'alls' business. But if you *must* know, no, I'm not fucking her. And no, I'm not tryin' to get her in the mood. She's new in town, and I just want to feed her the best food she's ever had. Nothing more. Nothing less. That so hard to believe?"

Maria snorts in reply.

"The oysters speak for themselves," Kip says. "I'll go ahead and get everyone seated. And yes, chef, before you ask, Olivia's going to get the best seat."

"Best seat?" I ask.

Kip wags his eyebrows, tilting his head toward the dining room. "One where she can see you. So y'all can, like, make eyes at each other all night or whatever."

"Eye fucking." Maria is still nodding. "Best kind of foreplay there is."

Chapter Eight
OLIVIA

I gawk shamelessly at my surroundings as Kip, the sprightly manager who immediately introduced himself when I walked into The Pearl a few minutes ago, leads us to our table.

The restaurant is take-your-breath-away gorgeous. There's a hefty sense of place about it. You *know* you're in Charleston the second you step inside. Lest you forget, there's the exposed brick walls, antique wooden beams, and miles of roughed up leather banquettes to remind you. It's like a 1920s speakeasy and a hipster-y gentleman's club had an especially stylish baby.

There's dark paint for days. Artsy brass light fixtures. An enormous bar with a mirrored wine cellar beside it.

I see Eli's touch everywhere.

The whole vibe is so sexy it's literally turning me on. I press my legs together, willing my body to behave itself.

The dining room is filled with a good-looking but casually dressed crowd. Every table is occupied; the bar is two or three people deep in most places. I hear the clank of ice in a cocktail shaker, followed by a distinct *crack* when the bartender—bearded, just like every other guy I've seen in this city so far—opens it and pours a drink.

It smells ridiculously good in here. Like meat roasting in a wood burning oven.

My stomach grumbles.

The noise of the crowd dims for a second, and I catch a strain of music. *Daughter* by Pearl Jam.

I'm not sure why this makes me smile. But it does.

We move away from the bar, and the gleaming white kitchen comes into view. A large, open window is cut into the wall between the kitchen and the dining room, allowing diners to watch the kitchen staff at work.

There, front and center, is Eli. Wearing a crisp white chef's jacket he fills out to perfection, JACKSON embroidered in simple black letters above the breast pocket. Tattoos peeking out from underneath the sleeves. Dark hair slicked back neatly from his handsome face.

A face that is a mask of concentration as he holds a plastic bottle over a plate and gives it a quick squeeze.

My stomach does a backflip. Only instead of landing, it keeps falling.

Eli looks so handsome it *hurts*. Those *hands* and *forearms* and *shoulders*.

So different from the reedy guys in crisp collared shirts I've dined with in the past.

I might as well be a million miles from home. From who I am there.

I feel a pang of guilt that I'm about to enjoy what is sure to be an extraordinary meal without Ted. This is exactly the kind of thing we'd do together.

But then I remind myself that I'm not here to think about Ted. I'm here to write. To *experience* things that will inspire my creativity.

And I find Eli and his food all kinds of inspiring.

Kip points us to a long trestle table that runs parallel lengthwise to the kitchen. When I try to sit at the far end, he grabs me and seats me smack dab in the middle of the table instead. I'm facing the kitchen.

Facing *Eli*. Head on. Ten feet—probably less—the only thing separating us.

As if he knows I'm staring at him, Eli looks up. He smiles at me. Winks.

I smile back, my face growing warm.

My hands shake when I pick up the menu. I feel like a teenager again. A little sick with longing.

Longing I don't want to feel. But there it is.

I imagine this is the kind of longing the heroine of my novel feels for the hero. It's forbidden. Exciting *because* it's forbidden.

Already a scene is taking shape in my head. The hero and heroine meeting eyes across a crowded room. Everything and everyone else falls away as wordless, primal understanding passes between them. Sounds, sights, smells—it's overwhelming and distant, all at once. Time slows and goes too fast.

Anticipation thickens the air.

Maybe—just for tonight—I give in to this longing. Not *give in* give in—like in the biblical sense. But maybe I let myself feel it. Maybe I pretend that I really am a writer, and I really am living here, and I really am free to lust after Elijah Jackson the way my heroine lusts after her hero.

I try it.

I give in, meeting Eli's eyes across the restaurant. For strictly literary purposes, of course. He smiles. So do I.

The sommelier pours the wine for our first course. It's an Albariño, a crisp Spanish white that tastes like green apples on my tongue.

Then there's the food. Course after course of fresh,

inventive, supremely satisfying amazingness. We start with biscuits that are served with something called pimiento cheese, made in house. It's so good I literally can't stop eating it. When we run out of biscuits, I beg our server not to bring any more. I'm worried I'll ruin my appetite for the real meal.

After the biscuits comes oysters on the half shell and a salad of pickled shrimp and green beans. Then broiled local snapper on a bed of collard greens cooked in coconut milk. Gnocchi made out of sweet potatoes follows, served with this tangy, yummy, buttery cream sauce that's so good I have to resist the urge to lick my plate.

I feel like my senses are turned all the way up. It's all too much. The wine and the food and Eli holding court in the kitchen. I find myself closing my eyes, willing myself to remember these moments, these flavors. This pure, fleeting bliss of just sitting and enjoying and *lusting*.

And often I find Eli watching me when I open them. Almost as often as I watch him working in the kitchen.

I can't stop watching him. It's full on competence porn. I stare as he grabs a pair of enormous tweezers from his breast pocket and uses them to painstakingly place a mint sprig on a perfectly round scoop of cream.

I feel myself getting wet.

There's something so steady about him as he works. His economical movements. The steady way he plates each meal. There's no rush. No second guessing. Eli is clearly in his element; watching him work alongside the other cooks, all of them putting these gorgeous dishes together without saying a word, is like watching a dance.

I drink my wine, my buzz so happy I feel it tingling behind my knees. The more I drink, the more I watch. The less I care about being caught watching.

No surprise that Eli catches me again. This time he

shakes his head, teasingly, like he's so sick of being the center of my attention. His eyes, though—they flicker with heat.

With a dare.

Keep looking, Yankee girl.

The guy's incredibly sexy outside the kitchen.

But in it? He's a god.

The kind I've only encountered in the pages of the romance novels that I love.

Finishing my wine, I feel a renewed surge of inspiration. *This* is how you capture a hero's strength. His virility.

This is how he should look. Move. Exist within his world.

I grab my phone and open the notes app. I jot down all the ideas I've had tonight so far. I can't wait to get back home to work on them.

By the time our server clears our dessert course—something called Coca-Cola sheet cake with ganache frosting that's so good I eat every last crumb, even though I'm beyond stuffed—it's late, and the restaurant has cleared out.

I notice everyone at my table is signing their bills and standing up.

Glancing around, I can't find my check.

"Excuse me," I say, flagging down our waiter. "I'll take my bill when you have a second."

He smiles. "I'll be right back."

My neighbor didn't finish his cake. Taking a quick peek around to make sure no one is watching, I swipe the tip of my finger in the frosting and bring it to my mouth.

"I saw that, Yankee girl."

I jump at the sound of the familiar, rumbly voice right behind me.

Turning, I see Eli standing there, looking bigger and broader and hotter than ever. The muscles in his forearms rope and bunch as he crosses his arms over his chest.

He's smirking. Ted would be horrified if he caught me eating with my fingers. Especially if we were out in public.

But Eli—he loves it.

The suffocation that has gripped my throat and squeezed for the past however many years feels so far away it might as well not exist. I can *breathe* here. Be myself—my messy, slightly drunk self—without being afraid of embarrassing or disappointing anyone.

A girl could get addicted to feeling like this.

"Guilty," I say, grabbing a napkin to wipe my finger. "If you didn't want me to be rude, you shouldn't make your food so damn delicious."

"You enjoyed it, then?" he says. There's a hint of uncertainty in his tone. A hint of hope.

It's cute.

A warning bell goes off in the back of my head. But I'm too far gone on wine and food and *him* to take heed of it.

"Hated it," I reply with a smile. He lets out the breath he's been holding. "So much so that I want to get my bill and get the hell out of here so I never have to come back. Speaking of—"

"Bill's taken care of," Eli says, waving me away.

I stare at him. "Stop it. Eli, you have to let me pay."

"Seeing the look on your face while you ate was payment enough. You wear your stomach on your sleeve, Olivia."

A new, more potent rush of heat to my face.

"Oh, Jesus, what kind of look are you talking about?" I ask.

His lips twitch. "The kind I like. C'mon, let's grab a drink at the bar."

Eli holds out his hand. I hesitate. Then, remembering to give in for the sake of my art, I take it. As he helps me down from my stool, an unmistakable charge of lust bolts through me from the place where my palm touches his.

I can't be the only one who feels it. But he makes no outward sign of acknowledgment. Just smiles at me, eyes meeting mine, and walks me across the restaurant.

Probably for the best.

He pulls out a stool for me at the bar and heads to the other side. The bartenders, who were busy loading the dishwashers and wiping down the counter, now nod at Eli and slip out of sight.

My heart is pounding. I know I should go home. Call it a night. But I don't want to.

Not yet.

"What are you drinking?" Eli asks, grabbing a shaker.

I look at the wall of liquor in front of me. "I'm *really* full—nothing too heavy. What would you recommend?"

He narrows his eyes playfully, searching my face.

"I got you. Hang on."

Watching Eli work a cocktail shaker—the way he casually knows his way around the bar, the liquor, the glasses—

I am sweating. This town is turning me into a perpetually sticky, sweaty, *lusty* mess.

My body is practically throbbing by the time he slides a heavy bottomed glass across the bar. He's holding another in his hand.

"Cheers," he says, holding it out. "Thanks for coming tonight."

I touch my glass to his. "Are you kidding? Thank you for having me. And for treating me to the best meal of my life. Seriously. I've never experienced anything like it. The food here—the atmosphere—it's special, Eli. I'm in awe."

He grins, bringing his drink to his lips. His eyes are on me as I sip mine. Like he's a little nervous to know what I think.

A smoky-sweet flavor hits my tongue, cut with a refreshing edge of something cold and foamy and just a little bit tart.

"Stop blowing my mind already, would you?" I say, smacking my lips. "One time is enough."

Eli is still grinning. "It's the Mezcal. I've kind of been obsessed with it lately—it's a Mexican liquor made from agave, and it has this incredible, sexy smoke to it I can't get enough of."

Sexy. That's exactly how this drink tastes.

That's exactly how I feel when Eli looks at me.

Chapter Nine
OLIVIA

"It's delicious," I say, looking away. "Everything you make is delicious. Watching you work in the kitchen gave me so much inspiration."

"Inspiration?" He arches a brow. "For what?"

I freeze, holding my cocktail in midair.

I hadn't meant to say that.

I meet Eli's eyes. They're dark. Handsome.

Earnest.

I think about what Ted said when I told him about my romance author aspirations.

Then I think about what Eli said the other morning over breakfast. The stuff about doing what makes him happy.

Maybe he'd get why I want to write.

Or maybe he won't.

Either way, I kind of want to try on Writer as a profession. Just this once. If I can't do it here, in a place where literally no one knows me, I never will. There are no friends to make uncomfortable. No colleagues to go running to my department head with the alarming news that one of their up and coming academic stars is writing a bodice ripper. No boyfriend to disappoint or embarrass.

It's not like I'd be lying about it, either. I *am* writing a book.

My heart thumps once. Twice.

"Inspiration for my novel," I say, squaring my shoulders. "I write historical romance."

Eli blinks. Then his face cracks open with the biggest, brightest smile I've seen on him yet.

My heart, suddenly light, flutters around my chest like a drunk butterfly.

"You write romance?" he says. "That is the coolest fuckin' thing ever! I don't know if you saw the bookshelf at my house—"

"I did," I say, grinning.

"But I love to read. I've met a lot of magazine writers in my day, but I've never had the pleasure of meeting a *novelist*. Least of all one who writes about love. You officially win the prize for Most Badass Profession Ever."

I laugh, bringing my cocktail to my lips to hide the rush of warmth to my cheeks and chest. His excitement is infectious. So intensely flattering I'm not really sure what to do with myself or the insane amount of pleasure I feel just *being* with this guy. He's authentic in every sense of the word. Which makes me want to be authentic, too. Authentic to my secret, romance-writing side I've hidden for so long.

"Thanks," I reply. "I'd say that prize actually belongs to you. Writing romance is a hell of a lot less glamorous than it seems."

Not that I have much experience with it. Not yet.

Eli shrugs. "Same goes for being a chef. But you're doing something *different*, which takes balls. A lot of people—they don't get different."

My turn to blink. My throat thickens, suddenly and unexpectedly.

I look down at my drink. "They don't."

"When I opened this place, everyone thought I was off my rocker to keep my menu—and my food—so simple. They kept waiting for me to fall on my face. But I'm still here. Bruised. Worse for the wear. But still here," he says, raising his eyes to the room around us.

"Yeah, well. Doesn't hurt that you're extraordinarily talented," I say.

Eli shakes his head. "No more talented than any other asshole with a culinary school degree. I've just always been a hard worker. I keep goin' when everyone else quits. I've wanted to quit, too. Every time something went wrong, I was so tempted to hang up my hat and call it a day."

"But you didn't." I'm leaning into the bar now, the countertop cutting into my stomach. "Why?"

"Because I love it," he says simply, eyes softening with emotion. "Cooking itself can be hard and hot and stressful as all get out. But when I see a packed house enjoying these beautiful dishes we put together, comin' back again and again to eat the food I love to make—it's satisfying. Deeply, deeply satisfying, in a way I can't really describe. It fills me up. It's freedom."

I want to be filled up like that.

It's been so damn long since I felt *free* like that. Which is ironic, because I thought I'd finally be free once I had it all. But now that I do, my life feels more like a prison than a wide open sky. Makes me think that as much as I should want to be the highly accomplished other half of Ted's power couple, maybe I'm not that woman.

Maybe I'm *this* woman. The one who writes romance and does yoga and flirts freely with handsome, interesting, talented chefs.

What if I've been wanting the wrong things? Things that don't make me all that happy?

"So what period do you write in?" he asks.

I take a long pull of my drink. "Regency. Early nineteenth century. I'm a total sucker for ballrooms and breeches. I just adore the romance of that period. All the rigid rules they had back then make for some pretty delicious plots. Forbidden romance is probably my favorite—enemies-to-lovers is a close second. I love a heroine who really grapples with convention and turns the rampant sexism of that world on its head. And the heroes—nothing turns me on quite like a Duke or a rake or a bareknuckle boxer who's a gentleman in the streets but a *total* freak in the sheets."

I hope I'm not going too far. I just can't help myself. I've never been able to talk to anyone about this stuff. Now that I am talking about it, and with a handsome, smiling southerner at that, I can't seem to shut up.

But judging from the way Eli's eyes are dancing, I haven't gone far enough.

"Shit," he says. "Now I wish I'd gone into bareknuckle boxing."

I laugh, the sheer giddiness of having someone to trade jokes about historical romance with flooding every inch of my being.

"Not too late," I reply. "So, yeah. I basically write in the same vein as Jane Austen, just with *way* more explicit sex scenes."

"So *basically* you go behind closed doors with Mr. Darcy and Lizzie Bennet."

Oh, God, as if this guy isn't hot enough.

Now he's got to go and name drop characters from *Pride and Prejudice*.

Just my favorite book ever. No big deal.

"You know your Austen," I say, looking away lest I spontaneously combust into a ball of screaming hot magma. "I'm honestly surprised—didn't see many women on your shelves. Writers or characters."

Eli holds up his hands in mock surrender. "You got me there. I'm not perfect, Olivia. But I am willing to learn. How about I start with your books? Just give me the titles and I'll have my friends over at the Rainbow order 'em for me."

Seriously.

This guy.

I hadn't expected Eli to be so enthusiastic about my writing.

I definitely hadn't expected him to want to *read* my writing. Even if he is a big reader, guys don't read romance. They make fun of it. Belittle it. At least in my experience.

But looking at Eli, seeing that earnest glint in his gorgeous eyes, I get the feeling he wouldn't make fun of it the way Ted does.

He'd devour it.

Just like he's kind of devouring *me* right now. Or maybe it's me that's devouring him.

I keep saying this. But I've never met a guy like him. A man who cooks for a living, who's tatted up to within an inch of his life, who loves to read and do yoga and talk passionately about big ideas like romance and freedom and purpose.

He's one of a kind.

A kind that would make the people I know back home uncomfortable. They wouldn't be caught dead socializing with someone who works in a kitchen. They'd roll their eyes at his tattoos and his accent. Don't even get me started on how they'd feel about his walking-around-town-shirtless habit.

But right now, Eli is making me feel like a million bucks.

I'm hit by the wild idea that *that* is all that matters. Not what other people think. Not what other people expect. But how *I* feel and what *I* want.

It's a stupid idea. I can just imagine Ted shaking his head and sighing. A tired, disappointed sigh that he'd follow with something like *don't be ridiculous, Olivia, you're an adult, not some teenaged free spirit nursing a crush.*

Still. Why not try it on while I'm here? Doing things because I want to, because I feel like it?

Blame it on my excitement. The wine. The way Eli talks to me like I'm not insane for writing romance. But I feel like taking a chance. Maybe having some kind of accountability—say, turning ten pages into Eli every night—will be the push I need to get this novel off the ground.

It's ballsy. But if not now, then when?

"Actually," I say, wrapping my hands around my cocktail glass. "I could use some help with a manuscript I'm working on. I keep hitting these roadblocks. I can't seem to move past a few thousand words. I know you're busy, so I totally get it if y—"

"I'm in," Eli says. "I'm no editor, and I don't know my way around romance. *Yet.* Like I said, I'm willing to learn. I'd be happy to read what you have."

"Really?" I'm fighting a smile so big it actually hurts. "You'd do that?"

He grins. That slightly devastating, totally handsome quirk of his lips.

"'Course. Maybe then you'll be stoppin' by my place for breakfast more often," he says.

An almost violent rush of heat prickles in my cheeks. Between my legs.

I remind myself that with a personality as big and warm as his is, Eli probably flirts with everyone, men and grandmas and babies included. I'm nothing special in his eyes. In all likelihood, I'm the fiftieth person Eli's laid out with his charm in the past hour alone.

I'm nothing special.

Even if he makes me feel like the sexiest, most interesting woman in the world for just being myself.

Eli is called to the kitchen to deal with a crisis—something about a dishwasher and a waiter being caught *en flagrante* in the locker room—so he puts me in a cab ("Olivia, you're outta your goddamn mind if you think I'm lettin' you walk home alone in the dark") with a promise to look out for the first ten pages of my manuscript I said I'd have on his doorstep the next day.

I giddily skip up the stairs to the carriage house. Somewhere in the back of my mind, I know I'm exhausted. I haven't slept properly in what feels like years. But from the way I float through the kitchen to the bathroom, even doing a quick little twirl while I wipe off my eye makeup, you'd think I'm bursting with energy.

I *am* bursting with energy. I haven't felt this jazzed up to write in…forever. Cozied up in bed in my pajamas, I open my laptop and plug in my earphones. I turn off the internet—a first for me—and then I open a fresh new Word document.

My muse is *singing*.

I don't second guess. I don't edit as I go. I just write, letting the words fall and trip over each other as my fingers move furiously over the keyboard.

MY ENEMY THE EARL
By Olivia Gates

ROMEO AND JULIET meets Regency England

SOUTHERN CHARMER

(meets the tiniest bit of GAME OF THRONES)
The heirs of opposing families stoke an ancient feud by falling in love.

England, 1813
Castle West, Northumberland

Even in a ballroom full of dark haired, broad-shouldered warriors, Gunnar Danes, Earl of Garrick, stood out. He was enormous, made even more so by the thick leather pauldrons that covered his shoulders, the metal plackart stretched across his breast. It was only a costume, but on him it looked thrillingly real.

He wore his long hair in a knot on the crown of his head, emphasizing the sharp lines of his cheekbones. Lines that gleamed in the honey-hued light of the room. The stubble of a careless beard—redder than his hair—caught the light, too. A prickly fuzz.

And his eyes—they were a striking shade of hazel, more green than brown.

They were on her.

Her, Catherine Woodville. Spinster. The daughter of his great enemy and all that. Their families had been at each other's throats for generations.

Reason number one hundred and eighty nine why sneaking into the Dane family's annual Michaelmas ball was a bad idea.

But here she was, dressed in a borrowed gown and mask, meeting eyes with the one man on Earth she needed to stay away from.

This Romeo was much, much different from the thirteen-year-old lovesick Italian in Shakespeare's play. Indeed, Gunnar Danes was the kind of rough-hewn, medieval-warrior handsome that made Cate dizzy. She grasped the edge of the refreshment table, readying herself for the onslaught as he approached her from across the crowded ballroom...

Chapter Ten
ELI

I make a quick pit stop on my way to work the next morning.

Rainbow Row Books, the city's oldest and most famous indie book store, is housed in a tiny Charleston single that, thanks to the great earthquake of 1889, is leaning precariously to one side. There's no way you could stand up on its second story porch; it's slanted at such an angle you'd slide right off and land on your ass in the parking lot below.

Its kooky exterior gives way to an equally kooky, light-filled first floor that is packed to the rafters with books and rescue cats.

Charlotte, a Siamese cat who's missing a leg, is the first to greet me, rubbing up against my calf. Alice, Beverly, Ernest, and George are next. In the space of half a minute my jeans are covered in cat hair and my tennis shoes are practically vibrating from all the purring going on.

Making a silent pussy joke, I grin.

"Elijah!" Louise, the owner, quickly closes her book behind the register at the back of the shop. Dipping her head, she looks at me above the cloudy lenses of her reading glasses. "I'm always happy to see you, handsome, but that Vonnegut you ordered still hasn't come in."

Careful not to step on any stray tails or paws, I make my way back to Louise and press a kiss onto the papery skin of her cheek.

"I'm actually not here for Vonnegut," I say. "I'm here because I need your help."

Louise straightens in mock seriousness. "Talk to me, chef."

"I want you to give me a crash course in romance."

"Romance?" Louise blinks. "As in, romantic love, or...?"

"Romance *novels*," I say, laughing. "I'd like to focus on historical romance, but I'll take anything you can give me."

Using her first finger to push up her glasses, she peers at me, her eyes wide and owlish through the lenses. "Wouldn't have pegged you for a romance reader."

"Because of the Vonnegut?"

"Because of your penis," Louise says. She slides off her stool. "World would be a better place if more men read romance. Come on, handsome. I'm sorry to say we don't keep much of it in stock. We've just never had that reader base, and so much of that market has gone digital in the last few years."

Louise is right. Her romance section is pitifully small. It's the bottom two rows on a rickety metal bookshelf. Many of the paperbacks are so old their pages are yellowing.

I wonder what Olivia would have to say about this. She was so contained the other morning at breakfast, and then again at yoga. But when she talked about romance, it was like a dam burst. Her eyes lit up and her cheeks flushed pink and she laughed, really *laughed*, the kind that came from her belly.

She was so goddamn gorgeous in that moment I'd had to grip my cocktail, hard, to keep from reaching for her. Kissing that pretty mouth of hers. Which would've been a bad idea on many levels. Most important, I didn't have her permission. I also don't know her story. Well—the story about her romantic life, anyway. Maybe she has a boyfriend.

Maybe she doesn't. But even so, maybe she's not interested in a kiss for whatever reason.

This all started out as innocent curiosity about the beautiful stranger who showed up in my kitchen, hungry and tired and holding something in.

But now that I'm getting to know this stranger, I'm finding I like her. A lot. I'm intrigued by the dissonance between her calm, cool exterior and the fire in her eyes. I like that she has secrets. I fucking adore that she's a writer. I admire her for taking a chance and writing romance. I also like how I seem to forget all my worries when I'm with her. She has this way of taking up the whole room that clears my mind and lightens my mood.

I definitely wouldn't mind getting to know Olivia better. As a person. But also in bed.

See if we can recreate that just fucked hair she sported that first morning.

I'm only human, y'all.

I start when Louise guides a small paperback with a turquoise cover into my hands. *Say Yes to the Marquess* by Tessa Dare.

"Start with this one," she says. "Oh! And then the newest Sarah MacLean—*Wicked and the Wallflower*. So good…"

Half an hour later, I walk out of Rainbow with a stack of books and instructions to purchase an e-Reader, where I can download the list of titles Louise didn't have available at the shop. Good thing I'm a fast reader. I usually go through a book or two a week—more if I can manage it.

Time to get to know these dudes in breeches Olivia likes so much.

Later that night when I get home from the restaurant, I open my mailbox to find a neatly arranged packet inside, the pages held together by a small black binder clip.

The light of a nearby gas lamp catching on the first page, I smile. *My Enemy the Earl* by Olivia Gates.

I wonder if that's her real name, or if it's a pen name she uses to protect the innocent.

A post-it note is stuck on the page underneath her name. Her writing is even and careful.

Eli—

THANK YOU again for reading this. Excited (nervous) to know what you think.

—Definitely NOT the Most Badass Romance Novelist Ever

I glance up at her window. I feel a stab of disappointment when I see that it's dark. She's probably asleep. Most normal people are at eleven-thirty on a Wednesday night.

Still wish she were awake. I'd throw a rock at her window, high school style, and invite her over for a drink. Pick her brain about this Earl. Make her laugh again. The belly kind of laugh.

At least I have this chapter to read. After the day I've had, I'm grateful for any kind of distraction. I got more bad news about The Jam—we're running low on money even after my emergency cash infusion and the time I spend over there, and we're going to have to pull the plug in the next few weeks if things don't improve. Which doesn't seem likely.

Tucking the packet underneath my arm, I head inside. Billy lumbers over to say hello. I give him a good scratch behind his ears. Let him out in the backyard. I take off my shirt—sweet baby Jesus, I've been waiting all day to do that—and grab a glass of water before letting Billy back in.

The two of us head upstairs to my bedroom.

Turning on the light, an image flashes through my head. Me throwing Olivia onto the bed, the mattress dipping as I climb on top of her. She'd be breathless, I'd be hard, we'd be naked in five seconds flat.

No, scratch that. I would take my time with her. Kiss her hard and deep. Put my hands on every fucking square inch of her body. Spread her legs and eat her out for an hour, driving her so wild she'd be tearing out my hair, waking up the neighbors.

She'd be anything *but* careful and collected. I'd unleash the fire I saw in her eyes.

I blink, the image of Olivia on my bed dissolving into Billy, who has jumped onto the mattress and is now contentedly licking his nonexistent balls.

"Dude, come on," I say, trying to urge him to the other side of the bed.

He doesn't budge.

I sigh. Dog's getting too comfortable up there.

Been too long since I had another human in my bed.

I take a quick (cold) shower, washing away the smell of the kitchen, and brush my teeth. Then I grab a pen from the drawer in my bedside table, prop myself up against the pillows, and get to work on *My Enemy the Earl*.

I don't know what I was expecting. But I'm immediately struck by the seductive mix of beauty and humor in Olivia's prose. I can hear her voice, clear as day, in the structure of her sentences. In the word choices she makes. One of my favorite paragraphs comes when Gunnar, the hero, is eye fucking a stranger across the ballroom—a stranger he'll later discover is Catherine, the daughter of his family's enemy. The Juliet to his Romeo.

Gunnar opened his eyes, and the beautiful stranger was there. A few strides and he'd be at her side. Inside his veins his blood warmed. He tried to fight it. He knew this feeling—the devil inside him, simmering to life. He should run, find a freezing pond to leap into, a priest.

I can fucking relate to that, man.

The story sucks me right in. Everything about this book is *ardent*. The characters. The angst. The sexual tension.

The *vulnerability*.

This isn't the work of the girl in the Chanel sunglasses and silk dress.

This is the work of the girl who looked like she was coming while she ate my food. The girl whose eyes flashed, naughty and bright, when she talked about dukes who were good in bed.

The girl who is burning up inside.

She is so fucking talented. Which strangely enough makes me question if I'm talented enough to be with her. If I'm good enough to be with someone who so clearly has a bright future ahead of her. Because my future is looking pretty fucking bleak right now.

What if I'm too simple, like that one critic implied? Too stupid for someone as smart as Olivia?

Holding up the pages, I look down to see that I'm pitching a tent. Intelligence has always been a huge turn on for me.

I'll take care of my dick in a minute. I gotta find out what happens after Gunnar and Cate's first witty exchange.

So I shove those nasty thoughts from my head and keep reading. When I flip a page, only to find it's the last one—Goddamn it, Olivia gave me exactly ten pages, not a sentence more—I literally curse out loud.

"Are you fucking kidding me?"

Billy looks up from his pretend balls. We meet eyes.

"What?" I say. "It was just getting good. Gunnar was about to give Catherine a 'private tour'"—air quotes—"of his castle."

If Billy could shrug—*who gives a fuck?*—he would right now.

He goes back to his butt.

I re-read the ten pages. Then read them again.

I make a few notes. Mostly about trimming stuff down.

I read and I write and I *want*. Reaching down, I give myself a few light strokes. My dick feels hot and huge in my hand.

I want to see more of this woman. The one who writes with such playful verve and eroticism and obvious skill.

I stroke a little harder now. I feel my orgasm approach at lightning speed. I'm so hard it hurts. One, two vicious strokes, and then I come, my hips bucking off the bed as I spill into my palm. Jet after jet of hot cum.

After I clean myself up, I get back to Gunnar and Cate.

I have read exactly zero romance up to this point. But I've read enough novels in my lifetime to recognize quality storytelling when I see it.

My Enemy the Earl is top quality.

I can't help but notice the way Olivia wrote longingly about freedom and choice. It comes across loud and clear that her heroine feels trapped by her life. By convention.

Cate lost herself in Gunnar's world, wondering what it would be like to be him. A handsome man, whose life was freedom and possibility. A life that was much, much different from her own.

I keep coming back to that line. I make a note to ask her about it.

As much as I feel like I'm getting to know Olivia—the real Olivia—by reading her work, I also feel like I have more questions than answers about her. I know Catherine is a fictional character. But how much of her is based on Olivia's own experiences? Why choose *freedom* as a theme if it wasn't something Olivia wrestled with in her real life?

It's after two by the time I put down *My Enemy the Earl*.

I'm tired and turned on again. Frustrated and curious. Hopeful but cautious.

I'm learning Olivia. The more I learn, the more I want.

I'm never one to deny myself. If I want something—someone—I go for it.

But what if Olivia isn't there for the taking? What if I reach for her, only to have her slip through my fingers? I'm about to lose a restaurant. Losing a girl just might push me over the edge.

Running a hand down my face, I will the thought to go away.

I'm being ridiculous. I've known the girl for all of, what, three days?

I turn off the light, determined to sleep off this second hard on.

Determined to stop wanting this girl so damn bad.

I'd be lying, though, if I said I'm not thinking about what food I should bring over to her tomorrow morning along with my edits.

Someone's gotta keep her fed so she can finish this story.

That someone's gonna be me.

Chapter Eleven
ELI

I climb the carriage house steps, the first chapter of *My Enemy the Earl* in one hand and two foil wrapped egg-and-pimiento-cheese biscuit sandwiches, still warm from the oven, in the other. The plastic handle of a travel coffee mug dangles from my pinkie finger.

Knocking on the door with my elbow—more like thudding—I wait.

My heart's doing this funny little dance in my chest. I glare down at it, like I can will the damn thing into submission.

I'm tired as fuck—I don't sleep much these days, thanks to everything going on at The Jam—but I feel strangely decent. Energized, even. Like the passion in Olivia's writing has reignited my own or something. I found myself wide awake before seven, wondering if I had enough butter in the fridge to whip up a batch of Grandma Mae's biscuits.

I had just enough.

So here I am, two hours later, flour in my hair and a stupid fucking smile on my face, waiting impatiently for Olivia to open her door.

When she does, I feel like I've been punched square in the gut.

Her wide blue eyes light up and she smiles. This wide, unguarded, totally gorgeous smile of surprise. She's wearing a sweatshirt and these tiny little pajama shorts that show off her muscular, lithe legs.

Her dark hair is everywhere.

I'm struck speechless. *Literally* speechless. I just look at her.

Her. The girl who writes so vulnerably about longing and sensuality and freedom.

The girl I'm smiling at like she hung the goddamn moon.

Lord above.

"Hi!" she breathes, suddenly a little shy when her eyes flick to the pages in my hand. "Oh my God, don't tell me you already read it."

I clear my throat. "First thing I did when I got home last night. You kept me up *late*, girl."

"Is that a good thing?" Her smile fades. "Or a bad one?"

I hold up the pages. "This? *This* is one of the best damn things I've read in a long time."

Olivia blinks, her lips parting in happy disbelief. Her cheeks flush with pleasure.

"Really?"

"Really. I'll tell you more if you let me come in and feed you some breakfast," I say, nodding inside.

She bites her lip, opening the door wider. "You really have to stop being such a great neighbor. I'm never going to be able to pay you back."

"I don't want to be paid back." I follow her to the tiny but stylish kitchen. The whole place is actually pretty stylish. No surprise there. I've met the owner of this place, Julia, and she told me she was into antiques. "I just want you to eat. And to write more. Gunnar and Cate's chemistry burns right off the page. Please tell me they're going to get it on soon."

Olivia is still smiling when she turns to grab a couple plates and some napkins.

"I have to torture them a bit first," she replies.

I move beside her, opening cabinets until I find two coffee mugs.

Her arm brushes mine when she reaches inside a drawer for spoons. My skin prickles to life.

The air between us tightens. Thrums with a low current of electricity.

"Sorry," she says, quickly retreating to the safety of the small island.

I glance at her. She's studiously unwrapping the biscuits, not looking at me.

Her cheeks are pinker than they were a second ago.

Is she uncomfortable? Embarrassed? Aroused?

"Torturing the characters really amps up the tension," she continues, still not looking up from the biscuits. "As delicious as the sex can be, I happen to think the stuff leading up to it can be even juicier."

I unscrew the top from the travel mug and pour the coffee into the mugs. I already put half and half in it, just in case Olivia didn't have any.

"Interesting theory. What kind of juicy stuff are we talking about?"

"All *kinds* of juicy stuff." She looks at the biscuits, bits of melty pimiento cheese oozing out from the sides. "Christ, Eli, these look incredible. Don't tell me you—"

"Made them from scratch this morning?" I grin. Hand her a mug. "If you think I'd ever serve you anything from a freezer, then you don't know me at all, Yankee girl."

Olivia looks down at her mug, the expression in her eyes tightening.

"Eli," she says slowly. She looks up. "Why are you being so nice to me? First the grits bowl, then the chef's tasting. Now homemade biscuits and a glowing review for my romance novel. I can't help but feel like I'm having a *Fight Club* moment."

My brow puckers. "Does this have something to do with those bareknuckle boxers you like? Because I'm a fast learner—"

"No," she says, laughing. "I just—I feel like you're so kind and so..." Her eyes stray to my bare chest. "*Shirtless* that I must be making you up."

I pick up a plate and hand it to her. "This biscuit sandwich I made you is real. So am I."

"You promise?" Her blue eyes flick to meet mine. My stomach drops.

"I promise," I reply. "I gotta admit, Olivia, your question worries me a bit. People not nice to you in New York? This is just how we are down here."

Her lips twitch against the lip of her mug. "Half-naked?"

"Hospitable. Neighborly." I put my hand on the island and lean into it. "Look. I know you don't wanna talk about it—because if you did, you would—but I see the pain in your eyes. You're goin' through something. Something that hurts. If I can make it hurt a little less by feeding you, makin' you smile—hell, I'm gonna do it. If it makes you uncomfortable, just tell me to stop. I'll never bother you again. But I'd like to help out if you'd let me."

Olivia swallows, the sound audible. She blinks.

"Thanks," she says at last. "And you don't need to stop. I really appreciate everything you're doing for me. The food *definitely* makes me feel better. I guess..." She shrugs. "I guess I'm not in the habit of accepting help. Can't help but feel suspicious of it."

I take a sip of coffee, eyes still locked on hers. "I want to make it clear that I expect nothing in return. Except maybe a few more chapters of *My Enemy the Earl* if you write them. Which you should."

Olivia grins, the tension in her expression melting.

"We're friends then?" she says.

I nod. "Friends with a shared appreciation for grits and good books."

I don't mention that I'd like to be more than that. For obvious reasons.

We settle on the stools at the island and dig into the biscuits. In true Olivia fashion, her eyes roll to the back of her head as she eats and she makes these little noises—moans of appreciation—that have me covering my lap with my napkin. I feel like I'm in eighth grade sex ed again, hiding an inconvenient hard-on underneath my desk.

If the fact that she writes passionate, angsty romance didn't give her away, this does.

Girl's got a sensual side.

"What *is* pimiento cheese?" she says, licking at a stray bit with her tongue.

I bite the inside of my cheek. Jesus *take* me now.

"Everyone's got their own recipe. But the basics are shredded cheddar cheese, chopped pimiento peppers, and mayo. I add bourbon and a good handful of parmesan to mine and let it sit for a day or two. Let the flavors really meld. Always keep a quart of it on hand at home for just such an occasion." I nod at our plates.

Olivia has already finished her biscuit sandwich. She's using the pad of her first finger to dab at the crumbs on her plate.

"Wow," she says, swallowing. "Eli, just...*wow*."

I grab the first chapter of *My Enemy the Earl* and set it between us. "All right. Enough about the food. Let's talk about Gunnar and Cate. Anyone who knows me knows I don't give out compliments easily. I mean it when I say this is fucking *good*, Olivia. One chapter in, and I'm already hooked."

"Thanks." Using both hands, she pulls at her mouth with a napkin. Then she folds it, setting it neatly on the counter. "I've rewritten this first chapter a million times. I can't ever seem to get it just right. In my head, I'm juggling character arcs, themes, symbolism. I'm thinking about what reviewers might think about this word choice or that plot point. It's paralyzing."

I pick up my coffee and take a sip, meeting Olivia's big blue eyes. They're tired and conflicted and on fucking *fire*.

"I've obviously never written a book," I reply. "So take this with a grain of salt. But when I'm in the kitchen, whether I'm cookin' or coming up with new recipes or whatever, I've learned to keep things simple. I focus on the food and that's it. Do I enjoy making it? Do I enjoy eating it? Those are the only questions I ask myself. Everything else is just noise. Noise that I block out so *I* can tell *my* story—only I'm tellin' it with food instead of words."

Olivia's eyes are still on mine as she takes this in. I can practically see the wheels turning in her head.

"But how do you block it out like that? You're one of the few people I've met who genuinely doesn't seem to care what other people think. My whole *life*—" Her voice catches. "Well. I've definitely struggled with being a people pleaser."

"I noticed you touched on the idea of freedom a lot. The lack of it. The yearning for it." I open the packet and flip to a passage I underlined.

But as a spinster, Cate had nothing to lose. This—flirting freely behind a mask with Gunnar Danes, like she was pretty and young and he not forbidden, not out of her reach—was fun.

It was fun being someone else, being something other than a proper lady, for a change.

"Yeah," Olivia says, nodding. "Cate is definitely tied

down by society's rules. She's a woman, born to a good family, so she's got to always be ladylike. On top of that, she's a spinster, and kind of a plain looking one at that. Back then, everyone viewed spinsters as these, like, tragic burdens on their families. So she feels this need to help out as much as possible to make up for the fact that she's basically a loser in everyone's eyes. She's terrified of disappointing people, her parents especially. She tries to be well behaved and quiet and inoffensive. Even though, deep down, she's anything but."

I nod. "So what's tying *you* down?"

Olivia blinks.

"You know, no one's ever asked me that question."

I hold up the pages. "No one's ever read your book."

She swallows again, slowly, and rolls her lips between her teeth. "Not too long ago, if you would've asked me if I was tied down, I would've laughed in your face. I feel like I worked so hard to have it all—everything a thirty-something woman is supposed to want. Great career. Great house and car and a closet full of great clothes. And I do—did—have it. But then after a while…" Olivia shakes her head. Sighs. "I don't know. I started to feel suffocated by all these things I was supposed to want. All these things I'd worked *hard* to get. I had them, and I am—was—I *was* proud of them. But none of it really felt right. I felt like I was living in someone *else*'s dream world. I think that's because I had to hide so much of myself to fit into that world. I thought if I just tried hard enough, the person I hid would kind of just…disappear. I mean, really, who in their right mind wouldn't want the best of everything? But I'm realizing that maybe I can't *change* who I am, as much as I want to. And I really, *really* want to be the woman who has it all. I want it so badly I'm not sure I can let it go."

Her voice wobbles a bit on that last sentence. I resist the

urge to reach for her hand. She could probably use a little moral support at the moment.

"Sounds a lot like expectation's the thing that's holdin' you hostage," I say, picking my words carefully. Olivia is opening up to me, and I don't want to scare her away. "People—your parents, maybe, your peers—expect you to live a certain way. You're wantin' to please them, so that's what you've done. You're responsible. Practical. Dutiful. Even though deep down, you're anything but."

A ghost of a smile plays at Olivia's lips. "Maybe. I don't know if I have the balls to be anything other than responsible, though. Where I'm from, people are obsessed with keeping up with the Joneses. They don't—they don't value authenticity—" She shakes her head and straightens. "Anyway. Thanks for the advice about keeping things simple."

"Olivia," I say, spearing her with a look. "You're changin' the subject."

She meets my eyes. Hers are wet. Pleading.

My heart twists.

"I'm not used to talking about this stuff with anyone, Eli. Least of all a shirtless stranger. Give me time. Please."

I don't wanna give her time. I want to peel back her layers and tear down her walls and get to the center of who this talented, interesting, *tortured* woman really is.

But that's not my place. She's not my girl.

Although the more I get to know her, the more I'm thinking I'd like her to be.

"Take all the time you need, Yankee girl." I offer her a smile. "And I'm not a stranger anymore. I'm a friend, remember?"

Olivia smiles at that. Genuinely smiles.

"Yeah." She digs her teeth into her bottom lip. Her gaze flicks to my mouth for half a heartbeat. "You're the first friend I've made down here."

I offer her a grin. "I'm honored. You're somethin' special, Olivia."

I look at her. She looks at me. The space between us crackles. Begs me to make it smaller, to step forward and take her face in my hands and kiss her soft and deep and good.

She's attracted to me. I can tell by the flicker of white hot heat in those big eyes of hers.

But she just asked for time. She's not ready for me.

Not yet.

I stand up, gathering our plates and empty mugs.

"I gotta head over to The Jam in a bit," I say.

Olivia walks me to the door. We pause in the threshold, awkwardly. She's trying not to look at my chest.

Trying, and failing.

I shove my hands in the back pockets of my jeans to keep from reaching for her.

"When can I expect the next installment of Gunnar and Cate?" I ask.

That makes her grin. "I have plans to find a coffee shop and write it this afternoon."

"Need a suggestion for a good spot?"

"I'd love one."

"Holy City Roasters. Cute little place on Wentworth Street. Their iced coffee is second to none, and you can walk from here. I happen to know the owner—she's my sister. Tell Gracie I sent you."

"Your sister owns a coffee shop? How cool! Thank you for the tip." Olivia looks up at me, suddenly shy. Before I know what she's doing, she's wrapping her arms around my neck and pulling me into a hug. "And thank you for breakfast. And for reading my romance. *And* for listening to me. Basically, thanks for being such an awesome human being and letting me be myself with you."

For a second I just stand there, too dumfounded by her

words, by the press of her body against mine, to formulate a coherent thought.

She's not wearing that expensive perfume today.

Instead, she smells like coffee. Clean sheets. A smell that fills my head and chases away whatever anxiety hovered at the edges.

I wrap my arms around her waist and pull her as close as I dare. She's all curves and softness against me.

I close my eyes and breathe her in. Her head is tucked into the crook of my neck. She fits perfectly there.

Damn it. I *want* her.

I wanna take her home and make her come and stay up late, talking and eating and fucking. I can only imagine how good Olivia would be in bed once that inner fire of hers is let loose.

But I can't take her with me. And that's kinda killing me right now.

"Anytime," I say, forcing myself to step back. "I'll look out for chapter two tonight."

Chapter Twelve
OLIVIA

It's not as hot today, so the fifteen minute walk to Holy City Roasters is actually pleasant.

I head north on King Street. It's Charleston's main artery, cutting the peninsula in half lengthwise. I'm starting to recognize certain landmarks. Certain brightly colored houses. The old time-y men's store on the corner of King and Broad that marks the end of the residential area and the beginning of the long, crowded shopping corridor. The cute art gallery I'd like to check out when I'm done writing for the day.

I think about what to write as I walk. The fresh air must be good for my imagination, because ideas swarm inside my head like bees in a hive.

Or maybe it's Eli's excitement about Cate and Gunnar—his certainty about the merits of their story and my skill—that's making my muse sing.

I don't need his stamp of approval. I'd be writing this book with or without his help. I've wanted to write it for a long time. It's taken me years—and a botched proposal—to finally screw my courage to the sticking place and do it. I am making this decision on my own.

But it is nice to have Eli in my corner. It's too easy for me to get stuck inside my head. To give up on myself and just do what everybody else is doing. Hell, I've built a whole life around that. But Eli won't have it. He's pushing me to give my dreams—*my* dreams, not everybody else's—some breathing room. And maybe I just needed that push—that nod of encouragement—to get the ball rolling. I needed to see how another creative person took their head out of their ass and just *created*.

The actual creating, though?

That's up to me.

Hanging a left on Wentworth Street, tourists give way to students wearing shorts and backpacks. I can feel the familiar energy of a university in the air. The students are smiling as I pass. They're talking to their friends, slowing down to peek inside shop windows and pet dogs.

It makes me smile. The sunshine and the wide open blue sky certainly don't hurt, either.

Neither does the fact that I'm going to write a *novel* on a *Wednesday* afternoon.

Pinch me.

A shadow moves over my sunny mood when I remember I only have three and a half weeks before I have to report back to my old life.

My real life.

But I decide that today I'm going to take a page from what I did the other night at The Pearl and *give in*. I'm going to pretend this is my real life. I'm going to pretend that I live here and that I'm a writer and that dreams—ridiculous, silly dreams—really do come true.

I take a deep breath. Let it out. That sense of freedom, familiar now, washes over me. I'm wearing shorts and a cruddy t-shirt. I'm not worried about who sees me or what they might think. I'm not trying to impress anyone. I'm not running around. I'm just doing what I want to be doing.

It's really, really nice.

Holy City Roasters just might be the cutest, coolest coffee shop I've ever been in. It's on the small side, buzzing with students and professors and handsome hipsters. Couples flirt over mugs so big they look like bowls. A woman with the most gorgeous tattoos on her arms is tearing at a flaky chocolate croissant with her fingers while she peers at some kind of design on her laptop screen.

The earthy scent of coffee hangs so heavy in the air I can taste it.

I order an iced coffee and a cupcake—because why not?—from the woman behind the counter. She's wearing thick, tortoiseshell framed glasses and bright red lipstick. Emboldened by her friendliness, I ask, "Are you Grace?"

She grins, holding out her hand. "I am. And you are?"

"Olivia. Eli—Elijah Jackson—he said to tell you he sent me. He's my new neighbor."

"I'm so sorry," she teases, her grin deepening. "My brother can be *such* a pain in the ass. Thank you for putting up with him."

I laugh. "No problem. He's actually been a pretty great neighbor so far. He saved me from those birds—you know, the ones that wander around in the street?"

"The Guinea Fowl! Yes!" It's Grace's turn to laugh. I recognize the way she laughs with her eyes. Eli does that, too.

My pulse skips a beat.

"Where the hell did they come from?" I ask.

"No one really knows. But I guess there are enough gardens and trees in your part of town to provide a little makeshift habitat for them, because they've been around for a while and they keep having babies."

"They're fearless," I say. "I almost ran them over when I

first got into town a few days ago. I think I'd still be sitting in my car, playing a game of chicken through my windshield with them, if Eli hadn't shooed them away."

Grace rolls her eyes. "He's a show off. Have you eaten at one of his restaurants yet?"

I smile. "I actually did the chef's tasting last night at The Pearl. It was probably the best meal of my life."

"It's pretty ridiculous," she says, nodding. "I don't see him nearly enough, because he's always working. But I am super proud of him. His food is the best in the city."

"You should be. He's a really talented chef, and an even better guy."

Grace studies me for a second, her grin knowing now. Almost wistful. I feel myself beginning to blush.

"Welp, welcome to Charleston," she says. "Please make yourself at home, and don't hesitate to come find me if you need anything. I'm glad Eli's found a new friend."

Friend. I know I was the one to put that label on my relationship with Eli. And as nice as it sounds—as *safe* as it sounds—I'm surprised to discover I kind of hate it when someone else says it.

I don't allow myself to dwell on what that means.

"Thanks for the warm welcome," I say, and I mean it. Seriously. Is *everyone* in this town so friendly? So willing to help out a total stranger?

It's quickly becoming apparent that things are done differently down here.

Priorities are different.

I settle down at a table by a side window. I open my laptop, fully expecting a repeat of last night's magical, super productive writing session.

Popping in my headphones, I start to write chapter two.

At first, it *is* a super magical session. The chapter opens with this angsty, sexy kissing scene, where, after Gunnar gives her a tour of his castle, Cate pushes him against a wall in the medieval chapel. He smirks. She burns.

He was her enemy.

And she was going to kiss him.

Gunnar was looking down at her, the angle of his bent neck so very, very enticing. Strands of wavy dark hair framed his face.

Cate wanted to kiss him.

For once, she did not think. She did what she wanted.

But then, after the kissing ends and Gunnar and Cate go home to their respective castles, I hit a wall.

What the fuck do I write next?

I start a new scene—one where the two of them run into each other the next morning at church, as one does in Regency England—but every word is like pulling teeth. Some raunchy Shakespeare lines about fatal loins and virginity float through my head. I try to cleverly incorporate them into Cate's inner dialogue, but it slows me down so much I end up taking two hours to write two paragraphs.

At this point, I'm so frustrated by my lack of progress—my lack of direction—that I open my old friend The Internet. I promptly fall down a celebrity gossip hole wherein, like one possessed, I hunt down every hilarious Instagram comment Chrissy Teigen has ever posted.

And she's posted a *lot* of hilarious Instagram comments.

The longer I dick around, the more frustrated I become with myself and my writing.

My dissertation was painful to write. But I was expecting that. Writing romance, though—the kind of delicious, sexy, angsty romance I love to read—I thought it would be fun.

Easy.

Especially because the story came on to me so strongly at first. I plowed through that first chapter in a burst of inspiration.

Writing this book isn't supposed to feel like work. This is

supposed to feel like a dream coming true, right before my eyes.

Dreams aren't supposed to make you want to chuck your laptop across the room.

The urge to quit for the day is strong. I could go for a walk. Shave my legs. Do anything other than work on this goddamn story.

I feel a smidge of regret. Maybe the grass really isn't greener. Maybe I really *don't* want to be a writer deep down.

I expect the thought to make me feel better. It would mean all the choices I've made up until now were the right ones. It would mean I could go back to New York and say yes to Ted without any qualms. Without any of the uncertainty I felt when he proposed.

But instead, the thought depresses me. I guess I wanted to love this writing thing more than I allowed myself to admit.

Then again, maybe Julia was right when she said writing is the pits eighty percent of the time, no matter what you're working on. Writing requires focus. Your brain needs to be firing on all cylinders. At the same time, it can be boring as fuck. At least that was the case with my dissertation.

I thought this kind of writing would be different, but maybe it's not.

Maybe all writing is difficult and boring. But maybe it's also worth it in the end. Drafting my dissertation, I hated every minute I was chained to my computer, typing and worrying and typing some more. When I was done for the day, though, I would feel such a huge sense of accomplishment. Three quarters of the time, I hated writing itself. But having written?

Best feeling in the world. And if I felt that way after finishing a dissertation on nineteenth century social mores, I can only imagine how I'll feel after finishing the book of my heart.

So, because I clearly have zero self-control, I download an app that locks you out of the internet for a set amount of time. Two hours of just me and a blank page.

Keep it simple.

Eli's words echo in my head.

Simple. Right.

Forget the Shakespeare. Literature nerds like me might appreciate that. But all readers appreciate a well told story.

That's all I'll focus on today. The story. Two damaged, lonely, sexually frustrated people falling in love. Saving themselves and each other in the process.

Nothing more. Nothing less. I can always go back and embellish once the bones of the book are there.

I put my fingers on the keyboard, and force them to move.

Chapter Thirteen

OLIVIA

It takes me all afternoon to finish the next chapter. Every sentence is a struggle. But knowing Eli is expecting the next installment of Cate and Gunnar's story tonight is terrific motivation.

By the time I'm done, the sun has started to set. I'm beat. I feel like I ran a mental marathon. I can practically see the steam coming out of my ears when I duck into the bathroom on my way out of Holy City Roasters.

As tired as I am, though, it feels good to get all those words down. Like they'd been building up inside me. Bottlenecking. Making me anxious. But now that they're released, I feel satisfyingly empty—content—*calm* in a way I haven't in a long time.

Waving goodbye to Grace—these friendly southerners must be rubbing off on me—I step out into the sunset and take a deep, cleansing breath.

I don't even know what time it is.

I don't care. All I know is that I'm famished, and I could really go for a gigantic glass of ice cold wine.

I *could* go back to the carriage house. Do some laundry.

Answer some emails. Have a glass of wine there. Maybe have Julia over.

But it's such a beautiful night. The sky is a rainbow of pinks and oranges and purples. Spotless. The air is warm, the humidity falling.

I decide to take another page out of Cate's book and do what I want.

I want to explore the city. Meet her people and taste her flavors.

So I pop into the art gallery I passed earlier. Turns out there's a little gallery crawl going on in this neighborhood, The French Quarter. I accept the glass of champagne an owner presses into my hand and drink it slowly while I browse alongside casually dressed patrons chatting in drawls. I meet a painter, a real estate developer. A gynecologist who moonlights as a pirate tour guide.

The neighborhood is gorgeous. A little buzzed from the champagne, I get lost walking down a cobblestone street. I find an adorable wine and cheese shop. Duck inside for a decadent wedge of French goat cheese and a deliciously crisp glass of rosé.

I'm learning that Charleston is a very easy place to fall for.

I keep wandering, approaching The Pearl. For a second, I consider popping inside for a drink. Eli will be there.

The thought makes my stomach dip and my heart skip a beat.

But as much as I'd like to see Eli-the-kitchen-god at work again, I'm enjoying my own company. I kind of want to experience the city by myself.

I walk past The Pearl, and belly up to the bar at another restaurant nearby. I order a salad and, on the bartender's recommendation, quail, which I've never had before. It's all insane. I finish the meal with an oyster shooter—vodka, house made Bloody Mary mix, and a raw oyster—and head back out into the night.

The moon is out on my walk home. It's late for a Wednesday—past ten—and while the city is quiet, there's still this energy in the warm autumn air. This sense of history and movement. I'm stuffed. The branches on a nearby Magnolia tree block out the moon. A man makes his way down the opposite side of the street, walking two chubby dachshunds on leather leashes.

A gas lamp flickers beside a glossy door.

The smell of the ocean permeates everything, blowing in on an easy breeze.

I could live here.

The thought's ridiculous, I know. I've been in Charleston for all of a few days. This is the honeymoon period. Of course I'm going to fall in love with it when it's so new, and so exciting, and so *different*.

It's also not real life.

But today was kind of the perfect day. Biscuits and Eli in the morning. Writing in the afternoon. Good food and good wine at night. I can breathe here. Be myself.

I feel a pulse of guilt, same as I did last night at dinner. Here I am, starry-eyed, enjoying myself, while Teddy's at home waiting for me. Yes, he agreed to a break. But for the past three years, all the traveling I've done has been with *him*. All the good meals I've eaten have been with him.

I almost feel like I'm doing something wrong by enjoying myself without Ted.

Then again, I wouldn't be upset if Ted enjoyed himself without me. I *hope* he's enjoying himself right now.

Does that mean something?

Have I missed being on my own? During my single days before Ted, I remember being desperate to have someone to experience things with. I felt so lonely. When he and I started dating, I dove in head first. Never coming up for air until now.

I want to miss Ted. But I don't. Just like I want to be his perfect other half. But maybe I'm not.

Being away, writing my sex, eating alone—I kind of love it.

Maybe the fact that Ted and I were okay with taking a break—with each of us potentially sleeping with other people—means we don't love each other enough to get married.

Shit.

Shit shit shit.

I have this creeping sense that I was wrong to think being in Charleston would make me realize how happy I am back home.

Instead, being down here is making me realize how *unhappy* I've been.

It sounds so stupid. How could I not know if I'm unhappy or not? But then I think about how inextricably linked other peoples' happiness and my own are inside my head. I get a huge sense of pleasure from pleasing people. I love the praise I get for being a good daughter, a good employee. A good girlfriend. I feel so satisfied when I meet or exceed peoples' expectations.

But once the rush of satisfaction fades, am *I* happy?

And why do those expectations matter so much to me in the first place?

I wonder if the reason why I feel so suffocated is because I constantly—to the point where it's second nature—put everyone else's needs and expectations above my own. Ted's especially.

My life—my own goddamn *life*—doesn't even belong to me. If it did, it would feel like this more often. I'd be able to be myself. Truthfully. Fearlessly. I'd do what I wanted without second guessing myself. Without apologizing.

Maybe, without even knowing it, I came to Charleston to take back my life. Not just as an experiment. Not just as a "reset". But as a real, permanent choice. If that's the case...

I squeeze my eyes shut against the burn of tears.

I don't want to think about what that means. It's terrifying. I don't think I'm strong enough to pull off a stunt like that anyway.

Taking a deep breath, I keep walking. One foot in front of the other. That's all I have to do right now.

I just have to keep going.

Back at the carriage house, I print out chapter two from *My Enemy the Earl* and head over to Eli's. I secretly hope he'll be home. I could use some company. I need to get out of my head a little. But the lights in his house are out. When I knock, all I get is a scratching sound on the other side of the door. Billy. I should offer to walk him for Eli. I imagine Chef Jackson keeps long hours over at The Pearl, which means Billy is here by himself all day.

I drop the pages in his mailbox and head home.

I call Julia, who picks up on the first ring. She's eating something, smacking her lips as she talks.

"Sorry," she says. "Late dinner. What's up?"

I let out a breath. Then I blurt it all out.

"Do you ever get the feeling that you're hiding who you really are to fit in? Do you ever want more? Not more stuff, but a life that's more *you*, you know? I feel like a jerk saying this, because I already have so much, and I feel like a glutton for wanting someone—no, wait, some*thing*, I meant to say some*thing*—else. But this desire for more won't go away. I want it to go away, Julia, because I think it's keeping me from being happy with what I have. God, I really am a glutton, aren't I?"

Julia stops chewing. I hear her swallow.

"Olivia," she says, lowering her voice. "Have you been smoking weed? It's cool if you have, but we both know how paranoid you get—"

"No drugs." I look down at my (very) full glass of wine. "Just wine from a box."

"Oh, God, that's even worse. Dump that shit in the sink. *Now*. Before I have to call poison control. Jesus Christ, Olivia, you're going to give me a heart attack. I'll be there in ten with a few bottles from daddy's cellar. You're welcome."

Ten minutes later, Julia and I are sitting in bed together, a bottle of expensive wine in my lap, a twelve inch sub from Jimmy John's in Julia's.

"Had a busy day," she says. "Haven't had time to eat. So I'm having two subs for dinner. Please don't judge me."

"No judgment here." I watch her stuff half the sub into her mouth. "How's your dad?"

"Okay," she says around a mouthful of turkey bacon club. "But c'mon, Olivia, no changing the subject. I'm here to talk about you. Why don't you think you deserve to be happy?"

My throat tightens. Taking a slug right from the bottle— much better than the boxed stuff—I wipe my mouth with the back of my hand.

"I didn't say that."

"Yes you did." The butcher paper on her lap crinkles when she drops the remains of her sub onto it. She wipes her hands on a napkin and looks at me. "You said you felt like a glutton for wanting to be yourself. Which is a huge part of being happy. Tell me why you think that's such an enormous ask of the universe."

"Because," I say, my voice thickening. "I already have it all."

Julia furrows her brow. "According to who?"

"Everyone. Society. Teddy. My life is perfect. On the outside, at least."

"So the inside doesn't count?"

I take a deep breath. Let it out. Julia was never one to beat around the bush. Still, I didn't expect her honesty to hurt so much. I didn't expect her to find my sore spots so easily.

"Look, I'm just playing devil's advocate here," she says, putting a hand on my leg and giving it a squeeze. "It's important to suss out your reasons. I think it will help."

"Okay. I'll try." I swallow. "I guess I thought the inside would follow the outside, if that makes sense. Like if I got all these things everyone was telling me I should want, I'd actually start to want them myself, you know? There had to be a reason why everyone wanted the same things. The big fancy job, the big fancy house."

"Big fancy diamond," Julia adds. "You still haven't shown it to me, by the way."

I nod at the dresser on the other side of the room. "It's in there. I don't want to look at it right now."

"Fair enough. So now you have all this stuff—"

"And I'm proud of it. I worked hard for it. But now that I'm staring down the barrel of committing to it all for the rest of my life, I feel..."

Julia looks at me. "You feel what, Olivia?"

I grasp for the right word to capture that feeling of suffocation. Of doubt.

"Stifled," I say at last. "I feel stifled. But then I think, hey, maybe that's just part of the deal. Everyone feels like that sometimes. Life is hard. Yeah, maybe I felt pressured to live this way. But I'm the one who actually *chose* to. There's this voice in my head that tells me to shut up whenever I feel unhappy, because it's my fault. Maybe the problem isn't society. It's me. Why can't I be happy? Hell, I have everything."

Julia's eyes soften. "Do you really talk to yourself that way?"

Tears flood my eyes. I blink, hard, making them tumble down my cheeks.

"I've always been hard on myself."

"This is different." She shakes her head. "Being hard on yourself can be a good thing. Like when you're trying to write the best damn dirty romance novel you possibly can. But it can also be toxic. Like when you tell yourself over and over again that you're fundamentally flawed when really it's the world that's fucked up. I'm not sure you even realize you're doing it, Olivia, but you've really internalized this message that happiness and authenticity aren't meant for you."

I wipe my eye on my shoulder. "Why would they be? I'm far from perfect. What could my 'authentic self' offer the world anyway? I'm on the run from my boyfriend, writing sex all day, wandering around town drunk."

"Happiness is meant for you because you're human." Julia wraps her fingers around my wrist and looks me in the eye. "No one is perfect. But everyone deserves to be happy. Including you. And if your life in New York isn't making you happy, then you should think very, very seriously about changing it. Who cares if you have the perfect house and the perfect guy? Maybe your mom and your friends are impressed by that crap. But you're better than that. You're *smarter* than that. I think deep down you know that's not who you are. So *be who you are*. If not now, when?"

Tears are spilling out of my eyes left and right, slipping down my neck onto the coverlet. I take another swig of wine.

"I can't just leave my life in New York."

Julia is still looking at me. "Why the fuck not?"

"I'll break Ted's heart," I reply hotly. "I'll break everyone's heart."

"You're going to break your own heart if you go back to him."

I know she's right. But part of me would rather break my own heart than disappoint the people I love.

I wrap my hand around Julia's.

"I don't know if I'm brave enough," I whisper.

"You don't have to do it alone," she replies. "We can figure it out together. But you have to be the one to actually make the call."

I nod. Swallow again.

"Just think about it," Julia says. "You still have time. Hey, it could be worse. You could be me—addicted to turkey clubs and masturbating nonstop because you can't find a real penis you're even remotely interested in."

That makes me laugh. I put my head on Julia's shoulder.

"We'll figure it out together," I repeat.

She grins tightly. "I know we will. I'm so glad you're here."

"Me too," I say.

And even though coming to Charleston could very well be the impetus for blowing up my life, I mean it.

Chapter Fourteen
OLIVIA

I wake up with a heavy head and a heart that aches. Part of me is still on a high from the near perfect day I had yesterday. And part of me is hitting a low now that I'm realizing I need to make some hard choices if I want to fix what's wrong with my life.

I'm almost afraid to check my doorstep for Eli's edits. His awesomeness is not making my thought process any easier. If I hadn't met him, maybe I wouldn't be so twisted up inside. Maybe I'd never know what I was missing out on.

If I hadn't met him, it'd be easy to go back to New York and pick up right where I left off. But now that choice is much more difficult.

I don't know whether to be angry or grateful.

I grip the doorknob, heart pounding. *Please*, I silently plead. Although I have no clue what I'm pleading for. Please let the doorstep be empty? Please let Eli be there so I can yank him inside and tear off his clothes and rub up against him for the rest of the day?

Taking a deep breath, I open the door. I find the edited chapter on the mat, a Post-It stuck to the corner.

On top of the pages, wrapped neatly in tin foil, is this perfect mini veggie quiche.

Clearly my cooking worked some magic on your muse, a sticky note says. *Loved this chapter even more than the first. Keep eating. Keep writing. Give me a ring at 843-234-8769 if you have any questions—E*

Butterflies take flight in my stomach. I suddenly feel achy not just in my chest, but all over.

A good, delicious kind of ache.

I look up. Look around. I don't want to see Eli. Seeing him will just make me want him more. And I'm not sure I'm ready to have him. I just have this feeling—this strong sense in my gut that being with Eli will change everything. And I don't know if I'm brave enough to embrace that change.

What if it causes a domino effect? What if I not only leave Ted, but I end up leaving my job, too? My parents? I'd be burning my entire life to the ground.

I look down at the edited pages in my hand. Something about his careful block script makes my stomach do a somersault.

Eli may be dangerous. But I do have to thank him for this. He's a busy guy. It's incredibly generous of him to take the time to edit my romance *and* make breakfast for me.

I go inside and dial his number.

He picks up on the second ring.

"Hello?"

"H-hi. Eli? It's me. Olivia."

"Yankee girl!" he says, the excitement in his tone radiating through my breastbone. "You get the quiche?"

I grin.

"I did. Thank you. Very much. You really don't have to keep making me breakfast."

"I want to make you breakfast. Gotta fuel you up so you can get through chapter three today."

"You're relentless," I say, biting my lip. "You know that?"

"I know." A pause. "How're you feelin' today?"

Confused. Terrified.

Joyful.

"I'm all right," I manage. "You?"

"Tired. You been keepin' me up late, Olivia, with these chapters of yours."

"Seriously, you don't have—"

"I *want to*. You gotta let me help you. I'm enjoying it. Truly. It's nice to use another part of my brain once in a while."

Oh, God, if there was ever a time when I thought my heart would literally burst, it's right now.

"Then let me help you," I say. "I know you work crazy hours. Can I maybe walk Billy for you? Hang out with him a bit during the day?"

"Lucky Billy. He'd love that. I keep a key in the pot by my back door—it's the one with the tomato plant in it. Feel free to come over anytime you'd like."

Toe-mata.

His accent is especially velvety this morning.

"So chapter three? I can expect it tonight, then?" he says.

"Yeah," I manage. "Tonight. I'll have it in your mailbox."

"Get to it, girl."

I do.

Over the next week, I settle into a nice little routine. For the first time in all my thirty-two years on this earth, I don't have to set an alarm. I get up early, practically leaping out of bed to discover what goodies Eli left me on the front step. One day it's scrambled eggs and sausage. Another, it's a grits bowl topped with bacon and chives. Oatmeal with candied pecans and brown sugar. A B.E.L.T.—bacon, egg, lettuce, and tomato—on thick slices of sourdough slathered in mayo.

The designer wardrobe I brought with me gets tight to the point of pain. I buy a pair of ripped up boyfriend jeans—inspired by Eli—and some flowy dresses, and I wear those instead.

Eli always leaves an impeccably edited chapter alongside the food. He edits in blue felt tip pen, his letters all neat, small caps. He tells me what he likes—*Cate's reaction is great here*. He tells me what he doesn't—*dialogue comes off stilted. Let them flirt!*

He makes a comment on chapter six—something about making Gunnar a beta hero outside the bedroom, but an alpha hero in it—that gives me pause. Those terms are *romance* terms. Stuff I only know about because I read a lot of it.

Makes me wonder what Eli is reading. No way he's reading any romance other than mine.

Right? The thought is too lovely to even consider.

I go through Eli's edits while I eat. Then I have coffee, do some research on publishing online. The weather is getting nicer with each passing day, the temperature and humidity dropping just enough to leave us these slightly crisp, gorgeously sunny days. So when I'm done eating, I grab Billy, and together we take long walks along the battery. Minus his gigantic poops, he's a great walking buddy.

Some days I squeeze in a yoga class.

Then I grab a shower and head over to Holy City Roasters for the afternoon. Grace and I chat for a while about her coffee and my book. My chapters are averaging about ten pages—two thousand words, give or take—and, sitting down at my usual table by the window, I don't leave until I finish a whole new chapter for Eli to edit that night.

Sometimes it takes me all of an hour and a half to bang it out. Other times, I'm still typing away at closing time.

On days when I finish at a decent hour, I take myself out on dates with the city. I go where I want, when I want. I peruse shops. Tour historical homes. Pop into bars. Try new restaurants.

People weren't kidding about the food down here. It's insane. Each meal is better than the last. Just when I think I've found a new favorite spot—an Italian place on Upper King Street that serves pizza with the best, crispiest crust ever, or the tiny French-Spanish restaurant that serves the most delicious gazpacho I've had—I eat another amazing meal at a new restaurant.

I'll meet Julia for dinner sometimes, or dessert. She introduces me to some of her colleagues at The College of Charleston. I have a great chat with the English Department head about their creative writing program (yes, it exists, but no, they're not hiring). One of the tenured professors, Kathryn Score, actually writes romance that she indie publishes herself. I meet with her twice to pick her brain. She writes contemporary romance, which means her market is a little different than mine. But she hooks me up via Facebook with a few historical authors who are also self-publishing their books. They are a literal treasure trove of information.

Slowly, slowly, I am stitching myself into the fabric of life in this city. I start to recognize faces around town. People stop to say hello. I run into Kathryn at Holy City Roasters, and we decide to have a standing writing date there every other day.

I have my favorite smoothie shop. My favorite place for takeout. My favorite bar (well, my favorite bar after the one at The Pearl).

I walk everywhere. My fancy car sits idle in the driveway. I don't miss it.

I walk so much that when I finally fall into bed at the end of every day, I pass out hard. I'm so tired that even the thoughts that have weighed so heavily on me lately don't have a chance to enter my mind before I'm asleep.

But I do have a thought first thing when I wake up.

That thought is always about Eli.

What he thought of last night's chapter.

Why I had an explicit dream about him. Again.

When I'm going to see him. As much as I love his edits, I miss *him*. Being around him. I like who I am when we're together. He's working, I know. Trying to save The Jam. Doesn't mean I don't wish our schedules matched up a little better.

He's making me forget myself.

Making me lose grip on the fact that this isn't my life. Which makes me wonder if it could be.

The following Monday, I wake up to an empty front stoop.

Puzzled, I immediately glance across the alley. Eli's house is locked up: doors shut, lights out. I have to admit I was really hoping to see him today. He told me he has Mondays off.

Is he okay? Did he not like chapter eight?

Did he not get to it because he took someone home last night? Someone he's probably worshipping with those big, calloused, knowledgeable hands of his...

I shiver, surprised by the stab of jealousy in my gut. I have no right to be jealous. I'm the one with a potential fiancé waiting for me at home. And I've known Eli for, what, a little more than one *week*?

Gorgeous, talented, tatted up guys like him probably go for girls who look like Gisele and paint like Picasso anyway.

Girls who can convincingly rock vintage Levi's, who have tans and talents and the kind of thick, wavy, ombre-colored hair that is just *made* for Instagram.

I am not that girl. I am his friend. He said so the other morning.

But when I head back inside to see my phone lighting up with a call from Eli, butterflies take flight in my belly anyway.

I pick it up.

"I was starting to get worried," I say. "I didn't find any edits or breakfast goods on my step this morning."

Eli laughs, the deep, extra rumbly sound making my heart stutter. Sounds like he just woke up.

The image appears inside my head and stays there. Eli on his back in bed, naked. One hand over his head. Sheets riding low over his hips. His scruff even scruffier than usual. Hair sticking up every which way.

I put a hand on the counter to steady myself.

"That's 'cause I'm holding 'em all hostage," he says. "I'm off today. Come over for breakfast—we can talk edits over coffee and sweet potato pancakes."

A wave of relief hits me head on.

So Eli *wasn't* with an ombre-haired painter last night.

I smile.

Shit. I don't want this information to make me smile. I don't want it to make me feel or do *anything*.

But it does.

Oh, does it.

"Do I have time to shower?" I say, running a foot over the prickly hair on my shin.

"Take all the time you need, Olivia," Eli replies. "Just let yourself in when you're ready."

Chapter Fifteen
OLIVIA

I take way too long getting ready. I don't want to dress up, but I *do* want to look my best.

Unfortunately, the "careless, casual, but cute" look I'm going for takes a lot of freaking effort. I try on every item of clothing I've bought recently. Eventually I settle on my boyfriend jeans and a long sleeved t-shirt. Simple, but comfortable.

By the time I get out the door, I am absolutely starving.

It's already a glorious day. Fall is really in the air this morning, the leaves on the trees turning almost violent shades of yellow and red and orange. I walk next door, my hair fluttering in a soft, crisp breeze.

I breathe in lungful after lungful of air. It's scented with salt and sun. Turn my face up to the wide open sky and close my eyes for a minute, just soaking it in.

Just *being* in this perfect, perfectly content moment.

Never thought my weekday mornings would ever look or feel like this. Usually I hate weekdays, dread sitting like a brick in my stomach from the second I crawl out of bed to the second I fall back in it, too exhausted to even read.

That's just how it is, my mom says.

Adulting sucks, my friends say.

Think about our future, Teddy reminds me.

But standing here in the sun, ideas for my novels taking shape inside my head, a day of good food and good writing time ahead, I get this pressing, urgent feeling that maybe I really can do things differently.

That maybe there's a different way to live.

Maybe I want to live like *this*. Happy and free and excited about my day, rather than dreading it.

But is this even real? Can this feeling last? Is being true to myself just an exercise in idiotic self-indulgence? And what about all the people I'll have to hurt or disappoint to stay here?

It's such a huge risk. A huge, *huge* risk. One I am not sure I'm prepared to take.

Then again, is *anyone* ever prepared to take a leap into the great unknown, no safety net, no guarantee they won't fall on their faces?

Are you ever ready to look yourself in the eye and acknowledge who you truly are? That takes guts.

I have never been a gutsy girl. I was raised to be a *good* girl.

And now I'm starting to realize what a prison that has become.

I also realize I haven't thought about Ted all that much this past week.

I glance at the pretty brick house, its doors thrown open to the morning, ahead on my right.

I've thought about Eli instead.

Eli and Gunnar. A chef and a fictional Earl. Both of them handsome. Dangerously talented with their hands. Smart.

Neither of them the man whose ring is sitting in my drawer.

The scent of bacon yanks me back to the present. My stomach rumbles.

Despite the crush of thoughts inside my head, I smile.

Breakfast is waiting. And I'm not going to let my confusion, my indecision, ruin a meal made by Chef Elijah Jackson.

Billy greets me when I step into the kitchen, but Eli is nowhere to be found.

There's something warming in the oven. It smells so good it almost makes me dizzy.

I call Eli's name, but I get no answer. I move through the house, looking left and right. Only when I look out the windows into the tiny backyard do I find him.

He's lying in a hammock—shirtless, of course—his ankles crossed. All smooth skin. Biceps. Chest hair.

He's reading a paperback book.

The door is open. I step out, the grass rustling beneath my feet.

When I get closer, I catch a glimpse of the cover. It's bright yellow.

The Duke of Midnight by Elizabeth Hoyt. One of my all time favorites.

Turning a page, Eli chuckles. A low, masculine rumble.

My heart seizes inside my chest. It's like the wind got knocked out of me, seeing this man—this gorgeous, talented, half-naked man—in a hammock reading Elizabeth Hoyt and chuckling out of sheer enjoyment.

Billy appears at my side. I pat him on the head, a silent thanks for his moral support in this moment of extreme distress brought on by too much joy and lust and longing.

"Eli," I say, a little breathless. "What are you doing?"

He looks up from the book. His eyes, clear and warm in this light, catch on me. He smiles.

"Just brushin' up on all the greats in your genre," he

replies. "Figure it'll help me help you make Gunnar and Cate really shine."

He folds down the corner of the page and closes the book, getting up.

I feel like I'm living inside a movie as I watch him stride across the lawn, bare chested and smiling and heading for me.

Holding the book he's reading for *me*. To help *me* make my romance the best it possibly can be, because that's my dream and he wants my dreams to come true. No matter how weird or difficult they might be.

Eli is a dream come true.

He wraps me in a hug and says my name and cracks a joke about oral sex in the nineteenth century. If I didn't know it before, I know now that I am falling for this man.

Hard.

Fast.

I don't want to. I didn't mean to. But here I am, curling into his enormous arms, wanting more than anything to be with him. All day. All night.

My body leaps. My heart does, too.

Maybe I've taken the big leap without even knowing it. Makes sense: he's the only person I've ever been able to truly be myself with.

I cling to him. Too scared and too turned on to let him go. His body feels *so good* against mine. So certain.

"You okay, Yankee girl?" he murmurs into my neck, his beard scraping against the sensitive skin just underneath my jaw.

A bolt of desire lands right between my legs, spreading liquid heat throughout my body.

I have never, in all my life, been as attracted to someone as I am to Eli. I always thought chemistry like this only existed in romance novels. But now I know that it's real, I know it's terrifying, too, and so painfully sweet part of me thinks I've died and gone to heaven.

Teddy and I are on a break. We agreed it was okay to be with other people. I wouldn't be doing anything wrong by hooking up with Eli. I just—

I'm scared.

We already get along so well outside of the bedroom. What if we get along inside it, too? What if the sex is great? (I have a feeling it'd be really, really great). I'll keep falling for him—how could I not?—and suddenly it will be the end of October, and I won't be able to go back to Ted because I'm in love with Elijah Jackson.

Am I really ready to make that choice?

"*I don't know*," I say, more to myself than to Eli.

He holds me a little tighter. Pulls me a little closer against him.

"Wanna talk about it?"

"I'll be okay."

"You don't sound okay."

How can I be okay when I'm falling in love with a guy and a life that are completely at odds with everything I've ever worked for?

"I'm overwhelmed," I offer, relieved that I don't have to look him in the eye right now. I don't think I could handle it. "As usual, Eli, you're overwhelming me with your awesomeness."

He begins to lightly stroke his thumb over the small of my back. I can't help it; I arch into him, wanting more. It's a tiny movement, but it's turning me on in a big way.

I love the feel of his hands on me.

I just love the way he makes me feel, period.

"If you need to go, Olivia, just tell me. I hate that I'm upsettin' you."

"You're not—" *Upsetting me. You're turning me inside out.* "That's not it. You've been nothing but excellent, Eli."

Eli pulls back, arms still looped around my middle, and looks down at me, brows pulled together in concern.

"I'm never gonna push you, Olivia. But one of these days, I'd really like to know what's goin' on in that head of yours."

I swallow, searching his eyes. Like Julia said, I need to figure this out for myself. It's obvious I'm too swayed by other peoples' opinions. I don't want to involve Eli in my decision making. I don't want his opinion. Not yet.

I need to learn to trust myself.

"I know. I'm sorry. I need some time. I just—I guess I wasn't expecting you and I—I didn't expect that we'd get so close. I wasn't prepared for you."

Eli grins, reaching up to tuck a stray bit of hair behind my ear.

The simple gesture—the handsomeness of his blunt tipped fingers—sends my pulse into a tailspin.

"Good thing I was prepared for you. I always make extra food, just in case beautiful women show up at my door."

I laugh. Always so charming.

"C'mon," he says, tilting his head toward the kitchen. "Let's go eat. You'll feel better with a full belly."

Chapter Sixteen
ELI

Olivia cleans her plate in record time. Watching her enjoy my food makes me feel better than I have all week. It's been one shit storm after another at work. The Jam is on life support. It's obvious we're going to have to close it down. I was fine with that in theory, but now that it's happening, it's a bitter pill to swallow.

But being with Olivia chases all those heavy thoughts away. When she asks for another pancake, and then slathers it in butter and syrup, I have to stop myself from saying what I've been thinking about a lot lately.

I wanna be more than friends, Yankee girl.

I want to take her upstairs and peel her clothes off. Fuck her for a week straight. Wake up next to her.

But she just asked for time. When she's ready, she'll let me know. This whole thing just feels so delicate. One wrong move, and I'm worried I'll send her running.

I'll just enjoy her company in the meantime. I'll take whatever she's willing to give me.

"So you never really told me why you write what you do," I say, filling her mug with more coffee. "Why romance?"

Olivia sets her fork on her plate and sighs. A contented, sexy as hell sigh. My dick takes note. Which is just perfect, considering I'm going commando in sweats right now. You can see everything. I mean *everything*.

I look down to confirm. Yep. Even the ridge on the head of my dick is visible through the thin fabric.

Fuck.

I hang out on the other side of the island so Olivia can't see the very obvious wood I'm sporting.

"I came to the genre as a reader first," she says, cupping the mug in her hands and settling her elbows on the counter. "Reading romance is kind of what got me through my twenties. I plowed through everything I could get my hands on. I loved the adventure in the stories. The way the heroines had real agency—a real say in how their lives ended up, despite the horribly repressive society they lived in."

I nod, sipping my own coffee. "Their bravery is admirable. So is their willingness to make hard choices. I think that's what I like best about romance. How the main characters never take the easy way out."

Olivia's eyes soften when they meet mine. For a second I think I've upset her again. But then she blinks, clearing her throat, and takes a large swallow from her mug.

"You're a very perceptive reader."

I smirk. "It's what makes me a good editor."

She scoffs, smiling and rolling her eyes.

"Anyway," she continues. "The few friends I told about my romance reading habit weren't exactly supportive. They thought it was kind of a joke. They called it escapist trash."

"Small-minded bastards."

"Right? But I'm kind of like, wait, I think the escape actually improves our reality. I know my life is fuller and better and more interesting because I've read romance. Don't we have a lot to learn from one of the few genres that openly embraces female ambition and sexuality? Isn't it nice to see women in books having killer lives and killer curl-your-toes orgasms? I also love that romance always ends with a happily ever after. It's such a nice reminder to stay hopeful, you know?"

I look at her, my heart thumping in my chest. Her mention of orgasms is doing nothing to help my hard on situation.

"I do. It's a nice reminder that happily ever after exists. That it's possible, no matter how shitty your situation is."

"Exactly." Olivia's throat moves as she swallows. "I love the *variety* of happily ever afters. It showed me there are a million different kinds of happy endings for women. Not just the ones I saw in my own life."

This piques my interest. She hasn't talked much about her life before.

"What kind of endings were you seeing?"

She shrugs. "All of my friends back home, my family—well. None of them have ever really pursued any kind of interest or passion. Which has always been kind of difficult, because I *do* have this thing I'm really passionate about. I mean, I know not everyone is going to be a weirdo who binge reads romance and wishes Mr. Darcy was a real person who really looks like Colin Firth. But I just—living where I'm from made me think actually pursuing my passion was silly, because I'd never seen it done before. Then I read about a heroine who was passionate about justice, so she became this kickass FBI agent who takes down all these bad guys. Or the heroine whose happily ever after was running a taco truck with the boyfriend she felt no need to marry or have babies with."

"So romance gave you the go ahead to be who you are," I say. "To seek out your own version of happily ever after."

"Kind of," she replies, eyes flicking to meet mine. "I'm

still figuring that part out. Seeing that kind of passion at work in real life is definitely helping."

I step around the counter and stand next to her. I can't help it. She's magnetic when she talks like this. Full of heat and truth and excitement.

"Oh yeah?" I sit on the stool beside her. Our elbows brush. My blood jumps when she doesn't pull away. "Where are you seeing that kind of passion?"

Olivia's eyes are still on mine. They radiate heat. Want.

"Right here." Her voice is barely above a whisper. "In this kitchen. In the kitchen at The Pearl. You're clearly *yourself* when you're working. You're doing something you love, something that lights you up. I want to be lit up like that."

Her praise—her belief in me—fills me up. It's fucking nice to hear someone still has faith in what I do and who I am. I've been plagued with so much doubt lately. Doubt about my future. My ability. My path. In my darkest moments, I doubt my ability to provide for a girl like Olivia. She deserves the world. But what if I can't give that to her?

Now, though, her confidence makes *me* feel confident. In her eyes, I'm still the capable, successful chef I've worked my whole life to become.

Makes me want her so bad I'm sick with it.

"You wanna find your happily ever after," I say, "so do it. Start looking."

We're sitting close. Real close. She's looking at me like *that*. Eyes flicking to my lips.

Do it, I silently beg. *For the love of God, kiss me.*

For half a heartbeat, I actually think she's going to. She leans in, just a little, her pupils dilating until her eyes are more black than blue.

Her mouth looks ripe and soft. Like a fresh peach.

Is she that soft between her legs, too?

I don't lean in, but I don't pull back, either. Can't spook her.

We meet eyes. Understanding, lightning quick and hot, passes between us.

Want.

Olivia draws a sharp breath, blinking.

Then she falls back and puts her palm on my chest. She wants to keep me away.

I'm crushed.

Fucking *crushed*.

I can't take it anymore.

"Olivia—"

"I should go," she says, standing. "I'm sorry, Eli."

I can't even formulate a response. I just watch her set her mug down and shove her hands in her pockets and turn to leave.

Spearing a hand through my hair, I let out a long, low breath.

For chrissakes, why won't this woman let me in?

Chapter Seventeen

OLIVIA

I'm shaking when I get back to the carriage house. I close the door behind me and pace in the tiny kitchen, unable to stand still.

I almost just kissed Eli.

I wanted to, more than I wanted my next breath. That *mouth* of his. It's juicy. Infinitely kissable. And the way he was looking at me—the way he was asking such intelligent, interesting questions about romance and happy endings—

I grab onto the back of a stool. Oh God, I'm an idiot. I totally should have kissed him.

It would've been just a kiss.

Who am I kidding? It would've been so much more than that. It would've been a leap. A choice that changed everything.

I just don't want to hurt anyone. And if I kiss Eli, I'll be hurting Ted. I'll be disappointing everyone I know in New York.

But sparing Ted meant hurting Eli. The look in his eyes when I pulled away just now—that was hurt, raw and real.

I'm hurting the guy who's been nothing but wonderful to me.

I can't keep doing this to him. I need to make my choice already. I know that.

I just wish I had more time.

I just wish I wanted him less.

Eli

Yoga usually clears my mind. But after an especially intense hour and a half class later that afternoon courtesy of Peter, I still can't stop thinking about Olivia.

I'm dying for this girl. I can't remember the last time I wanted someone so bad.

I want her body, yeah.

But I also want inside her head, too. Want to know what's got her all twisted up.

Want to know what private parts of her inspire such passion.

She's hurting. I'm doing everything I can to help her feel better. But until she tells me the whole story—not just parts of it, not just what she wants me to know—there's only so much I can do.

Olivia is just so fucking *hot*. Everything about her is hot. Her body. Her eyes. The way she's chasing down this dream of hers to write a novel.

She burns.

Damn it, I want to burn with her. I miss burning like that. I've been so wrapped up in the business of food that I've forgotten the joy of just creating.

Lines from *My Enemy the Earl* swim across my thoughts.

The devil in Gunnar wanted more, wanted to peel back the layers of Cate's clothes and make her bloom with his hands and his body...

Cate's belly muscles tightened beneath Gunnar's palms, her body winding tight, curling into his caress...

That night Cate lay awake in her bed, touching herself. She imagined Gunnar doing it, his fingers on and inside her body...

I can't help but wonder—foolishly—if Olivia is writing about us. About me doing those things to her. Cate and Gunnar are fictional. But Olivia's admitted to mining her own experience for inspiration.

Was she thinking about me when she wrote about Cate touching herself?

Aw, fuck, I'm hard.

I'm so turned on—so lost in thought—that I almost run someone over when I turn onto Longitude Lane without looking.

"Jesus *Christ*," I say, spearing a hand through my soaking wet hair.

I need some relief. Right now. Before someone gets hurt.

Inside my house, I turn the knob in my shower all the way to cold. But the water does nothing to calm my raging hard on.

What in the world are you doing to me, Yankee girl?

My skin is throbbing as I lather up. Every inch of my body feels overly sensitive. Needy.

Turning away from the shower head, I draw a sharp breath through my teeth when my palm brushes the head of my dick. Instinctively I thrust into my waiting hand.

I see fucking stars.

The soap provides just enough lubrication to let me slide easily in and out of my grip. My balls tighten; already sensation is gathering in my head, threatening to explode.

I shut my eyes. Take a shaking breath through my nose.

I'm on the edge. And just the thought of Olivia is enough to push me over into the abyss.

I imagine it's her pussy that's gripping me tight and warm. I imagine her opening her mind and her legs to me, trusting me.

I want this girl to *trust me* already. I don't know why, but I need it.

Tightening my hand around my cock, I thumb the seam on the underside of the head. Water beats down on my neck. The blades of my shoulders.

Would Olivia take charge in bed? Or would she melt into heat and softness?

Soft thighs and soft noises and soft, swollen, perfect cunt.

Heaven. *Help me.*

I start pumping my hand, hard, messy, jerking strokes that would make my fifteen year old self roll his eyes at how artless they are.

But I don't care. I am desperate for relief. Any way I can get it.

My hips surge forward, thrusting my dick into my tight grip one last time, and then I come.

I come so hard it's *painful*. I cry out, squeezing my eyes shut against pulse after pulse of sensation.

I'm in deep with this woman. But she won't let me in. I don't know what else to do to scale her walls. Bring them down.

I am a patient man. You have to be if you want to climb the ladder in the restaurant business.

But then I meet this woman, and suddenly I am a greedy, desperate shitbag, insatiable and impatient and indescribably horny.

I put my palms on the tile, cool to the touch, and lean my weight into my arms, hanging my head. Letting the cold water course down my back as I try to catch my breath.

Catch my feelings before they run away with Olivia again.

I need a drink.

Many drinks. Good thing I have the night off.

Luke and I have our traditions. Among them getting banged up when we're having girl problems. Nothing like Fireball and fried food to clear the mind. I don't necessarily approve of blacking out. But if blacking out means forgetting Olivia for a minute, a second, an hour—means making a light bulb go off that might help me win her over...

Well.

Desperate times call for desperate measures.

The bartender, Jake, pours Luke and I a shot of Fireball. Then he pours one for himself and holds it up.

"Thanks for stopping by tonight, Chef," he says.

I pick up my shot glass and touch it to his. "Thanks for helping us get fucked up."

"It's an honor," Jake says solemnly. He knocks back his shot.

I do the same. It's been a while since I had Fireball. It's somehow way worse and way better than I remember. The sticky sweet cinnamon liquor burns its way down my throat, leaving an astringent, slightly spicy trail of warmth in its wake.

I cover my mouth with my fist to hide a gag.

"Oh, God," Luke says, wincing. "We're too old for this shit."

"Yeah, but that means we're old enough to know the lyrics to almost every damn song those guys're gonna play." I gesture to Buns 'n Roses, a band of middle aged, man-bunned dudes who are setting up on the other side of the patio. Best eighties cover band in town, hands down.

It's one of the reasons we chose to come to the The Spotted Wolf tonight, my favorite dive bar downtown. Granted, it's gotten less dive-y as of late. But the crowd, the drinks, and the music are still on the right side of skeevy, and the patio is the best in town. It's actually the hollowed out basement of an ancient mansion that used to occupy the site. Original brick arches are open to the night sky; strands of Edison bulbs form a kind of open-air ceiling.

"Fingers crossed they play some MJ." Luke gestures to a tall blonde in a far corner. "Ten bucks says that girl gets *down* to 'Billie Jean'."

I hold out my hand. "I'll take that bet."

"Done." Luke shakes my hand, then nods at Jake for another round.

The second shot goes down easier than the first. I roll back my shoulders. Roll my head, releasing the tension in my neck. I catch a woman, cute and busty, checking me out. She smiles.

I blink, waiting for the familiar tingle of interest.

None comes.

I turn back to Luke, bewildered. Been a long ass time since one girl ruined me for all the others.

"So, Olivia," Luke says. Man's got an uncanny ability to read my thoughts. "I take it you haven't figured out her story yet."

Grabbing the Bud Light Jake slides across the bar, I take a long pull.

"Nope," I say. "Not for lack of tryin'."

Luke sips his beer and meets my eyes. "Ever consider that maybe she's just not that into you? Meanin' no offense."

I raise one shoulder in a half shrug. "Could be. But I just get this *feeling* about her. The way she looks at me. Smiles at me. The way she writes—"

"She writes?"

"Yep. Romance. Smart, sexy, *hot* romance."

Luke takes a swallow of beer, eyes suddenly wide. "Go on."

"I could go on for hours," I reply. "But suffice it to say I fuckin' love her writing. Writing that she's sharing with me. No one else. Just yesterday she came over, and we talked for pretty much the whole goddamn morning about her book, about other books, her life. I swear to God she was gonna kiss me at the end. I could see it in her eyes—how bad she wanted to do it."

"But she didn't," Luke says, furrowing his brow.

I shake my head, taking another pull from my bottle. "Nope. It's like—almost like she's holding back. Fighting it."

"And you made it clear you wanted her to plant one on you," he says.

"Just short of puckerin' up, hell yeah. I was looking into her eyes. She's got these gorgeous blue eyes, Luke." I shake my head again. "She called me a friend. But I want to be more than that, and I think she does, too."

"Huh." Luke takes a thoughtful sip. "I get that this girl is special. But the fact that you're wantin' her to kiss you so bad—that you're so in your head about this girl—I don't know. Makes me think it has something to do with your restaurant being in trouble."

"What?" I pull back, feeling a rush of indignation. "Writing's been on the wall for a while now at The Jam. You know I've made my peace with it."

Luke cocks an eyebrow. "You really gonna tell me you're feelin' *just fine* about a restaurant you poured your blood, sweat, and tears into failing? Never mind the fuck ton of money y'all are gonna lose. And all those jobs...c'mon, E. This time last year, you stood in this very spot and told me The Jam was the restaurant you've always wanted to open."

"I stand by that statement," I say hotly, before sucking on

my beer like my life depends on it. "Was I upset when I found out The Jam wasn't the hit The Pearl was? Yes. But I'm still proud of the food we made there. And I still got The Pearl. Which is still makin' money hand over fist."

Luke settles his back against the bar and looks me in the eye. "I'm saying this as a friend, E. But maybe you're ignoring the fact that you're feelin' a little lost right now. You gotta give yourself time to mourn The Jam. Part of me thinks you're wantin' this girl to kiss you to distract you from the fact that you failed. 'Cause let's face it, Elijah—you've never failed at a damn thing in your life until now. I don't buy that you're over it already."

I set my empty bottle on the bar harder than I mean to. Jake looks up from the glass he's wiping clean. He nods when I motion for another beer.

I'm angry. Which means Luke is probably right.

Doesn't mean the things I feel for Olivia aren't real, though.

Doesn't make her any less special. So maybe I pump the brakes a little. Let our friendship deepen. But I'm not giving up on her.

Not yet.

I settle my elbow on the bar and let out a sigh. Jake hands me a fresh beer. "Luke, I appreciate the honesty. I don't disagree with what you're saying. Maybe I am jumpin' in a little fast with Olivia. Maybe I am still a little upset about The Jam. But that's all the more reason to have a good time tonight. I promise to slow down, all right?"

Luke opens his mouth to say something when I hear a familiar voice at my elbow.

"Well well well. If it isn't my long lost brother."

I look to see my baby sister Grace standing beside me, beer in hand. Smiling, I pull her into a hug.

"Hey Gracie," I say.

"Hey yourself." She pulls back to examine my face. "I was *this close* to filing a missing persons report, Elijah. I haven't seen you in almost a month."

I run a hand up the back of my head. Gracie's got mama's death stare down pat.

"I'm sorry. I know I been a shit brother lately. But with everything going on at the restaurant—"

"And everything going on with your new *friend*, Olivia."

I blink. "How'd you know Olivia and I are…whatever we are?"

"Word travels fast in this town." Grace smiles. "Also, she talks about you a lot when she comes into the shop. Like, a *lot* lot."

My heart skips a beat.

"She does?"

Grace's smile deepens. "Oh, you got it *bad* for this girl, don't you?"

"That's none of your business." I sip my beer. "But if you must know, then yes, I would very much like to see more of Olivia."

Luke steps up beside me.

"Grace," he says. "You look…great."

Still smiling, she replies, "Hi, Luke. I haven't seen *you* in forever. How've you been?"

"I've been all right," he replies. "What about you? I hear you're killing it over at Holy City Roasters."

Her smile turns teasing. "Sure am."

She goes in for a hug. He lets her. When he steps back, he looks at her for a beat too long.

Grace is blushing. Luke is staring.

She only looks away when her phone starts to ring. She glances at the screen.

"Sorry," she says. "I have to take this."

Turning around, she moves away from us and brings the phone to her ear.

I take the opportunity to spear Luke with a look.

"What?" he says, sipping nervously at his beer.

"You know what. I saw the way you were looking at her."

He turns bright red.

"I'm sorry, E," he says. "I didn't mean anything by it."

"Look," I say, turning to him. "Grace is a grown woman. She can make her own choices. I wouldn't usually interfere with stuff like this. But she's been dating the same guy for a while now, and she says she's really happy with him. So leave her alone, all right? I don't want you fucking with her head."

Luke runs a hand through his hair. I can't read his expression.

"Of course. Gracie's a friend. Nothing more."

I look at him. "Good. You understand, right? That I just want my sister to be happy?"

"Of course," he repeats. "I want the same thing for her, Eli. Always have."

I keep my eyes on him for another beat, trying to figure out what's going on. He looks like a lost puppy dog. It's pitiful.

Whatever. Luke's love life is none of my business.

I turn my back to the bar and lean against it as I scan the crowd.

That's when I lock eyes with a gorgeous brunette who steps through the side entrance nearby.

My heart skips a beat *again*.

It's her.

Holy shit she's here.

"Eli!" Olivia says, eyes going wide with surprise.

Chapter Eighteen
ELI

"Olivia!" Can't help it. My gaze flicks down her body. "He—*hey*."

Of course.

Of *course* Yankee girl shows up to The Spotted Wolf looking hot as hell five seconds after I decide to *pump the brakes*.

What a sick fucking joke.

Thanks for nothing, universe.

Olivia, bless her, is wearing blue jeans that are tight tight *tight*. Her white button down would be prim if it wasn't partially see through. The red lace bra she's wearing underneath—

I can't.

I focus my gaze on her feet instead. She's wearing cute Chuck Taylors that are a little scuffed up.

Her hair falls in loose, unruly waves around her shoulders. I bite the inside of my bottom lip, hard, to keep from winding a lock around my finger. I imagine how silky it would feel. How her lips would fall open and her cheeks would flush when I gave it a tug.

I can smell her shampoo. Something clean and herbal.

She smells good enough to eat.

"I finished my chapter early today, so I thought I'd do some exploring. I saw the lights from the sidewalk and came in for a quick drink..." Olivia puckers her brow. "Eli? You all right?"

"Yep," I bite out, blinking. "Sorry, I just—uh. Long day. Beer—" *Bullshit*.

I go in for a hug. It's awkward, all thanks to me. Olivia has to go on her tip toes to reach me, and I kind of half crouch, half bend over. My brain screams *slow*. But my body—

Well. There's a reason I keep my crotch region bowed away from her.

I fall back. Luke gives me a not so subtle nudge.

"Don't be rude, Elijah," he says. "Introduce us."

I tug a hand through my hair. "Olivia, this is my friend Luke. Luke, this is my new neighbor, Olivia."

"Nice to meet you," Luke says, aiming his all-American-baseball-player smile at Olivia while extending his hand. "I hear you're new in town."

She takes Luke's hand. "I'm already smitten with it."

"Charleston's a great city. Only downside is that this grump lives here." Luke points his thumb at me.

"I'm not a grump," I bite out.

Luke shrugs. "See what I mean?"

I resist the urge to punch him in that handsome mug of his.

Grace gives Olivia a hug, and they chat for a minute. It's obvious they're friends, both of them laughing and gesticulating wildly as they catch up. I have to say that seeing how well they get along makes me feel all warm and mushy inside. Olivia's a natural conversationalist. Good listener, thoughtful talker. Grace shoots me a look, grinning.

I like this one.

Because Olivia wasn't great enough. Now she's got to go and be wonderful with my sister, too.

Yet another reason to think I might not deserve this girl. I'm gripped by the terrible idea that I have nothing to offer her. Which, in my rational mind, I know is ridiculous. I'm feeding her. Editing her book. Encouraging her to chase after this incredible career she wants. I'm inspiring her in the same way she's inspiring me.

That counts for something. It has to.

Has to.

"Let's get you somethin' to drink," I say to Olivia during a pause in their conversation. "What're you having?"

Olivia glances at my beer, then at the empty shot glasses on the bar. "That looks good."

Behind the bar, Jake nods, checking out Olivia before turning to grab the Fireball.

My grip tightens on my bottle. I am not a jealous guy. But all of a sudden I'm fantasizing about clocking every dickhead in this bar who dares to so much as glance at Olivia.

I spear Jake with a look when he turns back around. He takes the hint, quickly pouring our shots and handing Olivia a beer before busying himself with the dishwasher.

She picks up the shot glass and gives its contents a sniff. "It's been a long time since I've taken a shot. What the hell is this stuff? Smells like candy."

"Tastes like it, too." Luke grabs his glass and taps it to Olivia's. "Actually, that's a lie. It kind of tastes like fiery death. But it gets the job done."

Olivia cocks a brow, smiling. "Fiery death. All right then. I'm in."

We take the shot together, my eyes glued to her face the whole time. She winces, blinking hard, after she swallows. Her eyes water a bit. I can tell she wants to sputter, or maybe gag, but instead she just shakes her head and grabs her beer, taking a long pull.

"Whew," she says, pressing the back of her hand to her mouth. "That is...interesting."

I'm smiling now, too. God damn she's cute.

"Yep. You're definitely gonna feel interesting tomorrow morning, that's for sure," Grace says.

The patio is really getting packed. People hang out in front of the stage, waiting for the band to begin. I look up when the lead singer from Buns 'n Roses introduces himself into the microphone. A beat later, the band bursts out into a loud, throbbing version of "Pour Some Sugar on Me" by Def Leppard.

Immediately the front half of the patio turns into a dance floor. Hands are in the air, there's hollerin' and hootin' and some pretty egregious dry humping going on.

I turn to Olivia, half hoping she's got a look of disgust on her face because she hates eighties music and/or Def Leppard. I need a reason to want her a little less. A reason to help me pump the goddamn brakes.

Instead, her face is lit up with a smile as she mouths the lyrics, nodding her head in time to the beat.

"You like Def Leppard?" I say, raising my voice so she can hear me.

Olivia nods, digging her teeth into her bottom lip. "Love 'em. Although Bruce Springsteen is probably my favorite. From the eighties, at least."

My uncle introduced me to The Boss when I was a kid. I've been obsessed ever since.

I meet Luke's eyes over her head.

Good*ness*.

I'm in big fucking trouble.

As if on cue, Buns 'n Roses plays "Dancing in the Dark".

Olivia looks at me. I look at her.

"Wanna dance?" I ask.

She chews on her bottom lip. My heart falls. She's gonna turn me down again. God, why do I keep doing this to mys—

"Would love to," she replies with a smile. She looks at Luke and Grace. "Are you guys going to be okay? I hate to leave you..."

"Y'all go have fun," Luke says, hardly giving us a glance as he turns to my sister.

I shoot him a dark look.

"You two behave." Then I nod my head toward the band. "Let's go, Yankee girl."

She follows me as I try to nudge my way through the crowd. It's slow going; the patio is *really* packed. I turn around to see some asshole cutting Olivia off, shouldering her aside.

"Hey!" I shout at the guy, stepping back. "Watch it."

Then I reach behind me and grab Olivia's hand. For a second, it stays lax in mine. I worry I've made her uncomfortable. But I don't want her to get lost in the throng. Shit—

But then she firms her grip, fingers curling around my palm. I glance over my shoulder and she meets my eyes.

"All right?" I ask.

She nods, her smile returning. "All right."

My pulse hiccups. Her hand feels small and warm in my own. She's *trusting* me.

I feel like I could fucking fly.

I turn back around and head for the stage, keeping Olivia close. Once, when I stop unexpectedly, she kind of crashes into me. I swear to God I almost bite off my tongue at the feel of her tits pressed against my back. Am I imagining that she lingers there for half a heartbeat?

I keep moving. I don't wanna do something stupid. We burrow our way to a spot in the middle of the dance floor. The lead singer has busted out a saxophone, and everyone around us is going nuts. Olivia comes to stand beside me, her hip brushing against mine when she shimmies.

I take a chance and give her hand a squeeze.

Olivia smiles, squeezing back.

I can't let her go. Not yet. I crave *this*. Whatever this feeling is.

I raise my arm and twirl her around. Then she raises her arm and attempts to twirl me, and even though I bend my back, I somehow manage to fuck it up, spilling beer all over the front of my button up shirt. Her eyes widen when they fall on the stain. She puts the flat of her palm over it. Over my stomach.

"Sorry!" she shouts.

My entire body warms at the simple contact. I don't wanna read too much into it. That she's the one touching me now.

But I do.

I *lean* into it. Into her palm.

Into her.

And she doesn't pull away.

"Don't give me an excuse to take my shirt off," I reply.

Olivia laughs, taking a step closer. "Like you need one."

I cock a teasing brow, my free hand going to the top button. "Should I?"

"I don't wanna get kicked out yet. Band's too good," she replies, swatting away my hand.

Her playful touching—her flirting—is driving me up the wall. It's such a fucking turn on. The blood inside my skin feels downright giddy.

I catch her hand, guiding it onto the back of my neck. Her eyes flash with heat, and she steps into me, sliding her other arm onto my shoulder. Pressing our bodies together.

The solid, soft feel of her against me is enough to make me wanna scream. Our bodies fit together perfectly.

Her curves are all over me.

My cock starts to feel heavy when she digs the tips of her fingers into the hair at the nape of my neck, gently dragging her fingernails across my scalp.

I curl an arm around her waist and hold her closer. Duck my head to murmur in her ear.

"I like that."

Olivia's nose brushes against the line of my jaw. I don't know if it's intentional or not. But it turns me on in a really big way.

"Thought you might."

Her voice is different. A little husky.

The band is playing "Jesse's Girl" now. Olivia pulls away a little. Just enough to meet my eyes as she starts moving her hips, her body practically writhing against mine.

Don't get a boner.

Do. Not. Get. A. Boner.

I'm terrified of scaring her off. She's never been so open with me. So *free*. Her fiery side has finally come out to play, and I'm not about to send it back into hiding by poking her with my badly behaved dick.

So I twirl her a few more times, hoping to put some distance between us. But then she turns around and presses her ass into my crotch, rolling it to the beat of "1999", the song the band plays next.

I brush her hair over her shoulder so I can lean down to her ear again.

"You tryin' to kill me, Olivia?"

She shoots me the sauciest, sexiest, hottest look ever over her shoulder. For a second I can't breathe.

"What? You really expect me *not* to dirty dance to Prince?"

Jesus, take the wheel.

By some miracle, I manage to keep my body under

control. The night is warm and the music is loud, and Olivia and I dance like we have nothing to lose. No worries. No disappointments. It's just us and Pat Benatar and U2 and Foreigner underneath a cloudy night sky.

At one point, I glance toward the bar. I let out a silent sigh of relief when I see Gracie there with her boyfriend Nicholas. Luke is MIA.

Good. Gracie's in safe hands. I don't have to worry. Which means I can focus on Olivia.

She's one hell of a dancer. Never would've guessed the girl in the designer shades would act out the lyrics to "Addicted to Love" in public while taking slugs of Bud Light. But here she is, laughing, making *me* laugh, rolling her hips and biting her lip and throwing her arms in the air as she sings about one track minds.

Throwing her arms around *me*.

It starts to rain. Just a sprinkling of droplets. No one seems to notice. Least of all Olivia, who's behind me now, hands on my hips as she encourages *my* ass to press into *her* crotch.

I oblige my lady, and give her as much booty as she can handle until I pull her around, her back to my front, and hold her against me, our bodies moving in tandem.

We're both sweating. Both breathless. My heart is going apeshit inside my chest. I feel like I've been plugged into a socket, blood electric, skin charged. Our chemistry is real.

My feelings for this romance writing, dirty dancing woman are real.

Feelings I would very much like to express physically. I'm too warm and too turned on. I want her too much.

It begins to rain in earnest, followed by an ominous rumble of thunder.

I look down at the back of Olivia's head. She's been raking her hands through her hair all night, making it messy.

Just how I like it.

The band calls it a night, blaming the thunder for their shortened set.

Without a word, I grab Olivia's hand and head for the covered bar. But we're not the only ones with that idea, and about five seconds later, the bar is packed and we're edging back out into the rain.

I notice Gracie is still here with Nicholas. I wave to her.

"You okay?" I shout.

She gives me a thumbs up.

"C'mon," I say, giving Olivia a gentle tug. "Let's get out of here."

"Okay," she replies, jogging after me.

We leave the bar, only to find ourselves on the crowded sidewalk. People are on their phones, trying to get Ubers. The rain is really coming down now.

I start to dig my phone out of my pocket, but Olivia tugs on my arm.

"Let's just walk. It's not that far. We're already soaked."

"You sure?" I ask. I move closer to her when I see I'm not the only one who's noticed her wet shirt is completely see through now. "I'm happy to get an Uber."

She grins. "I'm sure. Last one home is a rotten egg."

Then she takes off into the rain.

Chapter Nineteen
OLIVIA

Eli's footfalls are sure and even behind me, thudding on the wet pavement.

"Wait up, Yankee girl!"

I keep running. Keep smiling.

When was the last time my heart has pumped like this outside of a gym? Probably explains why I had my hands all over Eli tonight. I definitely didn't expect to run into him. I was just minding my own business, grabbing a drink on a Monday night at a cute bar I spotted in passing.

And then there he was, standing on the patio in all his scruffy, plaid-shirted glory.

I knew the second I saw him that I was a goner. The way his eyes lit up when they fell on me—the way they darkened when he watched me dance—

I've never felt sexier. More desired.

The touching started out innocently enough. He took my hand, and then I put my hand on his stomach. His rock hard stomach that literally rippled with muscle underneath my palm. Touching him made me burn with longing.

Him touching *me* pushed me over the edge. Having those big, capable hands on me made me lose my fucking mind.

So did his dancing. He was confident. But he could still laugh at himself. Still shimmy his cute little butt while singing Kenny Rogers at the top of his lungs.

I'm beginning to think there's nothing the man can't do.

I am hyperaware of his presence behind me. The rain, cool and insistent, does nothing to soothe the heat running just inside my skin.

My ribs ache from laughing. I had so much fun tonight with Eli. I loved the dancing, sure. But it was also cool meeting his friend Luke and running into Grace.

Speaking of Grace—I caught a glimpse of her at the bar as we were leaving. She was with some guy—it wasn't Luke—and she looked pretty miserable with him. Until Eli was waving at her, and then she managed a smile. It's clear the two of them are close. I like that. It's sweet.

Sweet *and* sexy. Eli in a nutshell.

I feel my heartbeat in my lips. They are tingly. Heavy. Full of blood and longing.

I have to make my choice already. I can't keep hurting Eli. Leading him on like this.

He catches up to me. He pulls at my elbow, slowing us both down. His fingers move down my forearm, capturing my hand.

I glance at him. He runs his other hand through his hair, coaxing the wet strands away from his face. I get that funny feeling again. The one I got over and over again on the dance floor. That weak-in-the-knees feeling of *joy,* just being with him. Just being *myself*, dancing and singing and smiling like an idiot.

He's unapologetically ardent in everything he does. He's not afraid of his heart. His body. Clearly he hasn't divorced them from his life in the name of having it all.

He made them his life.

Do I have the courage to do the same? Because damn does he make it look good.

Not effortless.

Not easy.

But *good*.

Then again, what if this is just momentary insanity? Who *wouldn't* be seduced by everything this sexy southern chef represents? Everything he does?

And as delicious as this world is, am I really ready to leave everything I have with Ted behind?

Bottom line: how can I trust myself to make the right choice when I may have been making wrong ones all along?

The questions flit through my head, somehow only heightening the potent *want* coursing through me.

"This way," Eli says, pointing to Longitude Lane.

"I know," I reply.

He turns his head to look at me. "You're learning the neighborhood."

"I am," I say proudly. "I've had a lot of fun exploring over the past week. Charleston's such a cool place."

He's still looking at me. The laughter is gone from his eyes now.

"I love that you love it."

The way his eyes search mine turns my heart upside-down.

We turn onto Longitude Lane. The rain is really coming down now. Eli's shirt is plastered to his chest and arms.

A stab of desire hits me right in the middle of my chest and lands in my clit.

It's so potent and I'm so overwhelmed by it that I have to drop his hand. I'm worried I'll spontaneously combust. I start to jog ahead of Eli. Jog to the carriage house and up the stairs.

My heart does a somersault when I hear Eli's footsteps thudding on the treads behind me.

"Gotta make sure you get in okay," he explains.

My pulse pounds low in my belly.

The laughter and the heat of the moments before turns to anticipation. Lust. Longing like I've never experienced before.

I want him to come inside. My God, do I want that, more than anything. My body is on *fire*. The flames inside my skin lick higher when I imagine the solid weight of his body pressing me into the mattress, those pouty lips of his on mine, teasing, pulling, moving down my chest to my breasts.

But there will be no turning back if I invite him in. Eli is forbidden fruit. Touch him, and I'll be eating from the tree of knowledge.

And we all know how that turned out for Eve.

Will it turn out the same for me? An unmitigated disaster that ends in his disgrace and my fall?

Eli has never been anything but patient and courteous and cute with me. But just the fact that he's *here*—his presence—it's pushing me up against all these questions I have, forcing me to confront them.

Forcing me to pick a side.

He's got me cornered, he's got me up against a wall, and that terrifies me and turns me on and makes me want to cry.

I feel the heat of Eli's body on the step behind me. Smell the woodsy smoke of his aftershave.

My hand shakes as I try to unlock the front door. I can't get the key into the lock. The enormous gas lamp above the door bathes everything in flickering shades of pink and orange.

Then Eli's arm appears above mine, and he's covering my hand with his, steadying my grip. Together we guide the key to where it needs to go. It slides easily into the lock. The muscles in his forearm pop against the skin as we turn the key, the deadbolt sliding back with a small *click*.

My breath catches at the same moment.

Neither of us moves. The feel of his skin on mine sends shockwaves of lust through my entire being. He's warm and smooth and *big*.

I'm wet in every possible meaning of the word.

I lean back, just the tiniest bit. Just enough so that my back meets with his front. We touched a lot dancing. But that was playful touching. Heat-of-the-moment touching.

This is different.

Shutting my eyes, I revel in the feel of him. The knowledge that he's *right fucking there*. That he's strong and solid.

That he could be mine.

Leaving my keys hanging in the lock, Eli slowly turns my hand palm side up. Then he presses the meat of his thumb into my wrist.

"Your heart is racing, Yankee girl." The softness of his voice is cut with an edge of gravel. Gravel I can feel vibrating in his chest. "And you're burnin' up."

I turn my head to meet his eyes. They are dark with unapologetic lust.

He wants to come in, too.

My heart pounds. One hard, decisive beat.

Yes.

This could be the dumbest decision I've ever made.

Or it could be the best.

Either way, I'm making it.

Right here. Right now. Everything changes.

Maybe I want it to. Maybe I'm actually *ready* and *deserving* and *allowed* to experience whatever's about to unfold.

Oh, but I'm shaking. So hard.

My voice does, too, when I finally gather the courage to speak.

"W-would you like to c-come in?" I ask.

It's really pouring now, the rain coming down in opaque sheets.

His eyes are dark. Hair soaked and wild.

"I would like that," he says, his voice an octave lower than usual. "Very, very much. But I need you to know something. I fucking adore you, Olivia. I been wantin' to touch you since that first morning you walked into my kitchen. I want you bad, sweetheart. So bad it's eating me up inside. But you asked for time, and I intend to respect that. Unless you tell me *right now* that you're ready. You gotta say the words."

For a minute I just stand there, letting the weight of his confession—his concern and his respect—wash over me.

Letting my skin and my heart and my thoughts absorb it. Revel in it.

"I'm ready," I say.

Then I reach out. Grab him by the front of his shirt and yank him against me.

Eli curls his arms and slides his hands onto my face in one smooth, swift motion. He's tilting his head, bending his neck in the most masculine, most delicious way possible. He guides my mouth up to his.

And then he kisses me. Or I kiss him. It's hard to tell.

All I know, a mere three seconds in, is that it's *the* kiss. The one I'll write about for years to come.

The one there will be no going back from.

Chapter Twenty
OLIVIA

Eli's mouth is soft and hungry against mine. I smell a hint of cinnamon on his breath from the Fireball shots. Taste it, too, on his lips.

Lips that move over mine slowly.

Erotically. Patient and knowledgeable and plump. He sucks gently on my bottom lip. Does it again before the tip of his tongue licks into my mouth. His thumb strokes over my cheek, the now familiar ridge of his scar lighting up my skin.

I'm melting against him, fisting his wet shirt in my fingers.

I can feel his heart throbbing. Alive and strong and beating *for me*.

Me. The *real* me. Not the perfectly put together Ivy League professor. But the messy, complicated, breakfast-loving romance writer.

Eli tilts my head a little and deepens his angle. He uses his tongue to open my mouth a little bit more. Then his tongue finds mine, lapping at me with intention. He drinks me in. Takes his time. Kisses me with light. Hunger.

Passion. The pent up kind.

The kind that literally makes my toes curl.

His scruff scrapes against my chin. I bring a hand up to touch his cheek, feeling the prickle of hair there. Blown away by the fact that I get to touch him like this.

That I'm being kissed like this. Like the world is ending.

I've never been kissed so...*thoroughly* before. This kiss—it's juicy and hot and the least practical thing I can think of.

To think I almost passed this up.

To think I was *this close* to going through life without knowing kisses like this existed.

The dissonance between Eli's rough, calloused palms on my face and the softness of his lips, his tongue, his touch, makes me want to howl.

I manage a whimper instead.

"You okay, baby?" he murmurs into my mouth, lips moving over mine like he can't stand to pull away, not now, not even for a second.

For as long as I can remember, I've hated when people use *baby* as a term of endearment. Just struck me as cheesy, I guess. What boy bands called the invisible object of their affection in saccharine pop songs.

But when Eli says it to me, less a word than a growly rumble, I'm hit by a surge of acute arousal.

I guide the wet fabric of Eli's shirt up over his belly. It sticks there, still plastered to his body. Then I slide my hands a little lower until I meet with the slice of bare abdomen over the waistband of his jeans.

"I'm okay," I reply.

His skin is hot. He's a wall of muscle here, rippled and ridged in all the right places. So different from my own body.

I reach behind me and somehow manage to open the door. I fall back, and Eli falls with me, catching my mouth with his. He shuts the door behind him.

His kiss deepens. He's kissing me hard now. We're breathing hard. I can feel him getting hard against my thigh.

Oh, Jesus, he feels *big*.

Really big.

The heaviness between my legs throbs.

I run my fingers over a happy trail of wiry hair arrowing from his bellybutton down to his taut waist. It disappears—tantalizingly, teasingly—into his jeans.

I slide my palms back up his torso, then grab the hem of his shirt. Wordlessly we work it up his chest, only breaking our kiss when he tugs it over his head. It lands with a wet plop somewhere on the floor.

Just like that, he's shirtless.

Back in his element.

His eyes meet mine. They're sharp. Glistening.

"So my Yankee girl likes me shirtless after all," he says, a half smile playing at one corner of his lips. I notice they're a little swollen.

He's so damn sexy I'd probably black out from looking at him if I wasn't so turned on.

I slide my arms around his neck, arching my body against his. The heat of his skin burns through my wet shirt.

My nipples prickle to life through my thin shirt. Eli notices, his eyes flicking down to my chest.

"Oh, you *definitely* like me shirtless." His eyes flick back up to meet mine. "I think I'd like you shirtless, too."

"I'll join your club." My voice is a little hoarse. "Although I don't think I'll quite compare to you."

"Shush," he says, reaching down for my shirt. "Stop comparin'. You're gorgeous."

I shiver when he pulls my shirt over my head, separating us again.

Keeping my eyes closed, I feel the heat of his gaze on me. I send up a silent prayer of thanks that I wore a decent looking bra today. It's red, a little lacy. Nothing crazy, but the cups are sheer, and it makes my tits look round and firm(ish).

I hear Eli let out a long, low breath through his nose.

The next thing I know he's pressing a scruffy kiss to my neck, just where I like it. Just where I can feel it in my clit.

I squeeze my legs together. Open my eyes and dig my hand into his hair as he bends down to kiss the rounded top of my left breast. The way he bends his neck—the thick cords of vein and sinew that pop against his skin—there's something overwhelmingly masculine about it.

"I've been wanting to do *that* since I walked into your kitchen the first time," I say.

The ghost of that delicious smirk of his plays at his lips.

"So do it." His eyes are a little hazy now. "Do what you want, sweetheart."

Rolling up onto my tip-toes, I curl my arms around Eli's neck and pull him down. I kiss him. I close my eyes and tilt my head and I kiss him.

In half a second flat the kiss is messy and hard and deep. I cannot get enough of it. Of *him*. The way he smells and the feel of his skin.

My pulse is hammering. A new wash of heat settles low in my core when Eli's hands snake down to my ass, giving me a squeeze before gently pressing me into his groin.

Oh, I can definitely feel his erection now. He's rock hard.

He kisses my neck. Sensation shoots through my skin to land squarely between my legs, making the heaviness there throb.

And then he says my name.

Olivia.

A half growl, half plea. That accent of his curling around the vowels, making it sound like something entirely new and entirely different and entirely sexy.

My knees buckle.

They fucking *buckle*.

I see it in my head. Me going down like a sack of potatoes, dragging him with me. One of us ending up with a bloody nose, the other a shattered elbow.

But I don't go down.

Instead, Eli catches me. His grip firms on my ass, moving to the backs of my thighs before he lifts me up, curling my legs around his waist.

He takes my gasp into his mouth. Kisses me senseless, tongue licking into my mouth, teeth nicking my bee-stung lips.

"I don't—" I manage.

Eli gives me one long, lazy stroke of his tongue. "Don't what?"

"I don't get all wobbly like that," I breathe. "Not with anyone."

Laughter rumbles in his chest as he takes my mouth with his again.

"You just did with me."

I roll my hips against his erection. He growls.

"Bedroom," I say, digging my fingers into his hair. "Just—just keep going back. Door past the counter."

Eli walks us across the tiny space of the carriage house. His lips never once leaving mine.

The ancient floorboards creak beneath our weight.

I am on *fire*. His scruff tickling my chin. Dick pressing into my pussy. The bare skin of his firm tummy pressed against mine.

Even though my eyes are closed, I can tell we're in the bedroom by the gentle sound of the rain pattering against the windowpanes.

He curls one arm underneath my butt. He glides the other hand up my spine to cup the back of my neck, cradling me.

"You ready?" he asks, pressing a kiss to the corner of my lips. "I'm gonna put you down on the bed."

I can only nod into his shoulder.

I'm speechless. I've never been held like this. Never felt cherished like this.

Or maybe I never allowed myself to feel this way. To be so vulnerable with someone else.

I just feel safe with Eli. Safe, and very sexy.

Eli sets me gently on the bed, and I untangle my legs from around his waist. A rush of cold air moves in where the heat of his skin used to be. I suck in a breath, shivering, and gather my arms against my chest.

The light from the window catches on Eli's face at the foot of the bed. There's a crease between his gathered eyebrows.

"I'm here," he says, and then he plants his palms on the bed and slowly climbs on top of me, the mattress dipping in time to his movements.

The *climbing*. It's so sexy I think my head might explode. The muscles in his arms and shoulders flex as he shifts his weight from one side to the other. His wet hair falls in his eyes. I reach up and brush it back.

I part my legs. Invite him in.

Eli's gaze sharpens.

My eyes nearly roll to the back of my head when he settles his groin against mine, giving his hips this little teasing, eviscerating roll before he grabs my leg and guides it up toward my torso, bending my knee. His body melts into mine. My wet jeans don't want to give; they tighten uncomfortably around the joint.

But when he bends his head and gathers my nipple in his mouth, sucking it *hard* through the fabric of my bra, all other sensations fade to the background.

I arch into his mouth, tugging my hands through his hair.

Lust bolts from the hardened point of my nipple straight to my clit.

As if he can read my body like a book, Eli rolls his hips again, making the seam of my jeans hit me *right there*.

"Eli," I moan.

In reply, he moves to the other nipple, then trails a fiery line of kisses on my chest, my neck. My jaw.

Then he captures my mouth in his, surrounding me in warmth and skin, settling his weight onto me as he draws a hand up my naked side and cups my breast, thumbing my already over-sensitized nipple.

He's hot. Huge. Heavy.

He begs me to give in to him. With his mouth and his body, he's asking permission to take charge. To do what he's wanted to do since he first saw me how many days ago.

"Yes," I breathe.

Chapter Twenty-One
ELI

Olivia gives her hips a tiny little roll. Just enough to meet me at the crest of my own roll, so the head of my dick hits her center just right.

I grunt, biting down on her bottom lip.

Leaning all my weight onto one elbow, I hold myself up and reach between her legs. Even through the thick, wet fabric of her jeans, I can feel how hot she is.

I can feel the beat of her pulse, too. It's going wild.

She's clawing at my chest. Digging her nails into my skin when I press my two fingers against the length of her slit.

She is *burning*.

Olivia does this thing—she lets out these little moans, so quiet I can hardly hear them over the rain outside, whenever I do something she likes.

She's moaning now into my mouth.

I feel like I died and went to heaven.

I want to unbutton these jeans and touch her for real. Slide my fingers into her soft, sweet heat. Spread her wide and taste her. See if she's as hot and bothered as I am.

Because good *Lord* am I hard. My dick feels swollen and huge inside my jeans. I'd like to unbutton them, too.

But I don't.

For starters, I don't want our first time to be some wet, thoughtless fuck after a couple beers at The Spotted Wolf. Olivia means more to me than that.

I want to give her more than that.

But more important, she's letting me in. She let the fire in her eyes spread to her body. She's feeling the passionate things she writes about in *My Enemy The Earl,* and she's trusting me to keep them from burning her to a crisp.

She's being truly vulnerable with me for the first time. Her trust wraps around my heart like a hand and squeezes, making me feel—

Capable. Strong.

Things I haven't felt since this whole business with The Jam began.

And if I'm as capable as Olivia seems to think, then I'd know not to reward her trust by pushing her. Even though I'm on top, she's the one in charge.

She's the one calling the shots.

So as much as I want to get her naked and give her an orgasm or five and make love to her the way Gunnar would make love to Cate, I'm not going to.

Not unless she specifically asks for it.

We'll stick to making out for the time being. Which I certainly don't mind.

Actually, all this dry humping takes me back to my teenage days in the backseat of my old beat up Ford. It's fun. I feel like I'm seventeen again, doing all this shit for the first time.

The way Olivia froze when I kissed her—the way she went boneless not long after—makes me think this *is* the first time she's been properly kissed. The first time she's been overwhelmed by desire.

Or maybe it's just been a while for her.

Whatever the case, I follow her lead, and do my best to give her what she wants. When her hands rove over my body, touching every inch of my skin with reverence and care and curiosity, I do the same to her. I walk my fingers over her belly, her breasts, her neck.

Olivia really likes it when I touch her neck. Especially when it's my mouth that's doing the touching. My mouth and tongue and teeth.

She's as soft as I imagined her to be.

My heart—that's soft, too. Soft and already sore from so much *wanting*.

I want to make this girl mine.

I think we're finally moving in the right direction. Thank fuck.

We make out for hours.

My lips are raw. So is my dick from rubbing up against the zipper of my fly all night.

But I still fight a pang of disappointment when Olivia's kisses become less ardent, and then stop altogether. I look down to see her nodding off, head lolling on my shoulder.

Her breathing evens out. I tuck her hair behind her ears. My arm is falling asleep, but I don't move. I don't want to wake her. Not yet.

I know I need to go. Olivia hasn't asked me to stay. Even though I want to.

Lord, do I want to stay. Curl her body into mine and fall asleep breathing in the scent of her skin. Wake up together.

Make breakfast. Talk books. Maybe get to third base before I have to go in to the restaurant.

With a sigh, I give my arm a little shake.

"Olivia," I murmur in her ear. "I'm gonna go. But you should take off your jeans. They're still wet, and I don't want you catchin' a chill."

She nods, not opening her eyes. "Okay."

"Can I see you day after next?" I ask. "I have a long day at The Jam tomorrow, but I should have some time the day after."

A pause. She rolls her lips between her teeth.

My heart contracts as I wait for her reply.

"Yeah," she says at last. "I'd like that."

I let out the breath I'd been holding. I gently roll her off my shoulder and sit up. Roll off the bed, careful not to disturb her.

"Promise me you'll take off the jeans. I'd do it for you, but..."

Her eyes are still closed when she nods again. Her fingers move sleepily to her fly. She undoes the button, raising her hips.

Even in the dark, I can see her nipples, puffy and perfect, straining against the sheer cups of her bra.

F-u-u-u-c-k.

"Two days." I quickly kiss her mouth. "I want to see you."

Wiggling out of her jeans, Olivia offers me a lazy smile. I glimpse the teeny tiny strap of a thong—red, too—and force myself to turn around. My cock is screaming bloody murder.

"Good night, Eli."

"Night, sweetheart."

Olivia

The next morning, I wake up on cloud nine. I finally took the leap.

I made my choice. I'm going to be with Eli. For real.

But then I promptly fall back to earth when I remember that making that choice means I'm not going back to Ted.

I take a trembling breath, running a hand over my face.

It's time. I need to call Ted. Tell him our relationship is really over.

I don't know if I'm in love with Elijah. Not yet. But after feeling so free and so happy in his arms last night, I do know there's no way I can marry Ted. As much as it's going to kill me to hurt him like this, I have to tell him the truth. It's not fair of me to allow him to hope we'll be getting back together. Because we aren't.

Ted is a *good* guy. I would have a *good* life with him.

But I can't be myself with him the way I am with Eli. Ted doesn't support my dreams. He doesn't enjoy the same things I do. He doesn't kiss me senseless. And he deserves to have someone be as crazy about him as I am about Eli.

So I need to end things. Before I hurt him any more than I already have.

My gut is telling me this is the right move. But a fresh bolt of dread moves through me when I grab my phone and pull up Ted's number. He's smiling in the picture I uploaded to his profile, looking handsome in his neatly pressed sweater and khakis.

I know I have to trust myself. I need to make this call. But damn it, I don't want to crush him.

Taking a deep breath, I hit his number. The ringtone blares in my ear, making my pulse jump.

I feel like I'm having an out of body experience. I'm really doing this. I'm breaking up with the guy I shared a beautiful, successful life with. The guy who spent a small fortune on a gorgeous diamond ring he picked out just for me. On paper, it makes absolutely no sense.

But my heart says otherwise. So does my gut.

I have no clue what's going to happen next. Ending a three year relationship is always terrifying and upsetting. If I'm being honest, though, I also feel this sense of liberation. Letting go of Ted means my life is my own again.

I want that. So, so badly. I see now that being with Ted made me feel tied down. Trapped.

But being with Eli? That feels like freedom.

When Ted finally picks up, his voice sounds different. Or maybe I'm just used to hearing Eli's voice these days.

We exchange our usual pleasantries. All the while my heart is beating hard. I feel like I'm going to throw up. *I'm so sorry*, I chant over and over again in my head. *I'm so sorry I have to disappoint you like this.*

There's a pause in our conversation. He waits for me to speak, like he knows I have something to say.

Taking a deep breath, I open my eyes and let it out.

"I am really sorry, Ted. But I have to end our relationship. For good."

Eli

The Next Day

I'm up early, elbow deep in biscuit dough before the sun is even up.

For the twentieth time, I glance at my phone. I wonder if I should call Olivia. Invite her over to eat.

And for the twentieth time, I look away. We texted a bit yesterday, but I was crazy busy at work. I thought about calling her when I got home, but it was almost one in the morning, and her windows were dark. I didn't want to wake her.

I also want to give her the space she needs. That's just becoming more and more difficult to do. I like the way she makes me feel too much.

I toss my phone onto the sofa. Best to keep it out of reach. At least until the sun is up.

Using the mouth of a mason jar to cut the biscuit dough into even rounds—Grandma Mae's old trick—my heart skips a beat when I remember the way Olivia surrendered to me the other night. The naked vulnerability in her voice when she said my name. *Eli.* Like she was begging me for something only I could give her.

I've missed feeling like I have what it takes to do something, and do it well.

I would *so* do Olivia well. I unleashed all that pent up sensuality of hers with just a kiss. Bet I could make her fucking howl if—when—we did more than that.

Thinking about all the possibilities is way too fun.

"Are you really humming 'I Want to Know What Love Is' right now? I guess that's one way of handling the news."

I start, almost dropping the bowl I was about to plop in the sink. Naomi is standing at the counter, twirling her keys as she looks at me with a slightly alarmed expression.

I guess I *was* actually humming. I'm never gonna live this down.

"Uh," I say, blinking. "No? Yes? Maybe?"

Naomi shakes her head. "Who are you, and what have you done with the foul mouthed chef I know and love?"

I roll my eyes, pretending to be absorbed in the dirty dishes I've piled up in the sink. "What news are you talkin' about?"

"You didn't hear?"

"Hear what?" I say, turning on the faucet.

A pregnant pause if there ever was one.

"Oh, Eli."

Her tone—quietly distraught—makes me look up.

Her eyes are wet. A tear slips down her cheek, and she looks away, wiping at it with the flat of her palm.

In the five years we've been working together, I've never seen Naomi cry.

My stomach plummets. The pleasant, happy warmth of a moment ago dissolves, and my blood suddenly rushes cold.

Naomi doesn't need to tell me The Jam is finally done.

I know it just from the look on her face.

I turn off the faucet and, not bothering to dry my hands, grab my phone off the couch. Sure enough, there are seven missed calls. Three from Naomi, one from The Jam's manager Katie, and the rest from members of the restaurant group who've been my business partners since I opened The Pearl.

Standing in my kitchen, I just stare at the screen. My pulse pounds. There's a ringing in my ears.

My eyes burn and I find it suddenly difficult to breathe. My lungs aren't working.

I blink away black spots that mar my vision.

I imagine this is what it feels like to be mauled by an eighteen wheeler.

"I am so, so sorry," Naomi says, taking a step toward me.

I take a deep breath through my nose. Try to shake the paralysis from my head. My heart.

It's okay. We'll be okay.

"We knew this was comin'," I say, the well worn lines spilling out of my mouth. "I have no regrets, and you shouldn't, either. We made food that I'll always be proud of. We stuck to our guns and stayed true to who we are as chefs and as people. This isn't a death sentence, Naomi. We learned a lot together, didn't we?"

The look in her eyes now—hell, is that *pity*?

"You know you don't have to be strong for me, right?" she says. "Don't feed me your bullshit. It's okay to admit you're torn up about this. I sure as hell am."

My fingers tighten around my phone.

"Of course it hurts," I reply. "But it's not a comment on our potential. Failure is not a death sentence, Naomi, it's—"

"An opportunity. You love that line, don't you?"

I meet her eyes. "What do you want from me?"

She takes another step forward. "Chef, I want you to *feel* this. I can't shoulder all this hurt and disappointment alone. I want you to acknowledge that this is a loss and that it fucking sucks. Stop pretending like you're okay. Because I know you, and you're not."

I'm gripped by a sudden, sharp surge of anger.

I don't do loss.

I don't do failure.

Spearing a hand through my hair, I look down at my phone. Another call is coming in. This time from Luke.

Like it always does in this city, word is spreading fast about The Jam closing.

I ignore the call.

"Look," I say quietly. "This is new territory for me. I gotta process it in my own way. I need—"

Well. I'm not sure what I need.

Scratch that. I need Olivia.

I need her, and I need to get away.

I run through the week in my head. With The Jam closing, I can send Naomi over to The Pearl. Put her on the line and let Maria cover for me while I'm gone.

I know I'm running with my tail between my legs. But I haven't taken time off—real time off—in more than a year. Maybe getting out of town, and getting out of the kitchen, will give me some much needed time to reflect.

Much needed perspective.

Looking up at Naomi, I say, "I'll call a meeting with everyone this afternoon. We'll iron out the details. Get you and the staff squared away, and start the ball rolling on selling off whatever equipment we don't want for The Pearl. Anything else, we can deal with when I get back."

Naomi's eyebrows leap to the top of her forehead. "Get back from where?

"The cabin," I say. "Where else?"

Chapter Twenty-Two
OLIVIA

It's late afternoon by the time I have a chapter ready for Eli. My hands shake a little as I gather the pages into a neat pile and fasten them together with a binder clip. I'm nervous to see him again.

I'm also still reeling a little bit from my conversation with Ted. I wouldn't say he was *cool* with me breaking up with him. But he was very civil about the whole thing. Calm, even. Suspiciously so. Which, again, makes me think we didn't love each other enough to be together. Much less to get married.

My gut was right. Breaking up for good was the right move. I guess I'm just a little stunned that this is happening, and it's happening so quickly.

But I've had a day to collect myself. I feel much better about everything than I did yesterday after the call. Yet another reason why Ted and I aren't right for each other. If I can recover in the space of a day from our permanent breakup, that's a pretty good sign Ted is not *the one*.

Maybe Eli is.

He's never home when I drop off my chapters. But imagining that he *might be* fills me with the kind of nervous excitement Cate feels when Gunnar walks into the room. I may or may not have written in a new kissing scene earlier, if only so I could put into words all the things I felt in Eli's arms the other night.

Cate and Gunnar shared a few hours, a kiss, nothing more. She did not know him. She certainly had no claim to his attentions.

She seduced him. She kissed him. And then she'd left.

Feeling anything but hatred for Gunnar Danes was forbidden.

Still, she could hardly breathe for the intensity of this decidedly forbidden thing she felt.

Reading those lines, I press my fingertips to my lips. I can still taste him, the cinnamon and the male sweetness that is so particularly Elijah Jackson.

The fact that I can't stop thinking about him assures me I'm making the right decision. I woke up this morning with the sun inside my chest, bright and burning. I could still smell him everywhere. On the sheets. In my hair.

With him all over me, I felt free and confident and *alive*.

My heart ached—still does—when I think about how he kissed me.

The sharp-edged softness in his eyes when he said *I want you so bad it's eating me up inside.*

My stomach dips forcefully. I press a hand to it, sucking in a breath.

No one's ever wanted me like that. Certainly not Ted, who's always responsible and even-keeled.

I want to see Eli again.

My gut is telling me to do it. To *go there*.

Taking a deep breath, I do.

I open the door and head down the stairs.

That's when I catch a whiff of tobacco. Not cigarette smoke. Something more earthy. Pleasant.

Eli's cigar. Same kind I smelled when he shooed away the birds in the street that first night.

Holy shit, is he actually home?

I clamber down the remaining steps, my legs suddenly numb. Turning onto the lane, my heart leaps into my throat when I see him shoving a cooler onto the bed of a humungous black pickup truck. He turns. Picks up a canvas duffel bag and throws that onto the bed, too. A cigar is clamped between his teeth.

Billy wanders around the back tires, wagging his tail and panting.

It's the fact that Eli is wearing a shirt—a broken-in white tee that his arms fill out nicely—that tips me off.

Something is wrong.

Does he regret what happened the other night? Did I chase him out of town with my ridiculous five hour make out session?

Clutching the chapter to my chest like a life preserver, I step forward.

Eli looks up at the same moment. His eyes are so, so green in the late afternoon light.

They're stormy. His brow is furrowed.

I start to shake all over again.

"Hey," I manage.

Plucking his cigar out of his mouth and balancing it on the edge of the pickup's bed, he stalks toward me. "Hey you."

Hey you. What is it about this man's accent that makes everything, even the smallest of greetings, sound like a promise of sex and adventure?

Eli wraps his arms around my waist and pulls me against him. A small wave of relief—arousal hot on its heels—washes through me when he presses a kiss to my cheek.

He smells like cigar and aftershave.

He's touching me with a familiarity and a desire that's new. His hands are sure as they slide from the small of my back to rest just above my butt. His pinkies flirt with my underwear, which peek over the waistband of my jeans. And he lingers a beat too long with his face half an inch from mine. His eyes flick to my mouth.

Mine flick to his. Did I really get to kiss those gorgeous, full lips?

Do I get to do it again?

Part of me was worried Eli would pretend we hadn't even crossed the line we did last night. Another part hoped he'd acknowledge it just like this. With touching and teasing.

He can't keep his hands off me. And I love it.

I loop my arms around his neck and hug him back, arching against him ever so slightly. A slow, warm beat of lust unfurls between my legs.

"What's going on?" I murmur into his neck.

His fingers graze my ass. "Hm?"

"This." I pluck at the back of his shirt. "It's not you."

A beat of heated silence. His chest presses against mine as he takes a breath. Lets it out.

"The Jam is closing," he says. "It's official."

Something in my chest catches. He sounded so...nonchalant, almost, when he'd talked about the possibility of losing his restaurant that first morning we met.

But now? Now he sounds defeated.

Not at all like the Eli I know. Poor guy.

I pull him closer.

"I'm so sorry. That really, really blows."

He swallows. "Yeah. It does."

Squeezing me one last time, he pulls back. He's still standing too close.

Or maybe not close enough.

"What can I do?" I ask, looking up at him.

"I'm leaving town for a few days. Need time to clear my head. I got a cabin out by the water." He searches my eyes. "Come with me."

My pulse leaps. I blink, ridiculously flattered—and ridiculously happy—that he'd ask me.

"I was just about to go knock on your door. I know it's last minute," he continues. "But I need a break, and you need a place to write. Cabin's perfect. It's quiet. Pretty. Just put a case of wine in my truck. And goes without saying I'll make you all the food your muse needs to keep writin'."

Goes without saying we'll fuck.

I mean, how could we not? It'll be just the two of us. In a cabin. With a freaking case of wine.

That alone makes me want to say yes.

But more than that, it's the hurt in his eyes that really pushes me toward going. He's distraught, even though he's pretending not to be. I don't know much about the restaurant industry, but I know closing a restaurant is a big deal. Especially after the success of The Pearl. Here Eli was, thinking he was on top of the world.

And then he's brought down into the mud.

I feel terrible for him. The man's been nothing but wonderful to me since we met. I want to return the favor. I want to help him out of this hole the way he's helping me out of mine.

"I'd love to," I say.

His turn to blink. He runs a hand up the back of his head and grins, letting out a breath. "I was hoping you'd say that. How much time do you need?"

"I'll just throw some stuff in a bag. I can be back down here in ten minutes. Is there anything you need me to bring?"

Eli shakes his head, his eyes going soft again when they trail down my body, then back up.

"Just you, Olivia."

I am not prepared for how hot Eli looks when he's driving.

One enormous hand on the wheel. The other hanging out the window, holding his cigar between his first and second fingers. He's wearing a pair of gold-rimmed aviators that make him look like an especially attractive off-duty cop.

He guides the truck along a series of country roads with well-practiced ease. He's master of this little universe.

And I'm wet. So wet I can feel it soaking my underwear.

The windows are down, but that does nothing to cool the heat that stretches between us. The air is thick with it.

My hair is everywhere. "I'm On Fire" is playing, because Eli is thoughtful like that and put on Springsteen even before we backed out of his driveway. Outside the windows, a fiery sunset paints the marshy low country landscape in shades of orange and purple and blue. Billy pants in the backseat behind us.

The smell of the ocean fills my head.

Ocean and Eli.

I venture a glance in his direction. Take in the square lines of his scruffy jaw. The sensual curve of his lips. His eyes are thoughtful behind his glasses, crow's feet deepening when we round a bend and sunlight slices through the windshield.

He's not usually this quiet. This contemplative. I can feel the hurt—the confusion—radiating off him.

"Y'know it's not polite to stare," he says, eyes darting to mine before returning to the road. One end of his mouth curls into a smirk.

I swallow. "Yeah, well. It's not polite to be so damn good looking."

"I could say the same to you." Through the lenses of his glasses, I can see his eyes flick over my bare legs.

A charge of electricity moves through my skin.

"Now who's staring?" I say, holding my hair back when it whips into my face.

He puts out the cigar in a tin container on the console between us. Then he shuts the container with a small, neat *clap*. "Me."

"You're not supposed to drive distracted."

His smirk deepens. "Can't help it. You're awful distracting."

"Try me," I say, wiggling my dress up a little more.

The truck swerves. Eli rights it with a grunt.

"Do you *want* me to drive us into a tree?"

"If it takes your mind off things, then yeah. Maybe I do."

"Aren't you sweet," he says, reaching over to playfully pat me on the leg.

My breath catches. Eli pulls back. Clears his throat.

"Sorry." He scratches his beard underneath his chin.

My heart is pounding. I fucking *loved* the feel of his hand on me.

He's being a gentleman. But I want the animal.

I reach over and grab his hand. Put it on my thigh.

"Don't be," I reply quietly.

He leans into me a little, turning his head to meet my eyes.

One hand on the wheel. One hand on me.

"I want to reiterate that I'm not expecting anything," he says, his voice different. Gruffer. "I meant it when I said I'm takin' you out here to write. Don't feel like you have to...do anything other than that. With me, I mean. Last night was great. Really, really great. But I'm happy to take things slow."

I bite my lip. Then I take his hand and slide it a little bit higher on my leg. My sex pulses at his nearness. His pinkie is a mere three inches, probably less, from where I want him most.

"I want *you* to know that I'd very much like doing things other than that," I reply. "But only if you want to."

Eli gives my leg a soft squeeze. "You kiddin'? I want to.

The other night—hell, Olivia, I haven't had that much fun in a long time. I admit that today I've thought a lot about picking up right where we left off."

I blink. I'm still not over the fact that this man wants me.

I'm not over the fact that I'm being so bold in expressing my want for him. There is a freedom in being upfront about what I want. In cutting through the bullshit and just *doing* what I want.

"I'd like that," I say.

He glances at me before focusing his gaze on the road. "Me too."

His pinkie brushes against the crotch of my underwear.

I smile. Even as I feel a tug of apprehension in my chest. This is all too wonderful. Too exciting. I'm worried I'm going to burn my whole life down for this guy.

I know I'm not going back to Ted. But what am I going to do about my job? My living situation?

I'm *worried*.

But not worried enough to have Eli turn around. Deep down, this feels right.

Chapter Twenty-Three

ELI

I can't help smiling when Olivia steps into the cabin and goes still.

"Wow," she breathes, sliding her sunglasses into her hair. "Eli, this is incredible."

Dropping her bags by the door, she walks over to the back windows. Puts her hands on the small of her back as she takes in the view.

Mother Nature must know I'm trying to impress a girl, because good Lord is she putting on a show tonight. The marsh expands to the horizon, alternating zig zags of dark water and tall grass. We've caught the sun just before it sinks into the water for good. The sky is enormous, wide open and fiery. The light catches on the water, making it burn gold and silver.

It catches on the gauzy material of Olivia's dress, too, allowing me to see the outline of her shapely legs and hips. I recall, in startling, visceral detail, what those legs felt like wrapped around me the other night.

The half chub I've been sporting for the entire two hour drive goes full salute.

I can't fucking wait to get this girl in bed. Get her hot and soft and ready so I can take care of her the way I want to.

If that doesn't clear my head—if that doesn't make me forget the disappointment that sits like a goddamn elephant on my chest—nothing will.

"I think so too," I say, coming to stand behind her. I want to kiss her neck, her bare shoulder. But I won't be able to stop there. And I want to properly seduce Olivia before I take her clothes off. Wine, dinner, dessert. *Then* sex. "I bought this property back when I got my first real payday. Been dreamin' about waking up to that view all my life. I've renovated the cabin over the years by bits and pieces."

Olivia's gaze moves over the cabin's interior. It's small—one bedroom, one bath, a kitchen, living room, lots of bookshelves, and then the deck out back—but exactly how I want it.

She smiles at me over her shoulder. "It's *you*. I love it."

I fall into her pretty blue eyes for a beat too long.

"Get comfortable," I say, blinking. "I'll pour some wine and get dinner started."

"Actually." Olivia crosses to the kitchen, where I set the cooler on the counter. She opens it and peers inside. "I was hoping I could make you a meal for once."

I smile, pleasure curling around my heart. She wants to take care of me.

It's sweet.

"I'm the cook," I say. "I don't mind doing it."

She lets the top of the cooler fall and looks at me. "I know. But you're always doing the work while I'm relaxing. Let me do it for a change. You've had a shit day. So put your feet up and relax. I'll take care of everything."

I laugh. "You know I'm not one to put my feet up. But if you wanna cook, then by all means—kitchen's yours. Can I be your sous chef?"

"What's that?" she says with a grin.

I shrug. "Your helper. How about I chop, and you cook?"

"Deal. Now please tell me you have a pantry."

"Of course I do," I say. I open the narrow door across from the refrigerator, revealing a pantry that's well stocked even by my standards.

Olivia comes over and grabs a box of spaghetti noodles and some cans of crushed tomatoes. "Perfect. I'll make a quick version of my mom's Sunday sauce."

Standing underneath my outstretched arm, she looks up at me. I'm overwhelmed by the desire to kiss her.

"All right, chef. Just tell me what to do," I say.

I open the windows. Open a bottle of good Barolo. Put on some Pearl Jam.

And then we get to work.

I dice garlic and onions while Olivia browns the meat in a big stockpot on the stove. Like the rest of the cabin, the kitchen is tiny, and we bump into each other with welcome regularity.

With Olivia in my kitchen and the smell of dinner in the air and Eddie Vedder singing in the background, the elephant rolls off my chest. I zone out as I chop, rocking my knife. Soothing motions I could perform in my sleep. Charleston and all my problems there slowly fade, until they start to feel like nothing more than a bad dream. Something my subconscious made up.

Olivia takes care of pretty much the whole meal. She does ask for help, once, when the sauce comes out under seasoned. I'm way too fucking flattered by her trust in me to fix it, and it feels good to help her out in this small way. In that moment, I felt the opposite of the way I've been feeling for the past six months. I felt like I knew what I was doing. I felt like I was needed.

I felt at home in my skin, and in the kitchen, too.

A nice little reminder that I don't always suck.

We eat outside at the picnic table on my deck. Olivia talks to me about places she's visited and loved in Charleston. I give her all the gossip on restaurants and bars. Deadbeat owners. Who's fucking. Who's cheating. Who makes the best shrimp and grits in town.

I get the feeling she's intentionally keeping the conversation light. Which I appreciate, more than she knows. The last thing I feel like talking about is my own restaurant.

My own fuck ups.

I also just like talking to her. She could be talking about the mating habits of the crickets that surround us, and I think I'd still be enthralled. The words she uses, the stories she tells. She's got this way of commanding the conversation—this confidence that actually reminds me of my teachers at culinary school.

Makes me wonder who—what—she was in her previous life. Before she became a writer.

I am a patient man. But the more time I spend with Olivia, the hungrier I become for her story. I want to know everything there is to know about her. I want to know what she's running from.

I want to know if she makes love as passionately as she writes.

The stars are pulsing against a pitch black sky by the time we bring our empty plates and wine glasses inside. Olivia puts hers in the sink, already piled high with dirty dishes. She turns on the water and starts scrubbing.

I sidle up behind her. Put my arms on the lip of the sink on either side of her waist, caging her.

Leaning my front into her back, I press a kiss to the nape

of her neck. Her hands go still. A rush of blood stiffens my cock. I been waiting all damn night to do this.

"Leave it," I murmur against her skin, nipping at it with my teeth. "I wanna take you to bed."

She draws a shaky breath. After a beat, she turns off the faucet. Then she lets me work my way down the slope of her neck to her shoulder. Her skin is covered in goosebumps. I lean into her a little more, canting my hips so my hard on glides between her ass cheeks.

Her hand finds mine on the sink and squeezes.

It's quiet in the kitchen. The only sounds coming through the open window. Crickets. The distant rush of the ocean.

"I'm so—" Her eyes flutter shut when I nip at her earlobe. Her breath catches. "Jesus, Elijah, I am so turned on it hurts."

A grin tugs at my lips. She's already falling apart.

She is already coming apart in my hands, and I've barely even touched her.

She's gonna fucking lose her mind when I make her come. Because that is something I can give her. I may not have the biggest bank account. I may have failed.

But I know what I'm doing when it comes to this.

I pull her hand off the sink and hold it in mine, turning her around so she's facing me.

"Then come to bed. I'll take good care of you, baby." I search her eyes. The trust and the desire I see in them flattens me.

I really do have it bad for this girl.

Real bad.

The sinews of her throat move sensuously as she swallows.

"I know you will," she whispers. Then she pushes off the sink and, turning around again so she's still facing me, pulls me slowly into the bedroom.

Chapter Twenty-Four
ELI

My heart is pounding when I kick the bedroom door closed behind us. Billy's got a bad habit of showing up just when I don't want him to.

I want to have Olivia all to myself tonight.

A breeze blows in through the windows. The air is crisp. A little cool.

Her eyes never leaving mine, Olivia drops my hand. Steps out of her flip flops. Tugs at the tie near her hip that holds her dress together.

My mouth goes dry when it opens, revealing a slice of her milky white belly. Makes the candy apple red bra she's wearing really pop.

She's got on different panties today. A nude thong.

Olivia rolls back her shoulders. The dress slides down her body, pooling in a pretty gauze heap at her feet.

I can't move. I stand in front of her like a slack jawed idiot, devouring her body with my gaze. She's shaking, small tremors in her leg muscles and arms. But she keeps her eyes locked on mine. Blue eyes lit up with fire.

Trust.

She's not touching me. But I feel like she's reaching inside me anyway, carefully rearranging all the soft parts in my chest cavity. I feel the ghosts of her fingers brushing against my lungs. Her thumb giving my heart a tender swipe.

"It's not polite to stare," she teases, a little breathless.

I take a step forward. Put a hand on her hip, dipping the long edge of my index finger into the lacy strap of her thong.

"I just—" I swallow. "I need a minute."

I rake my gaze up the length of her body. Her slender, girlish legs. The curve of her hips, accentuated by the naughty cut of her panties. I can see the dark shadow of her pubic hair through it.

Strong lines of her belly.

Her breasts.

I can't help taking one of them in my hand. Cupping its soft weight, I look up to see Olivia's mouth fall open when I pluck at her nipple with my thumb and forefinger. It pebbles to a hard point.

So responsive to me.

I press the flat of my palm against it. Olivia's hands find my shoulders. Her fingers dig into my skin. Like she's holding on for dear life.

Running my finger underneath her thong, I say, "You gonna let me?"

Earlier today in my truck, she already told me she wanted to pick up where we left off last night. But I'm not asking her to let me fuck her.

I'm asking her to *let me in*.

I'm asking her to share everything with me. Her secrets. Her sighs.

Her story.

I want her to let me see it all.

Her eyes go hazy when I tug the strap down. Her panties catch between her thighs. Another soft tug. They fall with a whisper to her feet. I lean down, hovering my mouth over hers.

"Let me."

My fingers are between her legs now. Her eyes search mine. Lips open and pink and a little wet.

I duck my head. Capture those lips in a quick whisper of a kiss.

"*Let me*," I say, slipping my first two fingers inside her sweet little cunt.

I groan. She's wet. And hot. And so damn swollen-soft I could die.

A surge of need in my groin, sudden and enormous, makes me dizzy.

I glide my fingers through her slit, front to back. I dip the tip of my middle finger inside her. Hot and soft here, too. Tight.

I move that finger to her clit. Circle it, slowly and firmly. Just once.

Her fingernails bite into my shoulders. Her tits brush against my chest as she breathes. Rapid, uneven breaths.

"Okay," she says, her eyes fluttering shut.

"Nu-huh." I press my finger against her clit. "Come on, baby, you gotta look at me when you say it."

Breath catching, Olivia opens her eyes. They're wet.

She is wet everywhere, she's as desperate for me as I am for her, and I love it.

I move my other hand to the small of her back. Trail my fingertips gently up the furrow of her spine. She curls a little closer into my body. Looks up at me. Vulnerable and warm.

I have to take a breath. My heart's gonna burst.

"Yes," she says steadily. "*Yes*, Eli."

I guide her mouth to mine, tilting my head so I can get a good taste of her sweetness. Wine and Olivia.

I want her to trust me with her story the way she trusts me with her body.

I want that more than anything.

Olivia opens her eyes, eyelashes tangling with mine. The naked faith I see there—hell, I'm a goner.

"Touch me like you said you would. I can't—God, Eli, I can't *take it* when your hands aren't on me."

I don't need to be told twice.

I dip my finger all the way inside her pussy this time. She arches against me, and I take the opportunity to unhook her bra with the hand I have on her back.

Looking down, I take in her nakedness. Her tits are gorgeous, full and round, her nipples pink and puffy and hard.

My clothes suddenly feel twelve sizes too small.

Pressing a kiss to her neck, I pull back.

"Make yourself comfortable," I say, nodding at the bed before I tug my shirt off. "I'm gonna go grab some condoms from my bag, okay? I think I left it in the truck."

"Okay."

Half a minute later, I'm back in the bedroom, condoms in one hand, my belt buckle in the other. I toss the condoms onto the nightstand.

I freeze when I see Olivia on my side of the bed. She's pulled back the covers and is lying in the crisp white sheets, head on a pillow, hand between her legs. Her fingers move slowly over her pussy. Her knee falls off to the side, spreading her wide open so I can see her. Pink and slick.

Perfect.

Her eyes lock on mine. She bites her lip, back arching when she hits her clit.

"I'm sorry," she pants. "I was dying without you. Had to."

My cock *jerks*.

Yankee girl is in my bed. *Playing with herself*. Because she's dying for me.

"Oh yeah?" I rip off my belt and jeans. "Tell me where you like it. Tell me how you want me to make you feel."

Olivia lifts her leg to her chest, spreading herself even wider. She runs the pads of her first two fingers over her clit.

"I like it here. And here." One of those fingers disappears inside her cunt. "I like it at the same time. Sometimes here, too." Her pinkie taps once against the pucker of her asshole.

I tear at my boxers like a man possessed.

Her other hand moves to her breast. Her back arches again when she thumbs her nipple. Eyes fluttering shut, she breathes, "Eli, I'm—oh, I'm close."

"Don't you fuckin' *dare* come without me," I bite out. "That orgasm is mine."

Her eyes open. They are so blue I get lost in them. My whole being goes still.

"Then come here," she says. "I need you."

Damn fucking right you do.

I tear the covers aside and climb on top of her, pulling her hand from between her legs. Gathering both her wrists in my hand, I guide them above her head, resting my weight on my opposite elbow. I lean a little weight into her. Just enough so that our bodies fit perfectly together. Skin on skin on skin. She's breathing hard, eyes at once teasing and vulnerable.

My dick bobs between us, head sliding against the hot skin of her groin.

For a second I fantasize about making love to her bare. The ultimate act of trust. I'd hook her leg over my shoulder and kiss her hard and work my cock against her pussy before finding her entrance and burying myself inside. Raw. Baby making style.

Soon, maybe. But not yet. Even in my lust-addled state, I know that's too big of an ask for Olivia right now.

Especially the baby making part. Where the hell had *that* come from?

I shake the thought from my head. I blame it on the temporary insanity I'm experiencing thanks to Miss Olivia Gates. If that's even her real name.

I don't even know her real name.

But I'll be damned if I don't get to know her in other ways tonight.

With her hands trapped in mine above her head, she's at my mercy. I work my mouth down her throat, her chest. I take her nipple in my teeth. I keep going down until I kiss her belly one last time. Then I urge her legs apart with my hips and, moving between them, settle back onto my haunches.

Dropping her hands, I grab her thighs and pull her roughly towards me. She gasps; I grin.

I reach for her breast. Curl my fingers around it. Play with her nipple.

With my other hand, I reach between her legs. Using my thumb, I gently part her folds and meet her eyes. Her dark hair is spread in a wild halo around her head. Her cheeks are red.

"You are beautiful," I murmur, rolling my thumb once, twice, against her clit, like I'm working the dial on one of those old-fashioned locks—the ones where you have to roll a series of numbers in place to unlock it. "And I'm gonna make you come."

Olivia moans. Her hips rise to meet my gentle strokes. I pinch her nipple, and her legs start to shake.

"So quick?" I say, equal parts smug and astonished.

She nods, her eyes catching on my dick. They darken. "For you? Yes."

I give her tit a firm squeeze. "All right, baby. Come for me, then."

I keep working her clit with my thumb. I bring my other

hand down, and sink two fingers into her pussy. I thrust them once, twice. Three times. Her walls flutter around me.

And then Olivia *explodes*. She fists around me, arching her back and crying out as the orgasm cracks through her. Pulse after hot pulse milks my fingers. She reaches for me, saying my name, and I can only watch in wonder, my dick throbbing, as she rolls against me, riding out the wave.

I'm gripped by the need to be inside her. To make this moment—this orgasm—truly my own. I wanna hold her. Be as close to her as humanly possible while I still have her with me.

I could climb over her right now and take my pleasure all night long. And she'd still be the one who'd end up taking.

She'd still be the one I want to give everything to.

The fingers of my right hand still inside her, I reach across her body with my left and grab a condom.

Chapter Twenty-Five
OLIVIA

"Yes," I manage as I watch Eli tear open the foil packet with his teeth. "Eli, *please*."

I'm boneless. Body still pulsing with the aftershocks of the orgasm to end all orgasms. I can only lie here helplessly, back sinking into the soft mattress, and watch and salivate and burn as this huge, gorgeous man rolls on a condom.

His dick is just as gorgeous as the rest of him. Smooth, pink skin. Pointing straight up. Proud. Perfectly made, if a little intimidating.

I notice Eli's hands shake a little. Takes him a try or two to get the condom all the way on.

He's nervous? For me?

The thought turns my insides to mush. I'm gripped by the fervent desire to be with this man for real.

For keeps. Could I really make a life with him in it—a life in Charleston, where I'm a writer—work? I'm not sure I'm capable of that.

But please, oh, *please*, in this moment, just let me imagine that I am.

Let me dwell in the sweetness of possibility.

He looks up, meeting my eyes. His darken. More brown than green tonight. They trail heatedly over my body. My nipples prick to renewed life. I feel so *sexy* when he looks at me like this. Like he's been starving for me all his life.

With a grunt, he leans down and kisses my mouth. I rise into his caress, spreading my legs wider. I love it when he puts his weight on me. Love the hot, slightly breathless feeling of being surrounded by him.

His skin is a little slick. Sweat.

He runs a hand down my side. Catches my leg and hikes it over his hip. Melting his body into mine, I whimper when I feel his latex-covered tip prodding my entrance. The pressure is already enormous. My pussy throbs with a new awareness of him.

A new sense of anticipation.

"Jesus, baby," he murmurs against my mouth. "I can still feel you comin'."

I nod, too overwhelmed to open my eyes. I just loop my arms around his neck and hold him close.

He buries his face in my neck. *Heaven.*

"Let me return the favor," I say, canting my hips so he slips inside me a little.

He hisses, the muscles in his neck and upper back flexing against my fingertips.

"Olivia," he half whispers, half warns. "If you do that—I can't control—I'm tryin' to go slow here, sweetheart. I don't wanna hurt you."

"You won't."

"You're so small," he says.

"And you're so perfect. Please." I cant my hips again. He's halfway inside me now, and it hurts. In the best way. "I'll tell you if it's too much. I want you to give me everything you've got, Eli."

He sucks in a breath. He's not convinced.

So I brush my lips against his. Open my eyes. He must sense me doing it, because he opens his, too.

Please, I plead with my gaze. *Please please* please.

Eli nudges my nose with his. Tender and sweet.

His eyes never leaving mine, he slowly draws back his hips.

And then he surges inside me, one long, swift, devastating stroke that buries him to the hilt inside me. I cry out. Pain and pleasure rip through me in equal parts.

There is nothing tender about this.

But it is still very, *very* sweet.

Eli pauses. Just for a second. Waiting for me to say it hurts. That it's too intense, he's too big. I'm too scared.

All of those things are true.

I still want more. I want to drink my fill of him. Want to know the kind of exquisite pleasure I've read about in my romance novels.

He searches my eyes.

More, I say with mine.

And that's what he gives me.

He thrusts, his body working above me in these delicious, masculine dips. Again and again and again. Filling me. Stretching me out. It hurts, but I drink it in. I try to be aware of everything. The woodsy-smoky scent of his skin. The feeling of sharp-edged satisfaction between my legs.

The way my heart seems to have dissolved into my skin. My entire being throbs in time to its beat.

Eli watches me the whole time. Brow furrowed with concentration. Concern, too. He takes note of my every movement. When I bite my lip after he swivels his hips—the angle made him hit my clit—he does it again, aiming for the same spot. When he thrusts into me especially deep and my body goes still, he reaches up and cups my breasts, one at a time, toying with the nipples and sending a new rush of liquid heat to my pussy so he glides in and out a little more smoothly.

It's not even attention. It's adoration.

I love how *loved* it makes me feel. Like I'm complete. Confident in my body's ability to meet his challenge.

Like I'm worthy of experiencing such urgent, overwhelming sensuality.

I have to close my eyes.

He captures my mouth with his. His strokes speed up to a punishing rhythm, our bodies slamming together. He's losing himself in me.

I feel something inside me tear. Come apart.

I hook my feet at the small of his back. Urge him closer.

"So good," he growls, his breath hot on my lips. "See how good it feels when you let me in?"

Tears press like hot thumbs against the backs of my eyelids.

I nod. It does feel good.

He swivels his hips against me one last time. Slams into me, *hard*.

Eli sputters, then goes still, his enormous body heavy on mine. His cock pulses inside me as he comes. I feel his abs working against my belly. He's struggling to catch his breath.

I open my eyes to see him looking at me. His are molten. Soft.

My heart hiccups.

Looking away, I press a kiss to his neck. But then he's using his nose to urge me back to center.

This guy's relentless.

He leans down and kisses my mouth. A slow, hot kiss that has me arching underneath him. I can't get enough of this man's kisses. He's unapologetically sensual and thorough in everything he does.

Pulling back, he looks me in the eye. Understanding

passes between us. That was *good*. Better than it was supposed to be for a first time.

Better than it's ever been for me.

I feel like I've been branded. I am different now. Changed in some irreversible way.

Can I ever settle for *safe* after experiencing how good *wild* feels?

I draw a trembling breath.

"It's okay, baby," Eli whispers, kissing me again. "You're gonna be okay."

I cling to him.

"I don't know," I whisper back.

He looks at me. "I do."

"Please stay," I say, drawing him closer with my legs. "Just for a minute."

Eli melts into my body, bracketing my head with his elbows. "Like I could ever leave you right now. Olivia, you're shakin' like a leaf."

I can't get a hold of my heartbeat. My face is on fire, and so is my pussy. I feel like I just lost my virginity all over again. Only this time I'm hurt because the sex was so good.

So, *so* good.

Eli holds me. Surrounds me. I listen as his breath evens out. Deep inhales. Deep exhales. Like he did in class that day at the yoga studio, he's trying to calm me down. I mirror his movements, breathing in, breathing out.

It helps.

Eventually I do calm down.

"I'm gonna go get cleaned up real quick," he whispers, brushing his lips against my forehead. "Okay?"

I nod.

We both wince when Eli pulls out of me. Lifting himself onto one elbow, he reaches between us to grab the condom. His hair falls into my eyes when he looks down.

He goes still. A muscle connecting his shoulder and collarbone pops against the tattoo of the bird there. He rolls off of me.

"Are you on your period?" he asks.

"What?" I ask, stiffening. "No. Why?"

"You're fucking bleeding, that's why." He looks up at me, nostrils flaring with anger. *Shit*. "Jesus Christ, Olivia, why didn't you tell me I was hurting you?"

He holds up the condom, streaked with blood.

My face goes up in flames again.

Oh my God, I actually *tore*. That wasn't just me imagining my heart being rent in two.

I made Eli hurt me.

With him looking at me like this—accusingly, angrily—I feel so vulnerable. So *embarrassed*.

What is wrong with me, wanting to be fucked like that?

Wanting to get so carried away I end up bleeding?

"I'm sorry," I say, closing my legs. "Did I get it on the bed?"

He looks at me. After half a heartbeat, he *tsks*, spearing a hand through his hair. His expression softens. Propping himself on his elbow, he bends his neck and kisses my mouth. My temple.

"C'mon, Olivia, that's not what I'm mad about. I'm mad I hurt you." He puts his hand between my knees. Sits up. "Let me see, sweetheart."

"I can handle it."

"Olivia. Let me see."

Swallowing, I let my knees fall apart. My entire being burns as he checks me out, hazel eyes cloudy with concern.

"Does this hurt? And be honest," Eli says, gently—very gently—pressing his fingertip to my entrance. It stings.

"Yes," I say.

"God *damn* it," he bites out. "Stay put. I'm gonna go get some stuff to clean you up and make you feel better."

"I can—"

"Olivia, *stay put*. Please. Let me take care of you, all right? I feel terrible enough as it is."

I go still at the raw anguish in his voice. Eli's upset. Which upsets me. I just had the best sex of my life with this man. I don't want this to ruin all the exquisite things I felt in his arms.

My stomach clenches. I need to explain myself.

I need to tell him who I really am.

A minute or two later, he comes back from the bathroom with a warm washcloth and a bottle of ibuprofen.

"I am so sorry," he says, pressing the washcloth between my legs. His touch is achingly tender. "I hate that I did this. Rough is not usually my style."

It's not usually mine either. But tonight, it just felt…right.

I just need to wring every drop of passion out of these nights with Elijah Jackson. I don't know how many I'll have. I'm not going back to Ted, but I still have to go back to my job. My students. My life.

I grab his wrist. Trail my thumb over the smooth skin inside it. "Don't be sorry. This is what I wanted. I loved every minute of it."

His eyes flicker with something I can't place when he looks at me.

"Why'd you want me do that to you?" he asks softly.

I blink. Look away. Then I sit up and close my legs. Glancing at the sheets, I'm relieved to see I didn't get any blood on them.

Swinging my legs over the edge of the bed, it's my turn to wince. I'm already sore. And still so wet I feel like I'm swimming in it.

Behind me, I hear the jangle of pills in a bottle.

"Take these." Eli drops two pills into my palm.

I put them in my mouth and press up to my feet.

"Let me get cleaned up," I say, swiping my dress off the floor. "Then we'll talk."

Chapter Twenty-Six
OLIVIA

I'm sticky with sex and sweat, so after I get dressed, I head out to the deck. Eli follows me. The autumn air is cool against my skin. The night is very dark around us. The world is quiet. Even the crickets have gone silent; the water barely moves. The tall marsh grasses sigh in a small breeze, once.

Then it's just Eli and me and the stars. The sky is so black I swear I can see the cosmic dust between them. Or maybe it's just more tiny stars, too distant to even make a pinprick in the darkness.

I sit in one of the weathered Adirondack chairs that face the marsh. Eli comes up behind me, setting a glass of cold white wine on the flat of my armrest before collapsing into the chair beside mine.

"Thank you," I say, reaching for the wine.

"Welcome."

The word is muffled. I look to see him lighting a cigar. Palm curled around the end as he holds a stainless steel lighter to it. His cheeks hollow out as he sucks, encouraging the embers.

He's barefoot. Wearing nothing but jeans. The skin on his bare shoulders glistens in the light from inside.

The bittersweet, earthy smell of the tobacco hits my nostrils.

Heat hits me squarely between the legs. I just had this man. And now I want him again.

Curling my legs into my chest, I take a long sip of wine. It's Chardonnay. Buttery and delicious.

A little liquid courage never hurt anyone.

I'm not really sure how to start. So I just dive right in to the heart of it.

"I'm not a writer," I say.

Eli leans back in his chair, looking at me from the corner of his eye. "Yes you are. You've written, what, half a book now? You sit down at your computer and you write. Therefore, you're a writer. And a damn good one at that."

A wave of emotion rises up in me. I don't know what it is. But I do know it makes me feel tingly. Happy.

"I mean it's not what I do for a living," I reply. "I'm a professor of nineteenth century literature."

"At the College of Charleston?" he asks, cocking a brow.

"I wish. I'd love to teach creative writing there. But no." I take a deep breath. "I teach at a university in New York."

Eli's mouth goes still around his cigar. At last he plucks it from his lips.

My heart begins to free fall as I watch the realization wash over his face.

"So you're not just from there," he says flatly. "You *live* there."

I nod, taking another sip of wine. "I'm on leave right now. My TA has taken over my class load. But her baby is due at the end of October. So I have to be back by then or—"

"Or what?" His eyes glisten in the darkness.

I roll my lips between my teeth. Look down. Look back

up. "Or I lose the tenure I've worked my entire career to get. I lose my salary. Insurance. My future as an academic."

He puts the cigar back in his mouth. Takes a long, slow puff, eyes on the ground.

"What about your writing?"

"What about it?" I shrug, the words sour on my tongue. "Right now, it's just a hobby. Something silly I've always wanted to do."

He spears me with a look. "It's not silly, Olivia. It's who you are."

My throat gets tight.

"What do you mean?" I ask, my voice barely above a whisper.

"Means I've read your work. And I can tell by the passionate way you write and the care and dedication you put into it that it means somethin' to you." He taps some ash onto the ground. "I can tell it makes you happy."

I swallow, hard. "How can you tell that?"

"The day we met—when you first got here—you had all this pent up energy. This pent up *passion*. I saw it in your eyes. You were holding it in. Hiding it. But now I see you releasing that passion onto the page. I see you lightin' up when you talk about romance. Writing. Gunnar and Cate. I don't know what your life was like before you came to Charleston. But you write an awful lot about feeling trapped. About being held back by other peoples' expectations. But it seems like you're free from all that bullshit down here."

Oh, Jesus, it's like I've swallowed the moon, and now it's stuck in my throat.

"Those are Cate's problems," I say, my voice wobbling. "They're fictional."

"The way you write them—they feel awful real to me, sweetheart." His voice softens. "So what exactly are you runnin' from, Yankee girl?"

The careful way he asks—the sincere concern in his voice—it's too much. I keep swallowing, hoping to clear the logjam in my throat. I'm having trouble breathing.

"A lot of things," I manage. "But the impetus for coming down here was getting away from my ex."

Elijah's fingers tighten around his cigar. "He hurt you?"

"No, no, it's not like that." I shake my head, looking down to pick at my yoga pants. I take a breath. Look up and meet Eli's eyes. "He actually proposed. I wanted to say yes. But I couldn't."

I can't read the expression in Eli's eyes. "Why not?"

"It didn't feel right. The life I'd be saying yes to is a good life. A beautiful one. But I wasn't sure it was *me*. I felt so stifled by it. After being down here, I understand why. I can't be who I am in that life. You know, the steamy book writer who bikes around town and splits her time between being terrible at yoga and reading romance."

That earns a small smile from Eli.

"You're not terrible at yoga," he says.

"I'm actually the worst. But you're sweet to pretend otherwise."

I take a sip of my wine. Eli puffs on his cigar.

"My life back home—everyone was always telling me how perfect it was. I have it all," I continue. "But now I'm realizing that none of it makes me very happy. There's no room for passion or creativity in perfection. It's bloodless."

He shoots me a look. All these damn *looks* of his. Dark and steamy and cutting in all the right ways.

All the *hard* ways.

"That why you wanted to bleed?" he says. "To feel somethin'?"

Yes.

I struggle to admit it out loud. So I tell him with my eyes instead.

He pulls on his cigar. Smoke rises from his lips, making him squint.

"I know it's fucked up. But I liked it, Eli." I shake my head. "Jesus. What is *wrong* with me?"

His brow puckers as his fingers go still. "Nothing is wrong with you. You're human. You wanted to feel alive. I just don't want to have to hurt you to get you there."

"Maybe I deserve to hurt," I say, looking away. "Considering all the people I'm disappointing."

I hear Eli swallow.

Looking up, I say, "I admit that when I first came down here, I thought for sure that I'd be going back to him. But now I can't. Not after being with you."

Eli's eyes glisten. He stubs out his cigar in the glass ashtray on the arm of his chair.

"That mean we're together?" he says slowly, glancing up at me. "That mean you're gonna stay in Charleston?"

"Yes." It's my turn to swallow. "And maybe. I can't make any guarantees, Eli. Not yet. But I do want to be with you. And I would love nothing more than to stay in Charleston, because I love it down here. I just don't know what I'm going to do about my job. It's obviously in New York. Yeah, there are some things I don't like about it. But I do love my students. And I've got a really bright future in my department."

Eli stretches out his legs in front of him. "What about teachin' those creative writing classes you mentioned at The College of Charleston? Do that and write on the side?"

"They aren't hiring. And even if they were, I doubt I'd get a position there that offers tenure," I say, shaking my head. "Most likely I'd be an adjunct professor. Which means I'll be working for very little money. I won't get any benefits. And there will be no guarantees of future employment. I do have some money in savings, but I imagine I'd burn through that pretty quickly living on an adjunct's pay. As far as my books go...I mean. I haven't even finished one yet. Much less thought about how I'm going to publish and market it."

Eli steeples his fingers, bringing them to his lips. He's quiet for a minute.

"Tell me something," he says at last.

"Yeah?"

"When we were in bed—tell me about things I made you feel."

Licking my lips, I take a breath through my nose. Consider my words carefully before I say them.

"You made me feel like I *could*. I felt so...sure with you in bed. So confident. Unafraid to be myself. To push boundaries and take chances, because we were there to catch each other if something went wrong. I could have my cake and eat it too, if that makes sense."

"So I'm the cake in this scenario?" he asks with a smile.

My gaze flicks over his bare torso. "Eli, you are all the cakes in the world combined. You're so delicious it's kind of ridiculous."

He laughs.

"See, I think you're lookin' at it all wrong," he says. "I think you're selling yourself short, thinking you can't create a fulfilling life for yourself down here that *works*."

"Eli," I say. "Come on. Do you know how hard it is to make a living as a writer?"

"'Course it's hard." He shrugs. "Doesn't mean you shouldn't try."

"I can't lose my tenure."

Eli tilts his head. "You'll give up your dream for *tenure*?"

My throat tightens.

"What if I fail?"

Eli scoffs. "Look at me! I've failed. Hell, I just failed spectacularly. In front of the whole damn world, too. All my peers.

The press. The city. But I'm still standin'. And I still get to wake up every day and spend my time doing something I love."

"Yeah, well. I don't have your talent."

"You don't need talent. You need confidence. And a hell of a lot of perseverance."

I shake my head, a tear spilling down my cheek. I wipe it away.

"I'm too scared."

"Join the club. We're all scared, sweetheart. But feelin' scared because you're chasing down your dream is better than feelin' nothing at all. You just let me hurt you so you could *feel* something. Think about that, baby."

I think about it. Wonder if the simple fact that *I am thinking about it* seriously means the scales are rebalancing inside my head. Am I more afraid to leave? Or more afraid to stay?

Can I really leave Eli? I'm sure we could try dating long distance. But he works crazy hours. And Ithaca is a long way from any major airports. It'd be really hard to make it work.

"When exactly do you have to go back to New York?" he asks.

"The end of the month."

His eyes glimmer. "Two weeks."

"Yep."

"All right," he says, nodding. "Two weeks."

Eli

I have two weeks to convince Olivia to stay.

Two weeks to convince her to give her dreams a shot.

Convince her to give *me* a shot.

Chapter Twenty-Seven
ELI

The next day is gorgeous. The marsh glitters beneath a spotless autumn sky. It's a little chilly, so I light a fire in the outdoor fireplace, wrap Olivia in a blanket, and leave her to write.

I grab my latest read—a romance about a marriage of convenience, quickly becoming one of my favorite tropes—and settle onto the couch inside.

Billy hangs with me for all of five seconds before he saunters onto the deck. Through the open door, I hear Olivia greet him, and his tags jingle happily as he lays down at her feet.

I smile. Look at the three of us, getting all cozy and shit together.

The sun is out. The fire's just starting to smell good. I keep smiling when I think about what I'll make us for lunch. I've got some fish and a pineapple-and-cilantro slaw, made from scratch of course, to throw together for fish tacos. Add an ice cold Corona, and I *know* my Yankee girl is gonna be a happy camper.

So am I. A sense of contentedness washes over me.

For a second it's overshadowed by nagging thoughts about The Jam. It won't be fun to deal with the fallout when we get back into town. People are going to lose their jobs. I've already lost a fuck ton of money.

News is probably hitting the papers right about now. I wince when I imagine what the headlines must be.

I haven't checked my phone—my bank account balances—and I don't want to.

I focus my attention back on Olivia. Nothing I can do about The Jam now. Which means I can enjoy my baby's company.

Because she is my baby. We agreed last night that we're together. Although we still have a lot to figure out. Namely, what we're going to do about Olivia's job. The thought of her leaving in two weeks fills me with an ache I don't want to name.

I already have a few ideas about convincing her to take a chance on herself. Because if she believes in her writing—in her ability to persevere—then I think she'll agree to stay in Charleston. I don't want her to go back to a job and a life she hates. I want her to be happy.

I want her to be happy with me.

I'd also really like her to move in with me. Sounds crazy, I know. But I like having her around. I love waking up next to her. This morning I about died when I woke to find her next to me, naked and dreamy and hungry.

I just feel *good* right now. I'm not thinking about The Jam. Not thinking about anything, really, except the girl sitting on my deck.

I imagine making escapes to the cabin a regular thing for us. So far, Olivia seems to love it here. We could sneak down once or twice a month. She'd write. I'd cook. When we weren't doing those things, we'd be in bed.

Good *Lord* I want to get back in bed with her.

I devour my book in big chunks. Every once in a while I look up to check on Olivia. She's moved chairs to be closer to the fire, and now she's facing me. I watch her type, her face a mask of concentration.

As the hours pass, and her fingers fly over the keyboard, her expression begins to soften.

And then she begins to *glow*.

She smiles. Bites her lip. Snaps her fingers, her eyes lighting up—I imagine she just hit on something good. Maybe Cate and Gunnar finally fell into bed with each other.

Maybe Olivia falling into bed with me last night inspired that particular lightbulb to go off. The thought soothes my bruised ego.

Writing in the sun, hair fluttering in the breeze, Olivia is nothing short of radiant. What the hell is she doing working a job at some hoity toity university in New York when she's clearly so happy here?

I kinda love the idea that I'm helping her *get* to that place of happiness. I've always enjoyed mentoring younger chefs in my kitchens. Maybe I'm mentoring Olivia in a way. Showing her the ropes of finding fulfillment. Honoring passion. Taking chances.

I hate the idea of her not taking a chance on her writing. She's too good to give it up.

I want her too bad to let her go back to New York. It'd be one thing if she loved her job up there. I'd never take her away from that. But it doesn't sound like she does. Clearly she's happier down south.

Olivia catches me looking at her. She smiles, this cute, pretty thing that flips my heart upside-down and brings my cock to attention.

"Hungry?" I call through the door.

She grins. "Ravenous."

"For me? Or for lunch?"

"Both."

"I think I can help you with that," I say, getting up. "Which do you want first?"

Olivia purses her lips as she pretends to think about it. "Let's do lunch first. Then I'll do you."

"I like the sound of this plan. I'll get the grill goin'."

Olivia moans and groans her way through the grouper tacos.

"Eli, this is *ridiculous*," she says, eyes rolling to the back of her head as she pops the last bite into her mouth. "Thank you."

"You're welcome, baby." I look at her. The question pops out of my mouth before I can think better of it. "Is Olivia Gates your real name?"

Olivia chews. Swallows.

"It's not," she replies, taking a sip of beer. "It's my pen name. Gates is my grandmother's maiden name. Apparently she was a big reader, like me."

"Tell me your real name."

She grins. "Are you always so bossy after lunch?"

"Yes. Tell me."

Still smiling, she says, "My real name is Olivia Josephine Wilson."

I roll the words around my mouth.

"Pretty," I say. "It's nice to meet you, Olivia Wilson."

She extends her hand. "Nice to meet you, too, Elijah Jackson."

I take her hand and give it a little tug. Laughing, she leans forward and lets me kiss her.

I'm hard as a fucking rock. I remember how hot and tight she was last night. The way her pussy fisted around my fingers.

I also remember that I hurt her.

"How're you feelin'?" I ask, my voice husky.

Falling back into her chair, she puts a hand on her belly. "Full."

I nod at her groin. "And there?"

A spark of heat lights in her eyes.

"I'm a little sore. Nothing too bad."

"Still bleeding?"

"No." Her eyes rake over my bare chest. I never, ever wear a shirt when I'm at the cabin. She gets up, dropping her napkin on her plate. "I think I'm healed enough. Let's go to bed."

Olivia's already tugged off her jeans and shirt by the time we get to the bedroom. She reaches behind her and unclasps her bra.

She isn't wearing underwear.

Climbing into bed naked, she looks so good I can't stand it. Her tits bounce when she falls against the pillows. Her eyes are on me.

I shuck off my jeans and boxers. Olivia watches my every move, her gaze darkening with hunger when she takes in my swollen cock.

I take it in my hand and give myself a slow, strong stroke. Sensation winds tight low in my stomach.

"Like that, baby?" I murmur.

She licks her lips.

"Come here," she says, crooking her finger as she gets on her knees.

I stand at the edge of the bed, and then she's curling her hand around mine on my dick, her thumb playing with the head as I lean down for a kiss.

Guiding her in another stroke, I pant against her mouth. I'm not gonna last long at this rate. But before we have sex again, I need to make sure she's really okay.

With my other hand, I reach between her legs. Gently—very, very gently—I part her lips and slip my fingertip inside her folds.

She's soaking wet and hot.

"*Yankee* girl," I sputter.

"I meant it when I said you turned me on, Eli."

I meet her eyes. Study them as my fingertip moves over her clit. Her eyes go hazy. My cock surges.

But when I move to her entrance, barely touching her, those blue eyes light up with pain.

Immediately I pull back.

"You're still hurt," I say.

"No!" she says, grabbing my hand. "No, it's fine, Eli, I promise. I *really* want to do this. I want you."

I search her eyes. "How about we try something different? Give you a little more time to heal before we—you know," I say, gently pressing the head of my cock to her pubic bone.

I grin when I see the heat return to her gaze.

"Something different," she says, eyes flicking to my cock. "I'm down for that."

And then, before I know what she's doing, she literally does go down.

She's on her hands and knees now, crouching in front of me on the mattress while I stand. Leaning all her weight onto her left hand, she reaches for me with her right. I see stars when she uses that hand to guide my cock to her mouth.

She takes me in, inch by inch, working her tongue over my head with slow, sensual strokes. Need rips through me. I bury my fingers in her hair. It's still warm from the sun.

Olivia looks up at me. Eyes wide. My dick in her mouth. Dark hair all over the place.

"Sweet girl," I whisper, rolling my hips the tiniest bit.

Closing her eyes, she takes me deeper.

And then she sucks.

She sucks and she strokes and she drives me so fucking crazy I feel my orgasm coming, not twenty seconds into this thing.

I'm in her throat now, her soft palate pressing against my head. She moans, the vibrations sending shockwaves through my cock.

She's *good* at this.

I gotta return the favor somehow.

Her legs are spreading wider now, opening her ass cheeks. I run a hand down the pretty slope of her back. Slowly, I curl my first two fingers between her cheeks, sliding them into her wetness from behind.

Olivia moans again, canting her hips to give me a better angle.

I go right for her clit, moving through her swollen, slippery folds with care. She starts bobbing her head when I circle my fingers where she wants me. She's winding up tight, just like me.

She's giving in. Being vulnerable.

Sucking me off with all that pent-up ardor I saw in her writing.

It does me in.

"Baby, I'm close," I say through gritted teeth. I move my hand from her hair to her chin, tilting her up so that she looks at me. "Lemme come in your mouth."

I let her know with my eyes that it's a question. She's the one calling the shots here. Always will be.

Some Neanderthal part of me just wants to mark her. Make her all mine. I hate the idea that she's got this shithead ex back in New York. She said she's not going back to him. But I'm still going to do everything I can to make sure she stays. I want to cross every line. Do all the wrong things the right way.

I just want to make her mine.

The blue in her eyes blazes.

In reply, she takes me even deeper, her tongue swirling soft and hot around me.

I roll my hips. Roll again, jerking a little this time. I feel my orgasm closing in on me.

My body stiffens, and I come. Hard. My eyes screw shut, and behind them neon fireworks explode as sensation slams through me. I feel pulses of my cum sliding down her throat.

"*Olivia*," I sputter.

She milks me with her tongue, then swallows. My knees nearly give out.

Now who's the wobbly one?

My fingers are still between her legs. As my orgasm fades, I carefully stoke hers to life. I glide my fingertips over her clit, again and again. She moves against me, guiding me to touch her just where she needs it.

I reach down to tweak her nipples with my free hand one at a time. They're puffy and so perfectly soft in my fingers I groan.

My dick is still in her mouth when she comes. I want to bury my fingers inside her so I can feel her spasms. But I know she's still hurt, so I settle for her moans and the way she goes boneless as the shockwaves subside.

I tilt my hips, pulling out of her with care. She falls heavily onto her back, fisting the sheets. She's breathing hard.

I climb onto the mattress beside her.

"C'mere, baby," I say, looping an arm around her middle and curling her into my body. Big spoon and little spoon. A breeze moves through the open windows, and I pull the covers over us.

My pulse is racing. So is hers.

I kiss her throat. She turns her head and lets me kiss her mouth. I can taste myself on her lips.

"I like you this way," I say, kissing her slowly. "Wrung out. My taste on your mouth."

She whimpers into my kiss.

"What?" I say.

"You," she says.

I pull back to meet her eyes. "What about me?"

"You overwhelm me, Eli," she replies, gaze searching mine. "I just feel...God, I feel everything when I'm with you like this."

My heart swells.

"I hope that means you'll stay a while," I say.

I press a kiss to her temple.

We fall asleep like that. Tangled up in each other. Warm and cozy and content.

I want to make this week last forever.

Chapter Twenty-Eight
OLIVIA

The days pass too quickly at the cabin. And the nights—those are never long enough.

By the end of the week, I'm exhausted. Neither of us has slept for more than a few consecutive hours at a time. Eli and I are too hungry for each other to sleep through the night.

He'll wake me at dawn, a wicked smile on his lips as he settles his head between my legs. I'll wake him in the dead of night, soaking wet and needy, and he'll wordlessly tear open a foil packet and roll his big body on top of me, making love to me slowly. Sleepily. His mouth on my mouth, my breasts, my neck.

He always cleans me up afterward, checking to make sure there's no blood. Satisfied, he'll pull me against him, his heart beating thickly into the center of my back as I drift off.

I wonder if I'll ever be able to fall asleep again without being surrounded by that soothing, confident sound.

Without being surrounded by him.

I'm not sure if it's the beautiful scenery, the good food, the incredible sex, or some combination of all three, but my muse absolutely *sings* out here. I spend the bulk of my day either in bed with Eli or in a chair beside the fireplace on the deck, churning out chapter after chapter. Eli edits as I write. He's falling in love with my characters.

And I am falling in love with him.

There is zero point in denying it. In playing the tough guy. I am so soft and so vulnerable being who I am with him. There's something incredibly romantic about opening myself up like this.

I think a lot about Eli's advice to keep things simple. Maybe this is part of that—simply letting my feelings be what they are.

Simply accepting them. Accepting myself.

Being free of all that self-imposed torture makes me feel like I can fly. I'm high on life. Eli is, too, for the most part. Every so often I'll catch him frowning when he checks his phone. And he'll get this troubled, faraway look in his eyes sometimes. Like he's somewhere else completely.

"Are you all right?" I ask one night during dinner. We're eating outside beside the fire, like we always do. We were having the best little chat about Gunnar's use of a French letter, the nineteenth century's version of a condom made out of sheep intestine, when Eli started zoning out again.

Eli blinks, shaking the frown from his face. "I'm sorry. You're wearin' me out, Olivia. I been walkin' around like a zombie all week."

"What were you thinking about?" I ask. "The Jam?"

His eyes flicker. Harden. Almost like a gate coming down. I can't tell what he's feeling.

"A little bit, yeah." He runs a hand through his hair.

I reach across the table for his hand. "I'm sorry. The whole thing sucks. I've wanted to ask you about it. But I know it's a sensitive topic, so I've kinda been waiting on you to bring it up. I'm always here if you want to talk."

"I know. And I appreciate that, baby, I really do." He

turns his hand over to grasp mine. "There's really not that much to say, honestly. We'll close for good on Tuesday. Naomi is takin' care of the bulk of what needs to be done." He shrugs, giving my hand a squeeze before standing. "But I don't want to think about that shit. It's depressing. I want you. You make me happy."

I look at him, the fire reflecting in his dark pupils. "I want you, too. Of course I want you. But if you're not feeling okay, I'd like you to tell me about it."

"The only thing that makes me feel better right now is being with you." His eyes are pleading. "So let me be with you. The way I want."

A voice in the back of my head nags me to push him on this. I'm delighted that I make him feel better. But I'm not doing that by addressing his problem. By talking him through it.

I'm doing it by fucking his brains out.

Something about that feels…weird, I guess. Am I some kind of sexual Band-aid?

But the feeling passes when he smiles at me and takes my plate and kisses me, hard. The kind of intentional, soul-searing kiss I've come to expect from him.

A man does not kiss a Band-aid like this.

So I make a mental note to ask Eli about The Jam later on. In the meantime, I am going to make him feel better.

Much, much better.

As we pack up that Sunday, I steal one of Eli's shirts, sneaking it into my bag. He doesn't seem to wear shirts all that often anyway. And I want to keep a little piece of him with me. Want to wear his shirt to bed so I can smell him when we're not together.

We drive home at sunset. My mind wanders as we make our way through the low country, the trees lit up in fiery shades of orange and yellow and brown. The fear of missing out has kept me on a straight and narrow path. Fear that I'll miss having it all.

I never wondered what I was missing out on by being *on* that path.

This.

I missed this. Eli's big hand on my thigh. Feeling deliciously tender and achy in every corner of my body. Crisp autumn air blowing through the windows, sending my hair flying every which way. Good, hard writing behind me. Good, hard writing ahead. No Sunday scaries here. I'm *excited* about tomorrow.

This is what I've been missing out on all this time.

It hurts to think about giving it up.

I look at Eli. Clean and confident and calm. Handsome as hell. The ache inside my chest and between my legs intensifies.

The cool air feels so good on my skin. It's overwhelming.

It's exactly what I didn't know I wanted until now.

It's dark by the time Eli pulls into his narrow driveway.

"Stay," he says, shoving the gearshift into park.

For a second, I think he's asking me to *stay* stay. The leave-New-York-and-stay-in-Charleston-forever kind of stay.

The answer comes to me with gut-quick certainty.

Yes.

My hand shakes as I reach for the door handle. The rumble of the truck's engine suddenly seems enormous, throbbing in time to my heartbeat.

Did I really just make my decision?

Am I really going to leave everything behind and start over?

For weeks now, that seemed impossible.

Now it seems inevitable.

I just don't know what I'm going to do about my job. I can't write full time. At least not until I have a better idea of how I can make real money doing it.

Christine having her baby also means I have no one to take over my classes in New York for the rest of the semester. There's a good chance that will fall to me. Which means I'm going to have to go back to Ithaca, at least until the end of December.

But I have contacts in Charleston now. I'm growing a small but mighty network. I'll start tapping into that. See if I can't figure something out. Piece together the beginnings of a new life.

Whatever the case, I think I might be ready to take the leap. The big one.

Eli's forehead scrunches when he takes in what I can only guess is the shell-shocked expression I must be wearing.

"It's cool if you don't want to," he says quickly, resting his wrist on the top of the steering wheel. "But I thought you and I could get up early tomorrow. Maybe grab some coffee and take a yoga class. I'm gonna need to sweat it out before I go into work and deal with the shitstorm that's waitin' for me."

I blink.

Right. He was talking about staying the night. At his place.

I manage a smile. "I'd love that."

Billy's tail thumps happily against the back of my seat.

We hit up Peter's yoga class first thing the next morning.

"Something to think about as you practice," Peter says as he makes his way to the front of the room. "Yoga is a union, or a bringing together, of all your various selves or beings. Your mental being. Your physical being. Your spiritual being. When we practice yoga, we practice bringing all these parts of ourselves into harmony. We strip back our layers to get to our most essential self. There's a Sanskrit phrase for this —*sat nam*. It means 'truest self.' Let's make that our mantra today. Say those words to yourself as you breathe. Far too often, the world encourages us to move away from our true selves. Yoga asks us to go *toward* that self. So try that on today and see how it feels." A pause. "Let's begin in child's pose."

I feel the heat of Eli's gaze on me. This is exactly the stuff we've been talking about over the past couple weeks.

Without looking at him, I settle into child's pose. I feel tired and full. Not at all in the mood to do this right now. To dwell on the very real possibility that I'll be taking the biggest leap of my life soon with no guarantees. No real safety net.

All in the name of seeking out this true self.

At first, I fucking hate *sat nam*. In my head it sounds like Satan. Which, considering how my shoulders and hamstrings burn during the opening sequence of sun salutations, seems appropriate.

But as I move, encouraged by Eli's graceful, steady movements beside me, my mind begins to clear. The burn begins to fade. I just keep going, silently chanting with my breath.

Half lift. *True*. Bow. *Self*.

My sweat patters softly on my mat as I sit into chair pose.

The more I chant, the more I think. I had no idea who my *true self* was before I came to Charleston. I was aware of the concept. But I didn't think it was important.

Having a big fancy job? Being a good girlfriend? Keeping

up with the Joneses? *That* shit was important. But finding out what I loved? Spending time doing it?

Nah. There weren't enough hours in the day to do that.

Standing here, twisted into eagle pose, breathing and silently chanting and peeling back my layers, I can't help thinking that the way I've ordered my priorities has been incredibly stupid.

What's the point of all this if not to enjoy it? To do good, meaningful work and laugh with those who know and love the real you?

And I know, with this gut-deep, jarring sense of certainty, that I can't enjoy life the way I deserve to if I don't fess up to who I am and what I want.

By the time we get to the torturous let's-do-200-bicycle-crunches portion of class, I can't tell if it's sweat that falls on my mat, or tears.

Which of course makes me think of Cate. All the tears she sheds as Gunnar pushes her up against her assumptions about herself and her life again and again and again.

Eli is doing the same to me.

Being in Charleston is doing the same to me.

I was afraid before. But now I'm grateful.

Eli is quiet on the quick ride home. A muscle in his jaw twitches as he guides the truck into his driveway.

I can tell he's anxious. He told me he has to let most of The Jam's staff go today.

Even though I'm soaked and smelly, I get out of the car and pull him into a hug.

"I'll be around all day," I murmur into his shoulder. "If you need me, just call, okay? You're going to get through this.

You're still Elijah Jackson, and your biscuits can still make me come."

He scoffs, holding me a little tighter. "They're that good?"

"They're that good." I give him a kiss on the cheek. "Hang in there. Your wounds are fresh right now. Today might be tough, but it will get easier from here. You just need some time."

"I just need you," he replies, pressing a hot, lingering kiss onto my neck before pulling back to look at me. "I should be done by midnight. I want you to be in my bed when I get home."

I cock a teasing brow. "So bossy. What if I want you to be in *my* bed?"

"Just leave a key under the mat," he says, grinning. "On second thought, don't do that, because someone else might find it and beat me to you. My bed. Midnight. Bonus points if you have a chapter for me to read. Can you make it happen?"

No please. No uncertainty.

No shame.

God, I love it.

"I should be able to work something out," I reply saucily.

"Don't keep me waitin'." He gives my ass a squeeze before he turns toward his house. I feel a neat, hot pulse of longing between my legs as I watch him go. Speaking of ass—his is perfect. Just like the rest of him.

I smile. And feel with a new, sweeping certainty that this crazy decision I'm about to make is the right one.

Chapter Twenty-Nine
ELI

"You're really not going to tell me where we're going?" Olivia asks, watching through the windows as we inch forward in the ever-present traffic on East Bay Street.

"You do know how surprises work, right?"

She shoots me a wicked little look. My cock perks up. God *damn* I love when my girl gets an attitude. It's been a week since we got back from the cabin, but my thirst for this woman has only grown. I can't stand to be away from her—to not be inside her—for a fucking second.

"Last time you surprised me, we didn't leave your bedroom for twenty-four hours," she replies.

I grin at the memory. "Was that really just yesterday?"

"Oh yeah," she replies. "I think we got our money's worth out of that thing."

The *thing* she's referring to is the vibrator I bought on my way into work the day before last. My girl gets sore too often for my liking. Considering what happened the first time we fucked, I want to be extra careful with her. But I still want to make her come. Often.

That fun little toy lets me do exactly that. No blood. No

soreness. Just Olivia's contented moans as she orgasms again and again and again.

Shit. I'm getting hard just thinking about it.

I *love* thinking about it. Only thing that gets me through the day is knowing I'll find Olivia waiting for me in bed at night. She couldn't have come into my life at a better time.

Makes me think timing really is everything.

I put my blinker on. Taking the turn, I guide my truck into the leafy Ansonborough neighborhood. Olivia gasps as we pass impeccably restored mansions, ancient oak trees towering over pools and carriage houses and secret gardens.

Never gets old, seeing how much she loves my city.

She's got a little less than a week left before she needs to go back to New York. I've been hard at work, trying to convince her to have faith in herself and her writing.

Trying to convince her she can build a life here in Charleston so we can be together.

I slow down to take the turn into the familiar parking lot. My blood buzzes with excitement. A little nervousness, too. Everything with Olivia feels like life and death these days.

In a way, it is.

Olivia ducks her head to get a better look at the small sign hanging out front.

"Rainbow Row Books," she reads, squinting. She turns to me, eyes sparkling. "Eli, this place is adorable."

"I'm glad you think so," I say. "But that's not the surprise. C'mon, let's go inside."

I put the car in park and unbuckle my seatbelt. Olivia hops out of the car before I can walk around the truck to open her door, like I usually do.

She's practically bouncing on her feet. She walks a stride or two ahead of me, allowing me to shamelessly check out her ass. Her jeans make it look nothing short of scrumptious.

Is it wrong that I already can't wait to get her back home and peel those jeans off her?

Clearing my throat, I give my crotch a discreet tug. Today is about books. Olivia's career as an author. Sex can wait.

At least for a little while.

I open the door for her.

Olivia bites her lip, looking up at me. "You know, you're always very polite in public. But in private—"

"I'm bossy?" I hold the corner of the door in my hand and lean into her. "Rude in my demands and needs?"

"So rude." She rises onto her tip toes and kisses me, quick and sweet, on the lips. Then she whispers, "Good thing I like it."

"I'm 'bout to get real rude if you don't go inside," I say, nodding at the bookstore. "Those jeans are killin' me."

Shooting one last heated look my way, Olivia heads inside. I follow.

Louise looks up from her usual spot behind the counter, which is strewn with brightly colored paperbacks. Her face breaks into a smile.

"Eli! Is this the romance writer I've heard so much about?" she asks, sliding her glasses onto the tip of her nose to get a better look at Olivia.

"Sure is," I say. "Louise, this is Olivia. One of the best damn historical romance novelists working today. I can say that now, because I've read a lot of historicals over the past couple weeks."

I put a hand on the small of Olivia's back, guiding her forward. She takes in the store as we move. The peeling paint. The cats. The bookshelves that groan beneath haphazard arrangements of bestsellers and staff recommendations. She takes a deep breath through her nose. I do, too, and together we inhale the scent of paper. Dust. Unopened stories.

She turns her head and smiles at me. I feel her joy like an arrow through my heart.

Goodness gracious.

Louise leaps from her chair and walks around the counter, pulling Olivia into a tight hug. Olivia laughs.

"It's so great to meet you," Olivia says. "Your store is absolutely beautiful."

Louise grins at the compliment. "Thank you. We've been in this spot since 1982. A lot's changed since then, but I'd like to think there's still some magic in this old bookstore. Which is why I'm glad you're here. I need your help."

Olivia looks at me, arching a brow. "Help?"

"I may have volunteered you for a small project," I say sheepishly.

"My romance section is pitiful," Louise explains, pushing her glasses back onto the bridge of her nose. "I don't know what to stock, and I don't know how to draw romance readers into the store. Since you're writing romance, I thought you might be able to help me fix that."

Olivia draws back. Her cheeks are pink with pleasure. I slip an arm around her waist, keeping her close.

"Me? Really?" She looks at me. Looks back at Louise. "But I'm not even published. Not yet."

Louise crosses her arms. "Have you read a lot of romance?"

"Yes," Olivia blurts. "I think it's safe to say I'm kind of addicted to it."

"Then you know which authors to buy. What's new and exciting. Debuts that are worth reading."

"Well. I'm no expert. But I have been keeping up as best I can, especially now that I have an eye towards publishing."

My turn to raise a brow. "You do, huh?"

"I do," Olivia replies easily, grinning. "I read a lot of romance blogs—it's a good way to find out about the books everyone's talking about. I signed up for an author profile on Facebook and Twitter, so I can follow reviewers and other authors. I've even reached out to a few with questions I have. And of course I'm always poking around the charts on my e-reader, looking for my next read."

Louise nods. "Sounds like you know a hell of a lot more about romance than I do. Would you be willing to help me grow our readership? I'm thinking together we can come up with a plan to spread the word and get readers inside the store. We'd pay you, of course. And we'll help out however we can when you decide to release your fabulous book." Louise's eyes dart to me. "Eli's talked nonstop about how great it is. I'm excited to read it."

Olivia's blinking, hard. My heart thumps inside my chest. If she commits to helping Louise, then she could very well be committing to staying in Charleston.

She could be staying with me. Writing her books. Chasing down her dreams.

"Yes," Olivia says at last. "*Yes*. I'd love to help! I'm so—truly, I'm so honored you guys thought of me. I already have lots of ideas we can start with. We can do signings—maybe get a few local romance authors to pop in. We could even put together a local book club that's dedicated exclusively to reading romance..."

My heart swells. Then it bursts.

I resist the urge to tug her in my arms and pick her up off the floor. I give her side a squeeze instead, pulling her a little closer against me.

I hope this means what I think it does.

Judging from the way Olivia's glowing again, I'd say the chances are good.

I wonder if she really would move in with me. We practically live together these days anyway. I know things are happening fast. But I've never felt more sure about a girl.

I'd like to think Olivia feels sure about me, too.

Maybe I'll bring it up on Monday. My day off. Make a big brunch. Make love. Then make my move.

Together, the three of us sit down behind the counter and chat everything and anything romance. Must buy authors, important new books. Topics to touch on. Covers that caught our eye.

Seeing Olivia and Louise hit it off over piles of romance paperbacks fills me with a deep sense of satisfaction. By the time we have to go, they've already exchanged numbers and email addresses, and have made plans to grab dinner later this week.

Olivia is vibrating with energy on the ride home. I think about how different the girl sitting next to me is from the one who walked into my kitchen how many weeks ago. That girl hid her passion. Suppressed it.

But this girl right here? She's blooming with it. It's in her eyes. Her smile. Her fingers and her mind and her body.

"So?" I say, turning my head a little to look at her at a red light. "Good surprise?"

Her gaze softens. She smiles, reaching across the console to put her hand on my cheek.

"The best surprise ever. Well. The vibrator was pretty great, too. All your surprises are great, Eli. But this one was extra thoughtful." Her eyes lock on mine. "Thank you. For everything."

I turn my head and press a kiss into her palm. The light is green. I turn back to the road.

"You're welcome, baby. I'm proud of you for how far you've come. And I really do think you're the perfect person for this job. I figure you can learn a bit about the book business while also meeting the right people—readers, other authors."

She rubs the pad of her thumb over my scruff.

"You really want me to make this book thing happen, don't you?"

"I really want to make *you* happen. The real you." I cut her a glance. "I hope this means you're gonna be staying in Charleston."

Her cheeks flush pink. "I'm hoping that, too. I still need to iron out some details. But I'm trying, Eli."

"You just let me know how I can help."

Olivia grins. A sexy, saucy thing.

"Just keep giving me ideas for sex scenes," she says. "If I'm going to write romance for a living one day, I'll be working on lots of those."

I laugh. "Done. Speakin' of—you're still comin' over tonight, right?"

Olivia wags her brows teasingly. "How about you come over to my place instead? I'd like to give *you* a surprise."

"I like the sound of that," I say, grinning.

She grins back. "I'll leave a key—"

"Not under the mat."

"Wouldn't dream of it. How about in the flower pot at the bottom of the stairs?"

My turn to grin.

"That'll work."

Chapter Thirty
OLIVIA

I walk my usual route through the College of Charleston on my way to Holy City Roasters later that day. There's nothing quite like being on campus on a crisp, sunny fall afternoon. I pass a pair of students—young, sophomores maybe—who are deep in conversation about the ethics involved in robotics. A knot of girls lingers around a bench, doing some last minute crunching together for an organic chemistry exam. The guy in front of me is on the phone with his mom.

"Yes, Mom, I promise, I'm fine," he says, clearly exasperated. "It's just a cold. No—no, really mom, please don't try to mail soup. Pretty sure that will end badly for everyone. I appreciate the thought, though."

I grin.

I don't miss my job. The pressure cooker environment. The awful office politics. I never think about the job itself; I only think about how I'm going to leave it. Between all the fictional sex I'm writing and the very real, very excellent sex I'm having, I don't have time to think about anything else. My new life in Charleston has swallowed me whole.

I couldn't be happier about it.

But I *do* miss teaching. Interacting with bright young people. Writing can be a pretty awesome gig. It does get lonely, though. Being part of a campus culture was one of my favorite things about being a professor.

I stop in front of the English Department. It's housed in a cute yellow Charleston single that looks a little worse for the wear. Through the old wavy glass windows, I can see people moving around inside.

My heart works double. I'm a little early for my appointment with the Department Head. But I want to make a good impression.

I can't live on my writing alone. Not at first. I don't want to blow through all my savings. Having a part time job teaching would be a nice little bridge between my old life and my new one. I know there are no openings at the moment, but I can at least toss my hat in the ring. Feel the Department Head out on openings in the future.

It would just be really, really cool to teach something different. Something I'm actually passionate about. No more moody Byron (thank God). No more Dickens. I want to teach Nora Roberts. Beverly Jenkins. And of course Jane Austen.

I'm nervous.

A feeling I kinda-sorta welcome. I've experienced the gamut of emotions down here. It's made me realize how numb I am back home. Or maybe how hard I tried to sweep whatever I felt under the rug, because it got in the way of living my "perfect" life.

Standing here in front of a crumbling house, wearing jeans and my heart on my sleeve, I'm about as far from perfect as it gets.

I'm also as close to my true, romance-writer-wannabe self as I've ever been.

Taking a deep breath, I climb the steps and go inside.

Eli's been working especially late this week. I've been trying to squeeze a nap in around dinnertime so I can be awake when he gets home. I have to admit I sorta love the fact that he comes straight to me after walking through the door. He doesn't put down his keys. Doesn't grab some food or a glass of water. He always makes a beeline for me, tearing off his clothes as he comes to tear mine off, too. Then we're up *late*. Fucking, then talking. Then fucking again.

Tonight, though, I'm too wired to nap. I'm bursting with good news. Exactly the kind of surprise I wanted to give Eli.

I finish up some emails to some indie authors I've been in touch with. After that, I read a few of my favorite romance blogs.

I head for the shower next. I want to give myself extra time so I can shave everything. I've never been bare for Eli before. I figure it might be nice to try something new.

Whatever he thinks of it, it definitely turns me on. My skin feels tingly down there. Soft.

Then I put on his shirt—the one I stole from the cabin that smells like him—and the lacy red thong I know he likes so much.

No bra.

I'm in bed reading over the chapter I wrote earlier when I hear a low *zip*.

The key being inserted into the lock.

A heartbeat later, I hear the door open.

"He*llo*," Eli calls.

The sound of his gruff voice makes my nipples pebble. I see him in my head. Holding his hair back with an enormous hand while he toes out of his sneakers. He'll smell like a wood fired oven and sweat. Skin.

"You here, baby?" he says. I hear him put something down on the counter. Open a drawer.

I leap out of bed, the pages falling from my lap onto the floor. I don't bother picking them up.

I can't stand the thought of wasting another second without him.

"I'm here," I say, mussing up my hair one last time in the bureau mirror before heading out into the kitchen.

For the split second before he sees me, Eli wears a somber expression. It hits me just how *tired* he looks. There are dark rings around his eyes, and his skin is pale. A few grey hairs dot his scruff.

But then his eyes meet mine and his face lights up in a smile. He's halfway through opening a frosty bottle of white wine, but he drops the opener and stalks toward me. His eyes flash with hunger when they catch on my nipples.

"Hey," I say, biting back a grin when he blatantly adjusts his hard on.

"That my shirt?" he asks.

"Yeah," I say. "I kind of stole it. Smelled too good to resist. Smelled like *you*."

"As sexy as you look in it, sweetheart, I gotta admit I want to tear it off you. You joined my shirtless club, remember?"

I laugh. "Of course."

He steps around the counter and pulls me into his arms. We're really good at this by now. I go on my toes, pressing myself against him. His hands go to my ass. Guide my groin into his.

He's always hard for me.

Always.

And my body is always eager to rise to the occasion.

A low thrum of electricity sparks in my core when he massages my ass cheeks, giving them a possessive squeeze.

He buries his face in my neck. Inhales, then grunts. A needy, primal sound.

"You smell good," he murmurs against my skin. I feel the prick of goosebumps. "Did you just get out of the shower?"

"I did," I reply.

"Oh? This have something to do with your surprise?"

"Part of it. Yes." I pull back, flattening my palm against his chest. "I have some news."

One side of his mouth curls into a half smile so handsome and so joyfully familiar it makes me weak in the knees.

"Oh yeah?" His fingers play with the hem of his shirt at the top of my thighs. "I'm dyin' to hear it."

"I spoke to the head of the English Department at the College of Charleston this afternoon. They aren't hiring for this semester. But I am first in line for any openings for next semester, and he's letting me put together a proposal for a commercial fiction class I'd like to teach."

His eyes go wide. "Seriously? You went in today? That's incredible news! Congrats, baby."

"He was impressed with my resume, and even more impressed with my knowledge of the romance market. Apparently they're trying to make the department a bit more career focused, so my specialty lines up nicely with that."

Eli tugs me into another hug, giving my whole body a squeeze this time.

"I can't tell you how happy I am for you, Olivia. This sounds like something that's so *you*. You love to write, and you love to teach. Now you'll hopefully get to do both. And in my city, no less."

I'm smiling so hard I worry my face is going to crack.

"Charleston's my city now, too."

His turn to pull back. He searches my eyes.

"You mean that?"

I bite my lip. Nod. "I do."

In reply, he dips his head and nips at my earlobe. My breath catches. So does a hit of lust between my legs. It feels slightly different on my bare sex. More tingly. Which just makes me that much more turned on.

"We should celebrate," he breathes.

"We should. I have another surprise," I say. "But first, that wine you brought looks good."

Eli groans, hooking his first finger in the top button I have done on my shirt. "You really gonna make me wait?"

"Delayed gratification," I reply with a smirk. "It'll make the payoff that much better. I promise."

Rolling his eyes, Eli reluctantly takes his hands off me and goes back into the kitchen.

I watch the muscles in his forearm pop as he uncorks the bottle.

"Cabinet above the stove," I say when he looks up for glasses.

He smiles. "I'm learnin', sweetheart."

I join him in the kitchen, taking the glass he presses into my hand.

His gaze flicks appreciatively over me again. His nostrils flare.

I'm hit by the juiciest wave of that feeling—the feeling that there is nowhere on earth I'd rather be right now than in this kitchen with Eli. Drinking wine.

Drinking each other in like horny teenagers.

He nods at my shirt. "So you gonna take it off or what?

I take a sip of wine. Sancerre. It's perfectly cold, crisp, just a hint of fruit. I close my eyes, allowing myself a second to enjoy the feel of it on my tongue.

"What are you going to give me to take it off?" I tease, opening my eyes.

Reaching up, he tucks my wild hair behind my ear. Takes a sip of his wine before setting it back on the counter.

"You know what I wanna give you, baby," he says, his voice lower and softer and rougher, all at once.

A new rush of heat to my pussy makes me squeeze my legs together.

I'm a little sore. Nothing new there. He's just so much bigger than I'm used to.

He fucks me harder and better than I'm used to.

I open my eyes to see him looking intently down at me. His eyes are soft.

Hungry.

My heart twists.

Jesus, I am *drowning* in this man. Just when I come up for air he pulls me under again. A look, a sound, a touch—that's all it takes to send me reeling. He never gives me a moment to catch my breath.

He steps closer, surrounding me, and starts unbuttoning the shirt. Case in point.

"How are you feeling?" he says, eyes not leaving mine. His concern is so sweet it makes me ache. Ever since I bled that first night, he's been extra careful with me.

Not to say he hasn't been ardent in his attentions. He just knows my body better now. Knows when to push and when to pull back.

His skill is intoxicating.

"Like I'm drunk," I reply honestly. "On you."

He laughs. "I can relate."

The top buttons are undone now. He reaches inside and gently cups my tit.

Runs a calloused thumb over the nipple, coaxing it to a hard point.

I arch into his touch, my breath catching.

"Eli," I plead.

His hand moves back to the buttons. "Keep drinking the wine."

I blink. "The wine?"

"You're enjoying it." The shirt is fully unbuttoned now. He parts it, putting his hands on my waist. "So keep drinking it."

He kisses my mouth. I rise into him, kissing him back.

He hooks his finger into the strap of my thong. "You have no idea how much I love these little panties of yours."

"I do, actually," I murmur. "But that's not the surprise."

Eli pulls back to look me in the eye.

"I like this game," he says.

Then he's trailing his mouth down the slope of my jaw. He kisses my collarbone, my chest. Stops to take one nipple, then the other, into his mouth, sucking gently at first, then harder.

Harder.

My clit pulses. Agony.

He crouches the further south he goes until he's on his knees.

Gliding his hands up my thighs, he gathers my hips in his hands and leans forward. Buries his nose into my crotch and inhales.

"You smell so good here, too," he says, pressing his lips to the red lace. "I can tell you're already wet."

His fingers are in the straps at my sides now. I'm bursting with anticipation.

My hand shakes as I bring the wine to my lips. I close my eyes and take a sip at the same moment Eli pulls my thong down.

His hands go still on my legs. Silence.

My heart flips. I drink the wine, letting it slide down my throat. I feel the start of a happy buzz inside my skin.

"You gotta be fuckin' kidding me," he growls at last.

I open my eyes to see him staring reverently at my bare pussy.

"You did this?" His eyes flick to mine.

My heart flips again.

"I like it," I reply. "Maybe not always. But it's fun to try something new."

He shakes his head, letting out a pained scoff. "*Fun*. Jesus Christ, Olivia, sometimes I think you're tryin' to make me stroke out."

"So?" I shoot him a look. "Are you going to have fun with me? Or are you going to have that stroke?"

In reply, he hooks one of my legs over his shoulder, spreading me wide. Then he twists my thong in his fingers and gives it a solid, savage tug, snapping it in two. He throws it behind him.

Turns his attention to my sex.

He uses his thumbs to gently prod me. He feels the smooth skin on my labia. Rubs it. I bite my lip to keep from crying out.

Watching his eyes darken with need as he looks at me, *looks*, turns me on so much it hurts.

His thumbs open my lips. Now I'm spread wide right in front of his face.

He's still staring at me with such intensity I want to scream.

He swipes at my clit, back to front, with the tip of his thumb. Just once.

A tremor claps through me. Making my legs shake.

"Yes," I hiss. "Dear God, *yes*."

He shoots me a dark, saucy look before gliding that questioning thumb through the length of me. Front to back this time. I'm slick enough that he goes easily. Smoothly.

My hips roll into his touch.

His middle finger finds me. Sinks inside me at the same moment Eli leans forward and kisses me.

He kisses me just above where my lips meet.

I dig a hand into his hair and give it a pull.

"I like that," I say.

Eli's eyes flick up to meet mine. "Don't forget your wine. Keep drinking, Olivia."

"How can I—"

"Do it. Otherwise, you're not getting this," he says. His middle finger slips out of me, and he gives my clit a hard pluck between the knuckles of his first and second fingers. I moan.

I tip back my wine and take a long, *long* sip.

"That's my girl. Good, right?"

It *is* good. My buzz is growing in tandem with the throb in my sex. The two of them together is sensory overload.

I love it.

And then Eli is slipping a hand onto my ass, his fingers toying with the crease. He kisses my clit next, and my need for release tightens. Becomes almost unbearable.

He tilts his head a little and then full on french kisses me. Takes all of my pussy—everything that I can see, anyway—in his mouth, laving at me with his tongue. His teeth. His lips.

Slowly. Oh so slowly.

I can't help it. I cry out his name. I feel myself getting weak. Losing my footing.

But Eli holds me up. One hand on my hip, the other still on my ass. His fingers are slipping lower inside my crack.

Lower.

I buck against his mouth when he presses a finger to my asshole.

He doesn't insert it. He just plays with my pucker, teasing me as he sucks *hard* on my clit.

I moan again.

I feel the wave coming. It's already huge and overwhelming.

"Why," I gasp, tugging at his hair. "Why do you have to be so good at loving me?"

Loving me. Panic lights in my belly at the words.

I hadn't meant to say that. I wanted to say those words when we weren't—well—doing this. It's important to me that I tell him I love him not in the heat of the moment, but in a moment I intentionally choose.

Shit.

"Because." He gives my pussy a long, slow lick before locking eyes with me. His are clear, free of lust. "I do love you, Olivia."

It's his eyes that do it. Yes, we're in the heat of the moment right now. But he's still somehow *clear eyed*.

That's all it takes to send me over the edge.

I come. The orgasm to end all orgasms.

Tears spring to my eyes at the bite of its intensity. I crumple against Eli as my limbs stiffen, then go slack. Beat after beat after beat of sweetness roils through my pussy. My blood.

My heart feels like an open wound inside my chest. It's bursting. It's tender. It's *vulnerable*, helpless against the onslaught of everything, everything Elijah.

I close my eyes.

I surrender.

Eli gives my clit one last kiss. I feel him rising to his feet, his body brushing against mine. He grabs my wine. Sets it on the counter. Grabs me and lifts me onto the counter, too, looping one arm around my waist to hold me upright as he settles between my legs. I'm helpless. I cling to him, too overwhelmed to move.

Above the furious working of my heart, I hear the tear of a foil packet. He pulls back for a minute.

Then he's prodding my entrance. He's using his arm to guide me onto his dick. He sinks slowly into me, letting out a hiss between clenched teeth.

He feels so good I can't look at him. I'm worried I'll combust. Be left in mangled pieces on the floor.

Capturing my mouth in a kiss, he begins to roll his hips. God, I love the way he moves inside me. Deeply and strongly and slowly. Great, rolling, athletic thrusts. He takes his time.

He's always giving me time. Time and space to be who I am.

I curl my arms around his neck.

"I love you too, Elijah," I say in his ear.

He goes still mid-thrust.

He pulls me a little closer, hanging his head.

"That's all I've ever wanted to hear from you," he says. His breath is ragged. "You're all I want."

I'm finally able to roll my hips, needing him. He rolls back, needing me.

Together, we bring him to orgasm. I feel him pulsing inside me, coming with a howl.

"I don't know how this keeps getting better," I say when he finally catches his breath. "But it does."

"I'm a chef," he says, pressing his lips to my neck. "You knew I'd eventually have to make love to you in a kitchen, right?"

I laugh, pulling him closer.

I can never get my southern charmer close enough.

Chapter Thirty-One
ELI

I wake up the next morning in Olivia's bed with a big stupid grin on my face.

She said it back.

She told me she loved me.

I've known for a while that I'm in love with her. Ever since—

Well. I honestly couldn't tell you the exact moment I fell in love with Olivia. Coulda been that night we danced to Bruce Springsteen in the rain. Or the moment she melted into me when we first kissed.

Coulda been that first morning she showed up in my kitchen. That fire in her eyes. The way she'd smiled after devouring the breakfast I'd made her.

I never had a chance, did I?

Olivia rustles beside me. She's on her side, her back to me. The sheets fall away, revealing her bare shoulder.

Getting onto my side, I take it in my mouth. She moans. Without rolling over, she wiggles her hips, settling her ass into my groin.

Grabbing her top leg, I pull it over mine, opening her. I reach around to slide my hand down the plane of her stomach and find her.

Lust bolts through me at her bareness. As if I didn't wake up hard enough as it is.

She's swollen. So slick her arousal coats my fingers.

I groan my approval, giving her clit a soft, slow massage with my fingertips.

"Mornin', baby," I murmur into her neck.

She presses her ass into my cock. "Please," she breathes.

"Not too sore?"

"Baby, *please*."

I grin harder. First time she's ever called me baby.

I fucking love it.

I grab a condom from the bedside table and roll it on.

Her leg still resting over mine, I guide myself to her cleft. I take her hip in my hand. Then I slip inside her, quick and quiet, biting the tendon that connects her neck to her shoulder.

"Oh," she pants, voice still raspy with sleep. "That feels—Elijah, that feels so nice."

I adore how she tells me what she likes. What she wants.

Olivia reaches down and starts playing with herself as I thrust gently in and out of her.

She comes five seconds later, clamping down on my dick like a vise. Then I come, too.

All this sex has made me feel so connected to her. She's become an essential part of me. When she's not with me, I feel like something is missing. I feel *sore*, like her absence is a literal bruise.

"I love you," I say.

Olivia glances at me over her shoulder. She smiles, those blue eyes flashing with happiness.

"I love you too."

My heart soars.

She sits up, letting the sheets fall to her waist. Her tits are nice and heavy, nipples puffy and a little red from the attention I gave them in the middle of the night.

I reach up and take her left breast in my hand, fondling it absentmindedly as she checks her phone.

"I have a lot of writing to do today," she says, turning to run a hand through my hair. "Would you be cool letting yourself out? As much as I'd like to stay and do this"—she motions to our nakedness—"all morning, I should probably grab a shower and get a head start. Cate and Gunnar are about to have their black moment, which means I'm pretty damn close to being done with the book."

I give her tit a gentle squeeze before letting it go.

"I'm proud of you, Olivia," I say. "Just promise me you won't torture Gunnar and Cate too much, all right? They're very real to me, and I'm gonna hate to see them hurt."

She grins, tapping her first finger on the tip of my nose. "Sorry, Elijah, but you know how I love to torture them."

"You're a sadist."

"That's a serious accusation." She wiggles her eyebrows. "Want to find out if it's true?"

I groan at a new throb of desire in my groin.

"Get in the shower. Now," I grind out. "Otherwise you won't be writin' a damn thing today."

Laughing, Olivia gets out of bed and closes the bathroom door behind her. I always want to join her in the shower—and I have, many times—but she didn't invite me today. And there's only so much sex a man can take. My dick is actually sore. Girl is tight. Means if she wasn't sore before, she probably is now.

Best to take a little time off, lest one of us suffer an unfortunate sex-related injury that keeps me from putting my hands on her for days rather than hours.

Billy's also waiting on me at home. I need to let him out.

I roll off the bed and tug on my boxers and jeans. Grab my phone from the nightstand. Wallet. Keys. I leave the handful of condoms I brought with me. There's already a stash I left here the other night, but you can never have too many of these things lying around.

I hear Olivia turn on the shower.

My gaze catches on the shirt on the floor by the foot of the bed.

My shirt.

The one Olivia stole because it had my smell on it.

I grin, flicking my gaze to the dresser on the opposite wall.

Two can play this game.

Shoving my wallet and keys into my back pocket, I put my phone on the top of the dresser and open the first drawer.

It's filled to the brim with bits of lace.

"Fuck. *Yes*," I murmur, sticking my hand inside.

All kinds of goodness catches on my fingers. I recognize the candy apple red bra. The nude thong. A naughty corset she wore the other night with see through cups and laces I couldn't get undone fast enough.

I'm more interested in the underwear, though.

I want one of those red thongs. The kinds she wears when she wants me to notice.

I keep digging. She's got a lot of lingerie. A lot of it looks new. I smile when I think about her buying it just for me.

My knuckles meet with the bottom of the drawer. Only—wait. It's not the drawer. It's some kind of box.

A velvet box.

My heart skips when I see that it's small. Square. Familiar. A jewelry box.

A *ring* box.

I feel a weird sensation in my ears. The growing roar of an approaching wave.

The velvet is suddenly clammy in my palm. Or maybe it's my palm that's clammy.

This box belongs to Olivia. She put it in a drawer for a reason. I have no right to open it. I had no right to be digging through her drawers in the first place.

I can't help it, though. Blame it on me being crazy for this girl. On wanting to know everything and anything about Olivia Wilson.

Blame it on me being a lovesick, anxious asshole.

Whatever the reason, I open the box.

My stomach drops.

A ring is nestled between the tiny white cushions inside.

No joke, the diamond is the size of a fucking walnut. It's huge. Sparkly and perfect, set in a simple platinum setting. It's something straight out of a Tiffany ad.

When I (briefly) considered proposing to an ex-girlfriend years ago, I went to look at rings. Diamonds a quarter of this size cost more than I have in my savings account right now. I imagine a diamond *this* big costs as much as what one of my sous chefs makes in a year.

Made. Made in a year. I had to let all my sous chefs at The Jam go because *my restaurant went bankrupt*.

I can't afford to buy a ring this nice for Olivia. A year ago? Yes. But after taking a major financial hit when I closed The Jam, there's no way I could swing something like this. Much less a wedding. The kind of big, beautiful wedding Olivia probably wants.

All the panic and doubt and insecurity I've tried to shove aside comes rushing at me all at once. It's like a tidal wave that hits me head on, leaving me reeling. I'm breathing, I'm blinking, but I feel like my mind has separated from my body, and I'm watching from above as the wave pulls me under.

Olivia told me her ex proposed to her. But she didn't tell me she kept his ring.

Who was this guy who proposed to Olivia with a five figure ring?

And why the hell did she keep the damn thing and bring it all the way from New York?

I wonder if she couldn't let it go because she wanted it so much. If she *still* wants it so much. Which kills me, because I don't know if I'll ever be able to give her something even half as nice as this.

A surge of white hot jealousy like I've never known slams through me. I'm really drowning now.

Olivia dated this guy for a reason. He's clearly successful. Probably has a cushy, stable corporate job.

Basically the opposite of me.

What if she starts missing the things he gave her that I can't? When the excitement wears off and she gets sick of the hours I work, my small house, my smaller bank account?

You're a fun fuck buddy, I imagine her saying after she falls for him all over again when she goes back to Ithaca to quit her job. *But you're clearly not long term material. Ted is.*

In some distant corner of my mind, I know I need to take a breath. Calm down and come up with a plan so I can have a productive conversation with Olivia about how this ring is stoking the feeling of inadequacy I haven't talked about much but I've been grappling with all month.

I know I need to keep my cool until I know the facts. Maybe he made her keep the ring. Maybe it actually belongs to her family. An heirloom passed down from her grandmama or something.

I glance at the ring. It's so brilliant and fiery I have to squint to look at it without being blinded.

Fuck that.

I cross the room in two strides and yank open the bathroom door, not bothering to knock. It bangs against the wall.

A voice in my head warns me to calm down. *This is stupid this is stupid you are being so stupid right now.*

I ignore it, and barge into the bathroom like a lunatic. Because that's what this girl has turned me into.

Chapter Thirty-Two

ELI

Through the foggy shower door, I see Olivia whip around, her wet hair sending a spray of droplets flying against the glass.

"Jesus, Eli, you scared me."

I hold up the open box. "What the hell is this?"

Olivia blinks. Then she goes still.

Panic grips my gut and squeezes.

The sound of the running water is enormous between us.

"You were digging through my drawers?" she says at last.

"I wanted to take a pair of your fucking panties. Repay you for stealing my shirt. I was being cute."

"I didn't know going through other peoples' stuff was cute."

My heart is really pounding now. "Olivia, tell me what the *hell* this ring is about."

She hesitates. Just for a second. Just for a breath.

But she hesitates.

Which means—

Christ.

"It's the ring Ted proposed with," she says.

I don't know if it's the close, steamy air in the bathroom,

or the enormity of what I'm feeling, or what, but I suddenly feel dizzy.

"But I thought you said you turned him down."

Olivia turns off the water and steps out of the shower, knotting a towel around her torso.

"I did," she replies. "Eli, I'm not going to marry Ted."

"Then why'd you keep his ring?"

She swallows. Looks away.

"Because he told me to wear it when I went back to him." She looks at me. "That's why. But I'm not going back to him. I'm going to return the ring, and then I'm going to be with *you*, Eli."

I search her eyes. "What if I don't believe you?"

A look of surprise crosses her face. Surprise that morphs into hurt.

Shit. I'm letting my jealousy, my insecurity, get the better of me. But I can't fucking stop. I feel helpless. Which makes me feel *angry*.

I'm struck by the wild idea that maybe she's been using me this whole time. Maybe I've just been a rebound for her. Yeah, things got intense between us. She told me she loved me. But that doesn't mean she won't wake up one day and wish I were the guy she left. Not Ted.

Ted, who proposed to her with the fucking ring that's a reminder of all the ways I'm falling short these days.

"Why wouldn't you believe me?" she says, eyes welling with tears. "I've been nothing but honest with you this whole time. I've let you see parts of me no one else ever has. I've been intimate with you in a way I've never been with anyone else. I'm in love with you, Elijah. Not Ted. *You*."

"I'm in love with you, too," I say. Then I hold up the ring. "Which is why this bothers me so much."

Olivia blinks. "Wait. Are you *jealous* of my ex?"

"Maybe I am."

"You shouldn't be." She takes a step forward. "Ted's a great guy, but I think I've made it pretty clear to you that he's not the guy for me. You are. I'm done with Ted."

I take a step forward, too.

"Then prove it. Move in with me."

Olivia

My heart lurches. I don't know what to make of this. One minute, Eli and I are having slow, lazy, quiet morning sex, and the next he's charging into the bathroom, red faced and ready for a fight.

"Move in with you? Where did this idea come from?" I say, genuinely distraught. "Eli, I know we're in love. And I know we've spent a lot of time together over the past month. But I still haven't figured out what my situation is going to be. What if my department in Ithaca can't find a replacement and I have to stay up there until after the holidays? And what if this new job at the College of Charleston doesn't pan out? I need time to get my ducks in a row."

His eyes are hard when they meet mine. "And I need an answer."

"Eli," I say, bewildered. "You're being ridiculous. We have plenty of time to talk about moving in together. Let's revisit it when I know more about my future."

"I don't want to revisit it," I say. "I want to talk about it now."

I blink, hard.

"But I don't understand. You've never brought this up before."

"I've been thinking about it for a while." His gaze

searches mine. "I like having you around. I *need* you around, Olivia."

I blink. He's never been so needy before. So...insecure.

This is not the confident, almost cocky, boyfriend I adore. "This isn't like you, Eli."

"I'm sorry," he says, his eyes softening. "But I want to know you're in this for real. I need to know you're really stayin'. C'mon, Olivia, think about how perfect it would be. You can write. I can cook. Billy will be happy. And you won't have to worry about payin' rent. Let me give this to you. Please. It'll lend you some breathing time to get back on your feet."

C'mon, Olivia. Eli says it exactly like Ted used to.

And funny Eli mentions breathing time when really, he's giving me an ultimatum. The opposite of this supposed freedom I'd have living with him.

I know this feeling. I felt it when Ted got down on one knee and asked me to marry him.

A noose, tightening around my neck.

"The only thing I want is *you*," I whisper, my pulse beginning to race. "Please don't do this, Eli. Please don't tell me you want to tie me down after I've just won my freedom."

His hazel eyes go wide. "I'm not trying to tie you down. I'm trying to give you the freedom to write without worrying about money."

"No. You're trying to trap me by forcing me to make a decision before I'm ready."

"I don't get it." He bends his neck. Our faces are inches apart. "Why aren't you ready? You told me you loved me."

"Because I'm new to this!" I burst out. "This city, this career, this *life*. I want more time to explore it. I need to try on different things before I commit to moving in with someone. Hell, Eli, I ended a three year relationship less than a month ago."

He blinks rapidly, jerking back. Like I hit him.

"So you want to try on different people?"

"No," I bite out. Tugging a hand through my hair, I sigh. "You're missing the point, Elijah. I'm begging you. Please don't give me this ultimatum. I want to be with you, but I need to take things slow. Why rush when we have the rest of our lives to explore this beautiful thing we just started?"

He stares at me for a second. Then he holds up his hands and shakes his head.

"I'm sorry, baby. But I need to know you're mine. With everything going on at work—just..." His voice breaks. He clears his throat. "Bein' with you is the only thing that makes me feel better, all right?"

My pulse skips a beat—my head throbs—as the realization hits me.

"Oh my God," I say, leaning against the vanity to steady myself.

"What?"

"You're not asking me to move in because you love me. You're asking me because you don't want to be alone." Tears flood my eyes. "Jesus, Eli this has nothing to do with me, does it?"

A flush of red creeps up Eli's neck and spreads across his cheeks. His eyes flash with anger.

"That's not true," he says. "You can't tell me I don't adore you."

My throat is so tight it makes my entire head hurt.

"Of course you adore me. But I've asked you so many times to talk about what happened at The Jam. You always blow me off and start talking about my books, or you start touching me, and we—well. You know. Which makes me feel like maybe you've been using me as a distraction or something."

"No," he says, voice shaking, clearly backtracking. "You're so much more than that, Olivia."

A heavy sadness settles on me as I search his eyes. He has the panicked look of a cornered animal.

"You're right." My voice trembles. "I did mean more to you than that. But now you're making me feel used. You're making me feel *cheap*. I think you know that what you're doing right now is wrong. You're doing it anyway, though, because you don't believe me when I say I am going to stay. Why don't you trust me?"

Eli looks at me for a long minute.

"I don't trust you because I realized I know next to nothing about your life in New York," he replies. He sets the ring on the counter beside the sink. I reach over and close the box. "Got me thinking that the guy who bought you that thing is the real deal, while I'm just some idiot you wanted to fuck."

His words are like a punch to the gut. I struggle to breathe. I can't believe it's Eli who's saying these things. The man whose kindness and faith in me changed my life for the better in so many ways.

"That is not at *all* how I think of you," I manage. "What do you want to know about my life in New York? I'll tell you anything."

He meets my eyes. "The only thing I want to know is whether or not you'll move in with me."

I just stare at him. Is he serious?

"I'm sorry," I say. "My answer is no. I can't move in with you. *Not yet*. But if you give me time—"

"You're always sayin' you need more time." He crosses his arms, making the muscles in his arms bulge. "Maybe you need more time because you've been planning to go back to him. Maybe you want to wear a ring like that. Be with a man like that—someone who can afford somethin' so big. I'm sorry, too, but I'm done waitin' on you. I've been nothing but patient, Olivia. But you can't even find it in yourself to be honest with me. Why didn't you tell me you kept his ring?"

My gaze flicks to the jewelry box on the counter between us.

"For the hundredth time, I am not going back to Ted. I'm sorry about the ring," I say, feeling a stab of anger. "If I knew it was going to upset you so much, I would've flung the damn thing out the window. That ring is part of my previous life. A life I am going to leave in the past. I didn't think you needed to know about it because you're part of my future. A future I chose. Really, Eli, you're better than this, and you know it."

"I'm better with you."

I feel another stab. This one is a stab of hurt.

No one tells you how much being yourself—*choosing* yourself—hurts sometimes.

"*I need time.*"

He swallows, making his Adam's apple bob. A tear slips out of the corner of my eye. I wipe it away.

"So that's really a no," he says.

I nod, rolling my lips between my teeth.

He takes a breath, making his big chest barrel out. Then he pushes off the counter, dragging a hand up the back of his head.

"All right," he says. "I guess that's that. I should go."

I nod again, tears spilling out of my eyes with abandon now.

He makes his way out of the bathroom. The sound of his footsteps has an awful finality to it.

My mind races to calm me down as I follow him. *You're standing your ground. You're being true to yourself. You're doing the right thing.*

But watching Eli clamp the doorknob in his hand for the last time still feels wrong.

His eyes, clear and wet, sweep up to meet mine.

"They say timin' is everything. Ours clearly sucks," he says. "Maybe we weren't meant to be together after all."

I don't disagree with that. But it still fucking *kills* to hear him say it out loud.

"I'm sorry about the ring," I manage.

His eyes harden. "I'm sorry, too."

And then he leaves.

For the last time.

I slowly slide down to the floor, clutching the towel to my chest.

I cry until I'm lightheaded.

Chapter Thirty-Three
ELI

I move through the days in a fog. I know I'm working too much. Drinking too much.

Listening to too much Post Malone.

I just fucking hate everything right now. I came home from The Pearl the other night and saw that Olivia's car wasn't in its usual spot in the driveway.

I haven't seen it since.

Even if I hadn't noticed her missing car, I would still know she's gone back to New York early. The air is different. Charleston is suddenly sucked of every color. Every delight. Even the sky has changed. The early October sunshine has given way to an oily cloud cover that blankets the city.

Olivia literally took the light with her. Because taking my heart and my pride wasn't enough already.

The anger I feel towards this woman burns night and day in my chest. A furnace fueled by embarrassment and regret and self-loathing.

But what was I supposed to do? Was I just supposed to just lay down and roll over after finding another man's ring in her drawer? I recognize that things moved fast between Olivia and I. But when you know, you know.

I know Olivia is the one. She didn't feel the same.

End of story.

I need to let her go. It's stupid, burning up like this over a girl who doesn't want to commit to me. I just—

I can't fucking stand coming home to an empty house. Billy is morose. I am an insomniac. I spend my nights smoking and drinking. Watching shitty shows in my ever dwindling Netflix queue. I'm in the yoga studio every day, sometimes twice, grunting my way through class. I'm constantly working, going, *doing*. Anything to keep me from thinking about her.

To keep me thinking about the things she said. *I'm just a distraction to you. You used me.*

I drink some more. Stay away from my phone and the internet. The papers, too.

My hands have started to shake when I'm working in The Pearl's kitchen. My cooks are circumspect enough to not mention it. But I see the way they look at me. Pity in their eyes. I catch Naomi and Maria conferring in hushed tones in the locker room more than once, stopping abruptly when I appear.

But only when Luke comes in to drop off a crate of pie pumpkins does anyone confront me face to face.

It's a Friday afternoon. A little past two, but the kitchen is already bustling as we prepare for the weekend rush.

I'm turned away from the door, so I can't see him enter. But I know it's him by the low, judgmental whistle he lets out.

"Damn," Luke says. "Is he really makin' y'all listen to Post Malone?"

I can *hear* the eye roll in Maria's voice when she answers him.

"He's been playing 'I Fall Apart' on repeat for a week

now," she stage whispers. "I can't stand it anymore! For the love of God, help us, before I start dreaming about pasty white men with face tattoos."

Luke drops his crate of produce on the counter next to me, making me jump, and hits the power button on my portable speaker.

"Hey!" I snap, looking up from the tilefish I'm fileting. "Put that back on."

My stomach dips at the look in his blue eyes. He's trying to hide his surprise, but failing miserably at it.

I must look pretty close to death to scare Luke. He's seen me at my worst.

Shit, maybe this *is* my worst.

"No more Post Malone," Luke says firmly. "You look like hell, and you smell even worse. Go home, E."

I'd rather chew off my own arm than go home. The silence—the emptiness—it just makes me think of all the ways I've fucked up. Losing The Jam. Losing Olivia.

Work is the only thing keeping me sane.

"I'm fine," I growl, turning back to the fish. "We got a full house tonight. Kitchen needs me."

Luke takes a step forward so that he's in my vision. There's no getting away from him now.

"That's a fuckin' lie, and you know it. C'mon—I wanna talk to you outside."

Without waiting for a reply, he grabs my arm and drags me through the kitchen and out the back door. I blink at the onslaught of natural light, even though it's pretty gloomy for two in the afternoon. My head throbs.

Luke grabs a couple crates from beside the dumpster and sets them against the building. He pulls two cigars from his pocket.

Cohibas. My favorite.

He holds one out to me, along with a cutter and a stainless steel lighter.

Fuck this guy. He knows exactly how to get me to listen.

"Sit," he says, nodding at one of the crates.

I take the stuff he's holding out and, with a grunt, do as I'm told.

He sits beside me. We hang out in silence for a couple minutes while we light our cigars.

I take giant puffs. My mouth tingles, then becomes pleasantly numb.

If only all my other shit—heart, head, dick—would do the same.

"Was I right?" Luke says at last, plucking the cigar from his mouth.

I clear my throat. "Right about what?"

"What we talked about that night at The Spotted Wolf. That why you and Olivia broke up? Because you're feelin' like shit and you were using her to feel better?"

Shrugging, I intentionally release a cloud of smoke between us so Luke can't see my face.

"One of the reasons, yeah. But it's not like—it's not like I don't love her, Luke. Because I do. I am so fucking in love with her. Things were great between us. But then I found this engagement ring her ex had given her. This gorgeous ring that could've belonged to the fuckin' Queen of England for how big the damn thing was."

Luke's eyebrows jump.

"Yup," I say. "Point is, she said she was done with this guy—she turned down his proposal. But I didn't believe her. Why *wouldn't* she go back to a guy who gave her a ring like that? So I asked her to move in with me. You know, I made this grand, romantic gesture because that's what you do when you're in love."

Luke's eyebrows jump even higher. They're practically on the back of his head now.

"I know what you're thinking. And you wouldn't be wrong. Seein' that ring—it just made me feel so shitty about myself. If Olivia wants a ring like that, then I wanna be able to buy it for her. But I can't right now. I don't know if I'll ever be able to buy somethin' like that again. Her ex, though? He can. And that—it really kills me, Luke."

He claps me on the back. "Did you ask her if she even wanted a Queen-sized ring? She *did* turn the guy down."

"No," I say. "But I can't imagine she hated the thing."

"So you asked her to move in with you because if you couldn't give her a ring like that, you still wanted to give her *something*. You wanted to know if she'd really choose you—a crazy talented, honest, hardworking man who treated her so well she told you she loved you after knowing you for all of three weeks—over the small dicked douchecanoe who needed to propose with a gaudy ring to get her to say yes. And even *then* she said no."

I laugh, shaking my head. "Damn. When you say it, it sounds kinda dumb."

"That's because it is dumb. I think anyone lookin' in from the outside would see what I do. That y'all had this intense, crazy month together where you hid from the world and—er—*hung out* a lot. I don't doubt the things you shared and felt together were real. I don't doubt they were earth shattering."

"I hate euphemisms," I say glumly, tapping ash onto the blacktop.

"I hate you," Luke shoots back. "At least I do when you're bein' an idiot like you are right now. Listen. Y'all had this amazing month, but it was still just a month. Thirty one days. Asking someone to commit to you after such a short time is fuckin' wild, man. Even for you. You gotta give this girl time. You gotta make sure you want her for the right reasons, E.

Honestly? I think we both know you're clearly still grappling with the fallout from The Jam closing." When I open my mouth to protest, he holds up a hand. "Don't bullshit me. We been friends forever. I know you're hurting. You just won't admit it."

I feel a rush of emotion. It rises through my throat and lands in my eyes.

I close them, pulling at them with my thumb and finger. I'm starting to feel dizzy from the cigar. When was the last time I ate? I can't remember.

"What should I do?" I say quietly.

Luke puts a hand on my shoulder. "I want you to face this thing. It's time, E. We're all here to help you through it. And when you're ready—when you've learned to get back up on your own, without using other people as a crutch—*that's* when you go after your girl. Not a damn second before, you hear me? Because then you won't need her to move in with you to feel good about yourself. You'll be feelin' good all on your own. And that right there is the basis of a healthy relationship."

Tears are spilling out of my eyes now. I'm too tired to care. I let Luke see them, wiping them on my rumpled white chef's jacket.

Luke is right. Usually is. You wouldn't think a manwhore baseball player-slash-gardener would have much self-awareness. But my boy has it in spades.

I think about what he's saying. I asked—practically begged—Olivia to allow herself to be vulnerable with me. But I didn't allow myself to return the favor. To be vulnerable with her. And that, more than anything else, is what hurt our relationship.

I hate myself for letting it go so far.

"I'll try," I say. Then I scoff. "'Cause I'm not hurtin' enough as it is."

He gives my shoulder a squeeze. "You are stronger than you think, chef. It'll be worth it in the end. I promise. Think about it this way: you're gonna become the man Olivia deserves."

I nod, blinking. I want to ask him *how* I do this thing. How I begin the process of facing my failure and learning to accept it. But I know Luke. He'll tell me I need to figure it out on my own.

Which I do. I know that.

But I'm terrified.

I look up at the sound of tires crackling on the flinty pavement. A familiar, bright red Jetta zooms into view, coming to a stop a few feet in front of us.

"Is that Gracie?" I say, peering through the gloom.

Luke jumps to his feet, almost making *me* jump. For the first time, I notice that he's kinda dressed up.

Well. Dressed up for Luke, anyway. He's usually in beat up jeans and a dirt stained t-shirt. Unless we're at a bar, and then he's in a *clean* t-shirt. Today he's wearing nice jeans—dark denim, fitted—and a pristine white button down. A tag sticks out of the collar.

He shifts nervously on his feet as he tamps out his cigar on the side of the building.

I glance from Luke to Grace. Grace to Luke.

"It is Grace," Luke replies, smoothing his shirt tails. "We're, uh, meetin' for some coffee."

I pin him with a glare. "For fuck's sake, please tell me that's not another euphemism."

"No, not at all. I'm serious, E." He holds up his hands. "She asked me to try a new Colombian blend she's been working on."

"But you don't drink coffee."

Luke looks up at Grace and smiles. I look up to see her waving back.

"I do now."

Lord have mercy.

Luke is a good man. But he's definitely the love 'em and leave 'em type. The idea of him doing that to my baby sister—

Well. I don't like it. Not one fucking bit. If Grace is into that kind of thing, then fine. Well, not fine. I don't want her getting hurt. But she makes the rules. She's an independent, grown ass woman. She's smart. Way smarter than I ever was. She can do what she wants.

Only the Grace *I* know is a serial monogamist. Last I checked, she was still dating Nicholas.

So what the hell is she doing asking Luke out for coffee?

Grace rolls down her window, brow creasing with concern.

"How ya doing, E?"

"Been better," I reply, giving my cigar a solid pull.

I hear her car gears clank as she puts it in park. "Need me to take you home?"

"Nah." I wave her away. "Y'all go. I'll be okay."

"You sure?" Luke asks.

"I'm sure."

I meet Luke's eyes. Tell him, as best as I can without saying a word, to *keep it in his fucking pants*.

I've seen the thing. It's become something of an Urban Legend. I hear girls whispering about it in bars as we pass. *The Luke Lady Dagger*, they call it.

A lady dagger that leaves behind a trail of destruction and heartbreak wherever it goes.

Luke shoves his hands in his pockets. "Of course. Think about what I said, yeah? And call me if you need me, E. We're gonna get through this."

Easier said than done, I think to myself as I watch my sister and my best friend drive away. Together. To "get coffee."

Seriously. Has the world turned upside down over the past week? Or is it just me?

I go home. I skip my usual four fingers of bourbon and take a long, scalding hot shower instead.

And I try to stop.

Stop fighting my feelings. Stop lying to myself.

Stop holding it all in.

Giving in doesn't come easy. I've built up my walls nice and high. I feel the flood coming, pressing against my defenses. Rising up, filling my lungs.

Until finally, as I stand underneath the shower head, the giant tidal wave of all the things I've bottled up for so long comes crashing over my walls. The impact is immediate and devastating. I feel *everything*.

Disappointment.

Frustration.

Regret.

Panic.

Loneliness.

Fuck this sucks. It hurts so bad that I can't stay still.

I beat the outsides of my fists against the tile until I feel a crack in my left pinkie finger. I've suffered enough hand injuries over my career—burns, cuts, accidental amputations of fingertips—to know it's broken.

Fuck fuck fuck.

My first impulse is to dull the pain with a bottle of Jack Daniels. But by the time I get out of the shower, I feel wrung out. Too exhausted to get drunk, or even go downstairs.

I've hit a new low.

All I can do is collapse into bed. I fall into a drowsy half-sleep, waking with a start whenever my brain conjures a fresh round of panicked thoughts to torture me with. It happens over and over. All night.

I worry The Pearl is going to fail next. I worry about the cooks and wait staff and bartenders I had to let go. I worry about their futures, and I worry about mine.

I hadn't realized how tied up my self-worth is in being successful. Here I was, preaching the importance of fulfillment and passion to Olivia, telling her I valued my convictions over money and fame, when part of me obviously *does* value those things.

The next morning, I call my sister, and then I call a therapist. I throw out all my bourbon. Go to yoga.

I don't know if I'll ever be the kind of man Olivia deserves. But if I need to, I'm gonna die trying.

Chapter Thirty-Four
OLIVIA

The drive back to Ithaca goes by too quickly.

I don't want it to end. Because when it does, I have to burn my old life down so I can start a new one.

I am scared out of my mind. Mostly because I know I am going to hurt people I care about. All my life, I've tried very hard to *please* everyone. That was who I was—the people pleaser. I got so much praise for being easy going. For not rocking the boat or causing trouble or being difficult.

I am about to be very difficult. And while I feel confident that, in the end, I'll be glad I chose to prioritize my happiness, it's still going to suck crushing other people's.

I call Ted to let him know I'm on my way—I plan to swing by and grab some things before I go stay at my parents' house. Just hearing his voice on the phone was enough to send me into a tailspin of doubt and guilt.

I drive and I cry and I don't eat a thing because my insides are in knots. I feel like I'm going to be sick the whole way. A voice inside me asks *if you're making the right choice, why does it hurt so much?*

Doesn't help that I can't stop thinking about Eli. The

argument we had was horrible. I replay it over and over inside my head. I regret not telling him about the fucking ring. I begin to think that I was a coward, too, for hiding that piece of my story from him.

I'm not sure if I'll ever come to terms with the mistakes I've made. It's such a hard thing, forgiving myself for not wanting the beautiful life I had in New York.

Forgiving myself for wanting *more*.

I want Eli, too. I miss him. Badly. But he wants commitment. He wants *the end*. And I'm only at the beginning of my story.

I forgot how quiet it is in small town New York. I feel like I'm a million miles from the energy and bustle of Charleston.

Ted is waiting for me at the door when I arrive.

He's smiling. Like I've come here to beg him to take me back. Not to return his ring.

Clearly something weird is going on.

He lopes down the front steps of our house—it's prettier than I remember, very New England with cedar shake siding and a gabled roof—and opens my car door, holding it while I climb out.

"I've missed you," he says, kissing my cheek. The citrusy smell of his cologne fills my head. So different from the potent, smoky scent of Eli's skin. "C'mon inside. I just decanted a nice bottle of Bordeaux."

I blink. "Ted. I told you I'm just swinging by to grab my stuff. I'm not staying."

He meets my eyes. Slides his hands into his pockets.

"Are you sure?"

"I'm sure," I reply. When he doesn't move, I ask, "What's going on?"

Ted shifts uncomfortably on his feet. "I thought you were coming back because you changed your mind. Clearly you're not staying in Charleston, so..."

I just stare at him, too angry—too bewildered—to speak for several beats.

"Ted," I begin slowly. "I came back to get my things. Like I told you. I have plans to return to Charleston at the end of the semester. I'm not staying."

"I know you said that," he says, a red flush creeping up his neck onto his face. "But I didn't think you were serious. C'mon, Olivia. You ran away to write a romance novel, for God's sake. What kind of future does that afford you? It doesn't even compare to the future we have here. The future we have *together*. I still want to marry you. And I think you want to marry me, too. Please say yes. One word. It's easy."

For several beats I just stare at him, the realization hitting me like a ton of bricks. So this is why Ted was okay with me seeing other people during our break. This is why he was so cool when I broke up with him for good.

He thought *I wasn't being serious*.

He assumed I'd be too scared, that I'd miss him too much, to ever be with someone else, or to stay in Charleston for good.

He didn't think I'd have the balls to do it.

I'm gripped by a sudden rush of anger. How incredibly condescending of him to assume such a thing about me. Ted has always been confident in himself. But I never thought he'd be so arrogant about me.

Maybe I was scared before. But I'm not scared now. I didn't come all this way for *easy*.

I didn't come back all this way just to end up where I started.

Looking away, I duck back into the car and dig the ring box out of my purse. I hold it out to him and meet his gaze.

"My answer is no," I say firmly. "And trust me when I say I am dead serious about not staying. Now if you'll excuse me, I need to go grab some things from inside."

I spend the night at my parents' house. They're stricken when they hear the news.

"You gave it back?" my mother gasps. "That flawless, gorgeous four-carat diamond ring? Are you crazy?"

My dad shakes his head, grabbing another beer from the fridge. "You're going to regret this, Olivia. You're making a mess of your life. I don't understand it."

Just wait until they hear that I'm quitting my job and moving to South Carolina to teach and write steamy romance. They'll be horrified by the ridiculousness of it. And I'll smile at the awesomeness.

After I went to see Ted, I stopped by my office to hand in my resignation. Like my parents, my boss was flabbergasted I'd give up the tenure I'd worked nearly a decade to get to *possibly* teach creative writing halfway across the country.

"How about you finish out the semester here?" she said. "If you're still sure you want to quit in December, then I'll accept this resignation. Deal?"

I agreed, but I already know I'll be handing in the same resignation letter the day my students finish their final exams. I may not have Eli to go back to in Charleston. But I do have a whole new life waiting for me there whenever I decide to return. A life I am very excited to begin.

Later that night, I dig my laptop out of my bag and Google "Charleston SC apartment rentals". My budget—and the places within that price range—are tiny. But I admit I feel a little thrill at the idea of having a place of my own. I get high thinking about what my new life is going to be like living there.

Then I crash, hard, when I think about Eli not being a part of it. I glance at my phone, half hoping to see a text from him. A missed call. It hurts that he hasn't reached out, especially after the things he said. I'm going through a lot at the moment—calling off engagements, quitting jobs, breaking my parents' hearts—and I could really use a little moral support right now. Eli felt like my North Star when I was in Charleston. A reminder that I was always headed in the right direction.

But maybe I need to go through this on my own.

Maybe I need to learn to be my own North Star.

As much as it sucks, I want to know I'm making this decision because it's what I want. Not what Eli wants. Not what my lusty pants feelings want.

What *I* want. Truly. Deep down.

Doing this by myself will hurt. It will be lonely and hard.

But I'd like to think it will be worth it.

I'm also not sure if I'm ready to forgive him for the way he behaved. My eyes still well up when I remember the look on his face when he said *I'm done waiting on you*. That was unkind. Unfair, too.

Maybe Eli's not the guy I thought he was.

Sighing, I close the internet and open *My Enemy the Earl*. I've missed these characters over the past few days—with everything going on, I haven't been able to work on them.

This has been a difficult book to write. Whoever said "do something you'll love and you won't work a day in your life" was full of shit. Writing always feels like work to me. It requires extreme focus. It's often boring. But when I wake up and read through what I wrote the previous day, I'm bowled over by a sense of joy and fulfillment I feel all the way to my toes.

I wrote this. *I* came up with these characters. This story. I'm so proud of it, and so scared of it at the same time. I recognize writing a book and selling it require two distinct skill sets. But I hope to get a good grip on both.

I make a note on my digital calendar to email Kathryn Score, the professor-slash-romance author Julia introduced me to down in Charleston. Then I get to work on Gunnar and Cate.

Cate made the most of what she was given. She'd thought her family was all she needed. They filled her days and her heart. But recently—since she'd kissed Gunnar beneath the stars at Castle West—something had changed. Something inside her shifted, was different. Like a light shone inside the dark cavities of her heart, revealing a starkness, a bleed, she hadn't noticed before.

And now that bleed consumed her.

Chapter Thirty-Five
ELI

I can't get out of bed.

A week passes. Another.

I have never been laid low like this before.

Then again, I've never failed like this before, either. Losing a restaurant—a dream—and a dream girl all at once is not for the faint of heart.

But I don't shy away from feeling it. The pain. I let it pin me to the mattress. I let it keep me there, sweating and praying. Swearing and hoping.

Friends come and go in a steady, quiet stream, leaving behind casseroles and bottles of ibuprofen and books. Grace tries to take Billy, but he refuses to leave my side.

I appreciate the moral support. I get so lost inside my head—so twisted up—but Billy is always there to bring me back to the present. The little yelps he makes when he has nightmares. The way he licks my face in the mornings. How he wolfs down whatever bits of casserole I can't finish.

He's my lifeline to the real world. Without him and my therapist, I'd be lost.

It's fucking weird not being at work. I've never taken

more than a few days off at a time. I want to check in. I want to *go* in. Lose myself in the screaming bustle of the kitchen on a Saturday night. It'd be so easy.

But that would defeat the whole purpose of this little sabbatical I'm taking. I'm dealing with my fuck ups all on my own. So I leave instructions with Maria to call me in the event of an emergency. Otherwise, she's in charge.

She hasn't called once. Knowing that my kitchen is in such capable hands is both a relief and a disappointment. I'm not as essential as I thought I was.

Not as important.

Which begs the question: who the hell am I outside of Chef Elijah Jackson?

I glance at the stack of pages on my nightstand. *My Enemy the Earl*. All two-hundred some odd pages of it, marked up with my notes. Olivia left it here the last time she spent the night. I've re-read it countless times since. Made more notes. Thought about possible endings. Possible sequels.

Reading Olivia's beautiful words makes me miss her so much I get downright rage-y about it. And hard. I'm angry with myself for chasing such a passionate, beautiful person out of my life.

For being such a fucking idiot. I feel horrible about the things I said to her. Things I can't ever take back.

I want to call her. Want to apologize and do my best to win her back. But I'm getting glimmers of a new understanding. And I understand that any reunion we may have has to be on her terms. I'm bettering myself for her as best as I can. Facing my fears rather than distracting myself from them. If she's still not ready for me whenever our paths cross again, though...

Well.

I'll deal with it. Just like I'm dealing with my failure right now.

But this editing thing is one of the few bright spots in my darkness. Who knows if I'm actually any good at it or not. But that could potentially be a fun little side hustle. Maybe I could edit cookbooks or some shit like that. I have no interest in writing my own. I'd rather be cooking than *writing* about cooking. But I like the ritual of sitting down with a manuscript and uncapping my pen and focusing my mind on words, sentences, ideas.

Or maybe I just like focusing on Olivia and how she's totally going to knock it out of the park if—when—she publishes this book.

Jesus, I'm dying to call her. I miss hearing her voice. I want to know where she is and what she's doing and if she really gave that ring back to her ex.

But I'm sticking to Luke's advice. I need to figure my own shit out before I give my grovel a go.

Olivia hasn't written that part yet in her book. I would love to know what Gunnar does to win Cate back. Might give me some clues as to how I can win Olivia back, too.

Just another thing I have to figure out on my own.

Olivia

I finish the semester in Ithaca. Just like I planned, I hand in my resignation the same day my students take their final exams. This time, my boss accepts it.

The day after Christmas, I pack my car, say goodbye to my parents, and drive back to Charleston.

My to-do list when I get into town is overwhelming.

But I tackle it one item at a time from the bed in Julia's carriage house, where we're both staying while I figure everything out. She's ecstatic I'll be living permanently in Charleston.

First things first: my employment situation. I set up a meeting with the head of the English Department at The College of Charleston. When I find out there's a waiting list of students for their creative writing classes, I convince him to not only create an overflow class, but to let me teach it, too. I also needle him a bit on my commercial fiction class idea. He says he'll consider putting it on the schedule for the fall semester.

Teaching the class pays next to nothing. I knew it wouldn't be much, but I'm still shocked by just how low the number is. I'll be teaching as an adjunct professor, too, which means no tenure, and pretty much zero benefits. But the department head sounded hopeful about expanding my role in the creative writing MFA program going forward. And then of course I have whatever books I manage to write and publish.

In the meantime, I have my savings to fall back on. It's a decent chunk of change. Enough to buy me at least six months of solid writing and adjunct teaching time.

The money makes me see my old job in a new light. Maybe this is why I worked a job I wasn't crazy about for so long. To save up, quit, and work a job I love.

The whole thing still feels very uncertain. The control freak in me rears her head in the middle of the night every so often, keeping me from sleep. I feel vulnerable. Like my skin's peeled back, revealing every vein, every organ. Every dark wish and desire. Some days, just walking around town is excruciating.

But as much as I worry, I also feel this ever expanding sense of excitement.

I'm doing this.

I am actually taking steps to honor who I am and make my dream come true.

Although it would be nice to make that dream come true with Elijah by my side.

I am terrified of running into him. I'm not ready yet. I want to figure out my new normal down here by myself. It feels important to do that. I fell in love with my life in this city before I fell in love with Eli. I'm determined to *stay* in love with it, whether or not it includes gorgeous, tatted up men who read romance.

I find an adorable apartment on the second floor of a circa 1880 Charleston single house on Queen Street. It's right on the edge of the French Quarter. It's tiny and quirky and it gets incredible natural light in the late afternoons—my favorite time to write. The sloping porch faces St. Philip's Church. You can just glimpse its stuccoed spire over the roof of the house next door.

Julia and I find an elegant writing desk with a busted leg at a store in Mount Pleasant one day while we're antiquing. The owner sells it to me for a song. Julia fixes the leg, and I put the desk underneath the wavy glass window in my shoebox-sized bedroom. I write there on days I don't feel like going out.

I sell my car and buy a mint green bike.

Every Friday, I ride it to Kathryn's house on the edge of the College of Charleston's campus. She hosts the Charleston Writers' Club's weekly meeting. Over gin cocktails and cheese straws, I pick every brain I can about agents, contracts, traditional versus indie publishing. Some of the people belonging to the brains I pick become friends. They invite me to their homes, and I am continually impressed by their warm hospitality. Also by how much they can *drink*.

Charleston is definitely a boozy town. And I don't mind that one bit.

I start teaching my class. I love my students and my subject matter right off the bat. The vibe in the department down here is much more relaxed than it was at Ithaca.

I visit Louise at Rainbow Row Books often. We set up some signings with a few big names in romance—friends of other writer friends—and lay the groundwork for that romance book club we chatted about.

When I'm not writing or teaching, I'm walking. When I'm not walking, I'm meeting up with friends, or faculty from the college. As the trees begin to blossom and winter bursts into spring with crystal clear blue skies for days, I settle into my new life.

It is wonderful. Not perfect. I cry my way through the slog of writing the last chapters of Gunnar and Cate's story. I cry again when I get quotes for health insurance.

But life here is still dreamy in so many ways. Still *better* and more me. I don't know if it's the spring air, or the fact that I finally finished *My Enemy the Earl*, but every morning I wake up and feel this searing sense of freedom. It's open windows and freshly brewed coffee and nothing but *writing all the words* and *teaching all the words* on my to-do list for that day.

Some days, I almost feel guilty. Like I'm getting away with something for actually liking the person I'm becoming.

But then I think, *wait a second*. If I don't deserve to feel this way, then who does? No one?

I fought so hard to get to this place. I know I still have a lot of fighting to do. But I'm not afraid to work hard if it means feeling like *this* most mornings.

My nights, though, are a different story.

That's when the longing hits me. I thought by now, months later, I'd stop missing Eli so much. Especially after that last conversation we had. He was so awful. So *mean*.

But I only miss him more. I sit on my porch with a glass

of wine and look out over the city, wondering where he is in it. The Pearl, most likely. Holding court in the kitchen, looking handsome as hell in his chef's jacket and slicked back hair.

He'll pop up in the local news every so often. I can't stand to look at his picture in the articles. That smile and the scruff and those *eyes*.

Makes me want to see him again, despite how awful he was the last time we spoke. But what if he's still not over losing The Jam? What if he *is* over me? There has to be a reason why he hasn't contacted me. Eli's not the type to play games. If he wanted to see me, he'd reach out.

And he hasn't.

I drink my wine and I watch the sun set. My thoughts are a jumble. My neck and shoulders ache from another long day hunched over my laptop.

Yoga classes aren't exactly in my budget at the moment. But maybe I could take just one. Just to clear my head and work these knots out of my neck.

I wonder if Eli still takes classes at Yoga First.

I shove the thought from my head. I'm practicing for myself. And if he happens to be there?

I guess I'll find out if I really want to see him or not.

Chapter Thirty-Six
ELI

I am back in the kitchen. Worse for the wear. But I am semi-functional, and I no longer play Post Malone on repeat. That has to count for something.

I am also seeing glimmers of my old self. The man who wasn't afraid. Who had character and conviction and a fucking wicked way with bacon fat.

He pops up more and more as the months pass. By Gracie's birthday at the end of February, I'm laughing again. The loss of The Jam still stings. I struggle not to fall into a black pit of depression whenever I think about it. But time is helping. I wake up every morning a little steadier on my feet. A little more confident. I feel my wounds healing.

Every wound except the one Olivia left.

That goddamn thing smarts and bleeds and *hurts* nonstop.

"So are you gonna call her or what?" Grace asks one morning when she brings a pound of her latest Ethiopian blend to my house.

I don't look up from the pot of grits I'm working on. "Can't."

"Why not?" Grace says, putting her first finger on the

bridge of her *very* loud glasses and pushing them up on her nose. She sits down on a stool at the island. "We're proud of you for taking the time—"

"We?" This time I do look up.

My sister blushes. I notice her eyes look…happier. Lit up.

"Yeah. Luke and I."

"I didn't know there was a 'Luke and you.'"

"There isn't. We're just—um. Friends. Good friends." She clears her throat. "Anyway. Like I was saying—we're proud of you for taking the time to work on your own stuff. But it's been *months*, E. You're clearly still torn up about Olivia. We—"

"You and Luke?" I tease, cocking a brow.

"Jesus, would you let that go? Yes, *Luke and I* think you've done the work on your own, and now you're ready to be with her for the right reasons. I mean, come on, E. You were just telling me the other day how you're drinking less, and sleeping more, and really coming to terms with everything that's happened over the past six months. Just the fact that you're *talking* about that stuff tells me you've changed."

I give the grits a stir, then set a lid on the pot. "That may be true. But the ball is in Olivia's court. I pushed her way too hard. She wasn't ready for what I wanted, and she balked. Understandably. I can't push her again. She's got to be the one who comes to me because *she's* ready. Not the other way around."

Grace furrows her brow. "I get that. And I like how cautious you're being. It's definitely important to take her feelings into consideration. But what if she's waiting for you to reach out? Like you said, *you* were the one who pushed *her* away. I know you're the romance novel expert these days. But doesn't that make the groveling your responsibility in this scenario?"

I tug a hand through my hair, groaning.

"Yes and no," I say. "I just—my gut's tellin' me to go gently. I do miss Olivia. And I do want to be with her. Which means my grovel's got to be perfectly timed and perfectly executed. I gotta hit it outta the goddamn park, Gracie. The timing's gotta be just right. Only when she's ready."

She purses her lips and nods. "All right. That's fair. But how're you gonna know she's ready if you don't talk to her?"

That's the million dollar question. I've heard from friends that they've seen Olivia around town. Which means she *did* give her ex his ring back. Just like she said she would.

Christ, I'm a piece of shit. A faithless, stupid piece of shit.

Apparently she's teaching creative writing at the college. Some small, mean part of me wanted to stalk her usual haunts so I could "accidentally" run into her. But that's wrong. I've never played games like that, and I don't plan to start now. So I've just stuck to my usual routine in the hopes of crossing paths that way.

"I don't know," I say, shrugging. "I guess if it's meant to be, it will be."

"I kind of hate that idea," Grace replies. "I'm a woman of action myself."

I grin. Isn't that the truth. I swear my sister came out of the womb with a planner in one hand and a cup of coffee in the other.

"I hate it too. But I'm kind of at a loss right now. If enough time passes—well. I'll reassess. In the meantime, I'm gonna go slow."

"As slow as you're bein' with this breakfast?" Grace sits up on her stool. "I'm starving."

I cock a brow. "You've never been a big breakfast person."

There it is again—that blush.

Something's up.

Not that it's any of my business. But I find myself hoping that *something* isn't sleeping with Luke.

"I've been…exercising a lot lately. My appetite has gotten, like, huge."

Oh Lord.

I give her a look. "There something you wanna tell me, baby sis?"

"I'm not a baby."

"Neither am I. Tell me why you got stars in your eyes."

Grace pulls back, disguising her embarrassment as indignation. "Work is going really well. Some awesome opportunities are coming up. I'm just excited, that's all."

"Nu-uh." I point my whisk at her. "Don't use that line on me. You always got awesome opportunities coming up. You know you're only makin' me more suspicious by blowing me off, right?"

"I'm not—oh, wait, Eli, your grits are boiling over."

I turn around and curse when I see creamy white grits pouring down the sides of the pot and landing in the burner with a *hiss*. I turn down the heat and lift the lid, giving the grits a calming stir. At least they smell good. I'll add in a little cheese, some scallions, and all will be right in the world again.

Scratch that. All will be right when Olivia is sitting on a stool beside Grace, cutting me hungry glances while the two of them poke fun at me.

I can't wait for that day. Although truth be told, I am starting to feel a twinge of doubt that it will ever come. Maybe I fucked up too bad.

Maybe Olivia will never be ready.

Blind faith that I'm wrong is the only thing keeping me going at this point.

Right now, faith is all I got.

I'm not usually late to class. Yoga has been a big part of my healing process—I'm in the studio three times a week, minimum, since Olivia left—and I like to get there early. Give myself time to land on my mat before practice begins.

But I spent the morning fixing a kitchen crisis. Our fish vendor ghosted with zero explanation. Kind of a big deal, considering we're doing a seafood tasting this week. I had to call in the cavalry. With Maria's help, we were able to piece together what we needed from a motley crew of local fishermen, generous restaurant owners, and sneaky sous chefs.

Crisis averted. At least until tomorrow.

By the time I pull into the parking lot at Yoga First, my usual 11 A.M. class is just beginning. Thankfully it's not crowded, and I'm able to nab a spot by the door at the back of the studio.

Even though everyone else is already on their sun salutations, I take my time warming up. Child's pose. Downward facing dog. I melt my heels to the ground and lift my belly to the sky, giving my hamstrings a good stretch. Lordy are they tight.

I move into my first sun salutation.

I get on my feet, sinking into warrior one, and that's when I see her.

Her.

Olivia.

I feel a sudden, sharp throb inside my chest.

It's definitely her. I'd know that wild dark hair anywhere. Those long, muscular legs. They glisten with a fine sheen of sweat.

I just stand there like an idiot, stuck in warrior one as I watch her move through her poses. Totally unaware of my presence behind her.

She's thinner than she was. Her arms tremble as she hovers in low plank. I haven't seen her in the studio since she left back in October. Has she not been practicing at all? Or has she just not been practicing here?

My pulse thrums inside my skin. It's too hot in here. I'm too close to her.

Too far.

Longing hits me like a freight train.

Jesus, *I miss her*.

I don't realize she's caught me staring until it's too late. She's in downward facing dog, looking at me between her legs. Her eyes are so blue.

So fucking blue.

My heart seizes when they widen. I can hear the force of her exhalation from across the room. She falls to her knees, and the instructor goes over to her, gently rocking her hips as Olivia settles into child's pose.

Legs shaking, I do the same. There's no way I can practice with her in the same room. I'm gripped by the wild idea of rolling up my mat, grabbing Olivia, and getting the hell out of here so we can talk.

I wanna talk to her so bad.

But talking is a big no-no during practice. And it's important I don't overstep my boundaries with her. Me wordlessly plucking her from a yoga class she may really, really need is definitely overstepping.

I try not to stare at her for the remainder of the class. I'm worried I'll combust and/or pass out, for one thing. For another, I don't want to fuck up her practice. I know first-hand how a great class can turn around an otherwise shitty day.

Fuck me, it's just hard to keep my eyes on my own mat. I feel like it's some kind of test devised by Satan himself. I *feel* her presence. Like she's the center of the universe, and everything—the floor and my feelings and my heart—is pulled in by the force of her gravity.

I wonder if she feels it, too. Or if she's moved on in a way I haven't.

I'm starting to think I'll never move on.

Approximately one hundred years later, class finally ends. I've had sixty minutes to think about it, but I still have no idea what I'm going to say to Olivia when I approach her. Or if I should approach her at all.

I want to wait for her to come to me. That's how this is supposed to go, because I'm not pushing her again, remember? But I also don't want to be rude. And what if this is the last time I see her for another four months? I can't fucking bear the thought.

With shaking hands, I roll up my mat and grab my water bottle. Sweat drips down my temples onto my chest as I stand up.

"Hey."

I nearly jump at the sound of Olivia's voice. I turn around, and immediately my heart melts. She's a fucking mess. Hair sticking up. Red face.

She's *smiling*.

I have never seen a more beautiful woman in my whole goddamn life.

Stay cool stay cool stay cool.

"Olivia," I say, pulse beating a drum inside my ears. "I'm—wow. I'm really glad to see you."

She looks at me for a long beat. I look back. Something moves between us. Something *good*.

Letting out a breath, she tucks her rolled up mat underneath her arm.

"How have you been?" she says. Her voice trembles a little.

She's nervous, too. Good sign? Bad?

"I'm okay," I reply. "What about you?"

She nods. "I'm okay."

We're looking at each other again. After a stretch of uncomfortable silence, we both laugh at the same time.

"Sorry," she says. "It's just...been a while since I've seen you, Eli."

Four months, thirteen days, and one-point-five hours. Not that I'm counting.

"How's the book coming?" I say.

"It's done," she replies, brightening. "Gunnar and Cate nearly killed me toward the end. But I clawed my way through the story. I actually just sent it to my ARC team this morning."

I arch a brow. "ARC team? I don't know what that is, but if it has something to do with *My Enemy the Earl*, then I want in."

Olivia laughs again, and I worry I'm going to melt into a literal puddle of goo at her feet. I love the sound of her laugh. Love the way it touches her eyes.

"It's a team of reviewers you send ARCs to—advanced reader copies. The thinking is that bloggers and reviewers who like the book will post glowing reviews of it, and that will help spread the word about it before publication."

I nod, impressed. "Word of mouth is the best kind of marketing there is."

"Exactly."

"Did you decide to go through a publishing house? Or are you publishing it yourself?"

"I'm indie all the way," she says, proudly. "I've done a lot of research. Traditional and indie publishing each have their pluses and minuses. But I like the freedom I get with self-publishing. Plus it gives me a good excuse to hone my marketing skills."

As if this woman could get any sexier.

"'Cause you're the boss."

"Yup."

I shift on my feet. I resist the urge to ask her out for a cup of coffee or something. She's gotta be the one to make that call.

I find myself praying that she will.

"Welp," I say. "Congratulations. I'm happy for you. I can't wait to find out how the story ends—you know I've been a fan of Gunnar and Cate's from the very beginning."

Olivia bites her lip, her eyes moving over my face. I get the feeling she's weighing the scales in her head, too. Wondering what to say next.

"Release day is next Thursday," she says at last. "I'm doing a signing over at Rainbow Row Books to celebrate. You should come."

My heart sputters inside my chest.

I don't want to read too much—

Fuck it. I'm gonna read too much into her invitation whether I'm supposed to or not.

"I'd love to," I reply. "I'll get the details from Louise."

Olivia's smile deepens. "Great."

"Great. I look forward to seeing you again."

We say our goodbyes, and then I pretend that I have to talk to the instructor about something so Olivia can leave without me awkwardly following her out.

My mind is already racing. I can't let this opportunity slip through my fingers. I'm shaking I'm so excited. And so nervous.

Time for the grovel. The grand gesture.

I need to talk to Gracie. And Luke. And Louise. And anyone else who can help.

This has to be perfect.

Chapter Thirty-Seven
OLIVIA

I straighten the stack of paperbacks on the table at Rainbow Row Books for the millionth time. I can't get over how gorgeous they are. I splurged and hired a well-known cover artist for *My Enemy the Earl*. She did a fantastic job. The cover is just colorful and different enough to stand out, but historical romance readers will recognize some familiar elements: gorgeous, scantily clad couple, cursive script, and a sweeping, sunlit background.

I also can't get over that these paperbacks *exist*. Touching my book—all three hundred and eighteen pages of it, in the flesh—is as surreal and joyous an experience as I fantasized it would be. I'm so damn proud of it.

Which means I am also terribly, terribly nervous about sending it out into the world.

"You think I brought too many books?" I ask Louise.

She looks up from the cheese plate she's unwrapping and grins. "I think you brought just enough."

"Sorry," I say, smoothing my sweaty palms down the front of my dress. "I'm just worried. What if no one comes?"

Louise tosses the plastic wrap in the trash and gets to

work uncorking a bottle of my favorite $4.49 Trader Joe's Pinot Grigio.

"You're going to do great." She yanks the cork free with a grunt. "And I don't think you need to worry about people coming."

I resist the urge to grab the bottle from Louise's hands and take it to the face. I bet I could finish the thing in less than sixty seconds.

I flip through a paperback instead. "But I'm brand new. No one knows who I am."

"All the right people in this town know who you are," Louise replies easily. "As I'm sure you've discovered, word spreads fast down here. I promise you don't need to worry about attendance."

She pours wine into a plastic cup and hands it to me. I notice she's wearing a small, knowing smile.

"Louise." I take the wine. "Do you know something I don't?"

Wagging her eyebrows, she zips her fingers across her lips. "I don't know a thing. I am merely your assistant tonight."

My insides do a somersault, all at once. I gulp at my wine.

Because the idea that Elijah might come wasn't nerve wracking enough. Now lots of people are apparently coming to my humble little signing.

Save my soul.

Speaking of Eli. I almost had a heart attack when I saw him last week in class. He looked good. So, so good. And tired.

I wanted him to invite me somewhere. His bed, preferably. I wanted to climb in his truck and go back to his house and have hard, dirty sex over and over again until we were too spent to keep going. Then we'd lie there and talk. Figure out how we can make a relationship work.

Because I really, really want to be with him. I've had a lot of time to think about it. A lot of time to be on my own. And as much as I love my life as it is—and I love it, I do—I'd love it even more if he were in it. I miss the way his mind works. I miss his hands. His food.

His unwavering support of my dreams.

People start to trickle in. One by one. Then in pairs.

Then all of the sudden it's like the floodgates open, and people pour into the bookstore, crowding it with heat and noise and requests for autographed copies of my book.

I can't believe how many people come. I sit at my table and sign copy after copy of *My Enemy the Earl*. I take pictures with readers and chat with a local blogger. It's not long before my supply of paperbacks starts to run dangerously low.

But then Louise appears with a fresh box of them, which she unpacks on the table.

"From an anonymous fan," she explains with that knowing smile. "Here, let me get you more wine."

I sit and I sign, too bewildered—too overwhelmed—to really process what is going on. An anonymous fan? But who? My first thought is my parents. But while they're coming around, slowly, to the idea of me becoming an author, I know they would never encourage me like this.

Louise then? One of my friends from the writers' club or the university?

I stop to change Sharpies when my first one dries up. From the corner of my eye, I see someone step up to the table.

"Hi there!" I say, uncapping the Sharpie and grabbing a book. "Who can I make this out to?"

"Elijah Jackson, if y'please," a man says.

My heart stutters. My stomach dips.

That growly voice. That velvety accent.

That ridiculously perfect name.

I glance up and see Eli looking down at me.

I know I invited him to come. But I'm still so taken off guard by his hugeness and his smile and his searing eyes that I drop the Sharpie, my hands overtaken by a violent tremor. For a second, I worry I'm going to be sick.

He looks delectable. Good enough to fucking eat. He's trimmed his hair since I saw him last week. It's still wet, and the ends are boyishly curled in the humidity. (Only in Charleston would it be humid at the end of March.)

I can smell him. I have a full body reaction to that smoky sandalwood smell. My skin lights up and my sex clenches and I'm overwhelmed by a wave of longing so powerful it knocks the wind out of me.

He's here.

Holy shit, he's here, and he wants me to sign a copy of the book he helped me to write.

The book that has changed my life in so many insanely rewarding ways.

"You came," I breathe.

His eyes get warm. Soft. "'Course I came. Wouldn't miss your debut for the world."

My mouth has gone dry.

"Nice turn out you got here," he says, looking around the store. "Looks like I'm not Cate and Gunnar's only fan."

"But you were the first," I reply, and I suddenly feel like I'm going to cry. "Which is the most important fan."

He looks at me and smiles.

I have to look away.

Sign the book. Right. He's here for the book.

My hand shakes so badly that I can hardly write. *To Elijah—Thank you. For everything. This book happened because of you. Xx, Olivia.*

"Thanks," he says when I hand it to him, meeting my eyes. "I'm proud of you, Yankee girl."

His words wrap around my heart and squeeze.

I manage to give him a tight smile. "I would have never kept writing if it wasn't for you, Eli. I mean it—thank you for everything. Thank you for being *you*."

He taps the book against his palm, once. Twice. He wants to say something, I know he does. I can tell by the gleam in his hazel eyes.

Eyes that are currently locked on my face.

Oh, I want him to *say it*.

But then he draws a breath and straightens. "Don't want to take you away from your fans." He glances over his shoulder. "I'll be hangin' out with Louise if you get a breather. Although that doesn't seem likely. There are a lot of people here."

"I know," I say. "I have no clue where they came from, but..."

Eli looks at me, and I'm struck by an idea.

No way.

He didn't.

Did he?

Before I can ask him, he's turning away.

"I'll look out for Max and Jane's story next," he says, referring to secondary characters in *My Enemy the Earl* who clearly wanted to suck each other's faces.

And then he disappears into the crowd.

A young woman approaches the table and smiles, clutching my book in her hands.

I manage a smile. "Thank you so much for coming. I'm Olivia. What's your name?"

Chapter Thirty-Eight
OLIVIA

It's well past closing time when I sign the last of the books.

My hand is cramped. My mouth feels tacky from talking so much to so many people. I'm wiped.

And blissed out beyond belief.

My first signing for my first book was a success. I lost count of how many readers told me they heard "amazing things" about *My Enemy the Earl*. I don't know how they heard about it.

But I have a good idea.

I make a quick trip to the bathroom. When I come out, I look around the room at the few remaining people. I see Louise, popping the last of the cheese into her mouth. Eli's sister Grace, getting awfully cozy with Luke in the Nonfiction section.

But I don't see Eli.

"I don't know where he went," Grace says when I ask, glancing up from the book on gardening Luke holds. Then she gives me a pointed look. "But you should definitely find him. He wants to talk to you."

Luke gives her a gentle nudge.

"Fine." She rolls her eyes. "*Maybe* my brother *quite possibly* would like to have a *potential* conversation with you. But only if you want to, too."

I look from Luke to Grace and back again. They stare at me expectantly, like I'm supposed to know what the hell they're asking me to do.

"Right," I say at last. "I'll go find him."

I get stopped by a few people on their way out of the shop.

They open the door. And I catch a glimpse of a broad-shouldered figure in the parking lot. I see the end of a cigar light up. An ember in the darkness. A beat later, I'm hit by the earthy scent of tobacco.

I nearly sag with relief. I didn't miss him. Eli is still here.

"Louise," I call over my shoulder. "I'll be right back."

"Don't hurry!" she replies.

I can hear the smile in her voice.

I step onto the porch and quietly make my way down the front steps. The parking lot is dark. It takes a second for my eyes to adjust.

And then he's there. Enormous man standing beside an equally enormous pickup truck. The smoke from his cigar creates a haze between us.

I feel his eyes on me. My nipples prickle to life.

Crossing my arms, I move toward him, the gravel crunching beneath my boots. I stop a few feet away, scared that I'll reach for him if I get any closer. And I have no idea where we stand. Or if he still feels for me what I feel for him.

"It was you, wasn't it?" I say. "You're the anonymous fan who told everyone about my book and bought extra copies for me to sign."

The tip of his cigar lights up again as he pulls on it. His eyes are pools of green. So translucent they seem to glow.

My God he looks so handsome. Standing beside his truck.

Dark hair, plaid shirt. Juicy lips and beard and intelligent eyes.

My knees begin to wobble with a familiar weakness.

"I didn't force anyone to come," he says. "People just trust my taste. They know I read a lot. So when they asked me what great books I've read lately, I mentioned yours."

I bite my lip. "You also mentioned the signing."

His lips curl into a smirk. "Well, yeah. I had to mention the signing. Your book's so good that I told them they'd want a signed copy. I said I had the pleasure of reading a first draft and that it was one of the best romances I've read. And I've read a *lot* of romance."

His eyes flick over my body, once.

The space between us thrums.

My eyes fill with tears as a laugh escapes my lips. "Of course you have."

"Olivia."

Eli puts his cigar on the edge of the truck bed and takes a step toward me. My body leaps at the tidy determination of his movements. I have to look up as he approaches, tears spilling out of my eyes.

His sneakers catch in the gravel. "Please don't cry."

He searches my eyes. He's so close. So, *so* close. I'm overwhelmed by the need to touch him. To be held by him.

"I miss you," he says, words thick with emotion. "I've missed you so damn much. I haven't stopped thinking about you, Olivia. Not for a minute. I'm still so fucking in love with you it hurts. I'm sorry if that's not what you want to hear, but it's the truth. I'm even sorrier about the way I behaved that day in the bathroom. You were right. I was feeling insecure after fucking up with The Jam. I was using you to kind of soothe that sting, and that wasn't fair, and it definitely wasn't right. I'm really sorry I didn't trust you. I pushed you when I should have respected your wish for more time. I have no excuse—"

He doesn't get to finish.

He doesn't finish, because I'm stepping into Elijah. I'm taking his face in my hands and bringing his mouth down on mine. Hungry and hot and salty with his tears.

He kisses me. With all that pent up passion I adore. That light and intention.

And oh, that tongue.

My knees give out. He catches me, curling an arm around my waist and pulling me close. And then the kiss becomes his. He kisses me so hard and so well I see fireworks behind my closed eyelids.

I fist the fabric of his shirt in my hands. The joy of touching him again after not knowing I ever would is exquisite. My mind clears and my body throbs.

I feel weak with relief.

"Oh, baby," he says, breaking the kiss. He wipes away my tears with his thumbs. "Thank you. *Thank you.*"

"Thank you for your apology," I say. "It means a lot."

He nods. "I learned that I needed time, too. Time to process all the shit that went down at my restaurant. So I've spent the past four months trying my best to face my failures head on by myself."

I just look at him.

"That must've sucked," I say, breathless.

He laughs. "It's been the suckiest time in my life. For a lot of reasons. But you know what? It's supposed to be. The fact that it hurts so much is a testament to how much I love what I'm doin' with my life. Failure's awful. But it's also taught me a lot. Mostly that it doesn't last forever. And that it won't kill me. Although it will turn me into a bourbon soaked Post Malone fanboy."

"Post Malone?" I say, smiling.

Eli licks his lips, shaking his head. "Long story. My point is, I'm workin' on being a better man, and I want to be that better man for *you*. I love you, Olivia Wilson. I wanna be the partner you deserve. I wanna make you breakfast and edit your books and roll out my mat next to yours for the rest of my life."

"Elijah," I whisper.

"I'm not asking you to move in with me," he continues. "I mean, of course I'm still open to that idea. Always will be. But if you're not ready yet, I'm totally cool with that. I just wanna be with you. Whatever that looks like. Whenever you're ready to be with me—I'm ready, baby. I'm ready to live out our own version of happily ever after."

My heart is stumbling around in my chest. Punch drunk on love. I rise up onto my toes and kiss Eli's jaw, his chin. His mouth. Still bewildered that I'm in his arms again.

I inhale his scent. I inhale the knowledge that he's changed. Not just for me. But for himself, too.

I don't need to think about my answer. I'm certain. As certain about this man, and this new life, as I was *un*certain about my previous life in New York. My gut is screaming *yes*. My head is screaming *yes*.

So is my heart.

"I'm ready," I say.

He smiles, a devastatingly beautiful flash of white teeth.

"Was hopin' you'd say that."

"I've done a lot of thinking. A lot of writing. Every thought I've had is about you, truly. Every hero I write—Eli, I want him to be just like you."

"Selfish and scruffy?" he says, a shadow of a smile playing at his lips.

"Smart and sexy," I reply. "They'll like to cook, and they'll have dogs with human names. How's Billy, by the way?"

"Miserable without you." He bends down to kiss my neck.

His scruff catches on my skin. "He's gonna lose his fuckin' mind when he sees you're back. Although I plan to keep you to myself for a little bit here."

A beat of familiar heat unfurls low in my belly. I squeeze my legs together. I'm already getting wet.

Really, really wet.

Guess that's what four months of longing for this man will do. I feel like I'm going to go up in flames at any moment. I need relief.

I slide my fingers into the hair at the nape of his neck.

"Do you have to work tonight?" I murmur.

Eli's hands slide to my ass, and he gently presses me into his groin.

My clit throbs. He's hard as a fucking tree.

"Nope."

I turn my head to glance at his pickup truck. He takes the opportunity to nip at my earlobe.

"Let's go for a drive," I say.

The ridged bed of Eli's truck digs into my back. The air is chilly; I can just barely see my breath.

But I couldn't care less. We're parked in the middle of nowhere. It's quiet. The sky is wide open, strewn with stars and a big, heavy moon. The clean, crisp scent of pine trees fills my head.

And Eli is reaching up my dress and pulling my thong down. He guides it over my legs, kissing the inside of my thighs, my knees, my shins.

I squirm, the cool air soothing against my throbbing sex.

I am *dying* for him.

He plays his old trick and hooks one of my legs over his

shoulder, spreading me wide. Then he looks up at me from between my legs.

"I can smell you," he says, voice barely above a growl. "You smell so sweet, baby. So fucking sweet."

He ducks his head and licks me. Parts my folds with his tongue. Up and down. Up and down. He groans; I cry out.

He takes my clit in his lips and sucks, nipping at me, and I buck against him, digging my hand into his hair.

"I'm close," I manage. "I want you inside me when I come."

His eyes meet mine.

"And I want to be inside you bare. That gonna be a problem?"

My heart softens, even as my desire skyrockets.

"I'm clean," I say. "And I'm on the pill."

Those eyes of his flash. Darken. I'm trusting him. He's trusting me.

We're as vulnerable as we'll ever be right now.

"Good." He gets up on his knees and unbuttons his fly. "I'm clean, too. I don't want anything between us anymore."

My lips part when he takes himself in his hand. He gives himself a lazy tug, curling his palm over the head.

He's huge. Bigger than I remember.

Leaning down, he brackets my head between his forearms. Kisses me. Then he reaches down and notches himself at my entrance.

"I'm yours," he says.

And then he sinks inside me. One slow, *deep* thrust that buries him to the hilt.

It feels so good to be filled by him like this. So good to be raw and open and shaking like this, on the precipice of something huge and beautiful.

"Oh, sweetheart," he moans. "You feel—"

But his voice thickens. He loses himself in the moment. The trust. The completeness of it all.

I reach down, and all it takes is one quick flick of my finger against my clit. I come, tears spilling out of my eyes, and Eli kisses them away. Every one of them.

He moves over me with his usual athletic, rolling sensuality. I love it.

"I love you," I say.

"Always," he says. "I'll always love you, Olivia."

He comes a heartbeat later.

Curled up in the warmth of Eli's body, I press a kiss to his cheek.

He turns his head. Reaches over to tuck my hair behind my ear.

Kisses my mouth. A long, lazy post-coital kiss.

I pull back to laugh.

"What is it?" he asks.

"Nothing." I shake my head against the ball of his shoulder. "Just when I was driving into Charleston last September, I heard this song—it was about a guy making out with his girlfriend in the back of his pickup truck. I remember thinking how nice that would be. And now here I am, making out with you in the back of your pickup truck."

Eli looks at me intently.

"Do you like it?"

I grin. "Hate it. Totally the worst."

He pulls me closer. "Welp. I think you're officially a southerner now. You eat grits. You know the locals. And now you get naked in pickup trucks. I've taught you well."

"I hardly recognize myself anymore," I say, laughing again.

"I recognize you." Eli's still looking at me. Eyes searching mine. "The *real* you. That woman is satisfied and happy. Hopeful, too. I'm lucky as all get out to be your friend."

"More than that."

He smirks. "Way more than that, Yankee girl."

A beat of contented silence passes. My heart feels so full it's about to burst.

"But then I'm not Yankee girl anymore, am I?"

"Guess you're not. What would you like me to call you?"

I think about it for a second.

"Just Olivia," I reply. "When you say it, it sounds brand new. Just like me. Just like us."

"Just like us." He smiles. "All right, Olivia. You gonna let me make you some biscuits tomorrow or what?"

I bite my lip, then lean forward to kiss him.

"I'd like that," I say. "Speaking of biscuits…"

I reach around and pinch his butt. He laughs.

Then he rolls on top of me.

From then on out, it's just his mouth and the stars and the wild feeling of being *free*.

Not a bad way to begin again.

EPILOGUE

Eli

Six Months Later

Three parts bourbon, two parts lemon juice, one part sweet potato simple syrup.

I measure the ingredients and pour them into a cocktail shaker. Clamping the lid on, I give it a good shake over ice. The cocktail is just the tiniest bit foamy when I pour it into a rocks glass.

"Whatcha makin'?" Luke says, sidling up to the bar.

"My own version of a whiskey sour." I take a sip. Damn, that's good. "Thought I'd make a signature cocktail for the party today. I'm calling it The Olivia."

Luke grins. "A little on the nose, don't you think?"

"It *is* her birthday. Here, try it."

I hand him the glass. While he sips, I glance around The Pearl. We closed the restaurant for the party, and even though we're only serving a fraction of the food we usually do, the place is still bustling. The kitchen is a hive of activity as my cooks prepare the five course meal. My sommelier is in the wine vault, sniffing a glass of what I assume is our very best Malbec—Olivia's favorite. Busboys are busy setting the enormous family-style table we set up in the middle of the restaurant. We're expecting quite a few guests tonight; in the short time she's been in town, Olivia has managed to make a lot of friends. Other writers, other professors, neighbors, chefs—they'll all be here. I've even convinced her parents to fly down as a surprise.

This is Olivia's first birthday in Charleston. I want to get it right.

We've got so damn much to celebrate. Her birthday, clearly. But then there's the success of not only *My Enemy the Earl*, but also the second book in the series, *My Deal with the Duke,* too. Olivia is working hard to build her platform, and it shows. Readers are already clamoring for the third book, which she's having a damn good time writing. Her teaching schedule is also picking up. She's so popular with students that the department head approved her commercial fiction class, which she'll be teaching in the fall.

"Damn," Luke says, taking another sip before handing the glass back to me. "That *is* good. I was doubtful about the sweet potato syrup—"

"Hey," I shoot back. "I made it with your potatoes."

"Probably why it tastes so fuckin' delicious."

"More like it's my superior mixology skills that make this cocktail so deadly," I say, holding up the glass.

"Keep tellin' yourself that." Luke reaches behind the bar and grabs a Bud Light, which he pops open on the edge of the counter. "We both know it's my potatoes."

He's grinning again.

A big, shit eating grin I haven't seen on his face in ages. He almost looks like a kid again. Minus the scruff and the beer.

"Hey," I say. "What's going on with you? You look different."

Luke takes a long pull of beer and looks away. "Nothin'."

He's looking toward the door now. Like he's waiting on someone to walk through it.

I narrow my eyes at him.

"You expectin' someone?"

"No," he says a little too quickly. "When does Olivia make her entrance?"

I check my watch. "Seven. Told everyone else to get here a little earlier so she walks into a full house."

"I thought this wasn't a surprise."

"It's not," I said. "Just feels right havin' her walk in to see this whole new community she's built, you know?"

Luke pins me with a look. "The community you've *both* built. You're a part of this thing too, Eli."

I nod, taking a sip of my Olivia. It's as delicious as the girl it's named after.

"I appreciate that," I say. "Olivia and I have been really good at that—encouraging each other. Including each other in what we're doing. I know I feed off her passion, and I'd like to think she does the same with me."

Luke's eyes are still on me. Although there's this faraway look in them now. His grin contracts.

"Y'all are really makin' it work," he says.

"Trying to, yeah," I reply. "She's what I been lookin' for all this time. I'm not gonna make the mistake of letting her go again."

"Good." He offers me a tight smile. "I'm happy for y'all."

"When am I gonna be happy for you?" I ask.

Luke shakes his head. "I don't know, man."

He pauses, like he's going to say more. But then the door opens and we both look up and Olivia's parents are standing there, looking around the restaurant with barely concealed awe.

Pushing off the bar, I smile. I may have lost The Jam. But we're killing it at The Pearl if I do say so myself. We're packed every night. There's a two month waiting list for reservations. Being able to focus exclusively on my food here has given me the time and space to experiment in ways I never have before. It's also allowed me to spend more time with Olivia—we're heading out to the cabin a lot these days. It's bliss.

I won't lie, the loss of The Jam still stings every once in a while. But knowing people are enjoying my food, and coming back for more, is enough to make me happy right now. Hard to say if I'll ever get the itch to open another restaurant again. I figure I'll deal with whatever comes my way. As long as Olivia's by my side, I can get through anything.

We can get through anything together.

I make my way around the bar and extend my hand to Olivia's mother. I've never met her parents before, but I recognize them from pictures Olivia has shown me on Facebook.

"Elijah Jackson," I say. "I'm so happy y'all were able to make it. Welcome to Charleston."

We all shake hands. Mr. Wilson clears his throat and smooths his hands over his freshly pressed khakis. Mrs. Wilson shifts awkwardly in her fashionably understated sundress.

I glance down at my chef's jacket and apron. My sleeves are rolled up, like always, exposing several tattoos on my forearms. I catch Olivia's mother eyeing them.

I bite back a smile. Bet that's something she doesn't see every day.

"So you're the Eli we've been hearing so much about," Mrs. Wilson says, eyes flicking to my face.

"I've heard a good bit about you, too. Olivia was saying you've never been down south before."

Mr. Wilson clears his throat. "We haven't."

"Y'all are in for a treat." I clap my hands and nod at the bar. "How about a cocktail?"

Mrs. Wilson's shoulders fall as she lets out a breath. "I'd love one. Please."

Luke introduces himself while I shake up two more Olivias. He's charming as hell, and flirts shamelessly with Olivia's mother. By the time I hand her a cocktail, her face is flushed and her eyes are dancing.

"People sure are friendly down here, aren't they?" she says before taking a sip. She smacks her lips. "Wow. That is—"

"*Strong*," Mr. Wilson says.

"Delicious," she adds, grinning as she takes another sip.

"Y'all be careful," Luke warns playfully. "Chef Elijah Jackson is famous for his deadly cocktails."

"Among other things," I say with a sly grin.

Other guests begin to filter in. There's Julia, Olivia's friend from grad school and my neighbor. She wraps me in a tight hug and plants a kiss on my cheek.

"Thank you," she says. "For making our girl so happy."

"Thank you for being such a good friend to her," I reply. "She loves you."

"She loves *you*."

I smile, giving Julia a squeeze before she steps back. "I'm a lucky bastard, I know."

She fixes me with a stare. "You hurt her, and I'll hurt you. Got it?"

"Got it," I say with a quick nod. "I learned my lesson the first time."

"That's what I like to hear," she says, patting me on the chest. Her glance cuts over my shoulder to the bar. "What're y'all shakin' up back there?"

"Bourbon," I say.

Julia nods. "Don't mind if I do."

Louise and her girlfriend Mabel arrive next, followed by Kathryn Score, one of Olivia's closest writer friends. The entire Charleston Writer's Club arrives together, smelling like gin. Approximately half the professors at the College of Charleston come in next. Naomi walks in with Sergio. Maria ducks out of the kitchen to say hello.

It's starting to get loud inside the restaurant. Music is playing. Good smells are coming out of the kitchen. Shakers are going at the bar.

When Olivia finally steps through the door arm in arm with my sister, I think my heart's going to explode from too much happiness. Her face lights up, and Gracie laughs when Olivia pulls her close, clearly overwhelmed by the turnout.

Her eyes catch on mine. She smiles.

"Hey baby," she says.

I go to her and take her in my arms. I know the whole room is watching us, but I don't give a damn. I lean down and plant a big fat juicy kiss on her lips. Our friends erupt in applause and loud, lewd whistles. Olivia laughs against my mouth, looping her arms around my neck. I pull back to see that her eyes are wet.

"Happy tears," she explains. "You make me so happy, Eli."

"I love you," I say, thumbing away a tear. "Happy birthday, sweetheart."

Olivia smiles up at me. My pulse hiccups. Even now, almost a year since we first met, I still get butterflies when she walks into a room. This girl cracked my world wide open. I think I'll always be in awe that I was lucky enough to find her.

That we were lucky enough to find each other.

"You didn't have to do all this," she says, glancing around the room. "It's spectacular."

"I wanted to do it," I reply. "I don't know if you've heard, but I kinda like to cook, and I really like your friends, so... yeah. Figured I'd combine the two and throw a little party."

Olivia arches a brow. "Little? Eli, there's, like, thirty people here."

"Thirty-six to be exact." I shrug when her eyes go wide. "Don't blame it on me. You're the one who's the social butterfly."

Her eyes search mine. "Thank you. I mean that."

"Don't thank me yet," I say. "I invited your parents."

Olivia's eyes stay wide. "You did what?"

"They're over at the bar." I grab her hand. "Let's go say hello."

She's talked a lot about how her parents are slowly coming around to the fact that she's moved halfway across the country to write romance. She's also talked about wanting to invite them down so she can show them around the city she's fallen in love with. She's even floated a few dates with them. I would have never invited them if I knew she wasn't ready for them to visit. I figured what better time to come than Olivia's birthday? I know she misses them.

Case in point: she starts crying all over again when her mother wraps her in a hug and keeps her there.

"I don't know *what* they put in these drinks," Mrs. Wilson is saying. "But I love it. *Love* it, Olivia. I've had three already. I love you. And I love this city! And whatever is in this cocktail—I love that too. But I love you the most."

I cut a glance to Mr. Wilson. He shrugs in agreement, then raises his hand to order another cocktail.

There's a tug on my sleeve. I turn to see Gracie at my elbow, cocktail in hand, a smile on her lips. My sister has always been a pretty girl, but tonight she is nothing short of radiant. She's also dressed up to the nines. Nothing unusual for Gracie. But combined with the smile and the glow, it makes me take note.

Which makes me think someone else is taking note. Someone in this room.

"You look beautiful," I say, giving her a hug.

She's breathless when she replies. "Thanks."

I see something sticking out of the collar of her dress. When I look a little closer, I blink in surprise.

"Gracie," I say, nodding at her neck. "Is that a *hickey*?"

Her hand claps down on the offending spot. "Maybe it is. So what?"

I put my hands up in mock surrender. "It's no big deal. I've just never seen Nicholas...er, do something like that."

Grace takes a sip of her drink and looks away. Just like Luke did when I asked him about his love life.

Huh.

"It wasn't Nicholas."

"What?" I blink. "Then who did give it to you?"

"Give her what?"

I start at Luke's sudden appearance. He's standing across from Gracie, beer in hand, the other tucked into the front pocket of his dark wash jeans.

"None of your damn business," I say.

"Hey, Luke," Gracie says. There's almost something a little...shy about her greeting.

Shy, and knowing.

Luke's eyes darken when they fall on her face. "Hey, Gracie. You look gorgeous, as always."

"You don't look so bad yourself, handsome," she says, then steps forward to embrace him.

I watch the whole thing happen, frozen to the spot: Gracie going up on her toes. Luke's arms wrapping around her waist and pulling her against him. Guiding her body into his like he's done it before. For half a second his nose grazes her neck, right where her hickey is, and he inhales, closing his eyes.

Gracie holds on to him for a beat too long. When she pulls back, she's got those stars in her eyes again. Luke looks like he wants to tear her clothes off. His face is soft and hard all at once when her hand trails down his side to rest on his hip.

Oh no.

No no no *no*.

I know this look. The one Gracie and Luke are currently exchanging.

I know it, because it's the kind of look I've only ever given to one girl. My forever girl. Olivia.

The girl I'm hopelessly, helplessly in love with.

Gracie and Luke are in love.

Or at the very least, they're in lust.

What the fuck? I thought Gracie was happily dating Nicholas. And Luke is dating—well, everyone. I told him to stay away from her.

But before I can figure out what the hell is going on, Kip taps me on the shoulder and tells me it's time to make a toast. Waiters are handing out flutes of champagne to the guests. I grab one and make my way to stand in front of the kitchen. People crowd around me. Olivia ducks through the throng, her parents right behind her. They stand not far from me.

Taking a folded piece of paper out of my pocket, I clear my throat. The room gets quiet.

"Thank y'all for coming," I begin. "Olivia and I consider each and every one of you part of our family, and we appreciate all the support and love y'all have shown us over the past year. As many of you know, I was in a pretty bad place when Olivia came into my life. My restaurant was goin' under, and I was feeling really lost. Little did I know getting to know her—talking with her, reading her work, becomin' friends—was the beginning of my happily ever after. Going through the bad stuff was...Jesus, it was really shitty." This earns a laugh from the crowd.

"But going through it made me a better man. The kind of man that I hope deserves a girl like Olivia." I look at her. "I made it through the bad stuff because you were waitin' for me on the other side, sweetheart. I was lost, but you loved me anyway. I was a jackass, but you took me back anyway. Thank you for loving me just as I am. I hope to do half as good a job loving you."

Olivia comes to give me a hug. People are clapping. A few people are tearing up. So am I.

I unfold the paper. "I wanted to share one of my favorite passages from *My Enemy the Earl* with y'all. I think it really captures my feelings about love stories and happily ever after. And of course I always love showin' off my girl's talent." I clear my throat. *"'I may be named Gunnar.' His eyes flicked to meet hers. 'And I may ride a sinister black horse. But I am not afraid to admit I like a good love story, same as you, Cate.'*

She was looking down again, her hair falling around her face.

'It's easy to dismiss stories like that,' Cate replied. 'Love stories. People say they are silly. That they are fantasies. But I happen to think the fantasies improve reality. Make it more bearable, anyway. It's nice seeing how the happiest endings arise from the most hopeless places.'

Olivia, I was in a hopeless place when we met. But with you, I found my happy ending. I love you so much. Happy birthday, baby."

The room erupts in thunderous applause. Olivia is in my arms again, pressing messy kisses to my lips, my chin, my nose.

"Best. Speech. *Ever*," she breathes into my ear.

"Was the Gunnar quote too much?" I ask.

"Is me asking you for a quickie in the bathroom right now

too much?" she replies, pulling back to give me a sly little grin.

I wrap an arm around her waist and start to tug her across the restaurant. "Hell no. Let's go."

I hope you enjoyed reading Eli and Olivia's story as much as I loved writing it! In fact, I loved it so much that I wrote a BONUS EPILOGUE that may or may not contain a proposal (!!!!). If you'd like to find out how Eli pops the question, you can get the bonus epilogue for FREE by signing up for my newsletter at www.jessicapeterson.com.

The next book in the Charleston Heat Series, SOUTHERN PLAYER, is now available! Keep reading for an excerpt from Luke + Gracie's steamy book.

SOUTHERN PLAYER EXCERPT

Gracie

My heart is popping around inside my chest as I hit Luke's number and bring the phone to my ear. Not daring to breathe as the ringtone blares once, twice—

"Somebody's soaked through her pantalettes and is back for more," Luke says.

I smile. The *balls* on this guy.

Acute need twists low in my belly. Heaviness gathering, begging to be let loose.

"I would have soaked through them if I were wearing any."

A pause.

"You're naked," he says.

"Yes. I'm in my bathtub. Listening to *My Deal With the Duke*. And I got hungry."

"Romance makes you hungry, huh? Tell me more."

"It's a genre that stimulates the mind as well as the body," I tease.

"Deadly combination. Are you really in the bath?"

"I am." I lift my leg, making the water splash so he can hear it.

He groans. "Jesus Christ, Grace."

"What?" I ask innocently.

"Can you at least give me a chance to say hello before you get me all hard and shit?"

The image flashes through my mind: Luke lying down in his bed. One arm tucked underneath his head. The other reaching inside those fucking *jeans* and grabbing his dick.

My mouth waters at the memory of his taste. Salt. Skin. Him.

"Is now a good time?" I ask. "I don't mean to bother you—"

"Baby, you callin' for phone sex is never a bother. I always got time for that."

My chest swells a little bit. "You sure? And how'd you know that's what I was calling for?"

"Lucky guess. It's too late for either of us to travel. And your voice—I could tell by your voice. It's different. Little huskier than normal."

My entire body pulses. The water suddenly feels a little too hot.

"You don't miss much, do you?"

"Not when it comes to you."

I take a deep breath. Making my nipples break the surface of the water.

"Hi, Luke," I say.

"Hey, Gracie," he replies. He groans again, a little softer this time.

"What was that?"

"That was me lyin' down on my bed. Figure it's best to be comfortable for this kinda thing."

Oh Goooodddddd.

"Are you wearing a shirt?"

He chuckles. This masculine sound that makes my nipples harden.

"As a matter of fact, I'm not. Had a long day here on the farm, so I just showered. I'm wearin' a pair of sweats."

"That's it?"

"That's it."

"They don't happen to be grey, do they?"

Another chuckle. "Yes, they're grey. And yes, they leave very little to the imagination."

Picturing Luke in his big cozy bed, no shirt, smelling like the shower, uncut cock bulging against the thin fabric of his sweats—

I'm surprised I don't have a fembot moment, my head exploding from too much hairy sexiness.

"You sure you're okay with this?" I ask.

"Gracie. I promise I'm okay with this, and that you're not bein' a bother. I'd let you know otherwise."

"Okay." I let out a breath. "Okay."

A beat of uncomfortable silence. Now that we've agreed to do this, I feel a little...awkward. Since I'm the one who initiated, I need to be the one to take the lead here. I'm just not quite sure how to do that.

I try to focus on the sensations moving through me. Focus on what Luke said yesterday.

Tell me everything.

You got the prettiest little pussy I ever seen.

Yup, that's it.

"If you were here, you'd..." I say, switching my phone from my right hand to my left. How did this bathtub sex thing go down with Max and Jane again? "You'd come into my bathroom and kneel beside the tub."

"There bubbles in that bath? Or is the water clear so I can see everything?"

I glide my hand down my chest and cup my breast. "No bubbles. I use epsom salts."

Another groan. "What do your tits look like?"

"You look at them, and my nipples get hard. So you roll up your sleeve and you reach down, cupping one." My pulse is drumming. But I'm too turned on to stop. "You play with my nipple."

I start to do the same, running my thumb over it. A slow, patient circle. Just how Luke would do it. A charge of heat bolts through me, landing in my clit.

"Aw. Aw, yeah. Okay." He sucks in a breath. "Then what?"

"Then you'd play with the other. Eyes on my face the whole time. You'd make me wet. Really, really wet."

"You like it when I play with your nipples," he says.

"I'm playing with them right now."

"*Fuck*. Gracie—honey, I gotta touch myself. Tell me how."

I bite my lip. Luke took charge last night. But he's asking *me* to take the lead.

I am the one calling the shots.

The thought excites me.

I don't know why I'm surprised by this. I guess I didn't think I'd like dominating. Too much exposure to Christian Grey or something.

But I *am* turned on by it. The idea that I have complete control over this giant piece of man. No denying that.

Immediately resistance rises up inside me. *Too weird too dirty too embarrassing.*

I hesitate.

But then I close my eyes. Take a deep breath. Then another. My body blinking awake with awareness as I walk those negative thoughts back.

Luke is handing me one of my fantasies on a silver platter. I don't know when I'll have an opportunity like this again.

I have to take it. I owe it to myself to try.

My heart marks a staccato beat. *Try. It. Try. It.*

Try it.

I pinch my nipple.

"You gonna do exactly as I say?" I ask.

"Down to the stroke. Yes. But for fuck's sake, make it happen sooner rather than later. I'm hurtin', baby."

Another charge of heat. My body is winding up. Curling tight in anticipation of release.

"Take your hand and move it down your chest. Go slowly."

Luke lets out this little breath. I see him in my head. Phone cradled between his ear and shoulder as his big, broad hand wanders down his big, broad chest. Fingers catching in his wiry, blond-red chest hair.

"Now touch your nipples," I say, lust shooting through me as the words leave my mouth. "Pinch them."

I wait. And then—

Then he *hisses*. "I like that."

"Imagine it's me biting them. Licking them. Would you like that, too?"

"Ah. Ah, Gracie I—uh huh."

He's losing his shit.

He likes to be dominated as much as I like to dominate.

Time to jump in with both feet.

My hand dips below the surface of the water. "You want to wash me. So you take a washcloth. Get it nice and soapy."

"And then," he pants, "what do I do?"

"You wash me between my legs. They fall open, and my hips start to roll against your hand. Your thumb hits my clit through the washcloth."

"Fuck fuck *fuuuuck*. Baby, let me touch myself. Tell me to touch myself or I'm gonna die."

My middle finger slides into my folds. "Pull your sweats down. Not all the way. Just over your hips."

I hear him breathing hard. "Okay. They're down."

"Tell me how your dick looks. But no touching it. Not yet."

He sputters. "I'm—it's hard, baby girl. So hard for you. There's a little cum on the tip. And the vein—there's two that—you can see them. Baby, *please*. Lemme touch it."

I remember the feel of his cum on my lips. Slick, a little sticky. I was so vulnerable in that moment. So exposed. But I also felt powerful. Luke's obvious adoration—his barely restrained lust—it made me feel like a fucking rock star.

I circle my fingertip around my clit. My hips buck.

"Rub the cum over the head."

"O—okay."

"Now give yourself a stroke. One only."

He doesn't wait. I hear his sharp intake of breath.

"Aw, honey," he pleads.

I stroke myself again. "Another."

"I'm there."

"So you keep rubbing me with the washcloth. Your other hand—you lather it up with soap, keeping the soap in your hand while you glide it over my tits. You like how they look when they're all soapy and slick. You keep pressing against my clit with the other hand, the rough cotton of the washcloth catching on my flesh. Driving me wild. I'm moaning your name."

"*Gracie.*"

"I'm soft and spread wide open for you. I tell you that I want you to fuck me. But you say naw, naw baby, I'm gonna make you come first." My finger is really working my clit now. "Start stroking yourself."

"As much as I want?"

"As much as you want."

His breathing becomes labored. I imagine the sinews in his neck tightening and his mouth falling open as he works his hand in smooth, hard strokes.

"I grab at you. My orgasm is close. You lose the washcloth and touch me. I'm soft. Ready for you."

He lets out a strangled growl.

"Your first two fingers sink inside me as you use your thumb to make me come."

"You're coming?" he says, his voice cracking.

I'm pulling at my nipples now, working my clit hard with my other hand. "I come. Really hard."

"Then," he breathes. "Then what?"

"And then you pull me out of the bathtub. You grab me and spin me around and bend me over the sink. Water is everywhere. The pants you're wearing are soaked. But you don't care. All you care about is getting your dick out. I watch in the mirror as you lather yourself up with your soapy hand. Then...then youuuuu—" I lose my grip for a second when my orgasm threatens. "You say you're going to put it in my ass."

"Oh, *baby*," he groans.

"You work my asshole open with your fingers. *Stay fucking still* you tell me when I start to squirm. You use your knee to pry my legs open. And then you put yourself at my entrance. *You're ready*, you tell me as you meet my eyes in the mirror. I look away, but then you say *You look at me when I'm fucking you*."

I hear Luke's labored breathing. His obvious distress only eggs me on more.

"So I look at you. And you fuck me. Slowly at first. Sinking in one inch at a time. The pressure is unreal. It hurts at first. But then, when I get used to the feel of you, you start to move." My orgasm is *close*. "You grab my hair and you thrust again and again, putting that baseball butt to good use."

He scoffs. The sound half amused, half pained. "Gracie. I'm gonna come. Tell me it's okay."

"Can we—can we try to do it together? I'm close too."

"You're the one in charge. You tell me."

I focus on the movement of my fingers over my clit. I

close my eyes and imagine what Luke looks like on his bed, strung out on this little spontaneous fantasy I threaded together from bits and pieces of imagination. His chest barrels out with every breath he takes. Brow furrowed, dick hard but eyes soft.

He's *vulnerable*. Even though I'm not actually there, I feel his openness, his willingness to let his need show, through the phone. It's in his voice and his pauses. His sighs and his pleas.

All in the service of *my* fantasy. *My* needs.

The thought makes my chest contract. That ache I felt this morning—it's back with a vengeance.

I can't fucking breathe.

"Luke," I say, my body arching out of the water. "I'm ready, and I want you with me."

"I'm here, Gracie girl. I'm ready."

I circle my fingers faster. Their motion blurring my senses, my vision, every line I've drawn.

"Luke—I'm—"

"I'm there," he grunts. "I'm with you."

The explosion rocks me. I shout—what, I couldn't tell you—as my completion rips through me. My legs tremble, sending water over the edge of the tub. I feel myself unfurling, opening, *letting go*. I let go and ride the wave, praying I don't drown. Somewhere in the back of my mind I hear Luke shouting, too. My name. God's. Mine again.

He's twenty miles away, but I *feel* him here. Feel his warmth, his confidence. His certainty that this is right, and this is good, and that I'm the only one he wants this way.

I am the only one.

Just the thought sends my heart on a rollercoaster ride.

My God, I think absently, the orgasm pounding through me, *this is what I've been missing out on all this time*.

This.

This.

This feeling of being worshipped for who I am.

My orgasm fades. I lean back against the tub, just trying to catch my breath for several beats. I hear Luke doing the same.

I don't know what to say next.

Hey friend, how great was that?

Please don't judge me for fantasizing about you fucking me in the ass.

Luke, I'm starting to want you in ways I shouldn't, and it's making me feel all mixed up inside.

"Gracie," Luke says, bringing me back to earth. "Gracie, if I could high five you through this phone, I would. That was... the best phone sex I've ever had."

I grin, the heaviness in my chest lessening just a bit. "It's the only phone sex you've ever had."

"Doesn't mean it wasn't fuckin' awesome. 'Cause it was. Baby girl, you're a natural at this. I had no idea you had such —well. Imagination, I guess."

My grin broadens into a smile as something nice blooms inside me. "Are you saying my mind turns you on?"

"I'm lying alone in my bed with my phone in one hand and my cum in the other. I'd say your mind is a big fucking turn on, yeah."

Be careful.

How many other guys have complimented me, only to ghost after they'd gotten what they wanted?

A beat of silence passes.

"How was your day?" he asks. Because now the guy can read my mind in addition to reading my body, too.

I mean, didn't Luke get what he wanted? Didn't he come all over my tits last night?

But he's still here. He could say goodnight. Hang up.

But he's still listening.

"You don't have to do this," I say.

"Do what? Talk to you after putting my soap-covered dick inside you?" This makes me smile harder. "By the way, soap is never a good substitute for real lube. But whether or not I have to, Gracie, I always want to hear how you're doing."

Check out the rest of SOUTHERN PLAYER, available wherever books are sold.

Thank you very much for reading SOUTHERN CHARMER. I hope you enjoyed it! **SOUTHERN PLAYER, Luke and Gracie's story, is now available wherever books are sold.**

I included a Charleston travel guide in the following pages with all my favorite spots to eat, drink, and be merry in the Holy City. Enjoy!

I love nothing more than hanging out with readers, and I'm very active on social media. Here's how you can get in on the fun:

- Join my Facebook reader group, The City Girls, for exclusive excerpts of upcoming books plus giveaways galore!
- Follow my not-so-glamorous life as a romance author on Instagram @JessicaPAuthor
- Check out my website at www.jessicapeterson.com
- Follow me on Goodreads
- Follow me on Bookbub
- Like my Facebook Author Page

JESSICA'S CHARLESTON TRAVEL GUIDE

If you finished Eli and Olivia's story, then I'm sure you picked up on two things: one, that I absolutely love Charleston; and two, that I absolutely love to eat. I live about three hours by car from the Holy City, and my husband Ben and I try to sneak down there as much as we can. I thought I'd share our favorite places to eat, drink, and be merry in the Charleston area. Enjoy!

<u>To Do</u>

Charleston is a really great walking town. Some sights to check out on foot:

- **King Street:** Nice shopping, and you'll pass the College of Charleston's campus along the way. On the second Sunday of every month, the city closes the street to cars and hosts a pretty big pedestrian festival. Worth checking out!
- **East Bay Street/The Battery:** Get great views of the water. You'll pass the famous Rainbow Row along the way.

- **South of Broad Neighborhood:** This is where Eli lives. One of my all time favorite Charleston activities is wandering around the quiet streets, ogling the mansions and their gardens.
- **Saturday Morning Farmer's Market:** Held in Marion Square. Great food and people watching!

<u>To Eat</u>

I know I'm kind of biased, but I happen to think Charleston serves up some of the best food on the planet. Here are our current favorite eating spots:

- **Callie's Hot Little Biscuit:** Get there early (pro tip: they have an online ordering app) and treat yourself to a decadent breakfast of delicious coffee and homemade biscuit sandwiches. My favorite is the egg and pimento cheese biscuit. YUM.
- **High Cotton:** Their weekend brunch game is A++.
- **Cru Café:** Make a reservation for lunch at this Charleston staple. The best sandwiches and salads in town, hands down.
- **Xiao Bao Biscuit:** Funky lunch and dinner spot with funky, Asian inspired food. Dogs welcome at outdoor tables.
- **Rodney Scott BBQ:** It's a bit of a drive, but worth it for the pulled pork sandwich and sides.
- **The Darling Oyster:** For your oyster and seafood fix.
- **Chez Nous:** Tiny, romantic, tremendously delicious Italian-French-Spanish spot. Ben and I had the perfect date night here. We sat at the bar, an ocean-scented breeze floating through the open

windows, and stuffed ourselves silly. Can't wait to do it again.

To Drink

Charleston's got an amazing craft cocktail scene. Any of the restaurants above will have a stellar wine and/or cocktail list as well. These are my favorite watering holes:

- **The Bar At Husk**: Arrive when it opens. Grab a spot upstairs or out back on the patio, and enjoy some of the best cocktails and apps in town.
- **The Cocktail Club**: Perfect for pre-or-post-dinner drinks. Their cocktail menu is second to none.
- **The Blind Tiger**: I based The Spotted Wolf on this bar. A casual, fun Charleston staple.
- **The Gin Joint**: Tiny, *tiny* place that shakes up insanely delicious drinks. Get there early if you can!

If you have any questions, or need a specific recommendation, don't hesitate to email me at jessicapauthor@jessicapeterson.com. I love any excuse to chat about Charleston!

ALSO BY JESSICA PETERSON

THE SEX & BONDS SERIES

An outrageously sexy series of romcoms set in the high stakes world of Wall Street.

The Dealmaker (Sex & Bonds #1)

The Troublemaker (Sex & Bonds #2)

THE NORTH CAROLINA HIGHLANDS SERIES

Beards. Bonfires. Boning.

Southern Seducer (NC Highlands #1)

Southern Hotshot (NC Highlands #2)

Southern Sinner (NC Highlands #3)

Southern Playboy (NC Highlands #4)

Southern Bombshell (NC Highlands #5)

THE CHARLESTON HEAT SERIES

The Weather's Not the Only Thing Steamy Down South.

Southern Charmer (Charleston Heat #1)

Southern Player (Charleston Heat #2)

Southern Gentleman (Charleston Heat #3)

Southern Heartbreaker (Charleston Heat #4)

THE THORNE MONARCHS SERIES

Royal. Ridiculously Hot. Totally Off Limits...

Royal Ruin (Thorne Monarchs #1)

Royal Rebel (Thorne Monarchs #2)

Royal Rogue (Thorne Monarchs #3)

THE STUDY ABROAD SERIES

Studying Abroad Just Got a Whole Lot Sexier.

A Series of Sexy Interconnected Standalone Romances

Lessons in Love (Study Abroad #1)

Lessons in Gravity (Study Abroad #2)

Lessons in Letting Go (Study Abroad #3)

Lessons in Losing It (Study Abroad #4)

ACKNOWLEDGMENTS

In many ways, SOUTHERN CHARMER is the book I've worked my whole career to be able to write. Writing is never easy, but sometimes, when plot and character and theme come together *just* so, it can be absolute magic. I have never felt such joy working on a story as I did writing this one. I have many, many people to thank for helping me get here.

First, enormous thanks to my editor, Kristin Anders. Your belief in this book—and in my career—is what keeps me going on the hard days. You're insanely talented, and I am lucky to call you a friend.

I also want to extend a gigantic thanks to Jodi, my PA and all around savior/book doula/scheduling wizard/genius beta reader. I am so not kidding when I say you are single handedly helping me transform my career into the one I've always dreamed of having. I am so grateful to have you in my circle. Thank you lady for all the hard work you do—it does not go unnoticed.

I have the best beta team on the planet. Jodi, Heather, and Quinn—you ladies continue to blow my mind with your insightful comments. Also, thanks for catching my million and a half typos. This book would be pretty much unreadable without your help polishing it.

Thanks to Najla, my INCREDIBLE cover artist. You knocked it out of the park with this one, and on the first pass no less! I can't wait to see the work we'll do together in the future.

Thanks to Tandy, my awesome proofreader, for making this book shine.

Thanks to my insanely great, insanely enthusiastic ARC team. I so, so appreciate you taking the time to not only read my books, but to review them, too. Reviews make all the difference to new(ish) authors like me!

Thanks to my reader group, The City Girls, and to my incredible admins, Monique, Ingrid, Raquel, and Whitney. Y'all are so generous with your time and talent, and I am so stupid lucky to call you friends. Thank you ladies!

I am continually in awe of the amazing authors I've met over the past few years. There are too many names to list here, but I just want to thank you all for inspiring me, listening to me, and supporting me. Your generosity is humbling. Thank you!

And of course I have to thank my family, my friends, and ALWAYS, *always* my readers. Y'all are the reason I get to wake up and write every day. Thank you for making my dreams come true.

ABOUT THE AUTHOR

Jessica Peterson writes romance with heat, humor, and heart. Heroes with hot accents are her specialty. When she's not writing, she can be found bellying up to a bar in the south's best restaurants with her husband Ben, reading books with her adorable daughter Gracie, or snuggling up with her 70-pound lap dog, Martha.

A Carolina girl at heart, she fantasizes about splitting her time between Charleston and Asheville, but currently lives in Charlotte, NC. You can check out her books at www.jessicapeterson.com.